GOOD WITCHES DON'T DIE

Academy of Shadowed Magic - Year Five

S.W. CLARKE

FREE SHORT STORY: Liara Youngblood and Lucian the demon prince clash in the prequel story *The Fae and the Demon*.

Join S.W. Clarke's reader newsletter and get *The Fae and the Demon* for FREE only at subscribepage.io/swclarke.

CHAPTER ONE

The witching hour came with a howl.

Across from me, Eva shot up in her cot, her chest moving fast. Her eyes found mine in the dim, dancing firelight from the lantern on the ground between us. *You're awake*, she mouthed.

My reply was a single nod. I sat with crossed legs, my cloak wrapped around me, the weapon set over my lap.

I had been awake. I had never fallen asleep.

When I got up from my cot with a creak, her eyes followed me. "So that noise wasn't just in my dream," she said.

"It was outside."

"What was it?"

It had sounded like a wolf. But because it was the witching hour, I said, "I don't know. But I'm going out to check."

She swept her own cloak around her shoulders, threw her lavender braid back, stood up. Nodded at me to go ahead of her.

Farther back, Aidan and Liara and Callum remained still in sleep on their cots like none of them had heard the noise—I doubted Callum could have, anyway—and Aidan went on snoring lightly on his back.

When Eva and I crawled out from the tent and onto the leaf-strewn earth, I conjured a flame in my free hand. It illuminated the forest around us, the two dozing horses, the will-o-wisps floating at intervals out here as guards, and the edges of my enshroudment.

Almost the moment I had the Backbiter, my power had grown. Where before it was a struggle to wrap the enshroudment over another person for very long, it now encompassed our tent and a thirty-foot radius beyond it. The sight of it reminded me of Umbra's magic around the academy. But where hers glowed blue, mine shimmered orange-red.

I wasn't sure if I could maintain the enshroudment while I slept. I didn't dare try. Without it, we were exposed.

When we came outside, the horses' heads lifted, and Noir nickered, dark eyes flashing in the light off my flame. He didn't seem bothered—a good sign. And beside him, Siren swayed dozily on her feet.

Horses were prey animals. They would be the first on alert if there was something to be nervous about.

The wisps flew to me, gathering around my head in their natural arrangement: a half-circle from shoulder to shoulder, rising to a peak overhead. They whispered into my thoughts, reporting all they'd seen in the six hours since we'd made camp here in the woods a couple dozen miles from the academy.

Some deer. Rabbits. Squirrels. A mama bear and her two cubs.

"Nothing worse out there than a black bear," I said to Eva. "Apparently."

Eva stood beside me, her shoulder touching mine, eyes scanning the woods even though she couldn't see past my flame and the barest shadows of the trees nearest us. "The witching hour's only just started."

This was our first night outside the academy. Our first night spent fending for ourselves during the witching hour. Eva and Aidan both planned to call their families tomorrow, to pretend like they were still at the school. When really, we were on our own.

"Good point." With a thought, I sent the wisps out into the woods like the spokes off the center of a wheel, each of them moving in different directions to scout. They disappeared in a wink of blue into the deep forest.

Eva watched after them. "How far can they go?"

"That's a good question." I nudged her. "And we're about to find out the answer."

The faintest tick of a smile touched her lips, but she still shivered under her cloak in the night air. In theory, the enshroudment meant we couldn't be seen, couldn't be heard. But I had never used it like this, encompassing a whole campsite. What happened if one of the Shade's creatures stepped inside it? Would they see us? Hear us?

The howl came again from somewhere behind us. Eva and I turned. We waited for the wisps. This was a test: How far could they go from me before they hit an invisible tether? If a tether existed at all. They had traveled all the way across Europe to get to me when I was in Edinburgh, but that wasn't on my command. They were simply responding to the Backbiter, to its power, joining themselves with its wielder.

Now I needed to find out how far the Backbiter's wielder could push them.

A feathery touch brushed my leg, and I jerked away. When my eyes flashed down, Loki stood between Eva and me.

His emerald eyes lifted to meet mine. "Someone's a little jumpy."

"We heard a noise." My fingers shifted over the Backbiter in my left hand, the chain clinking lightly.

"Like a howl," Eva said.

"Could be Umbra," Loki offered, sitting down.

A tightness entered my chest, and I rolled my eyes down at him. "Thanks, Sherlock."

We still didn't know what had happened to Maeve Umbra, and all of us had speculated on and off as we'd traveled yesterday. Eva, ever the optimist, thought maybe she'd left on some kind of urgent quest. Liara and Aidan suspected she'd been kidnapped by Tristan Rathmore or the Shade's creatures.

And Loki, my macabre cat, theorized that she'd just croaked.

"If she's dead," Eva said, "she won't be howling."

"Unless she's now *un*dead," he said.

Eva took a step forward. "It's not safe in these woods."

"It's not safe anywhere during this hour," I said.

Eva ran a hand over her braid, pulling it over her shoulder. "With Umbra gone, it's not safe for us to be anywhere near the academy. If Liara and Aidan are right, and the Shade's creatures took her... We should have pushed farther today."

"It's two dozen miles off." I pointed back the way we'd come. "Over two bitchingly steep ridges, I should add."

Those ridges had been awful for the horses to scale and descend. We could have gone twice as far without picking our way up them and carefully finding paths down.

Eva turned back to me, pulling her cloak tighter. "You know how those creatures move. They can run twenty kilometers an hour. They don't get tired. Two ridges is nothing. Two dozen miles is less than nothing."

I straightened as something invisible tugged at my chest.

"What is it?" Eva said.

"The wisps," I said. "They're coming back."

The wisps had found their tether: half a mile. It was as far as they could stray from me—at least for now. When they came flying back, twelve blue stars converging outside the tent, their whispers filled my ears.

And one in particular stood out. The one that had gone straight south.

"What'd they see?" Eva whispered.

As if to punctuate her statement, the howl came again from the distance, yipping and then crescendoing.

"Wolves," I said. "Just wolves."

We were alone except for the wolves. I'd never thought that would bring me comfort. And it should have, but it didn't. Nothing did nowadays.

"Shall we head back in?" Eva offered.

"I want to stay out," I said. "At least until four. You can go in."

"If you're staying, I'm staying."

So we stayed, her and me and Loki. My cat lay down at my feet and curled up, and we stood in silence and tried not to flinch every time a leaf cracked. Every time a bough creaked. Mostly I managed it. Sometimes the Backbiter's chain clinked in my hands, and my eyes darted after a noise.

Nighttime like this—moonless darkness—could make anyone see things that weren't there. I'd thought I had gotten over this nighttime restlessness after a few years in the foster system, but I hadn't. Not at all. It had just been submerged.

After ten minutes of listening to her teeth chatter, Loki raised his head and said, "She doesn't have enough adipose tissue to stay out here."

"Adipose?" I said.

"Fat," he said.

"What are you two talking about?" Eva said.

"Your body fat percentage," I said. "Ignore him. He's weird. But you probably should go back in before you get frostbite."

She didn't move. "So light me a fire."

"Eva," I said. "I've got this."

Finally she sighed. "Don't stay out all night, all right?"

"Sure," I said. And I watched her disappear between the flaps of the tent, leaving me alone with the horses.

When she had gone, I beckoned the wisps to me. They came to their familiar arrangement around my head and shoulders, like a broken halo tipped vertical, and I counted them.

Twelve. Twelve wisps.

As they hovered around me, I said, "Do you have names?"

They didn't answer for a time. Finally, one voice said, *Forgotten.*

"Well, what did your mistress call you?" I asked.

Nothing, another responded. *Only commands.*

They spoke like they didn't have identities, didn't have full command anymore of language. I wondered if that was the effect of trapping a soul in a vessel for five hundred years, or if it was simply the lobotomy at work.

Maybe both.

"The first time you saw me," I said, "you said a phrase. 'Shadowend, you return to the ancient place.'"

They bobbed as if in recognition.

"What did it mean?" I asked.

Shadowend, twelve voices hissed at once in a strange, enthusiastic harmony.

"Thank you, class," I said. "Anything else?"

The wisps went on bobbing, floating above me, saying nothing. They weren't used to doing anything but taking commands. Executing orders. Obeying.

But what I needed most of all were answers.

I didn't have the will to explore their heads anymore. Not right now. And so as I stood guard outside our tent, eyes searching for shadows—creatures that pressed away light—the far recesses of my mind worked on the problem of how the hell to find Hell.

Liara was taking us to a person I "needed to meet." She'd been coy about who this person was, except to say we needed to get to Serbia. That was hundreds of miles from here, and it had only become clear at the tail-end of our first day of travel from the academy that she didn't have a great plan for getting there.

I would worry about that tomorrow, when she was awake.

The truth was, I needed Liara. If she hadn't shown up and told me I needed to go to Serbia, I probably would have turned in a circle with closed eyes and pointed, and that would have been the direction I'd taken. Because I didn't have any idea how to get to Hell.

Four years ago, the wisps had transported me to the Shade. I had taken hold of the liar's key outside Maeve Umbra's office, and when I did, I had arrived at what felt like Hell. Or the gates of it, at least.

My eyes focused on the wisps once more. This time, I needed to give a command. "Tell me where you sent me four years ago. When you offered me the key."

They went on hovering, bobbing, as though considering. Finally, one of the voices said, *Na dèan.*

That sounded like Faerish. "Translation, please?"

They didn't answer. "Tell me the translation of that word into English," I said.

Still no answer. Maybe there was no translation.

I squeezed my eyes shut, flitted my fingers through the air. With a thought, I sent them all scattering, heading back out into the forest to scan the terrain once more.

Na dèan. I'd have to ask the others about it.

Over the course of the witching hour, I sent the wisps out every ten minutes. They would reach the end of their tether, come racing back to me when they had.

Nothing. They found nothing.

And yet my heart wouldn't stop fighting its cage, pushing against my throat. The irony of the witching hour was that I was the only witch left alive, and it terrified me. This should be my hour. Instead, it was the one time of night I was supposed to hide.

Another thought came. Four people. There were four people who might know the way into the underworld:

Tristan Rathmore, Ora Frostwish, Tamzin Cole, and Callum Rathmore.

None of whom I had access to. Three of them would kill me if they ever saw me again, and one of them was six feet away, but soulless. Asleep. And I didn't know if he'd ever wake up again. I didn't know if Thom, the little soldier ghost boy, would return at all.

So of those four, I had one. Callum. And he couldn't speak.

The wisps returned, left once again. The witching hour drew on, and I remained in exactly the spot I had been standing since I'd left the tent. My feet hurt. I didn't care; all that mattered was staying awake.

Near the end of the hour, the thought came to me: I should just walk out into the woods. It was one sure way into Hell.

I could walk deep into the forest, yell as long and loud as my voice would allow. "You want the witch?" I'd say. "Here she is." And eventually, they would come for me. The Shade's creatures would come.

I could allow myself to be taken by one of them, slung over its back as I had been on that winter night. Not like I'd have a choice by then: they sapped all the energy from you, all the will to fight.

And then I'd find out where they took you. Where all those abducted mages ended up—the ones we couldn't save. It felt like death. Maybe it was.

I pressed out air through my nose, my fingers squeezing again over the Backbiter as they'd been doing all night. Even the thought of death was overwhelming. Mind-melting. How was I ever going to face her?

Anyway, it was a terrible idea. I'd be a captive, helpless, at the whim of whatever creature found me. *And so you're just going to stand here*, a small voice said inside me. *Fighting shadows all night.*

It wouldn't be the first time.

CHAPTER TWO

Aidan was the first to emerge from the tent in the morning. Only his head and his squinting eyes appeared as he slid his glasses onto his face. "Clem?"

I shifted to un-numb my legs, the weapon still seated across my thighs where I'd sat. Loki lay asleep next to me. "Hey, North," I said.

He crawled the rest of the way out. "Tell me you slept last night."

I glanced at him. "Good witches don't lie."

Loki woke, blinking blearily up at me, then Aidan, and let out an annoyed meow. Just that.

Aidan ran a hand through his bedhead. "Why'd you stay up?"

I shrugged one shoulder. "Had to protect us from the wolves."

"Uh-huh." He surveyed the scene: the wisps still at attention around the campsite, the horses eating their morning grass not far off, the enshroudment still shimmering over us. He didn't believe me at all. "If you won't sleep, will you at least come in for breakfast?"

Inside the tent, several stacks of Aidan's books—half of them probably taken from the academy—graced the far corner. Eva and Liara were seated on the floor near the back, a spread of conjured food between them: tea, coffee, hash browns, oatmeal, sausage. The smells of fat and salt couldn't have been more sinful.

Callum still lay prone on his cot, hands folded over his chest, breathing long and slow. Always the same. But his soul was out there—somewhere—and his body was kept alive by its presence.

"Clem," Eva said, her voice a bell of surprise and pleasure. Some days that alone got me through—Eva, always glad to see me. Then she eyed me. "You didn't sleep."

Liara took a seat next to them and lifted the teapot. "She's going to be as twattish as her horse."

"My twattish horse saves lives." I took a seat as the fourth part of the square, and Eva passed a platter of milk to Loki, who'd sidled up to her. I started piling my plate with my fork. "Eva, can you tangibly manipulate us some chairs in this place?"

"Working on it," she said with enforced cheeriness as she passed a bowl of grits to Liara. "We now have plates and utensils, you know."

I lifted the fork with ham speared on it, studying it. "Oh, so we do."

"And that was fast." Aidan accepted the grits from Liara, ladled them onto his plate. "Half the people in Goodbarrel's class couldn't even finish a pouch in a year."

"At the rate we're going"—I took a grossly large bite of ham—"it'll take that long before we get to Liara's Mysterious Person."

Liara's eyes slid over to mine. "We can't trust the leylines."

"Don't we know anyone in Serbia?" Eva asked. "If we could just find out whether one of the leylines there is uncorrupted..."

We all looked at Liara. She was the one, after all, who'd insisted I had to travel to Serbia to meet this person.

She shrugged under our gazes, unashamed. "I'm from Singapore."

"Then how do you know this person?" Aidan said.

A good question.

Liara's spoon trailed through her grits, eyes on her plate. She'd avoided talking too much about this Mysterious Person over the past day, except to say that I needed to meet her.

"Liara," I said, swallowing. "Just spit it out."

Her eyes caught mine, dark and severe. "Spit what?"

Aidan sighed, lowering his plate. "You don't know anybody in

Serbia, and you're avoiding telling us who this person is or how you know her."

"I'm not avoiding."

"I've known you four years." I nodded at her spoon, stuck deep and angrily into her grits. "And I know your tells."

She searched Aidan's and Eva's and even Loki's faces—all of whom must have been expectant, because she dropped the spoon. "When you arrived during the winter of our first year, Umbra called me into her office."

My eyebrows rose, but I didn't speak.

"She said you were a witch," Liara went on, shooting me the same loathing look she'd done so many times during our first year. "And while I may hate your kind, you were the last one left in the world. She made me promise that if anything ever happened to her, I would take you to a person in Serbia."

"You?" Eva said, almost offended.

"Right?" Liara shuddered, as though reliving the memory. "That's what I said."

"So Umbra disappeared," I said, piecing it together. "And you thought that qualified as 'something happening to her.'"

"Doesn't it?" Liara said. Before I could answer, she said, "I think having to make that promise made me hate you even more."

Aidan thumbed his mug of tea. "So you don't know who it is we're going to meet."

"Not a clue." Liara finally took her spoon up again, began eating as though to avoid more questions.

I glanced at Eva and Aidan. Why Liara? Why had Umbra made Liara promise and not Eva, my future roommate? Or Aidan, the responsible student ambassador?

And why hadn't Umbra told Liara *who* she was supposed to take me to?

All of this was a matter of trust now. Trust in Umbra.

I remembered again that I hadn't told anyone about what I had seen under Umbra's office. The tree encasing a perfectly preserved version of... me. At the thought, my hand went around the Backbiter, and I held down a shiver.

I didn't want to tell them. I didn't want to talk about it at all, or even think of it.

So I said, "I know a way."

"A way?" Eva said.

"To find out if any of the leylines between here and there are uncorrupted. Umbra taught me how to navigate them."

Liara's attention flicked from her food to me. "That was for guardian missions."

"Yeah," I said. "And since when do you care about rules?"

Besides, it wasn't just for guardian missions.

If I knew Umbra at all, nothing she'd ever taught me belonged to one circumstance, to one place. It was only designed to expand, to grow, until I wouldn't ever find myself helpless. She had trained me to be resourceful, because that was what she prided in herself. It was what she cared most about: survival.

I hadn't realized my eyes had unfocused until Eva said, "What are you going to do, Clem?"

I straightened, lifted my plate. "Conjure me something ink-black, because I'm about caffeinate until my eyes are ready to pop out. And then we're going to find the nearest leyline."

We broke down the campsite at dawn. The tent went into my cloak, and Aidan and Loki and I mounted the horses while Eva and Liara swept the leaves and grass in our wake, hiding our footprints and the horses' hoofprints as we set out.

I rode with the weapon across my lap, just as I had sat with it all night long. I couldn't seem to put it down anymore, couldn't even let it leave my sight.

"Clem," Aidan said when we were underway, "it's daytime. You can drop the enshroudment for a little while."

"Never know when a formalist will drop a metal box from the sky, North," I said. "Maybe that's what happened to Umbra."

"Oh, stop it." Liara flew by, eyeing me over her shoulder. "Send the wisps out if you're so paranoid."

Actually, that wasn't a bad idea. I sent the wisps out through the forest with a thought, their blue lights fanning in all directions.

Aidan half-turned atop Siren to watch them go. "How do you talk to them?"

"I..." I paused. "I just think at them."

"And do they talk back?"

"In a way. They'll say, 'Wolf' or 'Bear' into my head. Mostly they've forgotten how to make real sentences."

"Poor souls," Eva said as she flew. "I can't imagine five centuries trapped like that."

"Lobotomized souls," Liara corrected. "They probably don't even know they're trapped."

They do, I thought.

I didn't say anything as we tracked through the forest, but I was certain: the souls knew what they had been, and they knew what they were now. They served me as thralls, beholden to me through magic, and never disobeyed, never voiced any disagreement.

But they still knew.

I could feel it in their whispers. In their quickness to action.

I already knew what I had to do about the wisps. I just didn't quite know how to do it.

When they reached the end of their tethers and began racing back toward me, I slowed Noir to a stop as the twelve wisps converged. Their whispers flooded into my head in an instant, and I sighed out a breath. We were safe—for now.

With that breath, I dropped the enshroudment.

The shimmering veil dropped away, dissipating like stardust, leaving all of us open to the morning air. And I slumped in my seat, exhaustion filling me like it only does when you've stopped running, stopped moving. Then you become aware of it.

I was fucking tired.

A hand nudged my arm. Aidan, who'd brought Siren alongside me. When I opened my eyes, he held out a thermos with the lid off and steam rising from it.

I jerked my chin at it. "What's that?"

"Conjured coffee."

"Black?"

"What do you take me for?"

I took one hand off the weapon and accepted the thermos. The coffee was black as Ora Frostwish's heart. "I won't underestimate you again."

He half-smiled, started Siren forward with the press of his heels.

As we rode, I sent the wisps out once more on reconnaissance. Eva and Liara had taken to flying from tree to tree, crouching on branches. Their heads kept moving, scanning the area around us. And then I realized it was in their training as fae guardians. They'd fallen right back into our patterns from the last year: any time we were outside the academy, we'd had to be cautious, watchful.

I wasn't the only one who couldn't let my guard down.

"You know," Aidan said over to me as the horses made their way between trees, "I learned something interesting about fae."

Clearly he'd been watching me watch the two of them.

"Yeah?" I glanced over at him. "Please tell me they evolved from boggans. Then I'll have something to hold over their beautiful heads."

"Funny you say that." A daring look came into his eyes behind those glasses. "Because apparently demons were once fae."

I nearly dropped the thermos. "Demons, like the Rathmores?"

He gave a slow nod. "I'd always been told fae never turned bad. That there were no dark fae. Ora Frostwish proved everyone wrong on that point. And it made me wonder."

"And when you wonder, you turn into an egghead."

"I'm always an egghead, Cole." He directed Siren around a large tree, disappearing and reappearing on the other side. "Turns out, fae don't stay fae when they break bad. They lose their wings."

"Frostwish certainly didn't lose hers."

He shrugged. "That's what the lore says in the book I... borrowed from the Room of the Ancients."

"How many books did you steal from Milonakis's library?"

"More than a dozen and less than a hundred."

He did have a stupidly large pile of books in the back of our tent. I wondered where they'd all come from. Now I knew.

From his seat behind me on Noir, Loki let out a long meow. "Now we can never go back to the academy."

I laughed. "You know, North, you're going to be Milonakis's property for the rest of her life."

"I know," Aidan said, shaking it off like a bad thought. "I know."

"So Callum Rathmore descended from fae," I said. "According to lore." *And that's also how Tristan Rathmore hexed me—he was a demon, which means he has fae blood.*

"And guess what happened to turn the fae into demons?" Aidan said. "I'll give you a clue: it occurred five hundred years ago."

The Shade. It was always the Shade. She had made the Rathmores into her servants, generations of them born to be her hand above the ground. To swing a sword for her. To hunt down any witches who might contest her—like me.

And Callum had rejected that.

"She offered them power," I said. "If they would lead her armies. Am I warm?"

"Scalding. And," Aidan said, scrubbing his fingernails on the chest of his cloak, "if you want to know, I may be the first mage to ever make the fae-demon connection."

"I thought you said you read it."

"No," he said. "Only the hints of it. You see, in one illustration the Shade's lieutenant wasn't wearing armor like Lucian does now, but—"

I stopped Noir hard, his head jerking up. A second ago, one of the wisps had flown back to me with a whisper. "Eva, Liara," I called out, "what do you see on the ground thirty yards ahead?"

A pause. Then Liara's voice came from one of the branches above, "Should we see something?"

No, they wouldn't see it. Not now that it belonged to the Shade, palpating with her magic.

We had arrived at a corrupted leyline.

CHAPTER THREE

I swung down from Noir's back, and Loki hopped to the ground with me, trotting alongside.

"What do you see?" Aidan asked, still atop Siren.

"Corruption," I said, tracking through the forest toward it. The leyline ran north–south, and the Shade's magic rose from it like crystalline smoke, undulating and dissipating into the air two feet up.

Liara came to a nearly inaudible landing beside me. "I can't see it." She sounded almost petulant.

My fingers tightened on the Backbiter. "You haven't dealt with her magic like I have."

Eva landed on my other side, her feet equally quiet when they touched the grass. "You sure you can do this?"

"No," I said. "If I grow a second head, be ready to cut it off."

Liara snorted, and Eva stopped, staring at me.

Evanora Whitewillow, the one person who refused to doubt your truthfulness. Even me, the witch. Even after four years.

I kept walking. "Both of you hang back," I said, close enough that I could smell the dark smoke. "This will be messy." *If my experiences in Edinburgh's vaults are anything to go by.*

As Loki and I neared the leyline, I allowed the chain and blade to drop. The blade hit the grass, lightly dragging over it as I walked.

"Over there, Loki," I said, staring down the length of the corruption.

He'd already struck off to twelve feet away, and now sat to watch. "I wasn't about to hang around while you swing that thing."

I gripped the rod, lifting the chain-and-blade end higher for the first time in days. As I did, the Spitfire took in a deep breath in my chest, lidded eyes opening once more.

It had been asleep since Edinburgh. Now it commenced a soft purring, and I could feel the vibration in my chest as I swung the thief's blade up and around. At the far end of its arc it cleaved through the smoke rising from the leyline, dragging it away as it had done in the vaults.

And just like in the vaults, the smoke swirled up the length of the chain toward my hands. Somewhere in the distance I heard Eva's sharp intake of breath as the Shade's magic pooled its way up my body and between my lips, up my nostrils.

When it entered me, the Spitfire came fully awake. And so did I.

In a strange, half-conscious fugue state I sensed myself swinging again and again, drawing away more of the Shade's corruption from the leyline. Drinking in every offering the blade brought to me.

The magic sang, the Spitfire sang, the blade whistled.

I wasn't even sure I was clearing the corruption—I just knew the act resulted in intoxication like a drug, and if I stopped, all the rest of it would stop. My head swam, smoky and deluged, as my arms moved.

Voices spoke. Maybe the wisps, maybe the Spitfire, maybe Rational Clem. Eventually I recognized them as Aidan and Eva and Liara, all trying to get my attention.

I ignored them. I wasn't sure if I even had the control to pay attention to them—not that I cared.

Finally, somewhere nearby, Loki's paper-thin voice cut through the sound of my work. "Hey, junkie," he said. "You've weed-whacked the thing into submission."

My annoyance flared, but I didn't stop. Not until something landed on my shoulder and ten thorns dug into my neck.

That did it.

I swung my head around, found Loki seated across my shoulders. "What the hell?"

He retracted his claws from my neck. "Better question: Are you trying to dig your way there?" His green eyes flicked past me toward the ground.

"What are you—" I followed his gaze as my hands came to a halt, the blade dropping into the grass.

In front of me, the leyline glowed gold, this section free of the Shade's corruption. But the earth had also been hacked at again and again, deep grooves left in a swath of at least six feet.

I sucked in a breath, stepping back. "I only swung... three times."

"Three times?" Loki hopped off my shoulders, coming around to stare up at me. "Yeah, in the first ten seconds."

"How long was I at it for?"

Footsteps approached from behind me. I jerked around to find Eva approaching with Liara not far behind. "Twenty minutes," Eva said. "We tried to stop you after the first two minutes."

"I heard," I said. "I think." Their voices had felt so distant, so brief.

"Didn't make a difference how loud we yelled," Liara said. "Finally Loki had to jump in."

"Barely dodged that blade of yours," Loki said.

I winced. Even now, swimming in regret, I still felt the urge to turn back to it. To stalk up and down this leyline for as far as I could follow it, thieving the dark magic along the way.

It was that delicious.

"Your hands," Eva said. "They're shaking."

When I looked down, the chain trembled as my hands shook, still tightly curled around the rod. That was my desire at work.

"Maybe you ought to sit," Aidan said, approaching on Siren. He swung down off her back. "Rest a bit."

I did as he said, dropping to a cross-legged seat on the grass. The power that had filled me in the moments I'd taken the Shade's magic dissipated as quickly as it had arrived, leaving me drained. Empty.

It was like a current passing through me, empowering me only so long as it was in motion. Now that it wasn't, both the Spitfire and I wilted. "Five minutes," I said. "Then we'll find out where she goes."

I sat before the golden leyline with crossed legs, staring down at it. Last year, Maeve Umbra had taught me to utilize the leylines' power. To follow their criss-crossing paths across the world to get where I needed to go inside my head.

But it had been a while since I'd practiced. And so far, my attempts weren't working.

Liara came forward with a scarf, tying it over my eyes. Obscuring my view of the world. "Are you sure this is necessary?"

"No," I said. "But I for one would like to get out of this forest someday, and since I don't have wings like you, my best hope is recreating those lessons in the meadow."

Liara tied the scarf off at the back, her tug so hard I winced. "Do your thing, witch."

I tried again, focusing on the leyline before me. But my magic was already consumed by the enshroudment around us, my attention focused on maintaining it—and the blindfold didn't make a difference.

I had thought I could split my attention, especially now with the Backbiter. But as it turned out, it didn't make me all-powerful, and I had always been single-minded, anyway. My brain was so fixated on safety I couldn't begin to reach for more.

So it was either drop the enshroudment, or try growing wings.

"I have to let the enshroudment go," I said through tight lips. "For a little while."

"Nobody was asking you to keep it up all day," Liara said.

Nobody except the girl inside me still hiding under her bed, staring at the ebony sabatons of a demon standing in my bedroom. Nobody except her.

I allowed the enshroudment to drop, and I drew in a long breath of warm, pine-scented air. Better. This was better.

With the weapon across my lap, both hands seated on it, I envisioned Novi Sad. It was the one place in Serbia I had ever visited, and I remembered, too, the leyline we had used to arrive there. It ran straight through the central square, where a cathedral rose high. Maybe, long ago, mages had built the square around the leyline.

As I focused on my destination, wanting to be there, the threads of my magic dipped into the leyline before me. And once they did, everything happened quickly.

My magic, now infused by the Backbiter, traveled along the leyline's length faster than Noir could gallop, almost faster than I could control, finding a cross-line five miles north of us. That one was corrupted.

I backtracked, racing south along our leyline, and found another cross-line at almost the same interval. This one wasn't yet overtaken, and I raced west, heading toward Novi Sad.

Along the way, I encountered more corruption. Most cross-lines were corrupted, and I had to take a strange, circuitous route west, moving across fields and ridges and hills.

I recognized some of these leylines. I had used them on guardian missions over the years.

"Where is she, Liara?" I whispered. "This person."

"A monastery thirty miles outside Belgrade," Liara said, her voice distant. "That was all Umbra told me."

A monastery. A religious person? I pushed the thought aside, focused instead on finding the golden glow, the lack of corruption. So much of the world's latticework of magical lines was overtaken by it.

How? How had the Shade accomplished this?

When I did find a single, glowing leyline at the edge of Serbia's border, my eyes opened. I reached up, yanked off the blindfold with a tug. I stood, turning to face the others. I was about to say, "Let's go," except there was no one to hear me.

They weren't where they'd been a few minutes ago. Eva sat on a tree branch, legs swinging, eating an apple. Liara was nowhere to be seen. Aidan was brushing off the horses as they grazed.

And the sun was high, almost at its peak.

From somewhere on my left, Loki let out a meow-yawn. He rose, stretching from his place under a tree. "The prodigal witch returns."

That caught Aidan and Eva's attention.

Eva dropped with a flutter twenty feet to the forest floor.

"Where's Liara?" I asked.

"Having lunch over there," Aidan said with a thumb over his shoulder. "She said she couldn't stand our 'constant chatter.'"

Eva shrugged, half-smiling.

I glanced behind me, back at the leyline and the spot of tamped grass where I'd been sitting. Then at the others. "Let me guess—it's been three hours?"

"Four," Eva said. "How long did it feel to you?"

"Ten minutes." My teeth ground together; I'd never liked losing time, not even to sleep. "Anyway, I found a way through."

"Excellent," Aidan said. "How about you eat, and then—"

"No." I tossed the blindfold to Aidan. "I don't want to lose any more time."

CHAPTER FOUR

We passed through the veil and into a summery, green landscape, grass and hills and leaves jostling on the trees dotted everywhere. In the distance, cars struck down a single-lane highway, one every minute, the tall grass blowing in their wake.

Serbia in August was lovely.

"You said a monastery," I said to Liara as I stared out from atop Noir. "Where?"

"Thirty miles outside Belgrade," Liara repeated.

"In which direction?" Aidan said from Siren's back.

"If Umbra had told me that," Liara said, steely eyes flicking from me to him, "you can be sure I would have told you."

"It's fine." Eva slid her phone from her cloak. "There aren't many monasteries, and we have the world's knowledge in our hands."

"Finally," Loki said, "a fae with the common sense to use the only true magic humans have ever been able to create."

Eva's search turned up over fifty monasteries scattered in the hundred miles around Belgrade, and twenty within a thirty-mile radius of the city. She lowered her phone. "It's going to be a long day."

"We can't just go around knocking on the door of every monastery in the countryside," Aidan said. "How many people around here ride horses? We'll look strange."

"You already look strange," Liara said.

Aidan straightened his glasses. "Point that cannon elsewhere, Youngblood."

I stood staring at the leyline running off into the field. It glowed gold as it cut through the grass, a straight line toward the trees. One thing I'd noticed in my attempts to get us to Serbia: so few leylines had been uncorrupted, and this was the only line anywhere close to Belgrade that still remained pure.

Umbra had removed the corruption from the leyline outside the academy early into our school year. If she had that power, and I had that power, maybe someone else had that power, too.

Loki hopped onto my shoulder. "You're suspiciously quiet."

"I'm thinking."

"Hence the suspicion."

I pointed in the direction the leyline cut through the earth, raising my voice for everyone to hear. "We should follow this."

Liara and Aidan stopped bickering. Aidan squinted at me, lenses reflecting the sun. "The leyline?"

Without another word, I turned Noir and urged him into a trot along the leyline's course. As he passed directly over it, a strange sensation funneled up through me, like I could feel the vestiges of someone's magic running through it, an old scent.

It was familiar. Why was it familiar?

But I knew this was the way. It had to be.

The others followed, Aidan catching up on Siren, Eva and Liara in the air. We traveled while the sun was at its zenith, until we hit the trees and the leyline crossed with another.

Liara dropped to the ground. "The lines disappear after the cross."

"They don't disappear," I said. "They're corrupted."

Here at the crossing, the line was corrupted to the north and the west. It remained pure along the cross-line to the east. A perfect right turn, like a direction. Like someone was telling us where to go.

Eva dropped to a crouch on a tree branch. "Everything's corrupted except this one direction?"

"Yeah," I said. "Funny thing."

Siren stamped at the ground, and atop her, Aidan said, "Should we be concerned we're being led into something?"

I directed Noir over the pure leyline, and once again that familiar scent of magic came over me. It didn't feel evil. "No," I said. "Not concerned. Liara, you're sure Umbra said this person would help us?"

"No. She only said I should take you to her."

I hesitated on Noir's back. The horse itched to move, his back hoof rising and jerking back down, tail flicking. I should trust Umbra. But I couldn't—not fully. Not now that I knew what she was hiding under her office.

But I did trust Liara.

"What do you think, Youngblood?" I said. "Follow the golden thread?"

Her eyes narrowed as they glanced one way, then the next, staring after the leyline as it disappeared amidst the trees. "Yeah," she said. "But keep your enshroudment up."

We cantered the horses for the next hour, until Eva insisted we stop for lunch.

"I'd rather not," I said.

"Twenty minutes won't kill you," she said. "But falling off your horse from low blood sugar will. That would be a sad way for the last witch to go out, wouldn't it?"

Eva's motherliness was oppressive and logical. "You win."

Eva, ever prepared, pulled a thin blanket from her cloak, settling it across the grass while Aidan tied Siren's reins to a tree and I left Noir to graze nearby. We ate around Liara's conjured platter of char kuay teow, and Liara tilted her head as she watched the horses.

"You'd think he would run off," she said, nodding at Noir. "I know I would."

I swirled my noodles around my fork. "That's why you were made a fae and not a horse."

"He's bound to her," Aidan said. "Not like Siren. The mare never took especially to me."

Eva offered him a sympathy glass of water.

"Bound?" Liara said. "I thought horses were bound to magic. Not one mage."

"She isn't a mage," Eva said. "She's a witch."

My eyes lifted to Noir, who tugged hard at a patch of succulent grass. It was more than that. I was as bound to him as he was to me. "I don't think I would have made it," I said. "Without him."

"Made it where?" Liara said.

"Through my first year."

"You were kind of depressing," Liara said.

I dipped my fingers into the bowl of soy sauce, flicked it at her. "No thanks to you."

"She wasn't depressing," Eva said. "Clem just didn't trust anyone."

That was it. That was the thing I didn't want to say.

Liara swiped the soy sauce off her shirt. "But you trusted the worst horse at the academy."

"Yeah," I said, finally taking a bite. "It's easier to know what to expect from someone who doesn't trust anybody."

Nearby, Noir snorted, head lifting. He stared into the wind, mane blown back, nostrils widening. When his head swung toward me, eyes meeting mine, I knew it was time to go.

By the late afternoon the leylines had crossed once more. Again the corruption had been cleansed at a right angle, and we turned east, toward Belgrade. I could see the city in the far distance, and I could also make out old buildings amongst the sloping hills.

When we came to a high point in the land, I brought Noir to a standstill, tracing the path of the leyline straight toward those buildings. "Loki," I said. "What does that look like to you?"

"Old churches." He stared out from my shoulder. "A few of them clustered together."

Eva had pulled out her phone again. "We're almost exactly thirty miles south of Belgrade."

"They're monasteries," I said. "And someone was leading us to them."

For better or worse, we had arrived.

The leyline's purity ended almost exactly at the start to a dirt path that led to an old stone church nestled into a little rise amidst trees, a Greek Orthodox cross carved from the stone at the apex of the roof.

We paused at the sign, which read, *Tresije Monastery* in English beneath the Cyrillic. The church looked a thousand years old, and it might have been.

"Now what?" Aidan said. "We can't very well just walk inside, can we?"

"Even if we do, does anyone speak Serbian?" Eva asked.

None of us did. Of course not.

But a moment later, an ancient, creaking voice called from the distance, "I do."

Someone heard us.

But that wasn't possible. We were inside the enshroudment.

My head jerked around to where the trees were densest. There stood a bent-backed old woman, her eyes on us, one hand on a hip and the other holding a half-empty glass bottle by the neck. She was staring at me.

She sees us.

But she couldn't possibly do that, because she had no eyesight—her pupils were rolled back, eyelids fluttering. She was completely blind.

A bouquet of frizz hung long and unkempt around her head, veiling the sides of her sun-spotted, drooping face. She had to be ninety or a hundred or more. She wore nothing but simple brown robes, probably the same ones the priests at the monastery wore.

She looked homeless. Maybe crazy.

Eva appeared in a flash of wings, hovering by my side. "Clem," she said, "did that old woman talk to us?"

"Old!" the woman hooted, her body jerking with the word. "That's something coming from a fae."

Any question I'd had was erased. This woman could see through my enshroudment. But no one could do that except for Maeve Umbra.

Liara stepped out in front of us, placing herself between the woman and the horses.

"Oh, and what are you going to do?" The woman's head tilted to get a better view of Liara as the old fingers rose to twiddle through the air. "Sprinkle me with your fae dust?"

"You don't even—" Liara began.

"Or," the woman went on, her low, gravelly voice crowding out Liara's, "maybe you'll scowl hard enough to knock me right over. Careful, girl—a face like that will stick."

Liara straightened, and even from behind, I could feel her shock. Which made me smile. I kind of liked the crazy sass.

"Forget her," Liara said, turning toward the monastery.

"No," I said. "That woman is blind."

"So?" Liara said, practically vibrating with annoyance.

"Blind!" the old woman hooted again. "So both you and the fae have cueballs for brains."

"She's blind," I went on, "but she can see all of us. And she can see right through my enshroudment."

Liara stopped, staring up at me. "You didn't drop the enshroudment when we arrived?"

I swept an arm out. "See for yourself."

Around us, the enshroudment shimmered an iridescent red-orange, much good it did.

"Best you come out from under your little blanket now." The old woman hadn't moved, but she seemed to have gotten closer. Or maybe her presence had grown in my mind. "It's a paltry simulacrum of Maeve's magic, anyway."

I went stiff. Maeve. She knew Maeve.

I met eyes with Aidan, Eva, then Liara.

Is she the one? I mouthed at the fae.

Liara turned back, sullen fists clenched. "Gods, I hope not."

"I hope *so*," Loki said from behind me on Noir. "She's the most entertainment I've had since the sixties."

Eva flew closer, whispering into my ear, "She seems unstable."

The old woman chuckled low, as if she'd heard. She did seem unstable. But she also knew Maeve, and I had the sense she had other secrets, too. And power.

"What's your name?" I called out to the woman.

"You haven't earned that," she shot back, half-annoyed, half-amused. "For now, you may call me the Envoy of Pain."

I *did* like her. "Is that your wrestling name?"

Liara groaned. "Surely there's another monastery with a mysterious person Umbra wanted to send us to."

"Oh, it's most definitely me," the woman said. "Do I not look mysterious enough to you, fae?" Her hand went into her hair, shaking at the frizz like she was trying to dislodge a bird's nest from a tree.

The wisps flew lazily around her, as though considering her. They didn't seem to react to her in any real way, even when she reached into the air to pluck one out of her line of vision. It slipped away, went on circling.

I started Noir forward, allowing the enshroudment to drop away. As I walked him up to the woman, her fluttering eyelids opened wider, face turning up toward me. I swung down, boots hitting the grass. With her hunch, she only stood about four and a half feet tall before me. "I'm Clementine."

Her mouth worked as if deciding on words, eyes moving at strange angles. My spine lit up with a shiver, and a strange sensation came over me. The air around me seemed to change, to shift.

"Clementine," she said. "Let me guess, you fancy yourself special."

"That's not exactly the word I'd use."

A smile cracked her lips, revealing gaps. "You're going to be fun." Faster than my eyes could follow, the woman's arm flew out and she walloped me on the side of the head.

I dropped, face ricocheting on my neck like I'd been shot, and as the ground rose to meet me, I had one thought:

Definitely her wrestling name.

CHAPTER FIVE

I hit the ground hard, spinning until I landed on my hands and chest. My mouth hit the earth, and I felt one of my teeth cut into my lip in a burst of pain.

She'd hit me. The old woman had hit me.

And that wasn't any regular throwdown. She'd thrown me like six-foot-five Torsten during my first year in his combat class, but she'd been *faster* than him.

"'Special' isn't the word I'd use for you, either," she hooted above me. "Oh, and here comes the motley cavalry. Well, let's see your mettle, then. Quickly, before I get bored."

I raised my face to find Eva and Liara already rushing through the air, their eyes fixed on the old woman, lightning already crackling between Liara's hands. Aidan had urged Siren forward, his birthmark glowing at his neck.

And behind me, a hiss filled the space between me and the woman.

I pushed myself up, only to feel a hard force drive straight into my back. I thudded back down in a pile of hair and caught a glimpse of the old woman leaping ahead, landing lightly some three feet in front of my face.

She'd used me like a stepping stone.

When she turned, hands clasped behind her back, her head angled left to avoid a bolt of lightning. "Nearly singed a hair off!" she cackled. "Actually, I lied. You didn't even come close."

A burst of wind followed—Eva's attack—but she didn't even move. It simply blew her hair around her face, and she went on cackling all the while, still amused over Liara's lightning.

Her blind eyes fixed on me. "One old woman got you down, Tangerine?"

I huffed, went to thrust myself up and get my feet under me. But I couldn't—I couldn't move from the ground. It was like the old woman's foot on my back had permanently pinned me there, even though she wasn't even touching me anymore.

"Whoops," the woman cackled. "Should have done those morning push-ups while you had the chance."

I struggled against whatever force kept my chest to the ground, but the power of it was like a thousand-pound millstone on my back. "We didn't come here for this."

"Didn't you?" she shot back.

I needed the wisps—needed them to end this. *Stop her*, I thought. But nothing happened. I couldn't even see them. All I could see were the insane eyes and wild hair of the woman above me.

Liara came swooping in from the left with a growl. The moment her feet touched the ground, she sent a leg out in a roundhouse kick at the woman's chest.

The woman ducked under it. "That's a nice little move." As she rose, she swung her shoulder back to avoid Liara's palm hand shooting out toward her. "But not nice enough."

I stared as the two of them scuffled. Liara was a deft fighter—she'd kicked my ass over and over for the first year I'd spent at the academy —and moved faster than Eva and Aidan, and me on most days. She used every one of her limbs when she fought, and her magic, and her wings.

So as she and the old woman scuffled in the grass, Liara's hands and lightning and feet striking out and finding only air where the old woman had stood, I began to wonder if I was dreaming.

My tongue found the spot where my tooth had pierced my lip; no, not dreaming.

The Envoy of Pain didn't move like a woman in her nineties, or even someone half her age. She dodged, slipped, hopped, and never took a blow.

And she had *one hand tucked behind her back the whole time.*

A few seconds into the fight, one of Eva's vortexes railroaded toward the woman. She was nearly knocked over by it, but she managed to find her momentum at the edge of it, using it to propel her toward Liara, to give her thrust.

The woman struck out at Liara, nearly caught her with her fingernails across the cheek before Liara rolled away. The fae's foot flew out as she rolled, tripped the old woman.

The Envoy of Pain stumbled, caught herself in a somersault. When she came up to a crouch, her free hand before her for balance, she smiled. "So you've got some tricks in you after all." The hand she'd kept tucked behind her back came free now as her attention flicked to her right. "Well, so do I."

She launched herself at Liara. With a blast of air magic, Eva shoulder-charged the woman to knock her off course. But the woman used both hands to duck under the violet-haired fae, throwing her over her body and into the air as she spun through the blast of air. And as she landed before Liara, whose fingers crackled with lightning, the woman shoved the heel of her palm straight past the lightning and into Liara's chest.

It was a perfect hit. Liara was knocked away with a cry, her wings taking her airborne.

The old woman was quicker than all of us. Stronger.

"She broke my godsdamn rib," Liara breathed, dropping to the ground some ten feet away.

Eva was next to her in a second, one protective arm around Liara.

"Not broken. Just bruised." The old woman's hands clasped once more behind her back as she turned to the rest of us, her form still as hunched as a question mark. "The sour fae could be better. Both could be much better. Angry yet, Orange?" she said to me.

Aidan came alongside me on Siren, and as I angled my face up, I spotted blue fire on five of his fingertips. "Touch any one of them again," he said, breathing fast, "and I'll give you a burn like you've never felt before."

The woman's eyes ceased fluttering for a second, and her lips curled. "So you've got the otherworldly gift of the Norths." She observed him, head moving in a survey of his head to his toes. "Except you haven't got a clue what to do with all that power. Maybe I ought to strip you of it."

"I'll do you one better," I yelled from the ground. "Maybe I should strip you of your face."

She raised her eyes to the sky, a howl of laughter coming out of her. Tears formed at the corners of her eyes. She wiped at them, then glanced at Loki by my feet. "Does she always talk like that? I can't imagine why you've stuck around."

"For the milk," Loki said solemnly.

"Hey," I said. "Don't shit-talk me with my cat."

I tried again to summon the wisps, to make them obey. They still ignored me, floating idly around us like bugs.

She wiped away more tears, and finally the old woman's face went chillingly serious. "Huh, you tamp down your anger. That, or you don't have it in you."

What the hell is she talking about?

"Well"—in a blur of motion she was next to Siren, grabbing hold of Aidan's leg and yanking him off the mare—"I suppose I'll have to force out which it is."

Aidan hit the ground hard, his glasses flying off, bouncing away into the field. The woman was on him in a second, drawing him up with an arm around his throat and five fingers digging into his hair to turn his face aside.

"Look at this," she said, one half-inch fingernail digging into the artery just below his birthmark. "It's the birthmark that only comes around once in a century. Too bad you'll die with it."

Without a thought, I found myself on my feet, the Backbiter in my hand, the chain unfurling as the blade hit the grass. I had pulled it automatically from my cloak the second the Spitfire had flared with keening rage, the moment I'd seen her pull Aidan off the horse.

"*You'll die*," I hissed, only a fraction Rational Clem now. Most of me was consumed—instantly and thoroughly—by the creature. "*For that, you'll die.*"

This time the Spitfire felt darker than it ever had. More intense. Drenched in and empowered by the Shade's magic.

The woman's face lifted, her fluttering eyes gleaming red-orange as they reflected the flames dancing over my hands and the weapon. "There," she whispered. "That's what I was promised."

Somewhere Eva was calling out to me, saying my name. I couldn't answer her. Not now that I had let it out. Not now that the old woman had threatened to kill Aidan.

Not now that the Spitfire had consumed me.

I came at the woman with a yell, raising the weapon in an arc and bringing the flaming blade cleaving through the air toward her head.

She thrust Aidan aside, who stumbled off through the grass. "Good," she hissed, even as she ducked low, the flames nearly catching her hair. "Come at me."

I angled the weapon left, swinging the blade back the other way just as she straightened to her regular bent-backed posture. "It's very pretty," she said, one sandaled foot coming out to shove me backward. When it connected, I was thrust back with surprising force. "And you're very much inept with it."

I skidded to a stop, my chest blossoming with pain and anger. With a growl, I raised the rod high, the blade swinging high and fast over my head. The woman's face followed it like a cat's, her eyes on the prize, until I swung it low enough to sever her head from her neck.

Then she ducked, bull-rushed me. In a second I was on my back, one of her hands pinning my weapon-hand down to the grass with the same thousand pounds of force I'd felt before. Her legs straddled me, and though I kicked and fought, she loomed over me, eyelids fluttering with certain victory.

My lips curled back, and I raised my head with a hiss.

She stared back with those sightless eyes. "So that's how it looks from the outside." Then her face drew nearer, and she whispered, "Clementine."

With that whisper, her voice changed entirely. It wasn't an old woman's, but young. Soothing. Familiar. A remnant of who she'd been long ago. And hearing my name from her, even as I went on writhing, it was more of Rational Clem who did the fighting.

Eva's face appeared in my periphery, but the old woman snapped her fingers in the air. "Don't interfere, girl. I won't hurt her."

Seconds passed as I writhed, and soon I was breathing fast, and that was all. Just like that, the Spitfire had receded. It had never gone that fast. The fight had gone out of me against the unyielding force of her.

My fingers loosened on the Backbiter.

She took in a deep breath through her nose, let it out. Her grip on my wrist grew gentle. "Where are you trying to go, Clementine?"

"What?"

"I didn't stutter."

I blinked hard, opened my eyes to stare up at her. An earnestness had entered her face, that wicked smile gone. She really wanted to know. "I'm..." Where *was* I trying to go?

"It's a simple question," she said. "Everyone's going somewhere."

"Hell," I said, the word spat like a seed. "I'm trying to go to Hell."

She chuckled, a gritty, deep sound, and didn't seem at all surprised. "And you've come to a monastery to do it." She got off me, reached out a hand to help me up. And as I looked up at the old woman—the Envoy of Pain—I saw all the madness had receded. The eyelids only fluttered a little.

She was perfectly calm, perfectly sane.

I took her hand, and she pulled me to my feet. Patted her sandal print off the front of my shirt. "You did well. Now, let's have a drink."

My head reeled. "You saw through my enshroudment. No one can do that."

"With age you'll find that speaking in absolutes will fail you every time." Her head tilted as she glanced past me. "And that's your motley band, I suppose."

"Gods, do I love her," Loki said, now appearing at my feet. He'd been conspicuously absent the whole fight, probably spectating from the sidelines. *Ugh, my cat.*

The woman acknowledged him with raised eyebrows. "And a decent familiar found you."

"Decent?" I said.

She ignored me, turned on slow, careful feet in the other direction. Her arm swept out. "Come on, all of you. Nothing to be had from the head monk except those eternal half-smiles and dribs and drabs of wine he refuses to drink in more than small sips."

When I glanced back at the others, I nodded. They still seemed hesitant, but Eva flew forward. She would be with me no matter what. Aidan came next, and Liara last of all, refusing to fly. Instead, she walked with folded arms at the end of the line, following the procession up the hill alongside the monastery and into a thicket of trees.

We walked for maybe five minutes in silence, the sun drowned out more and more by the dense canopy. I should have been cautious, but I wasn't. She was one old woman, and we had two elements and a lightning fae between us, but it was more than that.

Loki liked her. I liked her, too.

We came to a small hut in a clearing, where a brown mutt began barking and dancing at us as soon as we arrived. Around him, the trees had been cleared out for maybe three yards, the hut not dilapidated, but definitely not in great shape, either.

The thatch roof was grown over with moss and age. The door sat partially ajar. The construction was wood, but not like a modern house —like someone had sawn the trees into halves and stuck them together with mud as grout. The windows fluttered with cloth, the small wood shutters open to the air.

It looked like a witch's house in the forest. Like how I'd envisioned Hansel and Gretel's killer luring them in when I was six.

Except for the dog. Who only had wild, intense barks for Loki.

"Oh, Bill." The woman swiped a hand through the air as she passed him. "Don't pretend. We both know you'd be beside yourself if that cat came within three feet of you."

As if testing that theory, Loki leapt from Noir's back to the ground as we approached. He trotted ahead, nearing the dog with his tail up, totally unafraid. The closer he got, the more the dog backed up, shrinking toward his mistress and the house.

"See?" The woman came to stand in the doorway, looking out at us. "Now you've gone and shown yourself for what you are."

Loki paused, tail flicking back and forth, observing Bill. Waiting.

Bill, who wasn't much bigger than a border collie, looked between his mistress and Loki and let out a final gruff. Then he was done, but he still skirted the cat as he trotted toward the hut.

"Well," I said over to Aidan, "she named her dog Bill. That either makes her harmless or great at seeming harmless."

Either way, I wanted to know more.

CHAPTER SIX

We left the horses to graze in the clearing. The wisps, too, whom the old woman refused to have flying around her hut. "Unsaddle and unbridle the mare, and don't bother closing them inside the lean-to," she said with a flick of the hand. "If they're mages' horses, they won't stray far."

The quartermistress at the academy had once told me that a mage's horse could never be without magic. Once they'd been around it long enough, they were bound to it. But how did this old woman know that?

Liara found my side, her face confidentially close to mine. "We're not really going inside that crazy old woman's house."

"There's four of us, and she's an old woman." I flashed a grin at her. "Afraid, Youngblood?"

"After what I saw her do?" She sucked in a breath. "Yeah, and I'm not ashamed to admit it."

I couldn't explain it to her, but I had a feeling. This was the right place—this woman wouldn't hurt us. Not more than she already had. "Come on." I slapped Liara's shoulder, starting forward. "You and I of all people shouldn't fear crazy."

As Aidan removed Siren's riding gear, the woman led the rest of us inside. Loki, daring as always, was the first one through the door of the hut.

When he'd disappeared inside, I heard him say, "Oh. *Oh.*"

"Good oh or bad oh?" I called out.

"He's found my oven for cooking you to tender morsels." The old woman's cackle echoed from somewhere in the hut.

"I wish I knew she was joking," Eva whispered, passing me by.

"Just get in here," Loki said. "Before the formalists find us."

"No formalists," the old woman's voice echoed. "Nothing that goes bump in the night will find you out here, I assure you."

I exchanged glances with Liara. Then I shrugged. "My cat thinks it's fine."

"Cats have good judgment, right?" Aidan called across the clearing.

"They're good at keeping their own tails alive, at least," Liara said, still hanging back with crossed arms. She was still bitter over the hit she'd taken to the chest, even though Eva had administered healing magic.

I went through first, pressing the door of the hut open. I'd expected grime, must, darkness. But when I came into the dark interior, I found it was as much an illusion as the door I'd stepped through into the academy that first night in the woods four years ago.

Past the other side of the darkness, the hut became a home. I stepped into a pool of light from a skylight—yes, with real glass—set into the roof, and around me, a cozy cabin spread much wider and taller than was possible from the outside.

I stood in the entryway, and to my right lay a fireplace and a living room with a three-seater, tan leather couch, two identical armchairs facing inward, a live-edge wooden coffee table, a square heather rug, and Loki already sitting in the middle of all of it, staring back at me.

He gave a smug meow.

Across the room before me, an oval dining table with four high-backed carved chairs sat near a pair of tall windows overlooking the forest. And to my left, a doorway led into another room, and a set of stairs disappeared up to a second level.

"Can you say tangible manipulations?" Liara whispered, arriving at my side.

Eva and Aidan pushed in behind me. And Eva was the first to gasp. "You have got to be kidding me."

The old woman, no longer bent-backed—but still with frizzy white hair—appeared from the doorway on my left with a pitcher of drink in each hand, one orange and one clear. She still wore the brown robes and sandals, but she moved more smoothly, her eyelids no longer fluttering. Still blind, though. And for the first time, I noticed old, white scars. They littered the skin on the backs of her hands, the patch of her exposed neck and chest, even her cheeks.

Was her appearance an illusion? I couldn't tell.

Bill followed her out of the other room, sticking close by, eyes darting from us to the cat seated on the coffee table with a flicking tail. He gave another gruff in our general direction.

"Which part baffles you, fae?" the woman said, her voice no longer ancient and gravelly—but still a much older woman's. "I must know. I am exceptionally proud of my work, and I so rarely receive guests to appreciate it."

Eva stared at her. "All of it."

She delivered the two pitchers onto the dining table. "I began with the structure. That alone took me twenty years."

"So you're a mage," Aidan said.

"Was," she said. "Now I just toy with the vestiges of what's available to me."

"What does that mean?" Liara shot back.

The woman turned, and even now two things were clear: she saw us, and she was also blind. "It means you've brought her to the right person, Liara Youngblood. And you really ought to stop scowling—life could be much, much worse than a bruised rib and the choice of red or white wine before your meal."

"I do love her," Loki murmured.

I took a step forward, out of the pool of light. "So you know Maeve Umbra."

"Knew," the woman said. "And she knew me as Samara."

"What happened?" Liara said with arms still folded. "You kick her in the ribs?"

Samara leaned against the table, setting both hands on it. Her blind eyes flashed at Liara with mischief. "In a manner of speaking."

"How can you see us?" I asked.

Her face shifted to me. "The same way Maeve taught you to use your magic to hear and see. Surely she wasn't negligent about that."

I shook my head, gaze drifting into nothing. She had taught me to layer my magic over other people's ears, their eyes, as a way of seeing. "She said it was for our guardian missions." But of course it wasn't. My face lifted, and I scrutinized her. "So you see yourself through our eyes?"

"It took a very long time to get used to." Samara retrieved five glasses from a cabinet as Bill followed her every move with his black eyes as he lay on his bed in the corner. "Now, if you'd believe it, I feel like I see as you do."

"You said you only have vestiges of magic." Eva turned a slow circle, hands going out. "But this place is incredible."

"And it took me forty-five years." She had set the glasses on the table, now lifted a pitcher to pour the orange drink. "I was never very good at tangible manipulations even when I was in my prime. Is Walter Goodbarrel still at the academy, by the by?"

"Professor Goodbarrel?" Eva said. "His name's Donald. He's taught at Shadow's End for thirty years."

Samara let out a laugh entirely different—softer, smoother—from the way she'd acted outside. "Goodbarrel's son carries on the legacy. I shouldn't be so surprised."

So she knows about Maeve and Shadow's End from more than thirty years back. Was she a student, or a professor?

"Is forty-five years a long time to manipulate a place like this into being?" Aidan asked.

Eva stayed silent, unwilling to say so, but Liara didn't hold back. "It's forever."

"Just as the dour fae says." Samara turned back to us, crossed to me and handed off one of the glasses of dark liquid. The red wine. "Everything comes slower to me now."

I accepted the glass. "Didn't seem that way outside."

"I had an advantage, you see." She brought glasses to each of her other guests, two at a time. Then she came to stand in front of us, palms out by her sides. "You all are terrible at fighting a witch."

Aidan had just taken his first sip of wine, and as Samara spoke, he coughed into it. A little geyser of the drink erupted over his face, sprayed on the floor. He went on coughing, pounding his chest.

Meanwhile, I just stared at the old woman, her frame shrinking away from me as though she was becoming smaller and farther away, the whole world kaleidoscoping around her.

A witch.

"Impossible," Loki whispered from his seat on the coffee table.

"A *what*?" Liara hissed.

Samara's white eyes flicked to her, the ghost of a smile appearing. "Maybe your bitterness has distorted your comprehension."

Eva came to my side, her arm pressing up against mine. "You can't be a witch."

"Is that a formalist decree?" Samara's glassy eyes flicked again. "Or perhaps Shadow's End now cultivates all fae to be so snappish and bossy."

"It's not a command," Liara said. "It's a fact."

"Willfully misinterpreting my willful misinterpretation." Samara twirled her fingers through the air. "Who's next in line? How about you, the clueless North with the once-in-a-century gift."

Aidan had finally stopped coughing, and he straightened, clearing his throat. "I thought that might have been a hex you cast on Clementine."

"Ah, so one of you is perceptive, at least." Samara pointed at him. "You Norths always were craftiest when you had the right prescription on your lenses."

My gaze snapped to Samara. That was a hex she'd cast on me when I couldn't stand from the ground. It wasn't a paralysis hex—I had learned that one and could resist it easily.

Maybe she was a witch.

As I studied her, my eyes traveled again over her hands, her frame, her hair. "You've cast a hex on all of us," I said, low. "Even now."

Samara's smirk deepened. She turned away, passing toward the table for the last glass. She poured herself water, and when she turned back around, her appearance was back to the old woman's, stooped and shuffling. With fluttering eyelids, she took a long sip of water. Then, lifting the glass away, she raised to me from her position halfway to the ground. "I salute you, young fire witch, heir to the prophecy."

Heir to the prophecy?

Before I could speak, she was shuffling off into the kitchen.

Eva's hand came to my arm, squeezing. She leaned toward me. "We can leave. We can leave now, if you like."

Both Bill and I were looking at the open doorway the old woman had passed through. The witch. There was another witch in the world. It occurred to me that might be why her magic had seemed familiar. "No," I said, "I can't."

I couldn't leave. Couldn't possibly.

From the kitchen, the sound of pots and dishes clanged. A pleasant, enticing scent wafted out.

"You led us here," I called out to her. "You uncorrupted the leylines."

"You led yourself here," her old woman's voice rang back. "I simply cleared the way should you ever desire to become a real witch."

My lip curled without my consent, and Liara and I exchanged a glance. She was a good one to turn to when you wanted to commiserate.

Hate her, Liara mouthed at me.

"And what makes you think anyone here is a witch?" Aidan called back, winking at me like he'd gotten one over on the woman.

From the kitchen, Samara hooted again. She said nothing else, just went on shuffling around as the pleasant scents grew stronger, more enticing.

I unwound my arm from Eva's and began a slow approach to the kitchen doorway. She was fascinating, alluring, this woman. And when I had crested the doorway and found her standing simply before a stove, stirring something in a large pot, she was back to her straight-backed appearance.

There was something awfully familiar in the way she stood. In the way she glanced over her shoulder at me. "It must be hard," she murmured, "to find out you are not the very last witch in the world."

I blinked, considering my feelings on it for the first time. And what I found there wasn't "hard"—not at all. Not difficult, not unpleasant, not unwanted. "No," I said. "It's easy."

For the first time since my mother and sister had left my life, a sense of aloneness I hadn't known the depths of wasn't there anymore. It couldn't have been filled, I realized, by anyone but her.

She was a witch. She knew it, and she knew what I was, and she didn't bear any hate toward me. Samara didn't have any hate at all. How did I know that? It was written over everything: her furniture, the way she'd crafted her home, the way her dog loved her, the way she stood over the stove.

But she had sadness. It lined her face.

"I understand why Umbra sent me to you," I said, leaning against the doorway as she went on stirring.

"Is that so?" Samara went on stirring, but I could hear her real intrigue.

"It's like you said: I'm not a real witch. Not yet." And no one could teach me to be one except another witch.

Her head tilted, long white hair shifting along her back. "Humility? Now that's a turn."

I smiled. "I'm sure you'll be disappointed to know you aren't the first person to kick my ass."

She snorted, lifted her spoon from the pot as she turned around. It was coated in red sauce, and as she set it on the counter alongside the stove, she said, "It's more than teaching you."

"Tell me what it is."

She looked past me, toward the doorway. "It's the ones you've brought with you. I can teach you to be a witch, but they have to know how to fight with you."

"With me? No—I'm fighting the Shade alone."

"Perhaps, if she were alone herself," she murmured. "But she never is."

"And where is she?"

"Why, she's in Hell," she said. Before I could snark back, she said, "And once a path to Hell has been trodden, it closes forever. Tell me, Clementine: Do you desire to return from Hell?"

I hesitated. "I haven't thought about it."

"Nonsense—of course you have. I sense a strong desire in you to live long enough for your hair to whiten."

I nearly stepped back, my hands finding the doorway's frame instead. Did I desire that? I hadn't really contemplated a future, not one beyond a few months, maybe years. Years at most, since I'd arrived at the academy.

But now...

"I'll have to ask them," I murmured.

Eva appeared in the doorway like she'd been summoned. "Don't be an idiot." She was flanked by Aidan and Loki piling in. "We're in."

"What she said," Loki declared as he trotted into the center of the room, evaluated the counter, and then leapt onto it with perfect feline grace, staring back at me.

Eva glanced around. Then, through the doorway, "Liara. Come here."

No response. The doorway remained empty.

Eva drew in air to call again, and then Liara's sour face appeared from the darkness. She stepped in, leaning against the doorway. "You'll make yourself hoarse with that shrillness, Whitewillow."

Eva smiled, turned back to Samara. "That means she's in."

Samara's arms folded, surveying the lot of us. "So you've brought me two fae, a North, and a cat who can't keep his paws off my counter. The training will take time, and a great deal of wine."

CHAPTER SEVEN

The training would begin at sunrise. After dinner, we were allowed to wander the witch's hut. No tour, because Samara couldn't be bothered with such things. We could enter any room "except for my bedroom," Samara said with a pointed finger drifting between us. "That's my space alone."

The downstairs consisted of the living room, two of the walls lined with bookshelves. Nearby lay the dining table we had eaten at, and through the doorway, the kitchen.

No witch's cauldron. No eyes or newts in jars. The stove was set in the corner, its pipe trailing out the ceiling. A farmhouse sink sat in another corner, and smooth wooden countertops lined the walls. Windows gazed out onto the forest, and I stood before them.

Eva came to my side, and I gestured to one of the windows. "This hut didn't have any glass, did it?"

"Of course not," Samara said from the other room. "At least, not visible from the outside. Cute trick, no?"

Eva leaned close to the windows, tapping a pane. "This is tangible manipulation?"

Samara chuckled, and it bubbled through the hut. "Young Donald Goodbarrel didn't teach you that, I suppose."

I wandered toward the second doorway, from the kitchen into a small library with a single armchair and four walls of books from floor to ceiling. New books, old books—mostly old books, and that was where I found Aidan, already seated in the armchair with a book in his lap.

"Is it in Braille?" I said.

His eyes lifted, eyebrows drawing down. "No. That's curious."

I picked a book off one of the shelves, leafed through it. No Braille. Not the next one, either, or the third one I lifted from a shelf.

"Samara," I called, leaning out the doorway, "all of your books are for people with working eyes."

"And working noses," she called back. "Who doesn't like the smell of them?"

Aidan shrugged, his eyes already back on his book. "Well, she's not wrong."

The library's other doorway led back to the hut's front door, and on the left, stairs leading to the second floor. I was the first upstairs, reaching the landing and turning a slow circle. Four rustic doors greeted me.

The first one led into a bedroom with a large bed with a quilt spread. The second one into another bedroom, this one with a second well-sized bed. The third led into a bathroom, and I took a second to stare at the porcelain toilet, wondering if magic could create a septic system.

That was the kind of magic I needed to learn.

Finally, the last door was locked. Samara's bedroom.

The whole house was clean and cared for. But when I wandered back into one of the empty bedrooms and untied my cloak, an instinct told me to kneel. When I looked under the bed, something gleamed back at me. I retrieved a corked, not-quite-empty wine bottle. Probably not the only one forgotten and lying around.

So we've entered a wino's lair.

Back downstairs, I found a broom sweeping all on its own. In the kitchen, it sounded like dishes were being washed. "You have a lot of beds," I said to Samara when I approached her on the couch. Then held the almost-empty bottle up. "And refreshments."

"Of course I have beds. Or would you rather the floor?" The woman had been reclining with Bill at her side and a thin-stemmed glass of wine on the table. The firelight gleamed over her scars, illuminating them so that she looked like she'd been drawn on. Her blind eyes turned up to me, fixed on the bottle. "Oh, I forgot about that one. A vintage, if I recall."

When I handed it down to her, she uncorked the bottle, sniffed. She made a pleased face and swigged at the bottle. "Definitely not for guests." Then she seemed to remember I was there. "Well, what is it?"

"Those animations," I said. "I've only met one person who could manage them, and she was the headmistress of our academy. It's supposed to be a rare, practically lost form of enchantment magic."

Samara's lips curled. "And what do you make of that?"

"I think Umbra must have shared what she knew with you."

She shrugged, took another swig from the bottle. "Keep an eye on what happens around you, heir to the prophecy, and you might figure it out."

What does that mean?

The old witch's attention was already back on the fire, her hand straying over Bill's head. A dismissal.

I went back upstairs, the warmth and post-food coma hitting me all at once. In the room where I'd left my cloak, I found Liara sitting on the edge of the bed with crossed arms.

She glanced back at me when I came in. "Close the door."

I did so. "Are we bunking?"

"Aidan snores."

I smiled, crossed to the window overlooking the nighttime forest. All I could see was my own reflection in the glass, wild red hair and tired eyes.

I could tell Liara wanted to talk, but if I said anything now, she would just close off, shut down. So I just leaned on the sill, hands braced beside me, waiting.

"We should leave," she said after a beat.

My eyebrows rose, head tilting. "Finally got tired of walking around with your arms crossed?"

"That woman's a drunk," Liara went on, uncrossing her arms. "And a witch. I don't know which is worse."

"Depends, I guess." I set a hand to my chest. "Me, I definitely know which is worse."

"This can't possibly be who Umbra wanted us to find." Liara stood, pacing toward the other window. She was a cocktail of fifty percent impulse, fifty percent revenge.

"There must be another powerful magic-user near a monastery in the middle of Serbia," I said. "If we get lucky, she might be a sober witch."

Liara groaned at her reflection. "Gods, why did she have to be a witch?"

The doorknob turned, and we both jerked toward the door as it opened. Eva and Aidan appeared, Loki scampering between their ankles. "Can we come in?" Eva said.

"We're just discussing the merits of my kind," I said. "What do you think of our host?"

The two of them closed the door and took seats on the bed after Loki had hopped up. Aidan had an armful of books he had presumably raided from Samara's library. Eva had some of Samara's fresh-baked chocolate chip cookies on a plate.

"Undecided." Aidan set the books on the end table. "But she's generous with her books, and have you seen that library?"

"Yes, Aidan," Liara said. "There are only three rooms downstairs."

Eva bit into a cookie. "And her baked goods are to die for."

"Love," Loki said, kneading one of the pillows.

"Gods, we're not evaluating her on books and cookies." Liara pointed in the general direction of the downstairs. "We need to know if she's the one."

"She's the one," I said, pushing away from the sill. "Wine, scars, the crazy eyes—all of it. I don't care. She's a *witch*, Liara, and Umbra wanted me to meet her. You can leave if you want. You've done your job. But I'm staying."

Aidan and Eva shifted their gazes to Liara, Eva still nibbling away at her cookie.

Liara's eyes went dull, lidded. She let out a sharp sigh, and after a beat, she gestured to Eva. "There'll be crumbs in this bed. I'm taking the other room."

"Who are you sharing with?" Aidan said as the fae crossed to the door and yanked it open.

"No one."

The door slammed behind her, and in the silence that followed, Loki went on kneading and purring atop the pillow.

"So it'll be the three of us?" Aidan said. "In one bed?"

"Four." I pointed at Loki. "He likes the warmest spot."

"That's your head," Eva said. "'Cause you're a guy."

The training began the very next morning. I woke with Loki on my chest and Eva to my left, Aidan snoring on the far end of the bed. Above me, the clean wooden boards of the ceiling were barely visible in the semidarkness.

I'd slept well. Better than I had in ages.

Downstairs we had a light breakfast, and then Samara brought just me out into the clearing in front of her hut. I stood off against the bent-backed old woman and Bill. Around us, the sun had just begun to gild the leaves in white light, illuminating the scars on her hands and chest and cheeks.

"I would speak to you," she said as Bill settled at her side, "before I invite the others out, since you are the reason they've come at all."

I gestured for her to go on.

Her hands clasped behind her back, and she eyed me. "Tell me, what has become of Maeve? And do not lie."

Why would she think I'd lie? That old teenage petulance flared up in me, the mold I'd slipped into as a kid: Clementine, the liar. "I don't know."

She had begun pacing, but stopped now, eyes fluttering as though she was considering my truthfulness. "How can you not know? She is the headmistress of the academy, is she not?"

"She is," I said, "but she went missing a week ago."

Samara went very still. A moment later, she rushed toward me, quick steps taking her right up to me, a quick-breathing frenzy entering her movements and face. "Tell me what happened to her," she seethed, her lips parting to reveal yellowed teeth.

I stepped back, nearly tripped over a root. "I didn't lie to you," I said, regaining myself. *She cares about her. She cares about Umbra.*

Her chest still moved fast, nostrils flaring. "She disappeared. And where were you?"

"Edinburgh," I said, my words coming fast, sharp. "Stealing the Backbiter. Destroying the Shade's labyrinth."

Samara stared, chest still moving fast like she wanted an excuse to blame me. To be angry. Finally, she jerked away, her back to me. It took two rounds of pacing back and forth before she swiped a hand across her forehead and settled.

"Maeve disappeared," she said. "And the enshroudment over the academy still stands?"

"As of a few days ago."

She sighed, slumping. "So she lives."

I didn't know what to say. *How do you know her?* Except my heart was beating too fast to speak; I didn't want her rushing me again with those teeth.

When she turned to face me, she said, "Today we'll begin. First, you should know there are no stupid questions. Ask me about the training, and I'll tell you what you want to know."

"Fine," I said. "How long will we be doing this?"

The old, hunched woman half-turned her head, stepping closer. "Say that again. I thought I heard you ask a stupid question."

"How long," I repeated, feet digging in, "will we be here?"

"Ah, so my hearing isn't gone." She shrugged. "Just a stupid question. We'll be here as long as it takes for you to figure it out."

"Figure what out?"

"All of it." Her hands went out to indicate the hut, the clearing, the trees. "You must learn how to resist me, how to fight me."

I tapped an invisible watch. "But we're on kind of a clock..."

"Tell me about this arbitrary thing known as time," she said. "Please."

Was she already inebriated? It wasn't even nine. "Okay, so no time-frame. Got a game plan?"

"Not so stupid a question. Here it is, Nectarine. You will leave when you've learned five things." Samara's hand shot up, the fingers splayed. She pointed at her thumb. "Hexes come first. You must know how to defeat them." She moved to the next finger. "Then we must hone your fire magic. Third, I will teach you how a witch would wield that weapon. Fourth, I will train you to fight together. As a single breathing, keening unit."

"And last?" I pointed. "Your pinkie finger."

She wiggled it. "This," she said, "is the culmination of everything—the final test. If you and your chosen defeat me in this, you'll truly be ready."

"If?"

Her hand lowered. "Has it ever occurred to you that you might not be the actual heir to the prophecy, Clementine?"

"Lots," I said. "But not since I dug out the thief's blade from under Edinburgh."

She huffed out a laugh. "Complacency breeds failure. Listen well, my young witch: there have been hundreds of prophecies delivered throughout history. Best you not believe it gives you armor"—she stepped forward, and in a moment, I was frozen—paralyzed—unable even to blink—"lest you realize the armor never existed in the first place."

CHAPTER EIGHT

Samara had complete control over me in this place in the woods. She could kill me here if she felt like it, using just her hands. And given the way she smiled at me, she knew it.

A moment later, she released me from the paralysis with a flick of her fingers. Then she called out for the others.

Aidan, Eva, and Loki came out together, Liara trailing behind. Bill trotted to her side, dropping to all fours as though he knew we'd be here a time. Samara got us all before her, and then she began.

"A witch"—Samara paced the empty space between us, once again the old, bent-backed woman—"does not act alone by nature. She desires a coven, but most of us have lacked them throughout history. In spite of this, no witch has accomplished more than Raven Murkwood. You all will know her best as the Shade."

I swallowed, hands behind my back, the wisps floating around me. It was strange to hear someone speak freely about Raven Murkwood, and it was also a relief. Finally, she was out in the open. Finally, someone besides me knew something about her.

"The Shade had her allies," Samara went on. "One fae who became known as Lucian the prince. The other was a human who went by the name of Catriona."

Catriona. That was who I had read about in *The Witching World*—the woman Murkwood had dedicated her book to.

"And it was only because of her allies," Samara said, "that the Shade obtained the very weapon Clementine now carries. It was only because of her allies that she rallied armies. And it was only because of her allies that she was able to fight the Battle of the Ages. Did you know, young ones, that the Shade obtained all these boons because she fought for the light?"

"That's impossible," Aidan said. "I read—"

Samara zipped her lips. "Quiet, North, before I sew those flapping things shut." She paused, eyeing us. Then, "Raven Murkwood fought a battle against darkness. Without her, the world would have been consumed by it. But then she changed."

"How?" I said.

Samara shook her head. "I do not know. It's said she became the first fire witch after that battle. It changed her. Had she not been betrayed by her closest ally, she would have become empress of this world. Witches would have reigned."

"And which ally was that?" I asked.

"Catriona," Samara said at once, to which Bill gave a bark. "The young mage Catriona had an attack of conscience about her lover."

"What did Catriona do to betray her?" Aidan asked with that fascinated tone he only ever had when learning history.

Samara stopped pacing. "She defected. They were mages who would not see a witch take over the world, and fae who knew if Murkwood won, their kingdom would be forced to close the fae portal off to our world."

Liara's arms unfolded. "But Murkwood didn't win, and the portal was closed anyway."

"But she did not die, either," Samara said. "And the fae considered her too great a threat, even from the underworld, for the portal to remain open between their world and ours."

"How could you know such things?" Eva said. "We don't even have that knowledge at the academy."

"Not in your library or in the Room of the Ancients," Samara said, one finger lifting to tap at her temple. "But the knowledge is there."

"We would know about it," Liara said, stepping forward. "We would have documented all of this in the Kowloon Library."

"Oh, a Singaporean fae. I should have known when I scented your arrogance." Samara resumed her pacing. "Well, you're wrong. Best get used to it."

"But how would *you* know all this?" Aidan insisted.

Now Samara was getting agitated; she wore it in her brow, in the sudden jerk of her head toward us. "Enough with your questions for today, you lot. I've not brought you out here to namsy-pamsy around with history lessons."

Bill gave another sharp report of a bark.

Samara pointed at me. "This is your witch, and you are her allies. When she says '*sabaid*,' you fight. None of you is the hero, which doesn't mean your lives are meaningless. Each and every one of you will matter if you wish to fight the Shade—including you, familiar."

Loki, who'd been standing by my ankle, gave a trilling meow of agreement.

I leaned toward Eva. "What does *sabaid* mean?"

"It's Faerish," she whispered back. "It's a command meaning, literally, 'fight.'"

Samara crossed to the center of the clearing, and as she did, she fanned out to four of herself. Five Samaras standing shoulder to shoulder.

It was the deception hex.

"All of you have been trained to fight to some degree of competency," said the Samaras. "That much I gathered when I evaluated you outside the monastery. But none of you have been trained to fight a witch. Today, each of you will begin your individual training."

"But you said we'd learn together," I cut in. "Fight together."

"So you shall, Nectarine." Samara raised a finger at me. "But until you know how a witch fights, you can't very well coordinate against one as a group."

"And how long will this take?" Liara said. "If you hadn't heard, the Shade is supposed to return to our world within the year."

Samara's blank eyes flicked to me. "Oh, I have heard. And as for you, dour fae, it shall take as long as it shall take."

Liara's frown deepened.

"Clementine," Samara said, her voice so sharp it could cut, "enshroud all of us. Now." She brooked no argument—not with that tone.

I did as she said, the enshroudment sweeping up from the ground in a half-circle, consuming the center of the clearing.

One of Samara's mirrors approached Liara, staring her down with wild, fluttering eyes. She walked slow, intent, silent, but the fae seemed unfazed and only stared back at her.

A moment later, Liara dropped to her knees in the grass, and a cry erupted from her throat as her head tipped back, mouth facing the sky. I had never heard Liara cry like that; it was the sound of someone caught completely in their own body, their own pain.

"I would hope you're familiar with that one," Samara's image said to me, focus never leaving Liara. "Young witch."

I stared down at Liara, protectiveness contending with absolute bewilderment. I didn't understand how Samara had done it; her lips hadn't even parted when she'd cast it. "It's the pain hex."

Liara's cry devolved into sobbing, her whole body wracked with the agony of her nerves on fire. Tears streamed from her eyes, which couldn't even blink. They stared like a child's up above, like she would rather die and ascend than endure this another second.

"Stop it," Aidan said with a quaver to his voice, and I knew he was remembering what Ora Frostwish had done to him back in Siberia. He'd never spoken of the depths of that pain, no matter how many times I tried to talk to him about it.

"Ah, that's a quaint name for it," Samara's image said, coming to stand in front of Liara with both hands still clasped behind her back. "Back when I learned it, we called it the agony hex."

My protectiveness finally pressed past my confusion. "Release her."

"Only she can release her," Samara shot back, frizzy white hair swinging as she spun on me. Her lips folded. "Ah, but you didn't know that—you can't even cast the agony hex."

Samara turned away in one definitive movement, and Liara was released. The fae dropped to the ground in a heap, still sobbing, breathing hard into her boneless body.

"In the end, you will meet her," the real Samara murmured as her mirror returned to its original place in the line. "If you wish to accompany this witch to Hell, then you will meet her agony hex, and you best be prepared."

After Samara's agony hex, Liara didn't talk back. She didn't talk at all, didn't respond to us or even look at Aidan or Eva and me; she only followed one of Samara's mirror images to a place in the forest, disappearing among the trees for her training with hard eyes.

"She'll recover," the real Samara murmured after her. "And with any luck, she'll be the better for it."

Anger flared in me. "Would you say the same if it were you?"

"It has been," she said, her voice even. "Many times."

The other mirrors led Eva and Aidan to their own spots in the forest, and finally the real Samara nodded down at Bill. "Show the familiar what's what, would you?"

Bill barked, tail wagging, and bounded toward Loki.

"Oh gods," Loki said, leaning toward my leg. "Don't make me. He calls me 'y'all.'"

I glanced between the two creatures. "You can understand him?"

"Barely," Loki sniffed.

Bill barked again, turning in a circle.

"What did he say?" I asked Loki.

Loki looked up at me with pleading eyes. "'Y'all come with now.'"

"He can teach you a thing or two," Samara said. "You might find that between the two of you, Bill's not the yokel."

Loki slunk away with his tail low. As they passed out of the clearing, he sent out a clawed paw at the dog when he got too close with his much-bigger head, tongue seeking to lick at Loki's ear.

The real Samara approached me with hands clasped behind her bent back, face rising as she neared.

"What you did to Liara," I said. "She'll hate you forever for that."

Samara snorted. "I'd rather she live forever to hate me than die at the Shade's hands. The girl has too much vim, not enough vigor."

I didn't know what to say to that. The old woman was harsher than Umbra, more volatile. Why did I trust her? It was implicit, almost from the moment I'd met her. Despite everything. "If you can change your appearance, why do you prefer this form?" I nodded down at her.

"You don't think it brings out the whites of my eyes?" Her eyelids fluttered. Then, "I don't leave the hut in any other form."

"Why not?"

She ignored that. Instead, she said, "I've seen you attempt to swing the weapon. Now show me your hexes."

"On you?"

Her hands went out. "Do you see anyone else?"

I took a step back. "All of them?"

"Gods, we'll be here all day with your questions. Yes, all of them, before you drive me to wine before noon."

I held back a smile. The first hex I whispered was the first one I learned: "*Pairilis síoraí.*"

Samara didn't move. She just stared back at me.

I smiled. "You want me to release it?"

Her lips twitched, and then her hands slapped her knees. "Oh, you thought it worked. Who taught you to hex like that, with your lips flapping and those poorly formed words coming out, young witch?"

My smile died. "It *has* worked. In the past."

"I suppose it might, in the way reciting the scale might work for a fourth-grade voice instructor at an out-of-tune piano."

This woman was going to send me to the burn ward. "Do you want to see the other hexes?"

"Who taught you?" Samara repeated.

"Ora Frostwish."

"A Frostwish?" Samara sighed, shaking her head with face down-turned. "They always did smell of paltry imitations. We have much work to do. Much."

"You knew a Frostwish?"

"Of course I did. You aren't the only generation to attend Maeve's academy."

Maeve's academy. "How old are you, Samara?"

"That"—she stepped toward me, and I stepped back again—"is of no consequence."

"Hey," I said as she stepped forward again, "we should probably talk about personal spa—"

I stopped moving. Stopped speaking. Instead, I was stuck in perfect stasis right in the center of the clearing with one foot lifted to get me away from Samara.

Who was still coming toward me.

And I felt proper pity for what Liara had endured on her knees that morning. Because as I stood in Samara's paralysis hex, I knew I was in the most powerful, irrevocable hold I'd ever experienced.

Next to this, Ora Frostwish's paralysis was a gentle pair of hands keeping me in place.

This was even worse than before. Samara had been toying with me the first time.

In Samara's true paralysis, the sudden, terrifying idea that I might never escape this spot, this clearing, this half-step, nearly overcame me. I was trapped. Trapped in my own body for as long as she desired, which might be forever.

I was trapped until she chose to release me.

"That," she whispered upon reaching me, fluttering eyes moving up to meet my own eyes, "is a witch's paralysis hex."

——————

CHAPTER NINE

——————

Four hours later, the sun massive and baking in the sky, I sat leaning on my palms in the clearing. I'd been paralyzed for at least two of those hours, and not once had I been able to do a damned thing about it.

The wisps floated among the trees, keeping to the shade. Samara hadn't spoken of them since she'd insisted they stay outside; she simply ignored their presence.

"You're very bad at this," Samara announced, standing before me with hands clasped behind her back, not a drop of sweat or line of fresh exhaustion on her forehead. "Surprisingly bad."

"I could resist Ora Frostwish," I breathed. "It isn't like I haven't seen the paralysis hex a thousand times."

"Frostwish this, Frostwish that." She turned a circle as though she was looking for something. "If I've told you once, I've told you twice: the Frostwishes should not even be on your barometer."

"Why not?" I sat forward. "The fae taught the Shade to hex. She's a fae, which means she ought to be more powerful."

"The fae taught Murkwood to *see*." Samara crossed the clearing, dragging an old, moldy lawn chair out from the side of the hut. She deposited herself in it across from me. "It was Murkwood who pioneered hexes."

"Frostwish could hex, though."

Samara set her face in her palm with dull eyes. "Please, do tell me more about Ora Frostwish and her party tricks."

She wasn't wrong. In the past four hours, Samara had redefined—and refined—my understanding of what a hex could be. She pierced my mind every time, a knife's blade straight into my motor cortex, and held me in a vise grip. And she did it without a single word passing her lips.

"When I cast the hex, you see my magic," she said as though reading my mind. Or maybe she was just picking up the same thread we'd been arguing about all morning. "Do you not?"

"Yes." Every time, her air magic was a deep red, blossoming from her like a flower unfurling its petals.

"Then why are you unable to get past the idea that I could paralyze you with a thought?"

I shook my head, eyes drifting. In fact, I didn't know why I'd been stuck on this point.

Samara sat back in her chair with a rusty creak. "It's because you don't trust me."

"I didn't trust Frostwish, either."

"Perhaps, but she was sent to you by Maeve, and you trusted your headmistress."

"You sure about that?"

"Maeve Umbra saved your life," Samara said. "When someone has done that, your trust in them can never be truly destroyed."

My eyes shot to her. "How do you know that?"

Samara's attention was caught by a yell from the trees. It was Liara, who came stomping into the clearing with thunderous eyes. "I hate witches," she declared, passing inside the hut. "I really, really hate witches."

"Ah." Samara turned to me, pressing herself up from the lawn chair. "Time to break for lunch."

Inside Samara's house, she resumed her straight-backed appearance as Eva and Aidan came stumbling inside. They were both sweaty, dusty, eyes lidded.

"Food," Aidan said the second he'd crossed the threshold. "Drink."

Samara laughed, a conjured spread already set across the dinner table. "Be at ease, young mages. At least for the next twenty-eight minutes."

Aidan had already sat at the far end of the table and held a chicken's leg close to his mouth. "Twenty-eight?"

"I'm not fond of half-hours," Samara said. "Or full hours. Or quarter hours."

She has a thing about time, I thought. I wondered if it was to do with the witching hour. I'd developed a thing, too.

"Weird." Liara dropped to a seat with a rigid spine, began picking at food and setting bite-sized portions on a plate, like if she took too much she would be relinquishing her hatred.

Eva simply stepped up to the table, poured herself a glass of water, and drank the whole thing without stopping. I'd never seen her do that. Or sweat, like she was doing now. Prettily, but still.

Loki appeared last of all, leaping silently atop the table and then lapping at a bowl of milk Samara had placed at one corner. His tail was curled around him, his whole frame bunched tightly.

"What did you do to them?" I said to Samara.

The witch sat on the first step of the staircase, rubbing one of Bill's floppy ears. "I made them fight a witch."

"It's not fighting when you're paralyzed the whole while," Liara said between hate-sized bites.

Aidan bit into a leg of chicken, then pointed it at me. "Samara makes you look like a toddler."

My sassier eyebrow popped. "Wow."

"A toddler who hasn't mastered walking." Eva set her glass on the table, then dropped into one of the empty seats and picked up two utensils, one in each hand, as she surveyed the food. "Or talking."

Liara just stared at me with an I-told-you-so grimace, like she knew all of this was a terrible mistake.

"Huh," I said, swirling my spoon in my tomato basil soup, "I guess the prophecy doesn't mention anything about the loyalty of my so-called allies."

"That reminds me." The step creaked as Samara stood. "I've been waiting to show you Catriona's prophecy in full."

I turned in my seat.

"Which prophecy is that?" Aidan said, alert as a rabbit.

Samara waved a hand. "*The* prophecy." She crossed through the doorway into a room I hadn't been inside yet, and I was left pondering if this was the same Catriona who'd betrayed Raven Murkwood. Whom I still believed Murkwood had been in love with.

When Samara reappeared, she was holding a fat old tome.

Aidan's eyes widened. "Is that the book I think it is?"

Samara brushed dust off it. "Too heavy for its own good and written in stodgy Old Faerish?" She crossed to the couch, set the book on the coffee table, flipping it open.

Aidan was by her side in an instant, seated shoulder to shoulder. "I can't believe you have a copy."

"You're not the only one who's 'borrowed' his books, North," Samara said.

Aidan stared at her. "I didn't..."

She waved him off, still turning pages. "Ah, I even marked it. Catriona was quite long-winded, you know—the prophecy itself goes on for some ten pages. Bet you just read the good parts, eh, North?"

Aidan was rubbing at his neck now, leaning closer. "This is the same book we have at the library, but some of the pages were ripped out."

"By the godawful one, no doubt."

"The godawful one?" I said.

Samara tapped the page, ignoring me. "No one has the full book but me. Because after Catriona delivered the prophecy, Edinburgh wouldn't have wanted anyone gaining this much power."

"They suppressed the full text?" Aidan said.

"Why?" Eva said from behind me.

My hand gripped the chair's back as I turned around to look at the fae, the answer coming clear. "Anyone who could defeat the Shade would be the most powerful mage in the world."

"Just so," Samara said, finally turning to me. "The Mages' Council would rather the Shade remain in chains—under control—than for anyone to grow powerful enough to defeat her."

"And that includes piecing her weapon back together," Liara said.

"Devious," Loki murmured, licking one paw.

"And logical," Eva said.

"But Rathmore heads the council," I said. "He's working to bring Murkwood back."

Samara raised a finger. "But he couldn't very well say as much, could he? No, each man who's assumed the title of the prince has worked with careful diligence over centuries to keep that goal under wraps."

"What did Edinburgh have before the Mages' Council?" I said. "Before the formalists."

"Four hundred and fifty years of monarchy," Liara said, eyes veiling. "Kings and queens who hated the Shade. And always a Rathmore nearby, working against the monarch."

"Until your father and Tristan Rathmore conspired to overthrow it," Eva said. "In the guise of a fairer council."

Liara nodded, slow and far away. "Until that."

Aidan was busy reading. "This is incredible. Everything's in here—the path to each piece. The key, the rod... Gods, this would have saved us so much time."

I stared at the back of Samara's head, her words from yesterday ringing in my mind. "You called me the heir to the prophecy. You knew."

"Why, of course I did." She flapped a hand as though dismissing me. "You swung that weapon around like a baby with a rattle, and none other in history besides one witch has wielded the Backbiter."

I sat forward. "How do you know so much about all of this?"

She straightened, and this time I sensed she was avoiding looking at me. *Squirrelly old woman.* "When you are one of the last witches in the world," she murmured, "you want to learn all you can."

Liara set her glass down. "You're hidden out here. What are you hiding from?"

A good question.

"Bloody hell," Aidan said, ignoring our conversation entirely, "Catriona's prophecy *does* mention allies. She said that one of them would be of great intelligence, sensitivity, and strength, and would 'keep the light when the flames go out.'"

"Not you, then," Liara teased.

Actually, that did sound like Aidan—if you interpreted "strength" liberally. When I met eyes with Eva, I knew we were thinking the same thing.

"What does the last part mean?" Eva said. "'Keep the light when the flames go out.'"

"Hell if I know," Samara said. She'd managed to slip past the question of why she was hidden out here.

"Samara," I said. "You're an air witch."

"And you're named after a fruit." She finally turned toward me, one arm resting on the back of the couch. "Are we just stating facts now?"

Of course she couldn't have been the heir to the prophecy—she didn't have fire. But... "You said you only have vestiges of magic left."

"When you're as old as me," she said, "you'll be glad to have vestiges of anything."

More deflection. In that way, she was just like Umbra.

Aidan scooted closer to Samara, edging her out. "And here it says, 'And through the passage the fae of yore will come in a time of direst need,' Clementine. But it isn't clear what passage."

My fingers drummed on the table. "How old are you, Samara?"

She was already up, Bill following behind, moving toward the kitchen—like she hadn't heard me. "I'd almost forgotten to bring out my favorite course. It's to die for. Watch out, dour fae." She cackled.

If she could have, Liara would have blown smoke from her delicate nostrils.

Eva had noticed Samara's behavior, too. In her lilting, carrying voice, she said, "Say, Samara. You asked about Walter Goodbarrel. How do you know him?"

"He was a student," she called back. "Destined to be a professor from the moment he set foot on campus. Brilliant with tangible manipulations."

Walter Goodbarrel—the father of our own Professor Goodbarrel—had been a student in her time. *She's older than even I realized.*

When she returned, it was with a pie in both hands, cream puff around the edges and black chocolate laced over the center. "There's nothing quite like a pie you've cooked yourself. It's almost a heady experience, never knowing whether each ingredient will come together right. Whether you'll overwhip the cream to butter, spill the chocolate, blacken the crust."

Aidan clapped his hands from his hunch on the couch, where he'd never moved from. "Brilliant. Clementine, you have got to see what it says here about the vessels—"

Samara cleared her throat, crossing to the couch and lifting the book from Aidan's lap with simple ease. She tucked it under her arm. "There'll be time for that, Mr. North."

Aidan turned, blinking behind his glasses. "Oh. Dessert."

Dimples appeared in Samara's cheeks. "This," she said, "is the finest pie you'll ever taste. And only the person who breaks through my paralysis hex during this afternoon's training will get a slice."

With a hoot, she disappeared—pie and all—back into the kitchen.

"Cruel," Loki said from his corner of the table. "What a queen."

In that afternoon's training, no one broke through Samara's paralysis hex. I didn't even wiggle a finger in it.

But afterward, the old witch served us her pie anyway.

Samara clearly took pleasure in her desserts. She ceremoniously served us each a slice and sat watching as we ate, and she wouldn't field any more questions that evening about herself, or the prophecy, or anything to do with our training. It was like a switch had flipped in her at a certain hour, and she turned off the witch.

She became simply Samara, and we her guests.

After dinner she sat in her living room with a wine glass in hand, an old LP on her record player filtering jazz into the room, and Bill on the couch at her feet. She told us we were free to go anywhere we liked inside or outside, provided we didn't stray much outside the clearing. "It's safe here," she said, "from whatever it is that frightens you at night."

It was only when she said those words that I realized I had slept through the night before. I had slept without a thought as to enshrouding us, protecting us, keeping us safe during the witching hour.

I hadn't even thought about the witching hour. I'd simply gone to sleep in Samara's hut.

I stepped through the door and into the clearing, where the moon gilded everything around me in a silver light, the wisps came to me from where they'd been floating listlessly among the trees. They reported to me in their whispers about everything they'd seen.

And they had seen nothing.

My eyes moved around the clearing and the trees beyond. I hadn't felt unsafe here because this was a safe place. From the moment I'd met Samara, I had known she was stronger than me. She was also benevolent, and somehow powerful enough to uncorrupt the leylines to lead us here.

Samara was wrong about me not trusting her. I did—inexplicably and immediately. And it was the inexplicable that made me doubt my trust.

That first night, I'd had no good reason to trust her. None except that Maeve Umbra had said to find this woman. This witch.

Aidan appeared next to me, closing the front door behind him. "Can't stand jazz."

"Really?"

"Call me uncultured." His glasses reflected the moonlight as he lifted his face. "My grandmother used to listen to it all the time."

"Aidan," I said, "before our training, you had mentioned something about vessels."

"Oh." He straightened from his lean against the doorframe, his posture made better by his thrill. "The prophecy said something like, 'Every generation the Shade will gather the power for one new vessel, and it is from among them one shall not break. This one shall be worthy of the gift.'"

"Vessels and gifts, huh?"

"What's interesting to me," he said, "is everyone calls *my* power a gift."

"And what's interesting to me"—I glanced toward the door to

ensure it was closed—"is that Samara didn't want you reading that part aloud."

She'd given Aidan the book, but she'd also taken it from him. She trained us hard and then she gifted us pie. She yelled and then she soothed. If I knew one thing about give and take, it meant conflict. This old witch was conflicted.

Umbra, I thought, *who was this woman to you?*

CHAPTER TEN

In the morning, I came downstairs to find Aidan the only one awake. He was seated on the couch in Samara's living room, hunched over the book with Catriona's prophecy. *So he took it back from her.* On the coffee table sat an untouched cup full to the brim with cold tea.

I dropped onto the couch next to him, conjuring myself a mug of steaming coffee. Instead of speaking, I held it between both hands and waited for him to realize I was there.

He only did so when I took a sip and cursed; I'd conjured this one scalding-hot. "Oh. Clementine." His eyes were bloodshot. "How long have you been here?"

"Too long for you not to notice me." I blew on the coffee. "Figured out the way to Narnia yet?"

He looked back down at the tome. "Not yet. But we're closer than before." He paused. "I have to call my grandmother."

I nearly tipped my mug. "Grandma North whose hair I burned off?"

"Yeah. She's still the family historian, even without hair."

"Think she'll pick up? Maybe if you tell her it's me."

"She will." He rubbed his hands along his pants and sat back on the couch. "She always picked up for me."

"Because you have *the gift*." I folded a leg on the couch to half-turn toward him. "Why call now?"

His eyes lifted toward the ceiling, where everyone else still slept. "I think there's some connection with that line I read you last night."

"About vessels and gifts?"

He nodded. "And Grandma would understand because she's obsessed with witches and prophecies and these damn blue flames. She's the person most likely to understand."

"What about Samara?"

His eyes shifted to me, and his voice lowered. "I don't trust Samara. Not that much."

I waited, eyebrows arched, for him to explain how he could trust Samara less than his own grandmother.

"She cast the agony hex on Liara. Made her suffer. She didn't need to do that, even if Liara was being an unmitigated arse." His gaze unfocused. "All those scars all over her body. The way she gave me the book and took it back when I'd read a part she didn't want me reading."

I rubbed my thumb over the mug. Aidan was right about those things, all of them. There was something hard and violent about Samara, the old witch. She was like... a flame. Volatile. Shifting. Moody.

"She's conflicted," I said. "But I don't know what about."

Claws sounded over the floorboards, and we both turned our heads to find Bill's face appearing around the edge of the couch. His black eyes shifted between us, and he gave a low gruff.

"What is it, Dog?" I nodded at the door. "Need to take a leak?"

"He's her familiar," Aidan said. "Not a dog."

"Loki's my familiar and a cat."

Aidan blew out air. "Don't tell him that."

"I would never. Except when he pisses me off, which is at least three times a day."

Aidan stood. He came around the back of the couch, leaning over it until his mouth was by my ear. "I think we came to the right place," he whispered. "I also think Samara isn't telling us who she is."

"What could be worse than a witch?" I whispered back.

A beat. Then, "A bad witch."

When he leaned back, we exchanged a long, meaningful look. A second later, Aidan was petting Bill, asking him if he wanted to go outside, to which the dog danced and panted.

Then they were out the front door, and I was left alone with Catriona's prophecy.

A bad witch.

I leaned forward, eyes drifting over the lettering. I couldn't read Old Faerish, not even a sentence, which meant I was completely dependent on the others.

I used to hate depending on people. Now it just prickled at my skin, that lack of control. And I was giving up some of that control to Samara, whom Aidan had a strange feeling about. And Liara no doubt felt the same way.

Which meant it was time to stop letting Samara set all the rules.

The old witch was true to her word. Every morning and every afternoon she paralyzed me in the clearing, and I had no choice but to accept it.

But when she released me, I always said, "Again."

She barked a laugh. "Did your mother teach you such theatrics?"

I ignored her, instead remaining intense, focused, pushing aside anything that wasn't strictly necessary to our training. She wanted to talk about my mom? No. We weren't going to do that. Because as soon as I began to talk about her, I knew exactly what the old witch would do. She'd indulge it a little, and then she would decide that was enough. Like she wanted intimacy, but she feared it.

In that way, she was the opposite of Eva.

Samara was a lot more like me. Or at least how I used to be four years ago, before all this.

During one of our trainings, I said, "How many hexes are there, anyway?"

"I only know of three," she said. "If you ever learn the trick to defeating this one, I will teach you all I am aware of."

The trick. I had no idea what the trick could be.

Late one afternoon after training, I passed out of the clearing toward where Bill and Loki disappeared to every day. When I found them, they were seated next to each other on a fallen log, both facing away from me in a strange silent communion.

Loki's tail swung like the pendulum on a grandfather clock, moving with metronomic rhythm and precision. He looked around first, his acute hearing clueing him in instantly. "Oh, if it isn't the creeper."

Bill hopped off the log with a gruff. Came up to me and licked my hand before he trotted off through the woods back toward the hut.

I approached Loki, who hadn't moved, and sat next to him on the log. "Glad to see Bill's training you every bit as hard as Samara is kicking my ass day in and day out."

"Suppose you'll never know," he said, "since you can't speak Dog."

"And you can?"

"We familiars have a language. You think we were just sitting here in pleasant silence?"

"Sure looked like it."

"As if. I can hardly tolerate the smell, and only then because he's quite wise. Did you know Bill is older than me?"

My eyebrows rose. "He looks kind of mottled, but not that old."

"A hundred and fifty," Loki said. "Had three witches before Samara. But of all of them, she's the most interesting."

"Is that what keeps a familiar bonded to a witch?" I said. "How much entertainment they provide?"

"If that was the case, I'd have left you long ago."

I laughed. "Asshole."

"Mine has certainly touched every surface of your living space." He blinked emerald eyes on me, surveying me. "You have a cut on your cheek."

I lifted a finger to my face, came away with half-dried blood. "I did that to myself. Trying to fight a fake Samara and sliced myself on one of those thin tree branches."

"So you hurt yourself in your confusion." He licked his paw once like he couldn't control the instinct, lowered it.

"Loki," I said, "has Bill told you anything about how he met Samara?"

"Gods, of course. He's a talker, I suppose because he's been alone in the woods with her for twenty-four years."

My eyes widened on him. "That's a long time." *As long as I've been alive.*

"It does explain why they're both half insane. Anyway." He lowered to a crouch on the log. "That was when he became her familiar. She was already quite old by then, and he said she just appeared one day in the streets of Belgrade, bloody and naked."

My confusion was obvious; I just sat there with parted lips, not speaking.

"We familiars tend to congregate around populated areas, you know. Because we need to eat to stay alive just like you. Bill was a street dog here in Serbia, and he scented her as soon as she appeared. She was covered in cuts that became the scars you see. Never did explain to him why—but since it had been ten years since his last witch was executed, you can imagine his excitement at finding another."

Executed. His last witch had been executed. And that wasn't even the most stunning part of the story he'd just told like it was light dinner gossip.

"Do you smell that?" Loki hopped off the log, leaving me in my shock. "I think Samara's made cheesecake."

CHAPTER ELEVEN

One morning, Aidan decided to call his grandmother but found his phone had died. And since Samara's hut had no electricity, he said he would take a trip on Siren to the outskirts of Belgrade, where he could charge it.

To which Samara only laughed and pointed at Liara over the dining table. "All this time you've known this lightning fae and she never once told you?"

"Told us what?" Eva said.

Liara grimaced. "I'm not here to be your battery charger."

My lips parted, and we all turned to Liara. "You can power a battery with your lightning," I said. "Of course you can."

A second later, Eva's phone was brandished face-up on the table. So was Aidan's.

Liara groaned and hid her face between her hands.

At the head of the table, Samara shoveled in a self-satisfied bite of hash browns and egg.

Later, when Aidan had called his grandmother from behind the closed doors of the library, he came out and found me waiting. "Well?" I said. "What did she say?"

He shook his head, pocketing his phone. "I couldn't get through. Tried four or five times."

I watched him pass me by and head out of the hut. "Where are you going?"

He stopped at the doorway, looked meaningfully back at me. Then jerked his head for me to follow.

When I did, he led me out of the hut, past the grazing horses and through the clearing. Together, we struck west into the forest, walking side by side in silence. "Where are we going?" I finally asked.

"Somewhere private."

I glanced over my shoulder. The clearing wasn't even visible anymore. "I think we're in private."

He stopped, nodded at the ground. "Put down the tent."

"Eva's tent?"

"That's the one."

I retrieved it from my cloak, and together we set it up on the grass amidst the trees. When we had, Aidan crawled inside first, and I followed him inside. There, I found him standing amidst the cots near Callum, staring back at me.

"This private enough for you?" I said as I pulled my legs in. "I could close Rathmore's ears if you like."

"It'll do." He raked his fingers through his hair, began pacing. "Like I've said: I don't trust Samara. Especially not with this. All my life, my family never told me the real story about my birthmark. They only told me something vague about it being a gift."

I sat on the edge of one of the cots, elbows on thighs. "I saw what you became that day we went to see your grandmother, Aidan." A creature of blue flame, wreathed and manic and unstoppable. "What was the story they told you about *that*?"

He blew out air. "I was always told I needed to keep myself steady, controlled. Because if I let myself get angry, that thing would come out. I wasn't supposed to have the gift, you see. I wasn't of the right temperament for it. I was too shy, too sensitive. Do you know, my grandmother discouraged me from crying? I wasn't allowed to cry, to be mad, or even to be terribly happy about anything."

"Well shit," I said, clasping my hands. "We might be neck and neck for worst childhood."

He finally stopped to lean against the square table near the back of the tent. His chest was moving faster than usual. "But because I have the gift, Grandma always picks up for me. Always. And I called at the exact time of morning she would be having her tea."

"Which means she's available?"

"She'd be sitting right next to her phone."

We sat there in silence, and I gazed at Callum. He looked paler than the last time I'd seen him, his eyes a little sunken. Or I might have been imagining he looked how I felt.

Finally, before I could stop myself, I said to Aidan, "Maybe she died."

"She can't die," he said. "She runs on watermelon, chocolate, and a voracious need to know everything."

"Maybe she ran out of watermelon."

He flicked me a glance. "You've seen her house."

"Fair. So what, then? Kidnapped?"

He stopped pacing. "No. I think there's something going on here. I think, somehow, Samara is interfering."

"With the cell phone towers?"

He shook his head; it sounded so ridiculous to both of us he squeezed his eyes shut. "I don't know. But I think we should consider leaving."

No, the immediate thought came. I didn't want to leave. I wanted to be strong—stronger, like Samara was. Plus, I hadn't worried here. I had slept peacefully. I had slept *at all*. "You can leave," I said, knowing it was a hollow offer. Aidan would never leave me here like this. "But I'm staying."

I was right. As soon as I said it, he sighed. Turned a circle. Sat down at the kitchen table. "Just keep an eye out, all right?"

"For?"

"Weirdness."

The next morning I contemplated what Aidan had told me as I stood stock-still in the clearing. What better time to do so? I had nowhere to go. I hadn't been able to move in two hours.

Across from me Samara sat barefoot in her lawn chair with a bottle of wine in the grass next to her, fingers moving over the Braille of a dime-store romance as she fanned herself with one hand. I didn't even know paperback romances came in Braille. How small-minded of me.

Yesterday, when Aidan and I had returned to the hut and gone into the library with both doors shut, he showed me Catriona's prophecy in Samara's old tome. I couldn't understand a word, of course, but he translated a new section for me: "'The blood pact will end,'" he read aloud, "'when the right vessel appears.'"

"Dramatic," I said. "'Blood pact,' huh?"

"Definitely don't get that. Or the constant references to a vessel."

Neither did I.

Catriona was a mage who'd lived five hundred years ago. We couldn't find anything else about her besides what I'd encountered in *The Witching World* and in her very own prophecy.

Focus, Clem. If I was ever going to fight the Shade, I had to learn the simplest trick: how to resist a witch's paralysis hex. It was Raven Murkwood's most uncomplicated hex, her bread and butter no doubt, and if I couldn't break free from this, I couldn't possibly defeat her.

The trick. I needed the trick.

I had been through a hundred different ideas for how to break the paralysis. Ora Frostwish's had been so easy to break, but in retrospect, she wasn't ever a terribly good mage. Cunning, a fine academic, loyal to the Shade—but a novice at hexes. I doubted her air magic was very good, either.

Her air magic. That tickled something in my brain. I was paralyzed. No part of me could move. Except for my autonomic nervous system—what allowed me to breathe. *Of course, you idiot.*

I was still breathing. My digestion was still working. I tested my reflexes, found the signal to my muscles to move made them twitch. Here was something I had never understood, and maybe that Ora Frostwish had never understood, but which came to me as a kind of obvious, sky-is-blue realization:

Hexes were never mental—no form of magic was. They were always elemental.

They were simple air magic.

I had been taught to see magic, but never to recognize it in a hex. But what if it was all around me? All I needed to do was heat my skin with my flames, sending it through all parts of me until the latticework of air molecules was made to spin so fast that it began to disintegrate.

And that was exactly what I did.

Samara's attention jerked from the book as flames burst along my skin, searing my clothes off my body. As my shirt began to drop away in charred pieces, Samara closed her book. "Well," she said. "You've finally done it."

"Finally?" I said as another piece of my shirt dropped away. "How long did it take you, then?"

She flapped a hand, reached over for her wine bottle. "That's neither here nor there. Douse yourself off and put on some fresh clothes."

Afterward, I came back out into the clearing and found she had folded up her lawn chair and leaned it against the hut. The romance novel and wine bottle were nowhere to be seen. "Much better," she said, evaluating me. "So you've figured it out, young Tangerine."

"I should have known right away. It was stupidly simple."

"Isn't it the stupidly simple things we never suspect?" She half-smiled. "Which makes them quite smart. Now, the next trick: you must dispel the likeness hex."

"Here's what I don't understand," I said before she could step away. "If it's just air molecules against the skin, why is the paralysis hex limited to witches and dark fae? All air mages should be able to use it."

"Paralysis and hexes have always been considered evil," Samara said without emotion. "They are a witch's creation, and you know how the world feels about our kind."

Our kind. I'd never heard her use that term before. Much as I tried to resist, I felt a small swelling in my chest.

"And," Samara said, "there is one other thing that a witch can do with hexes that no other magic user has ever managed." She paused, waiting for my guess.

I half-shrugged. "Make your victims clean the house? Scrub your dirty dishes?"

"Dirty dishes?" She broke into a howl. "You are so very young. I haven't even thought of that concept in decades. *Dirty dishes.*"

When she had finished laughing, she straightened as well as her bent back would allow. I still didn't know why she was the bent-over crone outside her hut and the straight-backed middle-aged woman inside, but I had a feeling it was a protection. A shield, to be the helpless old woman. I understood that.

"We can cast our hexes without speaking them," she said, finally serious. "A witch need only think the Faerish words and the magic flows out of her."

"And why couldn't Eva or Liara do the same?"

"Because we are creatures of passion," Samara said, stepping out into the clearing. When she turned around, many copies of her appeared, dozens of illusions littering the space. And all of them said to me: "And it is passion which precipitated the rise—and the fall—of every witch who ever lived."

CHAPTER TWELVE

Fifty bent-backed Samaras stood before me. Some of them with knuckles on hips, some with hands clasped, some laughing.

"Now," they all said as one, "it's time for your next challenge. Which one is the real Samara?"

Now that I'd undone the paralysis hex, the next trick came clear to me. It came at once.

I stepped toward all the Samaras standing, sitting, heckling me, and I dropped to one knee as I drove my flat palm against the earth. Fire spread from my hand in a wave, rushing over the ground in all directions. As it passed under all the barefooted Samaras, only one of them began dancing.

"Augh!" she yelled, hobbling. "Hot, hot, hot."

I stood up as the fire dissipated, reaching the end of its wave and wafting into smoke. "I found you."

When she finally stopped doing the hot dance, she lifted one bare foot, checking the sole no doubt through my eyes. Then looked at me with a grin. "You're cleverer than the average witch."

I gestured between the two of us. "Aren't we the average?"

She tsked. "Now you've jugone and ruined my compliment."

"Any other hexes for me to resist?"

"Just one," she said. "But that's for you to figure out."

"Pardon?"

She lowered her foot to the ground, ignoring me. Her hands rubbed together like things were just getting good. "It's time to learn to use your hexes like you use your fire, lest you sound like a toddler reciting the alphabet when you go visit the Shade."

Well, things *were* getting good. "So it's finally my turn."

"Yes," Samara said, both hands going out at her sides. "So paralyze me. Create your illusions. My only rule is that you must not speak the hexes aloud."

"But you know the tricks to resisting them both."

She rolled her eyes. "And I won't resist. I'm your willing test subject." She grew devious in her smile. "But I'll be surprised if you can attach one air molecule to me, or conjure a single likeness."

I did love surprising people, especially arrogant ones.

Pairilis síoraí, I thought, staring hard at Samara.

For a moment she didn't move—until she raised a polite hand to cover the magnitude of her yawn. When she was done, her eyebrows went up. "Oh, had you already started?"

This was going to be a long day, made longer by that smug goddamn smile.

When I had repeated the words a hundred times in my head without any effect, Samara raised a palm to stay me. "May I?"

I grabbed her lawn chair, dragged it over to where I'd been standing. "May *I*?"

"Impertinent witch," she said. Then nodded. "Go on."

I dropped into the lawn chair and conjured myself a glass of lemonade as Samara drew up air around one finger, twirling it like a basketball. "Consider that hexes are based in elemental magic. You know that now, having mastered the trick to the paralysis hex."

I sipped at my lemonade. "I do know that now."

"But the paralysis hex relies on air magic, and you are no air witch."

I lowered my glass. "Ora Frostwish told me all fire witches have an air witch inside them. Which is why we can use hexes at all."

"Did she?" A low noise came from Samara's throat. "And did she tell you how fire manipulates air?"

I half-shrugged. "She was more focused on being nefarious, I think."

"I am an air witch, but I know fire as well as you, Clementine. Fire consumes. It eats air, needs it to grow. And fire always seeks to grow."

And why would she know fire like me?

Before I could ask, she went on. "The way you were taught—to speak a hex—is how children were taught centuries ago. That's because in the process of breathing out the words, you also infuse the air with your magic."

I sipped at my drink, waiting for her to get to the point with wide eyes overtop my glass.

"But your magic," she said, "is fire. And when you spoke the hexes, it wasn't an air witch manipulating her element. It was a fire witch manipulating the air with *fire*."

"I never saw any fire." I sounded like a child, but I also felt a little bit like one. Might as well own it.

"Fire need not burn in color." She came to me, grabbed one of my hands. "Show me your flames."

I created a ball of flame in my palm, dancing over the surface.

She pointed. "You see how the gradient changes, darker near the inside, lighter near the outside." Her chin lowered. "Now summon a clear flame. You've done it many times without realizing it."

As far as I knew, I had never tried that—never even thought to try it. So I didn't get it right away. Every flame came out of my hand red and orange and wild.

"Not so much passion," Samara said. "Let it be simple. Speak the words, if you need to."

"Simple? You're talking to the wrong witch."

"Oh no," she said. "I have the right witch. Breathe. Be slow."

I did as she asked, slowing my air in and out of my lungs. "*Pairilis siorai*," I said, and in my palm I did manage a small, clear flame.

Samara's hand jerked away as soon as she felt for the heat, and she nodded. "That is what you have breathed into the air every time you've cast a hex. I imagine with a witch as headstrong and passionate as you, you brute-forced your way into it without realizing."

I stared at the iridescent flame under the sunlight. She wasn't wrong.

"And that clear flame," she said as she stepped away from me, "is what you will use to manipulate the air. Now for gods' sake, get out of my chair and paralyze me so we can eat lunch already."

A strange thing began to happen as time passed at Samara's hut. Time *didn't* pass. One day seemed to slip into the next, and we fell into a routine: Morning breakfast, training, lunch, second training, followed by dinner and evenings to ourselves.

I was aware of this phenomenon only on my periphery, only because I was doing what I enjoyed most—training, testing myself, growing stronger. Samara seemed to know this, and she made our schedule grueling. Every night, Eva would be healing one of us of bruises, sometimes sprains, and once, I even broke my wrist.

That hurt like hell, both to break and to heal. But I didn't mind as much as I should have.

On some level I was aware of the time dilation, but not on any level that mattered. Not really. I sweated every day, ate well, slept hard. The first time I paralyzed Samara without speaking the words, it felt like the greatest victory of my life.

And after that, the likeness hex came easy.

Somewhere I knew Rathmore and the formalists were searching for me. Somewhere under the ground I knew the Shade was growing in power, preparing herself for her moment of ascension. And every night, I knew her creatures roamed the Earth.

But not here. Here, we were safe. Here, Samara and the hut and the clearing were timeless.

One morning, during a break when I was half-sure Samara was disappearing to have a drink, I made my way over to where Eva was training with Samara's illusion. The two of them were sparring north of the hut, Eva leaping from tree to tree, her air magic rustling the leaves and shaking branches. She held an apparition of magic in her hands, like a massive triangular fan.

Once, she got stuck in place, and I knew the illusion had paralyzed her. Two seconds later, she was free. She dropped from the tree, flying at the illusion, cutting through the old witch's neck with her fan.

"Well done," Samara's illusion said, her neck wisping away like smoke, reforming. "Again. Faster this time."

I backed away before Eva noticed me, tracked over to where Aidan was training with ten illusions east of the hut. He knelt on one knee, a flaming bow nocked, eyes scrutinizing the Samaras before him. He must have mastered resisting the paralysis hex, and had moved on to the delusion hex.

With a hiss, he released his flaming arrow, whiffing past one of the illusions. They all ducked or spun or leapt away.

One of the remaining Samaras clucked. "For a North, you're wildly inaccurate."

"How about you stop referring to me as a North." His birthmark was reddening. "I'm Aidan."

Good. Aidan didn't show his anger often enough.

Last of all, I found Liara. She had blackened the trees around her, the forest charred south of the hut, the earth scorched. She wasn't building a resistance to hexes anymore. She was past that.

Now, she simply fought with a lightning whip in hand.

When I found her battling Samara's illusion, I could hardly call her a fae. She certainly didn't move like she used to. Her entire form crackled with lightning, eyes lit, and when she leapt through the air, she spun toward the illusion, branches of lightning racing off her the entire way.

She hit the ground on one knee, cracking her whip through the illusion, which evaporated into smoke.

Then she rose, lightning still dancing over her body. "Is that all, witch?"

Liara was progressing. She was progressing at the same pace as me. And that wasn't acceptable. Not with my competitiveness.

Not long after, Samara noticed the change in me. When I emerged from the hut the next morning, it was with dual flames in each hand. I came to the center of the clearing and lifted both palms to chest height, the flames dancing. "I'm done with hexes."

Samara's focus moved from the flames to me. "You haven't mastered them, witch."

"Haven't I?" My head tilted. "You can't paralyze me. Can't deceive me with your illusions."

Her lips curled. "So you saw the others, did you? You saw the dark-haired fae and got jealous. Well, I suppose you're right on those counts. But if you think making your flames dance is the way to master your magic, then you're quite small-minded."

"Expand my mind, then."

One crooked finger rose to point at my chest. "It's not about the flames. It's about the creature within you that controls them."

According to Samara, my fire didn't belong to me. Not really. It belonged to the creature I had always called the Spitfire.

"How do you know about it?" I said, feeling vulnerable. My hand closed over the flame, dousing it, and lowered to my side.

"It inhabits every fire witch," she said, as serious as I'd ever seen her. "And it is what grants you the flame. With it comes passion, anger. And when we met, it was stunningly easy to bring out of you."

"You did break Liara's rib."

"Pah. So what?"

"She's my friend."

She waved a flippant hand. "Much worse will happen below, young witch. I can promise you that. And when it does, if you let the creature take control then you shall lose your battle with the Shade."

"And why is that?"

She gestured me closer, and as I came up to her, she yanked my arm, tugging me down until we were eye to eye. Then, in a whisper as though if she spoke too loud the Shade herself would hear, "Because the creature—what do you call it?"

I stared. "How do you know I have a name for it?"

"Every fire witch did. And I'm sorry to say, I'm certain you're not wildly unique in that regard, Clementine."

I hesitated. Then, barely audible, "I call it the Spitfire."

"The Spitfire," she repeated. "Cute. Modern. Punchy." Her eyes fluttered as her mouth hardened. "The creature you call the Spitfire belongs to Hell, and there it would prefer to stay."

Now I dropped to my knees in the grass. One hand went over my chest as though I could hold whatever was inside there in. And within me, I felt the Spitfire's pleasure at being acknowledged.

Samara was right.

CHAPTER THIRTEEN

I needed to learn fire from a witch. I needed to learn how to harness the Spitfire's power.

"You're overeager," Samara said in the clearing. "That's good and bad for us."

"Seems all good to me."

She swatted a mosquito from her face. "It makes you quick and determined, but likely to cut corners. And you've already let the flame get the better of you quite a lot, haven't you?"

I set a hand to my chest. "Samara, that's a baseless accusation."

"Oh, fancy words for a fancy witch." She pointed to the path out of the clearing. "Old bent-backed woman decides she wants a piece of you by the monastery, and guess who shows up?" Her fingers curled to claws before her face, and her lips pulled back in an imitation of the Spitfire that made me smile. "Mr. Fire and Brimstone himself."

My head tilted. "You think the Spitfire's a he? I always thought of it as a guy, too."

She dismissed the thought with an irritable flapping hand, her favorite thing. "Male, female, it—you need to manipulate the Spitfire's flame in order to hex me, and you need it to strike me down. But you must not allow it to control you as it always has. Let's be on with it before the sun gets me first."

I had to control the flame. It couldn't control me.

We needed to start small; we started with shapes.

In the days that followed, we spent hours seated across from one another. I began with balls of clear flame in my hands, holding them to a perfectly round shape. When I had mastered that, I began manipulating their shape—squares, triangles, stars.

"Perfect angles aren't often found in nature. But we humans love them," Samara said. "We craft them into our weapons, into our clothing, into our homes. If you can shape fire into a perfect angle, you can do anything with it."

When, at the end of one training session, I finally managed a five-pointed star, and Samara said, "Good. Squelch it. Now think of the person you hate most, and then remake the star."

"Hate?" I said.

Samara stood, hands going to her back as she unfurled. "Loathe, despise, want to die. And no, it can't be me."

"I don't hate—"

"Don't lie." Her fingers pinched together. "You do hate me a little. Especially for what I'm about to do."

She left me there, wiping sweat from her forehead as she went. I was alone under the direct sun, cross-legged and trying to think of one person I hated. The Shade? No—I didn't, which surprised me. I didn't *know* the Shade to hate her. Hate was personal, deep, and it required a real memory. As a testament, the Spitfire remained sleeping inside me when I thought about the Shade.

I understood what Samara wanted. She wanted the Spitfire fully awake.

I sifted through memories. Maury, my old boss from the corner store who'd touched me that godawful night. The Spitfire cracked one eye, but it wasn't enough. My first foster family with the son who'd swung Loki by his tail. This made the Spitfire's other eye open, smoke trailing from his nostrils. But still, not enough.

The night they disappeared, my family. The night *he* showed up in his black metal armor.

The Spitfire's head rose. Still not enough. I couldn't pin one person as the source of the feeling.

But altogether, a knot had formed in my chest. All those years of anger, of frustration, of powerlessness. I was in a free fall from the age of twelve, my life never my own. My choices not my own.

That was what roused the Spitfire. That was what made his wings unfurl inside me, the flame in my palm bristling over a foot higher.

I hated the absolute helplessness I had felt for so long. I hated the man who'd taken my mother and sister from me. I hated the families who thought they wanted me, but changed their minds. I hated that I had no ability to control any of it.

Samara found me that way, seething with anger. She folded her arms. "Good. Now make the star."

My palm came up, trembling, and flames erupted high like a cook had just thrown oil on my hand.

"Hm," she said. "Not quite." And left me to my own devices once more.

It took days before I could bring the Spitfire's furor out, but temper it enough to create the clear fire in my palm—and even longer before I could shape it into a star. It was like trying to work with molten lava, the spitting kind.

But when I had done it, Samara came onto her knees before me and leaned close, inspecting it through my eyes. "You are a rare witch," she said when she leaned back. "Like none I've ever met."

I gritted my teeth to maintain the star. "But this is the first step to proper hexes."

She pressed herself to standing. "Yes, and most progress to hexes after they've learned to make a ball. I was taunting you with the star." She scoffed. "Ridiculous shape."

I closed my fist, staring up at her with slitted eyes. "This took me…"

She cocked an ear. "Yes?"

I didn't know how much time it had taken me. "A long time," I said, "a goddamn long time. And a lot of struggle and pain."

She half-shrugged. "Save your whining for your therapist." She crouched on her haunches before me. "You're finally ready."

"For what?" I hissed.

"The agony hex."

I stared at her. Uncertain.

She slapped a knife-hand on her opposite palm. "Focus. This one is the most crucial. It's what will end you if you aren't prepared for it."

If hexes were a dark magic, then the agony hex was, as Samara explained it, "off-the-charts forbidden." It was pure evil—just pain and suffering.

"But you used it on Liara," I said, "the first day we met."

"Yes," Samara said, dropping to a cross-legged seat in front of me, "because the Shade will surely use it on you. She'll do whatever she needs to do to survive, and you must know how to escape it."

I swallowed. "And now you're going to cast it on me, and I have to figure out the trick to it."

"There is no trick." She rubbed her hands along her thighs to the knees. "You simply refuse to succumb to the pain."

I paused. Then, "You're going to cast it on me like, a thousand times."

Her head tilted. "Do you want to defeat the Shade, or don't you? I can assure you, my agony will be *nothing* next to what Murkwood is capable of."

I sighed, pressing my eyes shut. "At least give me some wine first."

"Now that's what I like to hear." When my eyes opened, she was already standing. She brought me an entire bottle. "Drink as much as you like, Nectarine."

I drank half the bottle before we began in on the agony hex. And once we did, I wished I'd drunk the whole thing; when she cast it on me, the pain made every muscle in my body flex. I dropped to my side, in the fetal position, like I'd entered rigor mortis.

The pain was everything. Clementine was nothing.

Samara stood over me. "I've delivered microscopic needles of air magic straight to your nerves," she said, "throughout your entire body. No real damage is being done, but gods does it feel like it."

I didn't answer; I couldn't answer. I could only hear her words as a distant, far-off thing, like she was speaking to me through tempered glass. I just wanted to end it, to make it stop.

"The agony will end," Samara said, "when you resist. When you overcome. Pain is biological, but we are more than our biology, Clementine. We are the spirit within us."

I wanted to scream, but I couldn't. A thousand daggers pressed deep and deeper into me, somehow always finding more space to drive in.

Samara's face appeared before my eyes as she got on all fours before me. "Resist. Overcome. Push the pain aside and remember who you are. You're a fire witch, for gods' sake."

Resist. Overcome.

The words felt hollow the first time. And the second time.

But by the third time they'd repeated in my mind, they had begun to register. Resist. Overcome. They held meaning, and I was able to blink. I could use my eyelids.

"There it is," Samara said. "You've done the hardest part. Now place the pain in a lettered box and push it aside. Do what you must to stand before me."

I couldn't do that. Not the first time, and not the second or the third or the fourth. By the end of that day, I still couldn't do more than blink my eyes.

But days later, after hours of pain, I understood what she meant about the lettered box. I was able to visualize the pain, to imagine myself placing it into a box with a lid, and shoving that box into the corner of my mind.

That was when it became simply a part of my biology, and I became a witch.

It took minutes—first I had to find the use of my fingers, to press my palm into the ground. Then I had to get myself up to a seat. Finally I took a knee, and with five knuckles shoved into the earth, I stood on both feet, the pain still riding every nerve in my body.

"Now," I said through gritted teeth, "you'll teach me to cast it."

Samara didn't answer. With a flick of her eyes, the pain was gone. Just like that, it was a ghost of itself.

I doubled over, coughing and breathing hard. It had been all-consuming, and just the memory of it nearly brought me back to the ground. "Won't you?" I said up to her.

"I'd rather not," she said. "For it is as corrupting as the flame you carry inside you. The more it's used, the more it will become not the deliverance of absolute pain, but a tool. A weapon, and with every use it will sap away your empathy."

"I won't use it unless I have to."

She sighed, slumped cross-legged before me. "That's what every witch says."

It took her two days to teach me to use the agony hex. And at the end of those two days, I swore to her I would never use it unless absolutely necessary. I felt the promise, too—no one deserved that kind of pain.

Which meant I was finally ready to learn to wield the Backbiter. Properly.

I didn't want to show anyone the Backbiter. It was mine, my own, the weapon I had spent four years searching out and assembling. And yet I knew I had no choice; Samara was the only person who could teach me to wield it like a witch.

"Show me," she said as we stood outside the hut on a clear morning. "Show me the weapon."

I retrieved it from my cloak, bringing the cool metal of the rod into my hands, allowing the chain to unfurl until the blade touched the grass. Samara seemed to wince at that, as though it pained her to see any part of the Backbiter touching the ground.

"Lift it, impertinent witch," she whispered. "A blade such as that should never touch anything but its victim."

Samara came forward with slow, almost uncertain steps. Her breath seemed held, and as she stopped before me, her face turned up to mine. Both her hands went out before her, palms up to receive. "May I?"

My grip tightened on the Backbiter, an instinctive reflex. But I knew Samara was asking permission when she could have been asking forgiveness, and that was why I nodded.

I held the rod out, placing it into both of her hands. When I did, she dropped to her knees as though carried to the ground, staring down at the weapon in her hands.

"So heavy. I never thought I would touch it," she whispered, thumbs trailing over the orichalcum rod. "Once upon a time, every witch knew the lore of the Shade's marvelous kusarigama, the Backbiter."

"And the prophecy?" I said. "Did every witch know about that?"

She shook her head as her fingers slid to the chain, admiring it. "Catriona's prophecy was like a fairy tale amidst hundreds of other prophecies. Few bothered with it, and even fewer had access to what I've shown you."

"Why is it called the Backbiter?"

She hummed low in her throat as her fingers ran all the way to the blade at the end of the chain, lifting it into her hand. Her fingertip found its edge and began a delicate slide from stem to tip. "The Shade was considered so formidable, so fearsome, that the oral histories tell us her opponents often fled from her. It was then that the kusarigama's blade found its home between their shoulder blades."

"Brutal."

"Yes," she said. "It is said that as a magic weapon accumulates blood and lives, it carries with it a growing darkness. A weight. Have you noticed, Clementine, how heavy it is?"

"I thought it was the orichalcum."

"No—orichalcum is light. This weapon is weighted," she said, "with a great many lives. This is one of the reasons why mages do not carry them. Over time, the weight of their bloodshed exhausts not just our muscles, but our minds."

"So, what," I said, "this weapon will drive me insane?"

"Perhaps. It all depends on your inclinations, your predilections. A woman of passion like you might become a creature of impulse and fire. A witch predisposed to mania might go insane. By the time she was banished to Hell, it was said that Raven Murkwood had become wild, feral, unable to be parted from the Backbiter."

"Why didn't Murkwood get rid of it before then?"

"She fought for a different cause," Samara said. "She wielded the weapon justly, or so she thought. And it's our own delusions"—Samara twirled the blade so it whisked through the air—"that allow us to walk the thorniest paths. Remember this, Clementine: No man thinks he's evil. No witch ever set out to destroy the world."

Give it back, I thought, small-minded even as she spoke. In only a few weeks, I had become more attached to the Backbiter than even I was willing to admit. Right now, with it only two feet away from me, I craved to have it back in my hands.

With a sigh Samara rose, passing the weapon back to me with the same care she'd received it. "Thank you."

This time, I was the one to accept it with both hands, as though it had been imbued with new meaning. And for me, it had.

It was a cruel, famous weapon. And it had turned the tide of battles. I nodded at her, widening my stance. "Now teach me to use it."

CHAPTER FOURTEEN

Samara crossed to the side of the hut, where I heard the sound of sliding metal. A moment later, she emerged with what looked like a short scythe in hand. "Do you know who goes to Hell?" she said, the blade glinting under the light as she came before me.

"Bad people."

"Yes, and the worst of them are mages who wield weapons," she said. "Why do you imagine you weren't trained to use them at the academy?"

We had played with weapons in our first-year combat class as a way of fighting against opponents who would be wielding them, but never beyond that. I had no frame of reference for what mages did and didn't do—I had only accepted the way things were.

"Because weapons are useless when you've got magic?"

Samara raised the scythe, and the air began to distort around it. A moment later she chucked it at my head, and it spun end over end at wild speed, whistling through the air.

I had no time, no choice. By reflex, the Spitfire rose in me, flames bursting along my body. The scythe hit the barrier of flame, hissed, and dropped to the ground.

"Useless indeed," Samara said.

"All right," I said as my flames receded. "Let's just ignore the fact that you tried to kill me. I'm intrigued."

"That was a softball." With a snap of the fingers, a gust of air rushed against the scythe, flinging it back into her hand. She caught it in an unwavering grip. "It is against a mage's code of ethics to wield a weapon, and has been since the Shade razed entire countries with her kusarigama. That's why I've taught your allies to shape their magic into weapons—a bow, a fan, a whip. The weapons carry no blood memory, but you'll need them if you want to fight a witch with no compunctions about fighting dirty."

She swung the scythe through the air as though testing its speed. "A mage with a weapon is more dangerous than a mage without one. And a witch with a weapon? The most terrifying of all."

I nodded at her scythe. "Which is why you have that tucked away in the woodshed beside your house?"

"This is a kama," she said, "and at one time in my life, it was all that kept me alive. We witches don't operate by the magical world's codes, Clementine. We cannot, because the magical world wants us dead. You know that."

I did know that. It made my jaw harden, and I gripped the Backbiter tighter. "So you're going to teach me how to fight with the kusarigama."

"No," she said, swinging the kama once more. "I'm going to teach you to fight like a fire witch with the kusarigama."

She began simply, standing before me with the weapon in my hands. With delicate fingers she manipulated the Backbiter's parts. The rod could slide up the length of the chain to the blade, where it would slot into place. In that way it became more like a kama with a chain attached.

And at the other end of the chain was a small counterweight I had never noticed. That morning, she showed me how to hold the chain with slack at either end, to swing the orichalcum counterweight and lash out with it at her ankle or wrist or neck.

I swung again and again, missing most of the time. She didn't make it easy on me; Samara was in constant motion, either rushing toward me or dancing away. The first time I caught her ankle was after three hours, and even then the counterweight didn't wrap around it properly. It only fell away as she jerked her ankle back.

But by the time the sun was directly over us and we were both covered in sweat, I caught her wrist. The counterweight wrapped and held, and she grimaced. "Now don't hesitate—just yank."

I did so, and she was jerked forward, the chain tightening around her slender wrist. Her fingers opened, and she dropped the kama into the grass. "Gods," Samara cried, staggering forward with her other hand atop her wrist. "You've broken it. Why'd you yank so godsdamn hard?"

My heart went into my throat, and I came forward, dropping the Backbiter. The second I had, her bare foot shot out, connected with my chest, and a second later I was on my back and the wind was knocked out of me.

Samara's shadowed face appeared over me, her wild hair a halo around her head. "Gotcha." She burst into laughter and then disappeared past me. I heard the creak of the hut door opening and her laughter dying away as I lay in the sun trying to breathe. "Come on, fire witch. Maybe sandwiches and tea will improve your aim."

That woman knew exactly how to irritate me.

I practiced with the counterweight through the afternoon, that evening and into the night, and again early the next morning.

When we faced off again at mid-morning, Samara raised her kama and began, "Now let's pick up—"

I shot the counterweight out at her left ankle, where it wrapped and held. I yanked without hesitation, and sent her onto her back. When I approached, I hovered over her. "You were saying?"

Her lips twitched. "Impertinent witch."

* * *

The Backbiter's other end—the blade and rod—had multiple uses. The first and simplest of which was to revolve it over my head, the blade singing low as it swung fast and faster.

"That," Samara said, "is your defense. From here, you can strike out at anyone. Try me."

My eyebrow raised even as I kept swinging the blade atop my head. "Really?"

Samara's stance widened, the kama ready. "I always mean what I say."

I snapped the blade out, and it sliced through the air, the blade on a direct course with her left temple. When she didn't move, my eyes widened. "Samara!" I yelled, but the blade was already passing through her head.

As it came out the other side, Samara smiled at me, wisps of her illusion carried off with the blade like smoke.

The real Samara came around the side of the hut, clapping her hands. "I commend you for your conviction, young witch. You'd take your own teacher's head off."

Goddamn likeness hex will be the actual death of me.

I turned, the blade and chain coming to a swinging stop at my feet. "You were right—I do hate you."

She cackled. "Don't pretend you wouldn't do the same if you had a young, gullible witch to train. Now swing the blade again," she said. "And this time, I promise it's my real head you can take off."

I eyed her.

She set a hand to her chest. "You think I would trick you twice?"

I sighed, began swinging the blade. When I shot it out toward her, the edge of it sliced harmlessly through her chest, tearing away part of the illusory breast. And this time, the illusion burst out laughing, bending over with tears coming out of her eyes.

"Oh," she said, wiping her eyes, "you're more gullible than the light-haired fae."

"*Eva?*"

She nodded, wild hair bouncing. And as she eased upright, her face went serious. She disappeared as the real Samara stepped through her, a long-necked bottle of wine in her hand. She looked equally serious.

"What is it?" I said.

Samara's fluttering eyes gazed beyond me, up toward the bright sky just above the canopy. "We're short on time."

I glanced in the direction she was looking; only the golden sun shone back at me. "It's the middle of the day."

Samara set her bottle in the grass, retrieved her kama from the side of the hut. "I've wasted precious time, young witch, and for that I'm sorry. Come at me with your weapon."

I stood where I was. "You're screwing with me again."

In a moment she rushed me with a yell, the kama upraised, wind building around her and carrying her arm around in a vicious swoop at my head.

I hardly had time to swing the chain, deflecting the kama's blade with a clang. The two weapons bounced off one another, and I staggered two steps.

This was the real Samara.

Her hair rose in the wind around her, lips curling away from her teeth as she spun through a backswing at me. "The Shade is devious, a liar and a cheat and a thief. Treat me like you would her, and use your fire. Now."

I threw up the chain, caught the rod in time to block the kama with it. "Samara," I breathed.

"*Now*," she yelled, retracting her arm to dash under the Backbiter and swipe at my stomach. She had never been this severe, this wild. Not even the day we'd met outside the monastery. I had thought she was fighting us then, but she wasn't—that was simply a test.

I lowered the rod as flames burst from my hands and along the length of it. The kama hissed as it met the orichalcum, the scythe's edge of Samara's blade nearly grazing my abdomen.

The Spitfire's head rose as I called on its fire. *No*, I thought. *It's not time for you.*

I jumped back, swinging the blade high over my head and around, fire swooping up the length of it. The blade swung high as she ducked under it.

"Yes," she said, driving forward with another swing. "Use the Spitfire's power, just like this. But do not let it consume you. Never let it consume you."

I had never told her about fire riding and what Rathmore had taught me. No doubt Samara would disapprove of that. And as I swung the flaming ball-end of the chain toward her ankle, I wondered if I was already different for all the times I had let the Spitfire take control.

Maybe I was more a creature of impulse than I realized.

We sparred this way, fire versus air, until the sun grew low on the horizon and we could both barely stand. It was Samara who dropped to the grass first, breathing hard and fast, her white eyes once more on the sky.

"We might have two days," she said, hoarse. "Gods, if I wasn't so weak."

It was so strange hearing about time from her. I couldn't recall how long we had been here, or even bring myself to care all that much. I crouched across from her, balancing the Backbiter across my knees. "Weak? You nearly killed me."

Her lips faintly curled, and I could have sworn she rolled her eyes. "Don't patronize an old woman, Nectarine."

At that moment, Bill and Loki came trotting out of the forest, both their heads low.

"Rough day?" I said to my familiar. He ignored me, crossing to the hut. "You know," I called, "it's only polite to acknowledge the one who feeds you."

"Fine. You're acknowledged," Loki called back, pausing by the door. "As for my day, you'll know all tomorrow, won't you?"

"Tomorrow?" I said, but he'd already disappeared inside with Bill.

I turned back to Samara, who pushed herself up off the grass with a groan. She retrieved her wine bottle. "Two days. Tomorrow, you will all come together in this clearing. And the day after, you must pass the last test. Then, pass or fail, you'll leave."

"What's the test?"

"The test began long ago," she said as she passed me. "And you'll pass only if you understand what it is."

"But—"

Her hand went up as she walked. "Questions, questions. You'll do me in with questions."

I stared after her as she made for the hut. Leave. Why should I ever leave this place? Here it was safe. The horses grazed, we trained hard, we ate well, we slept harder.

I was perfectly happy to stay with Samara forever.

CHAPTER FIFTEEN

Back inside, I made it to the landing on the second floor and glanced at Samara's closed bedroom door. I hadn't tried the knob since that first day when I'd found it locked, and I had never gotten a glimpse of her going in or out.

In fact, I had never even heard the door creak.

I tamped my curiosity, began filling the bathtub with water from a bucket that somehow magically refilled itself every time I set it down. I'd never heard of such a thing, but apparently it was a branch of conjuration magic. At least, that was what Samara had said. She may have had running water, but she liked the old-fashioned way of bathing. "You'll never appreciate water," she'd said once, "like you do when you have to pour it on your own head."

Back before mages were so few, she'd told us one night that there were "servant mages" who knew simple magic: conjuring food, water, the barest minimum to animate brooms and scrub brushes.

But she wouldn't tell us how long ago that was.

When I had filled the tub, unclothed, and slid in, I stared out the window across from me. I had learned to control my fire, to defeat and cast hexes, but Samara had said there was one last test for me—but that it was mine to figure out.

But I had only ever encountered three hexes. Hadn't I? Paralysis, likeness, and the agony hex. *Except...*

I slapped the water to unlodge whatever was pressing at the edges of my brain. But nothing came loose as the water hit my face.

Samara was a lot like Maeve Umbra in that way. From the beginning when I'd sat barefoot in the forest outside the academy, Umbra had challenged me, forced me to come to conclusions on my own. To make discoveries, to sit with a problem until I got frustrated and obsessive.

Maybe there was a little bit of my own relentlessness in there, too.

Samara had made me figure out the tricks to the three hexes, and because of it, I *owned* them. It wasn't rote memorization—that moment of realization would stick with me forever, the exact instant the lightbulb flashed on in my brain.

And because of that, I was a better witch.

I need to stay. I want to stay.

When I had finished bathing, dressed, and came downstairs, it wasn't quite dinnertime, and everyone was on their own. Liara and Eva were sitting together on the couch, piecing a puzzle out on the coffee table. Aidan was in the library, deep into reading.

Samara wasn't around.

I went back upstairs and knocked on her bedroom door. No answer. But when I passed by one of the windows overlooking the clearing outside, I caught a glimpse of her disappearing between the trees. Like she was beckoning me.

I came outside, followed in the direction she had gone. After only a minute's walk, I came to find her standing very still, facing away from me. And before her lay two graves and two small wooden crosses.

I hadn't even gotten close when her head snapped around. I could feel her looking at me through her magic. "Hello, Clementine."

I sucked in air. "I shouldn't have interrupted."

"The dead don't mind interruptions." She paused, jerked her head. "Come."

When I came to her side, I found that the crosses were white, unmarred by age or wear. And the graves were smaller than average.

"They're unmarked," I said. "The crosses."

"Yes," she said. "They never did have names."

We stood in a graveyard of two, and my hands clasped in front of me like they never did. "Who were they?" I asked.

"I like to imagine they were two boys." Samara's lips pursed. "Do you know what a witch's son is called?"

I hesitated. "A warlock?"

She smirked faintly up at me. "He's called by his name." She paused. "Don't you think it's funny, Clementine, how you and I and every woman like us is called by a term that the world at large reviles?"

"Funny is one way of putting it."

She pointed at the two crosses. "Boys born of witches are a unique breed. They know their mother's pain, and they do one of two things with it when they carry it into the world. Either they become empathetic to all suffering creatures, or they become hardened."

Like Callum. His mother was a witch, killed by the formalists. By the very government his father now led in Edinburgh. When I'd met him, he had been hard. Unyielding. Sometimes he seethed. And I wondered what it was like to carry the pain of his mother being a witch, and on top of that, watching her die for it.

Maybe he'd been empathetic before then. That cruelty would harden anyone to the world.

"Samara," I said. "Why did you say that? You'd 'like to imagine they were two boys.'"

"Because they were never born," she said simply. "Never even conceived except in my mind."

My hands clasped tighter, and I didn't know what to say except, "Oh."

Samara eased herself onto a fallen log not far from the graves. She patted it. "Come."

I did so, sitting forward with my elbows on my thighs, eyes on the graves.

"I told you we witches are creatures of passion," Samara said, low and gentler than I'd ever heard her. "And it's that passion which brings about our rise and our fall. It can consume us quite easily, Clementine, and should that happen, we cease to be like normal women."

A tightness began to take hold in the center of my chest. So she had been passionate like me; I could still see it in her, but now it was dulled, dilute. "Even an air witch?"

"'Even an air witch.' We are no lesser breed, impertinent witch. Anyway, how do you suppose an air witch gains fire?"

"I was told it would happen if an air witch met a fire witch in battle."

"This is true of witches, and of any mage. But where do you think the first fire witch came from?" Before I could answer, her first finger pointed toward the earth under our feet. "Where the fire originates, Clementine. That is why your Spitfire is a creature of Hell."

No, a voice said, even as I knew it was right. She was right.

Of Hell.

One hand slid to my chest, clutching, as though I could hold the thing in there. Or maybe rip it out. "So I've got the devil in me. Must be why Mom gave me such a bright name."

She pressed out air through her nose, lips twitching with almost-humor. "Such is true of all humanity. We also carry a bit of Heaven, too."

"There's a Heaven?"

Her fluttering eyes lifted toward the canopy. "I don't know. I like to hope."

"And what happens if a witch's passion consumes her?"

"She becomes a creature of instinct, of will," she said. "If she's a fire witch, it eventually consumes all parts of her. Burns away her ability to create life. And if she is not already in Hell, the creature will take her there."

"There are multiple ways down," I said, "aren't there?"

Samara nodded. "But once you've trodden a path down, it closes to you forever."

My eyes drifted back to the two white crosses, clean and pure and simple. "I don't understand how you know all this."

Her hand fell on my knee, patted it. "I am the last witch to whom the histories were passed on before the formalists sought to erase us from the world. There's more, but it's not for me to tell you. Not yet." Already she was rising.

"I'm not ready." I stared up at her as she passed around the log and away from the gravesite. "Why can't we stay longer?"

"Because even magic is finite," she murmured as she passed through the trees. I watched her go, hobbling off through the forest back toward the hut in the late afternoon light.

What the hell does that mean?

When I turned around, my attention was caught by the light playing over one of the crosses as the trees rustled.

A piece of Hell inhabited me. I rose, and I left the graves alone.

CHAPTER SIXTEEN

For the first time since we'd begun our training, all of us—Eva, Liara, Aidan, Loki, and I—stood in the clearing with Samara and Bill, who sat by her side.

It had been a day or a week or a year. I couldn't say. All I knew was that we had all mastered escaping her hexes, I had learned to catch her in them, and she believed we were ready to fight her.

"Before we begin"—Samara nodded first at Eva—"show us a taste of your skill."

Eva nodded, stepping forward. Her hand flicked up, fingers splaying. The air distorted in an arc around her as she gripped an invisible fan with both hands, swinging it around and sending a massive gust at the far trees. In that moment I saw it: the yellow outline of her magic in her hands.

The wind blew over us so hard my hair was pushed straight back from my face and I had to work to keep my footing. A second later, the trees were rustling hard, and the recipient of Eva's massive gust cracked, one of the bigger branches hitting the ground.

Across the clearing, the horses started, snorting and wide-eyed.

It was the fan I'd glimpsed that day when I'd spied on her, but that had been a hand fan. This one was half as large as her body.

"Sorry, tree." The fan dissipated as Eva's hands lowered. "I never broke off a branch before."

"The tree will regrow." Samara gestured to Aidan. "Mr. North."

Aidan stepped back from the group, and we turned to find his hands flaming as the outline of a blue longbow began to take shape. With two fingers he drew through the air from bow to string, and a blue arrow appeared as he did.

When he had the bow and arrow in hand, he raised the massive weapon to his cheek, taking one-eyed aim. With a hissing twang, the arrow pierced the clearing and lodged itself in the trunk of a far tree.

Aidan lowered his bow, clenching his hand to dissipate the arrow's flames before they took on the bark.

"Liara"—Samara set the half-empty wine bottle she'd been holding on the grass—"if you would."

With a crackle, long trails of lightning danced to length from each of Liara's hands. They tapered as they reached the ground, their lengths sizzling and jumping.

She eyed the bottle for a moment, stepped forward, and brought one of her lightning whips overhead, cracking the lip of the bottle off. A millisecond later, she jerked the other straight up and straight down, carving the bottle vertically in half.

The bottle fell apart in three pieces, the end of the neck hitting the side of the hut, and the two tall pieces splitting in the center and dropping away from one another into the grass.

Wine gushed out, and Samara cursed, slapping her hands and shooting Liara a dirty look. "I pointed at the *lip*."

"Did you?" Liara jerked both whips back, and they receded into her hands. "Your fingers tremble; I couldn't be sure."

"Gods help me." Samara kicked away a piece of the bottle. Bill barked, and the old witch waved a hand. "Yes, yes, show them."

Bill rose, gruffing at Loki.

For the first time, I noticed Loki had fallen asleep in a particularly succulent patch of grassy sunlight not far from my feet. His front paws were in the air, body twisted in that acrobatic way in which only cats could sleep comfortably.

I cleared my throat. "Loki."

His emerald eyes opened on me, gemlike. "My turn already?"

Bill barked again, low and—if I read him right—annoyed.

Loki flipped onto his belly, blinked lazily at Bill. "Yes, yes, all right," he muttered, rising with a petulant lick of his paw. He trotted past us. "Give me some of your lightning, Liara."

Liara raised a palm, lightning brewing there. "I thought you'd never ask."

"Wait," I said.

Before I could intervene, she sent a bolt of lightning at my familiar. It hit the back of his neck, lit him up from nose to tail. He crackled with energy, almost too bright to look at. And a strange fizzing sensation began in my chest.

"Clem," Eva said. "Your hands."

I lifted my hands. Lightning danced over my fingertips—not painful like the times Liara had attacked me. It moved like it belonged to me. I turned a hand over, and the lightning flowed with me, racing up my arm.

"This is your familiar's unique ability," Samara said. "Unlocked through his training with Bill. Just as you are able to share your flames with him, he can absorb magic and share it with you."

"What's the catch?" I said.

Samara half-smiled. "Perceptive witch. He must be close enough for the magic to transfer to you."

"How close is close enough?"

"Eh, it's imprecise. Let's say your line of sight."

I nodded down at Bill, whose tongue hung out. "And what's his unique ability?"

Samara ticked her finger through the air. "Patience, young witch. You'll find out shortly."

"And by shortly," Liara said, flicking her whips back into existence at my side, "she means now."

Samara grinned, mischief entering her eyes. "What better time to fight than when your opponent is distracted?" She reached behind her, still bent-backed and wild-haired in the mid-morning. She was even barefoot as the kama came out, gripped in one hand.

She must have a tangibly manipulated spot where she keeps it.

"Clementine," she said, extending her arms as though presenting herself, "throughout your time here, I've trained your allies to fight against a witch, with a witch. Now, you must do the same against this witch."

"Now?" I said. "Right here? But we haven't——"

"We haven't got time," she spat, her voice grating and harsh and suddenly severe. "Just today. And today, you will fight me until all of you drop or I do. Make no mistake: Only those who overcome their fear survive in this world."

My eyebrows rose. "I can't tell if you're an angry drunk or finally sober."

With a yell, Samara swept her hands inward and up, drawing in air. Her hands surged toward us, a blast of red air magic in our faces.

This was going to be hell.

We did fight until someone dropped.

It was Samara.

The five of us sparred the old witch together, and it was clear the others had been trained to work as a unit. They had been taught to fight alongside me—which was slippery and hesitant at first, but soon enough we no longer had to call out each other's names. After the first two hours, we simply knew when to tag-team, when to drop back, how to combine our magic.

Along the way, Samara would say, "The two of you. Together—now!" And so it would go.

It wasn't really fair, five against a single witch. But then, she was an air witch with a ruthless kama that she swung even more ruthlessly. Once she even took a lock of Eva's hair off. Bill leapt and snapped and ran, weaving in and out of our legs with air magic trailing off him. Sometimes he moved so fast I couldn't keep my eyes on him, and when that happened the air magic trailing off him caught our ankles like a hand gripping us and we were pulled off our feet.

But we kept on.

After three hours and three water breaks, Samara slumped into the grass, one hand out to stay us. "Gods, take pity on an old woman."

Liara doubled over, wiping her forehead. I had never even seen her sweat before. "So we pass?"

Samara flicked a dismissive hand. "The others, fine. Not you."

Beside me, Loki snickered.

Liara straightened, ramrod straight. "Excuse me?"

"She's screwing with you," I called out between breaths, slumping against Eva as I set aside my weapon. "Where did you learn that thing where you surrounded me with the thing, anyway?" I said to Eva.

Aidan eyed us. "What *thing* are you two talking about?"

Eva examined her nails. I couldn't tell if she was just being extra, or if she really was concerned she had broken one. "Oh, you know." She rubbed her nails against her shirt. Definitely being extra. "Just a little move I practiced here and there."

Samara let out a bark of a laugh. "Every godsdamn day, morning, afternoon, and night."

"And," Eva said, "don't forget the move where Aidan did the thing with the arrow in Samara's bu—"

"Finish that word and I'll fail you after all," Samara growled.

Liara's hands had gone to her hips. "So do I pass?"

Samara pushed herself off the grass, pressing her sweaty hair off her face. "If it'll shut you up."

Bill gave a bark from where he sat next to Samara, tail swinging over the grass.

"Apparently I've passed with an A-," Loki said, his voice dour.

"A-*minus*?" I said.

Loki's face turned up to me, serious. A pause, then, "Yes. It's still an A." If I said anything else on the matter, I knew he'd injure me with his claws or teeth. Or both.

Samara clapped her hands together. "Tomorrow morning, you leave. If you can. What say we have dinner?"

I blinked twice. "Come again?"

"I propose wine," Samara mumbled to herself with an upraised finger as she disappeared through the doorway into the hut. Bill followed her. "My good vintage. Yes, the 1891 bottle..."

When I looked over at Eva and Aidan, they were both staring at me. "You heard that, right?"

They both nodded.

Liara clicked her tongue as she turned toward us. "I was the best of all."

"Get over it," Eva snapped. "She passed you."

"Whoa, Eva," I said. "Swapping out air for fire."

Aidan's fingers had gone to his hair, twiddling out a piece of it, his eyes distant. He was clearly in contemplative mode. It was the same face he'd made long ago when he'd told me something wasn't right about Samara, about this place. That felt like a different life.

"Aidan?" I said.

His hand dropped like I'd caught him. "Yeah?"

"Maybe we ought to search the forest around the hut for a secret oven," Loki said, glancing up at me. "Just in case she does plan to cook us after all."

"She said we're leaving tomorrow," I said. "I don't want to leave."

"Neither do I," Eva said.

Aidan went on twiddling his hair. "Me either."

I glanced at Liara, who had folded her arms, and waited for her answer.

She just shrugged. "It's not a bad place." I squinted at her, and she said, "What?"

"It's just..." I paused, unable to articulate what I was feeling. "Didn't you hate this place? That woman? You hate witches."

Liara's brow drew together as though she was searching her memory. "I do. I did. But I hate to admit it: that witch has taught me things about fighting. More than I learned at the academy."

"Same," the other two said.

"I'm dead tired," Aidan said, hand falling from his hair. He started toward the hut. "I call dibs on the tub."

"Damnit," Liara said, stalking after him. "If only you were that quick with your bow."

The two of them disappeared inside, and Loki followed.

Eva hesitated, setting a hand on my shoulder. "I thought it was strange, Clem. What she said. But maybe we can think about it after dinner."

"Sure," I said.

She began toward the hut, glancing over her shoulder. "Coming?"

"Yeah," I said, but I didn't move as Eva disappeared inside, her lavender hair trailing after her.

I crossed the clearing, crouched down to pick up the lock of hair that had been shorn off. When I straightened, staring at it under the early evening light, my other hand reached up to finger my own hair. All my life it had grown quickly.

But now?

CHAPTER SEVENTEEN

After our farewell dinner, Eva forgot to talk to me about the strange thing Samara had said. Everyone dispersed, keeping to themselves in different rooms of the hut.

And Samara?

She went out with Bill. She didn't say where she was going or why, but I assumed it was for an evening walk. I watched her disappear around the side of the hut as I washed dishes in the kitchen. Beside me, an animated cloth dried the dishes as I handed them off, from which they flew into a stack on a shelf.

Animations. They were a rare and mostly dead art, but now I'd met two women who knew how to use them. What were the chances?

I turned away from the dishes, thinking back on the things I'd felt and the thoughts I'd had on first arriving at Samara's hut. I had been filled with urgency, a need.

I needed to find the Shade and kill the Shade. The desire had filled every part of me for years.

That felt remote now. All I wanted was to prepare for bed, sleep dreamlessly, and train again tomorrow.

Dreamlessly.

I glanced right, into the open doorway to the tiny library. "Aidan?"

"Yeah?" he called back from an armchair.

"Can you remember your dreams from last night?"

His face didn't even rise. "Nope."

I pressed away from the sink, pushing past what I knew I wanted. What I knew would soothe me. Long ago, on that first night, Samara had told me there was one place in the hut I shouldn't go.

And as I started up the stairs, I remembered that I had once been a person who would ignore that rule. It was the memory of that Clementine that carried me up to the landing, made me turn around toward Samara's closed bedroom door.

It was the only place I hadn't been.

When I approached the door I found it locked, just as it had been on that first day I'd tried. Some part of me wished this was my first locked door. It wasn't. Not nearly—except before, I'd had paperclips. This time I had fire.

I set a finger to the slot where Samara's key would go, a tiny spear of flame appearing off the tip. She had taught me to manipulate air— or, at least, to recognize when I was manipulating it with my fire. And so it was with a swift manipulation of air that I pressed the mechanism like I would if I were using a paperclip.

Within a few seconds, the door clicked.

When I opened it, I didn't know what I expected. But my breath held as I pressed the door wider, and I knew I had developed a certain reverence for Samara.

She was a witch, like me. She was powerful even now. A drunk, sure, but we all had our flaws.

And she had trained me to be stronger. She had taught me things no one else could.

The door opened to reveal a simple, austere bedroom cast in shadows. The bed was just a narrow twin pushed against the far wall. The coverlet was made and smoothed. Beside it a low, circular nightstand offered a reading lamp with no shade, just a bare bulb. Across from me, a dark-wood dresser was set with a handheld looking mirror atop it.

When I crossed the room and picked it up, my face was haloed by the light from the hallway. I glimpsed freckles, mostly my curls. My thumb ran over the handle.

Why did a blind woman have a mirror?

I set it down. She had no closet. When I opened the top dresser drawer, I found folded clothes. The second drawer had nothing but an ornate, decorated box in one corner.

Lifting it out and taking off the lid, I was greeted by the smell of age and must. I picked out a photograph that sat on top of a pile of them and lit a small flame in my free hand for light.

There, staring back at me, was Maeve Umbra.

She wasn't any younger than she was now. An old woman, her lips closed but her eyes warm, and she had her arm around someone else. Except I didn't know who the other person was because at some point his or her face had been scratched out.

But I did glimpse the edges of curly red hair.

The next photo in the pile was the same: two young people sat on a log somewhere outside, separated in the middle by a person whose face had been scratched out. A young woman.

Finally, I came to a photo of a place I recognized. It was the meadow at Shadow's End, the very tree Umbra and I sat under when we had our daily lessons last year.

And whoever the young woman was, she was alone as she sat under the tree. She wore a school uniform, and someone had destroyed the section of the photograph where her face should be.

A noise behind me made me drop the photo, and I spun. My flame illuminated Eva's face peering in the door. "Clem," she whispered, "are you snooping?"

"Yes," I said, picking the photo up and holding it out for Eva to see. "Every single picture in this box is like that."

She stared a moment, shook her head. "Creepy."

It was more than creepy.

I set the photograph back in the box, picked up the handheld mirror. "Why would Samara have this? She can't see."

"Maybe she looks through Bill's eyes."

I snorted.

"Or maybe," Eva said, "it's sentimental."

"What do you mean?"

"Maybe once upon a time, she could see. Not everyone who's blind always was, Clem."

Now she was on to something. But I wasn't sure what.

"Eva," I said, "I came in here because a while back, Samara told me I had a final test to pass, but I wouldn't pass it unless I knew what it was. Weird, right?"

"Yes," she said at once, her eyes narrowing. "Weird."

I paused, a memory surfacing. It felt distant, remote. Important. "Do you remember when we tried to capture someone and you were hurt?"

"Yes," she said slowly. "What was his name?"

"I don't remember."

She hesitated. "I know he nearly caught you."

"He *did* catch me," I said, searching my mind with slow, slogging steps. "Fire. I remember fire all around me. But it wasn't fire. Not really."

Then it crystallized.

My fingers went up to my hair as my gaze fixed on Eva's. "Our hair hasn't grown." I turned to the handheld mirror. "And the mirror being out doesn't make sense."

"What are you getting at?" Eva whispered.

I spun back to her. "It's a hex." A moment later, I took a step toward her. "Eva?"

"Yeah?"

"Don't freak out, but your face is starting to melt."

And so was everything else.

Around me, the hut slid in on itself like melting chocolate. The roof collapsed, dripping toward the floor. The walls curled backward, revealing the other rooms. I could see outside. I could see downstairs.

"Clem," Eva said, the doorknob dripping from her hand, "you're melting, too."

I lifted my hands, found the nails slipping off their beds, my skin and muscle and bone all sloughing toward the floor together. Before I could react, the floor opened up beneath me. My stomach went into my throat in a nauseating free fall.

That was when my eyes shut.

I didn't hit ground. The free fall simply ended, and then a chill came over me as the wind slid over my bare arms.

"So you've done it," a gravelly, familiar voice called from not far off. "I'll be honest, I wasn't so sure."

My eyes opened. It was nighttime, but the moon was too far along in the sky for it to be just after dusk. And the night felt too cold, too desolate.

Beside me stood Loki, Noir behind me, and at my sides were Aidan, Eva, and Liara. The wisps circled my head. Beneath my feet, the path leading to the monastery, which lay in dark and shadows not far off.

We were exactly where we'd been when we'd first met Samara.

"How cruel," Loki murmured, sounding sleepy. "I'd just settled in by the living room fire."

When I'd finished turning a circle, I lit a flame in my palm and tossed it onto the ground ahead of me. Samara's blind eyes came illuminated some twenty feet away. She was hunched and frail. "What have you done?" I said.

A strange noise flowed through the trees—a clipped bark or a yell. Goosebumps came alive on my arms.

"I did what I was able," Samara said. "Now you must do the rest. This is the only way."

"You hexed us," I said. "Didn't you?"

"Yes," she said, her face dancing in the flame. "And you escaped in nine hours what some never do."

"Nine hours?" Aidan said. "But we were there for..."

"How long?" Samara shot back.

"Well, I..." Eva began. "Weeks, at least."

"Months," Liara whispered.

I shook my head, eyes darting around the darkness. What time of night was it? I needed to know the time of night.

"Nine hours," Samara said, hard and low. "Nine hours and you never wanted to leave. Such is the power of a witch's delusion hex."

That was what Tristan Rathmore had put me under. That was what I had escaped in Inverness.

"And now you must leave," Samara said. "I will hold them off as long as I can. Go, and do not come back for me."

"Hold who off?" Aidan said.

"So you ensnared us," Liara cut in with dark fury, her hands crackling. Beside me, those two lightning whips trailed toward the ground at either side of her. "For nothing. All for nothing."

"Nothing?" Samara hooted, voice echoing. "Look at what you hold in your hands, dour fae. It would be in your better interest to save them for what's coming."

Cold seeped into my belly. "What time is it?"

"I am sorry." Samara came closer to the flame, her steps shuffling. She seemed so uncertain, so ungainly. Her scars were white as ivory on her skin. "I am sorry for what I had to do. It was the only way to get you where you needed to go, young witch. Now you must ride and fly, all of you."

I set my hand to Noir's mane. "And you?"

"Clem"—Aidan grabbed my wrist, pointing into the sky—"look at the position of the moon."

My eyes lifted, found it hanging low and orange and round.

"It's the witching hour," he said.

"Fucking witch," Liara spat, her whips crackling as she lifted into the air. Her keen eyes searched. "They're everywhere, Clem. Those things are coming out of the trees."

"Many have come for you." Samara's hands began circling before her, the wind kicking up. "More than I can fight. I'll stay a few, at least."

I grabbed Noir's mane, swung up onto his back. Loki leapt onto my cloak, climbed his way up. The horse practically vibrated with pent-up energy beneath me. "Samara—"

"*Go*," Samara bellowed, and with air circling her in red strands, she stumbled out of the firelight and into the moonlight, only barely visible to my eyes.

"She's fighting them," Eva said with her keen fae sight. "But she's not nearly as good as she was inside the hex. She's slower. There's so many, Clem."

It was an illusion, I wanted to say. *It was Samara's illusion of herself we saw.* Inside the hex we'd encountered the capable fighter she'd once been, long ago.

And even in the hex, she was afraid to leave her house without an illusion. Protection against what lay outside her hut. *Why are you so afraid?* I wanted to ask.

But I didn't have time.

Aidan was already on Siren's back, and as soon as I spotted him up there, I squeezed my thighs and heels into Noir's sides.

The horse took off like a shot, from a standstill into a canter in two strides, and then a gallop by the time we'd gotten fifteen feet from the path.

"Clementine," I thought I heard Samara yell from behind me, "*Sabaid.*"

Or maybe I imagined it. Maybe that was what I wanted to hear.

Eva and Liara flew alongside as we headed for the trees. We broke the tree line and dove into shadow, the horses' hooves echoing back at me.

"They're closing on us." One of Liara's whips shot out, caught something in the darkness. The other followed. "They're coming from the sides."

Flames lit up my hands and arms, and in the circle of their light I glimpsed the Shade's creatures—darkness, pressing away light. I tightened my thighs, sending out bolts of flame that hissed when they made contact with the creatures. The wisps darted in and out, cutting through the creatures with silent certainty. "Keep going."

"Where?" Liara snapped from above, her whips flying out with retina-searing brilliance in the night.

Where. Where were we supposed to go?

Not the hut. Samara wasn't there at all.

The witching hour had only just started, and we had been spotted. Found. My enshroudment wouldn't protect us now—not with so many chasing. We couldn't keep galloping the horses for an hour.

Look at what you hold in your hands, little fae, Samara had said of Liara's whips. *It was the only way to get you where you needed to go*, she had said to me.

The hex wasn't for nothing.

And maybe I didn't have to run any longer.

CHAPTER EIGHTEEN

I reached behind me, into my cloak. There, I felt the cool metal of the Backbiter, and my fingers remembered exactly how to hold it. How to swing it.

The hex was the only way to get where I needed to go.

The wisps came to a hover around me as I sat up, leaning back against Noir's momentum. "Stop," I called out to the others. "You heard what Samara said."

"She's crazy," Liara called back, only her whips visible in the night. "She's a crazy old witch who entrapped us."

"Yeah." I spun Noir around, drawing the chain out before me, sliding the rod to its spot at the head of the blade. The feeling of the rod settling into place was familiar. I had done this dozens of times. "But she's also right."

Flames burst from my hands, surging along the length of the chain, illuminating the Backbiter in the night. It was brighter than anything else, even Liara's lightning. And in its light, I could see them. Hundreds of creatures in the night, all of them threading through the trees, pushing their way across the earth and floating through the sky, coming for me.

This had happened once before on the tundra, where the world was white and I only had half of a weapon I didn't know how to use. The sight of so much darkness had terrified me. I had wanted to—and knew I must—run. Run far, run fast.

Sabaid, Samara had said.

She had told us to obey her when she said that word. She had trained me for this and more, and if she was anything like Maeve Umbra, I knew she hadn't arbitrarily picked this time of night. And she also hadn't released me to my death.

"Clem," Loki said from my shoulder.

"Yeah?"

"Are you sure about this? You know, the whole running-headlong-into-a-hundred-monsters thing. Not that I'm judging."

"Yeah, Loki." The flames pressed past the weapon, up and down my body, wreathing my familiar and me in fire. "I'm sure."

Liara and Eva flew to the tree branches above, Liara's lightning crackling in both hands, and Aidan came by my side on Siren, drawing a flaming blue bow with an arrow nocked.

Inside me, the Spitfire raised its head. Wanting, wanting to be part of this fight. I was drawing on its power without giving it any control. Another thing Samara had taught me to do.

"*Sabaid*." I raised the chain, swinging it over my head. With a press of my heels into Noir's sides, the horse's head jerked up, his front legs lifting off the ground as he burst into movement.

The wisps fanned out before me, their light growing until the world was as clear as day, and everything I needed to kill was in my sight.

We were on top of the creatures in a single breath. I swung the flaming blade through a swath of them, cleaving through their bodies as they reached for me. The blade came around, swung through the ones on my left as Noir wove us through the trees.

Behind me, the others followed. A fae flew into my vision as the Backbiter clove through the creatures—it was Eva, sweeping a massive yellow fan of air magic around her body to coordinate our attack. What fire and air touched split in two, and those creatures dissolved into the earth.

Beside me, Siren charged to keep pace, Aidan's blue arrows whistling through the night, finding their targets with a hiss. And Liara ran, leapt, lashed out with her whips, slicing down the creatures with flaming arrows already protruding from their bodies.

We sliced, stabbed, electrocuted, and burned. We ended the strange half-existence of every creature of darkness that came to us, and we did so with the brutal efficiency of four students of a crazy old witch.

I had thought the Shade's creatures were the worst thing in the night. I was wrong.

It was us. We were the ones to be feared.

Inside me, the Spitfire seethed with desire. Every kill was catnip, every swing of the blade a whistling music to its ears.

But I was Rational Clem, and for once, this was my fight.

We burst from the tree line onto a rolling plain, and the horses' hooves were muffled echoes through the grass as we charged after the creatures visible under the moonlight and the wisps' illumination.

"Clem," Loki said by my ear. "Clem, look at them."

I swung the chain again, so focused on my mark I hardly heard him. "What?"

"They're not running toward us anymore," he said. "Look."

My attention flicked up, outward. The blade slowed in its revolutions. I squinted, surveying the expanse of plain.

Eva flew past me, sweeping toward the grass with a ruthless downward swing of her fan, cutting a creature with an arrow already in its chest diagonally in two. "They're running."

"Away," Liara said with a hiss of her whip, hovering a few feet above the ground.

Running... away.

I eased up on Noir, and Siren came to a canter alongside. Before us, the Shade's creatures scattered over the plain, receding toward the far tree line, spreading before us like a school of fish. The ones at a safe distance simply stood and stared back at us like wild animals.

Aidan kept his bow at the ready. "I don't understand."

"They don't run away," Eva said, still holding her fan. "They just don't."

She was right. For as long as I'd been a witch, that had been true: the Shade's creatures didn't run away, they ran *toward*.

But some fifty feet off, I could have sworn I saw one of them come to a stop and lower itself to the ground.

"Wait here," I said. "And don't let your guard down."

"Don't do something stupid," Liara said.

"Like wade into them?" I said as I trotted Noir forward, toward the creatures. They continued to spread before me, moving away from me, but more and more of them were moving into the same posture.

As I came upon one of the creatures on the ground, I sent a wisp above us to provide light. And what it revealed made me stop the horse.

The creature was cowering.

When I brought Noir closer, the creature raised its empty face and hissed at me like a cornered animal—a warning to come no closer.

I swung the flaming blade out at it, the lethal tip catching in the creature's strange, liquid-onyx back. And when I raised it up before me to eye level, the creature writhed and hissed and snapped with teeth I couldn't see—because of course it pressed away light.

It was a creature of Hell. Which was exactly where I needed to go.

Four years. Four years I'd spent terrified of these things. And now I had captured one, and it felt as small and light and unthreatening as a raccoon. Just a wild, scared animal.

The creature hissed at me, writhing on the blade. Not to get at me, but to get free.

Aidan drew Siren alongside me as Liara and Eva hovered nearby, neither fae wanting to touch the ground. Neither of them allowing their weapons to dissipate from their hands.

I didn't blame them.

"They've fled," Eva said, turning a slow circle. "They've all fled to the trees."

"And this one would if it could," Liara said, snapping one of her lightning whips just a foot from the creature. The two hissed in unison, lightning and monster, the sight and smell of its own death just twelve inches away.

"Tell me," I said to it, "the way to your mistress."

The creature continued writhing, caught in its own desire to be free.

With a thought, I sent the wisps to encircle it. And as their light drew close to the monster, it let out a squeal like I'd never heard from them. Loki's claws dug through my cloak and into my shirt as he pressed to my neck. Aidan's hands went to his ears. Above us, the fae recoiled in the air.

I just stared. The closer the wisps got, the more they ate away at the creature. It oozed away from them like smoke, dying right in front of me. I still couldn't make out its features, and I realized now that was impossible.

Complete darkness couldn't be illuminated.

"They're hellsbane," Aidan said beside me as the creature's squeal went on at the same pitch.

My face jerked to him. "Hellsbane?"

"Pull them back," Liara shouted, her whips gone and her own hands over her ears. "For gods' sake."

I sent the wisps to a distance of a few feet, and the creature slumped at once. The absence of noise left a ringing in my ears, and for a few seconds none of us said anything at all.

Finally, Loki said, "Is it dead?"

"No," I said at once, though I didn't know how I knew that. "Not quite."

"They can't be hellsbane," Liara said, her fingers going out as she drew near one of the wisps. "There's no such thing."

"I think we're past the point of 'no such thing,'" Eva said, her fan of air dissipating. "We passed it a long time ago."

"What *is* it?" I asked again.

"Perfect light," Aidan said. "In lore, hellsbane is perfect light."

I stared at the wisps, then at him. "As in, heavenly?"

"There is no Heaven," Liara cut in, her voice a blade.

"Wherever it's from," Eva said, "these wisps possess it."

Noir stamped beneath me, mirroring my own agitation. Confusion. Frustration. The wisps had belonged to the Shade. They were her pets. "How could the Shade possibly have possessed hellsbane?"

No one answered. No one knew.

But something Samara had said pinged at my brain. She'd told me once that the Shade had once served a different cause.

"She was banished to Hell," I went on as the creature began a slow and limp writhing on the blade, "because that was where she belonged. Because she was evil."

I was talking to myself now. Nobody had a response; if they did, they would have voiced it.

The Shade once had hellsbane. Perfect light. What was the antithesis of Hell if not perfect light?

The creature began a low and particular hissing, a stuttering and clicking in the night.

On my shoulder, Loki leaned forward. "I think it's trying to talk."

My eyes focused on the thing, and even though I couldn't see that it had a face or eyes, I got the sense it was also focused on me. Looking at me from the depths of its inky darkness.

"If it's trying to talk to me," I said to Loki, "it's doing a damn poor job of it."

"Talk?" Aidan echoed beside me, urging Siren a few steps forward. "They can talk?"

Eva had canted an ear toward it as the stuttering and clicking went on. "That's not English, or Faerish."

I glanced at the others. "Anyone speak Hellion?"

Aidan squinted at the creature. "Hellion's not a language, Clementine."

"Really? Because that thing's definitely talking to us."

We went on listening for another minute. There was a rhythm to its noises, like it was repeating the same thing over and over. Around us, the other creatures had disappeared into the darkness. This was the only one left.

And we only had it for as long as the witching hour lasted. That was what Samara had meant when she'd told us not to come back for her: we only had the witching hour. Time drew short.

I straightened on Noir's back, lifting the creature higher. "Doesn't matter what it's saying. All that matters is it can point us in the right direction."

"And by right direction"—Liara folded her arms—"you mean the underworld?"

"That's exactly what I mean."

"And Samara?" Eva said. "We ought to go back for Samara."

"Screw Samara," Liara spat.

"She can handle herself," I said, and I knew it was true. She was a capable witch, and she had meant it when she'd told us not to come back for her. She'd wanted me to use the time I had.

"I agree with Clementine," Aidan said.

I sent one of the wisps angling toward the creature, close enough that the thing felt its perfect, incandescent light. "Point me to Hell."

At first the thing didn't respond; it just hissed and wriggled and fought against the burning of the light. But when I repeated my command a second time, promising it the light would stop if it just pointed me where to go, the creature seemed to understand.

A beat passed, and with slow certainty one of its appendages extended from its body, lifting in the direction of the tree line.

"South," I said. "We're headed south."

CHAPTER NINETEEN

Noir set the pace. We didn't have time to trot, or even to canter—we galloped. I held the Backbiter in one hand, the rod balanced across Noir's withers, the blade dangling off to the side. The creature bobbed at the end of the blade, the thin tendril of an arm still pointing east as we rode through the Serbian countryside.

I should have been afraid. I had spent so long afraid of the deep night and Hell and the Shade. But all I felt was a spastic pressure in my chest, a thrill and desire and sense of absolute power, and I couldn't tell if that was the Spitfire or just me.

Maybe it was both.

Around us, the wisps illuminated everything we passed, turning night into day, shadows into rocks and fallen logs and tree trunks.

I didn't know where we were going. It didn't matter; all that mattered was getting as close to Hell as it could in the time we had.

I had a vision in mind, a place the wisps had taken me to once, four years ago—an open flat, a ravine and a river nearby. I had leapt into that river to escape the Shade during the witching hour.

And I had a feeling about where we were being led now.

"Keep up!" I yelled back at the others and caught a glimpse of Siren charging hard through the flying wisps of Noir's tail.

Eva and Liara flew overhead, disappearing amidst the trees when we hit a tree line, reappearing in glimpses and in the paper-thin sound of their wingbeats. They were both fast—I knew that from the times we'd raced, from the guardian trials—but I didn't know what kind of stamina they had.

I found out when, twenty minutes in, Eva dropped to a seat behind me, her hands going around my waist, her breathing hard. "Mind if I"—she paused to cough—"hitch a ride?"

I glanced back at her. "And if I did mind, would you get off?"

She coughed again, one finger stretching past my shoulder toward the fingernail moon. "The witching hour is almost done."

I leaned closer to Noir's neck, thighs and heels tightening, pushing him just a little harder, a little faster. He could take it; he and I had been together long enough now that I knew his endurance and his speed almost as well as I knew my own.

"Look," Loki said from my shoulder, "the creature."

My eyes flicked over to it. The appendage had shifted slightly, pointing a little more to the south. I raised my free hand, jerking it in that direction for Aidan and Liara to angle south.

We came to an incline, and the horses slowed as their hooves bit into the earth. I sent a wisp out ahead, and it lit a path up the hill, which grew even steeper ahead.

Liara flew by me. "It's a ridge," she called out. "We're going straight over a ridge."

Wonderful.

"Come on," I whispered to Noir. "Just a bit farther."

The horse pushed forward, willing, head jerking and lungs pushing in and out as he carried us up toward the ridge. He was still faster than any horse at the academy—Siren had fallen somewhat behind—but he couldn't outrun the moon.

Partway up the ridge, the creature began to dissipate like smoke. I stopped Noir as the wisps flew closer, illuminating the sight of it drifting off through the air. Only the blade was left, swinging and clean as though the thing had never been there at all.

I cursed, yanking the Backbiter back to hand and replacing it in my cloak. "Bastard left us on a hill."

On my shoulder, Loki sniffed the air. "No more dark magic around —just the smell of three stinking mages, two big beasts, and a witch."

Behind me, Eva sighed her chin onto my shoulder. "Never thought I'd hate to see the witching hour end."

"Can't say I mind," Aidan said as Siren trudged up beside us, coughing, head lowering as he patted her neck. "Nearly killed the poor mare."

Liara flew to a nearby tree, landing on a branch with one arm around the skinny trunk. "So what, now we have to wait until the next witching hour to nab another one?"

Good question. How else were we going to find one of the Shade's creatures, except during the witching hour?

"Even if we could grab one now," I said, dismounting Noir, "these horses wouldn't last another hour."

He was lathered in sweat, his head low, as I led him up to the top of the ridge. That was where we set up the tent and made camp for the night. I didn't even know what country we were in anymore, and I found as I fell into my cot in the tent that it didn't even matter.

The witching hour was over.

I didn't bother casting an enshroudment over the campsite. Didn't feel the need to sit outside and listen to the night. For the first time since we had left the academy, I fell into a hard void when I slept.

This wasn't like sleeping in Samara's hex, where I didn't sleep at all. Not really. This was a sleep so deep, my eyes closed and I was gone in the same instant.

When they opened again, daylight seeped through the crack in the tent. Aidan and Eva were chattering at the back, dishes clinking as a savory scent wafted toward me.

And Loki was on my chest, staring down at me.

"Is this real?" I said. "Or a hex."

His claws extended, digging through my shirt as he kneaded away. "What do you think?"

I winced. When I looked left, I spotted Callum lying on the cot across from me. He remained still, eyes closed, chest rising and falling, the same as it had since I'd found him in the crypts beneath Edinburgh.

Rolling my head back, I spotted an upside-down Eva and Aidan bickering over what size plates were needed for breakfast.

"Definitely real," I said.

In the morning sun atop the ridge, it was hard to believe last night had happened. We sat on a blanket under a tree, Loki eating a piece of conjured grilled trout between us, and debated what to do next as we dug into Aidan's conjured English breakfasts.

For the first time, someone had brought up Samara and the insanity of the hex she'd put us under. And we spent the next ten minutes commiserating and eating and eating some more, like the food could pack away the memories.

"We need to figure out the way to Hell," Liara was saying, "not explore our fee-fees about that old witch. In case you had forgotten, we have another hag of a witch to deal with."

"Fee-fees?" Aidan echoed.

I leaned toward him. "She means feelings, but she hopes if she calls them that we'll feel too ashamed to talk about them."

"She put us under a delusion hex," Eva said. "I felt great about it at the time. Now I feel kind of tricked, but also kind of grateful that she helped me. Where does that leave me?"

"Confused," I said with a solemn face. "Welcome to the club."

"Clem's been in that club for years," Loki said between bites of fish.

I waved a hand at Loki. "Quit meowing nonsense."

Aidan took a breath. "I think she had to do what she had to do to prepare us. I was mad at first..."

Liara groaned. "Oh, please do trail off as you consider your feelings."

"But I've put it aside for now," Aidan said. "Liara's right—we've got the Shade to deal with."

I raised my brows at Liara. "Bet you feel like a real ass now."

"The creature could have been lying to us," Liara said, keeping her eyes strictly off me. "When it pointed south, it could have been misdirection."

"The thing was terrified," I said. "It wasn't lying."

"They were all terrified," Eva said, her voice lowering on the last word as the memory of last night washed over all of us once more. The chase, the flight through the woods, the moment we stopped and turned on them. And then the slaughter and their fear and the strange appendage lifting to show us the way to the Shade's domain.

It was terrible. And we could never have done it without Samara.

I felt confused by what she had done, too. Angry, grateful, and deep, deep down, wishing I could be back in the safety of the clearing and the hut. Back in her hex of a world.

I'd felt safe there.

"Even if it wasn't lying, south could be *very* south," Eva said, eyes shifting out over the landscape and the hills in the distance. "Could be a different part of the world entirely."

"In which case," Aidan said, "at this one-hour-a-night pace, we might get to the entrance to Hell before winter. Maybe. Depends on if we need to cross any bodies of water."

I lowered my plate into my lap, gazing with Eva. "It's not so far."

"And you know, because..." Liara's eyebrow rose, visible only in my periphery. "Witches have a natural connection to Hell?"

I turned a smirk on Liara. "Maybe we do." I paused, letting the goosebumps rise on her arms. "Or maybe I remember the topography from that night."

"The night you got the liar's key?" Eva said.

I nodded, a finger tracing through the air, following the flow of the land around us. "That place was like this. Enough like this that we won't be crossing any bodies of water. At least, not oceans."

In the silence that followed, I looked between the others. Normally they'd have said something by now—disagreed, argued, teased me. They would have questioned how I could know such a thing. Liara loved to dig the knife in where she could.

But they kept on with breakfast. Eva cut her ham rasher with a knife and fork until it was in tiny pieces. Liara bobbed her tea bag in her mug. Aidan folded his toast to swipe up the sauce from his baked beans. Even Loki just went on devouring his fish.

It felt a little bit like Samara's hex. A perfect, unquestioning state of being. Life just flowed by.

But it wasn't. We had traveled far last night, and Samara was long behind us. Which meant the others were still in the habit of questioning nothing, or—worse, much worse—they had begun to see me differently.

Around us, the wisps danced among the tree like lightning bugs, their perfect light hardly visible except when they crossed past the leaves. The horses grazed, Noir's black tail flicking at flies. He was an absolute monster of a stallion, and the fact of his enormousness struck me just about every time I saw him. Last night, he'd made the ground vibrate with his gallop.

And in my cloak lay a weapon that had speared one of the Shade's creatures in the back. A weapon made of the hardest metal on Earth.

It wasn't Samara's hex that had led to this silence. It was me.

The others didn't see me as Clementine Cole anymore. They saw me as the witch—as something a little different, a little otherworldly, whose power they didn't understand. They couldn't apply logic to why I had perfect light—though I had heard Liara and Aidan whispering about it in the tent after they'd thought we were asleep—and that felt like the decisive moment.

Perfect light was perfect. Perfection wasn't a human trait, because it was impossible for us. Nothing we did or said or thought could ever be *perfect* because it was an unattainable, subjective thing.

But I wasn't perfect. I wasn't otherworldly.

And I needed them.

"Hey." I clanked my fork against my plate, a shrill sound. "Somebody tell me I'm wrong."

All eyes jerked up, even Loki's.

"You're wrong," my cat said, then went back to eating.

Liara eyed me overtop her mug. "How can we tell you you're wrong about what you saw that one night?"

"Because you're Liara Youngblood," I said, "and you tell me I'm wrong about everything."

She tilted her head, eyes drifting down as her lips curled. "All right, you're wrong about that entrance to Hell being close by."

"No I'm not." I pointed at the tree beside us. "I saw trees just like this one."

Eva turned her face up. "It's a pine tree."

I rolled a hand. "Yeah?"

"They're on most continents," she said. "So that doesn't narrow it."

Aidan had already caught on to what I wanted. "You said there was a ravine with a river at the bottom. That was how you escaped, right?"

"That's right."

He raised a finger. "Be right back." He got up and disappeared into the tent. Thirty seconds later he came back out with a bundle of large scrolls, laying them all between us. "I thought these would come in handy."

Liara leaned forward as Aidan unrolled the first one. She made a face. "Ever heard of Google Maps?"

Aidan pinned the edges down with his fingers. "Did I miss the rollout of Google Maps for mages?"

I studied the map before us. It seemed to be topographic, but strange lines ran across it—though maybe not so strange. I angled my head to see them from a different angle, and that was when I realized I knew these lines. I had studied them many times on the globe in the guardians' tree.

They were leylines.

Loki sat back from his fish, studying the paper. "A mages' map. Haven't seen one of those except in a book."

Apparently Eva also knew what it was, because she pointed to a high hill marked in Old Faerish near the border. "Apparently this hill is tall enough for a decently skilled mage to use it to part the veil."

Aidan patted the scrolls beside him. "Have them for every part of Europe. And a world map."

Liara shook her head. "Milonakis will see to your expulsion when she realizes you thieved these."

"Actually," Aidan said, "I didn't take them from the Room of the Ancients."

"Then where?" Eva said. "These maps are so rare..."

"Why are they rare?" I asked.

"Because they're mostly hidden from the world," Liara said, one hand sweeping across the map before us. "For many reasons, including that they're one of a kind."

"And they confer incredible tactical advantage," Aidan said. "My family used them to help our side win during the Battle of the Ages."

We all stared at him.

"What?" he said.

"Did you steal them from your grandma?" Eva whispered.

"It's not stealing if Grandma never notices," he said. "Right? Besides, she's got enough scrolls to last her the rest of her godforsaken life."

CHAPTER TWENTY

We studied the maps for the next few hours, looking for ravines and rivers—spots that could be used as points of power. Places that could have been *my* place, where I first met the Shade.

The problem, of course, was that Europe is full of rivers and tributaries and streams. The other problem was that not all of us could read Old Faerish.

By which I meant me.

So I sat mostly useless as the others conferred. When they had a likely spot, I stared at it, searching the ink etchings for what might qualify as a ravine—but since these maps were five hundred years old and a little faded, I had to get very close. And then I would shrug and say, "Maybe?" And they'd mark the spot as a potential.

When they didn't need me, I sat against the tree. Loki lounged beside me, tail flicking as he surveyed all the light could touch off the side of the ridge. I rubbed at his ears and wondered about Samara.

The witch had said we shouldn't come back for her, but I still wondered. Our time together had been an illusion, but I had *liked* Samara. I had gotten to know the witch, and sitting here on this hill, I began to think that if I somehow managed to survive all this and become old enough for white hair, I would like to be like her.

Irreverent. Witty. Incisive.

Maybe not so much wine, though.

"Clem?" Aidan called.

I got up, already knowing. That tone was in his voice—the pointed, no-nonsense one from when he tutored me in magical history.

When I dropped to a seat at one side of the map, he pointed at a spot. "You said there was a wide-open flat area where you met the Shade."

"Uh-huh." I squinted down at the ancient map, trying to decipher the topography from the smudges.

His finger circled the spot, where a river passed beside two crossing leylines. "Here, the Old Faerish says something interesting."

"And what's that?"

"'Don't,'" Liara said.

"Don't what?" I asked without looking up.

"Just don't," Eva said. "One word."

Now I looked up between all of them. *Don't?*

"Don't," Aidan said.

"Oh." I sat back. "I'm guessing the word 'don't' in Old Faerish, written all by itself, is just as ominous as it'd be in English."

All three nodded.

"So," I went on, "ominous is good. We want ominous. Where is this place?"

"Matka Canyon," Aidan said. "Northern Macedonia."

My head tilted, one eye squinting.

Liara pointed. "It's got a border adjoining Serbia. We can be there in a day if we ride."

I wiped dust off my pants. "You thought I didn't know where Macedonia was, but I was really just squinting because of the sun."

"Uh-huh." Liara stood, turning toward the south. Her wings twitched as though she was jonesing to fly. "We probably don't want to show up at night."

I stood too. "I've decided I don't mind nighttime so much."

She glanced back at me. "And if the baddies come out at night, what do you think they're doing during the day?"

"Sleeping," Eva said, rising as well.

"Uh," I said, "do hellions sleep?"

Under the tree, Loki gave a groan and stretched his paws out. "Everything sleeps. In a manner of speaking."

I eyed him. "Now that sounds ominous."

"From what all the stories tell us," Aidan said, rolling up the map, "the creatures of Hell go into a kind of stasis wherever the sun shines on the earth."

"Anyway," Liara said, still staring out over the landscape, "my point is this: we should use a leyline."

"The one by the canyon is bound to be corrupted," Eva said, "if it's an entrance to Hell."

"Clem doesn't fear the Shade's corruption anymore," Liara shot back. "Or does she?"

The flash of her eyes on me made my back straighten. I rolled my head around on my neck with a delicious crack. "Nope. Absolutely not. Zero fear. Nada."

"Please stop," Liara said.

Eva came to me, set a hand on my shoulder. "Fear's okay. You can't be brave without fear."

I pointed at Eva as the others began to take down the camp. "My roommate thinks I'm brave."

"Yeah," Liara said as she unhooked one leg of the tent from the frame, "and afraid."

We were on the move within ten minutes. The mages' map of the part of Europe now known as Serbia showed the ridge climbing to such a height that we could use it as a point of power when we reached the top.

So we climbed. The horses made their way up, picking past trees and fallen branches, while the fae flew and sometimes rustled trees as they came to a crouch in their canopies.

When we reached the highest spot, the trees had cleared to give us a view of the mid-morning earth and sky. I swung down off Noir, the wind picking up my braid and escaped curls, and I knew the map was right about this place.

I could part the veil here. I just didn't know what would lie on the other side.

If I was ready to fight the Shade, then I shouldn't fear her corruption. But I did. I had experienced it once before, and I never wanted to re-enter that lightless, damp place.

How much fear could you feel and still be brave? Did bravery mean raising a hand into the air without a tremble? Did bravery mean my ears wouldn't pound with the sound of my blood?

Just no panic attacks.

Those were the real killers.

I pulled the Backbiter from my cloak, letting the blade fall nearly to my feet, where it swung. Loki stepped up beside me, always nearby. The wisps came to a tight hover around my head, shoulder to shoulder, dimming. The others stood behind me, wordless.

My hand went up, palm perpendicular to the earth, and I cut down.

The first time I parted the veil, I might as well have cut through molasses. It was viscous, with little real give. I'd felt like I was cutting with childproof scissors—jagged, struggling, with too much effort.

On that ridge, I parted the veil with a single downward stroke. It split for me like a seam, straight from head to toe, and a frisson ran up my arms and down my neck. I hadn't known there could be pleasure in parting the veil just right. Nobody had told me that, which made it better.

I pulled it aside, found only a void staring back at me. The leyline on the other side had been corrupted. Of course it had.

I glanced back at the others. "I'll guide us through." I kept my voice even, digging in deep. "I'll get us to the other side."

Without waiting—and before I lost my will—I stepped through. Loki's tail brushed against me as he moved with me into the darkness. My next step was into a marshy wetness, slick and squelching. The air pressed in, thick in my throat.

Here again. This place.

As soon as I entered, I felt her. Or maybe the Spitfire felt her, or both of us. She was everywhere, all around—Raven Murkwood. This place belonged to her. But it wasn't Hell. It was an emanation of the Shade's power, a trap. This was her magic.

Footsteps sounded behind me, also wet, as Eva, Liara, and Aidan followed a half-second later. No hesitation. Not a word of objection.

"Can you see?" Eva whispered to Aidan.

"Not a thing."

"Even I can't see anything," Loki said by my feet. "And that's saying something."

But it didn't matter; they had followed me. They were here.

The thought came to me: *They'd follow you anywhere.*

"One, two, three, four, five," a voice echoed in the darkness. "Five souls."

The Spitfire's head rose, chest filling with purring flame. It was automatic at the sound of that voice. Even I felt drawn to it.

"Clem?" Eva said.

"It wasn't me," I said at once, though it had sounded like me. Just the same as my voice. "It was her."

"Or was it?" the voice said, lilting with humor. "Was it me, or her?"

Lightning crackled in the darkness. Liara's magic. "Don't toy with us, witch. If you want a proper fight, allow us to pass through."

"One fae soul touched by flame," the voice—my voice—said, unconcerned. "Delicious turmoil. I shall cherish you."

"Clem," Liara growled, "if you ever use a tone that smug, I'll kill you after I'm done with her."

"Murkwood," I said, "let us through. We're coming to you."

A murmur of laughter. "And aren't you with me?" The air pressed in closer, tendrils of it stroking my face with the kind of numbing coldness I had come to expect from the Shade's creatures. "You're here with me now. I can feel you."

"It's getting colder," Aidan said. "Isn't it?"

"I can feel her," Eva whispered, her voice chilling and low. "She's all around me."

The lightning's crackle died, and Liara cursed. "The air's smothering my magic."

Smothered? That shouldn't be possible.

"Clem," Loki said beside me, "just so you know, we're sinking."

My senses sharpened on him—and on my feet. Panic pulsed in my chest, tightening my throat. He was right: what had been semi-solid ground wasn't anymore. The cold was consuming my boots, pulling me in, slinking its way up my ankles.

I reached down, slipped a hand under Loki to yank him up. But he was stuck, already up to his chest in it.

"Be with me," Murkwood murmured as the marsh rose almost to my knees, pulling me deeper. It rose fast, so fast. "Five souls, mine to hold."

Eva began coughing, and then we all were. The air clogged, itched, poured down our throats. Consuming us.

But this wasn't Hell—we were still in the world. She couldn't take our souls unless we were down there, with her. This was the Shade's magic.

And two things didn't make sense: Where there had been ground, now there wasn't. The air had smothered Liara's lightning. The world had changed in too many ways, shifted too suddenly.

As the marsh touched my waist, Samara's face flashed in front of me. Her eyes, bone white, fluttered as her lips curled, and I understood that what she had done had been the only way to train me as she needed to.

She had taught me to fight the Shade's most dangerous, masterful hex.

And now I was inside it. I was inside the delusion.

"It's a hex," I whispered.

"A hex?" came Eva's feathery voice.

"What hex?" Liara growled.

The delusion hex.

As soon as understanding hit, the impulse came. A glow expanded around my head, and the wisps' perfect light illuminated the strange wetlands the Shade had created.

Black ooze came, revealed even as it was burned away. Only the tip of Loki's nose was visible in it, and then he was consumed by light. As the glow grew, it ate up the void, the delusion, washing it all away.

For a second, I caught a glimpse of a figure not ten feet off. Pale skin, curls, a small smile—she was me. And then she was gone, pressed away by the light. It consumed everything, blasted away all other color.

I had to squeeze my eyes shut, but they were seared anyway. When I opened them a crack, the air was soft and light again. The sun shone warm on my arms, and I stood on grass. Beneath me, the golden shimmer of a leyline.

My eyes lifted, and I glimpsed the others around me. All of us were intact.

We had passed through her corruption. I had passed through the Shade's delusion hex a second time in as many years.

So why had she let me pass through the first time?

CHAPTER TWENTY-ONE

We sat where we'd been ejected from the hex, all of us on the grass with our arms over our knees and our backs hunched as we recovered at Matka Canyon.

We had made it to the canyon in Macedonia; that much was obvious from the sound of water running through the nearby ravine, and the way the land sloped as it had on the map, where some fae cartographer had written, *Don't*.

The sun hadn't even moved in the sky. We had passed through the veil in no time, but the experience had been...

"Dreadful," Aidan said, adjusting his glasses against the sunlight. "That was really, truly the most dreadful experience of my life."

"Charmed life," Liara murmured.

"So that was Murkwood's delusion hex," Eva said, eyes unfocused. "How did you know, Clem?"

I pointed down. "The ground changed, for one. And she snuffed out Liara's lightning, for two."

"You picked up on it like that." Aidan snapped his fingers. "Well done."

I ran a hand over Loki's head, who lay under my legs. His fur was as soft and silky as ever, untouched, but a few seconds ago he had been consumed by ooze. It had felt so real—even more so than Samara's hex, if that was possible.

I saw now where Murkwood's power outstripped Samara's. Where the dark witch held not just the edge, but the absolute cudgel over any other magic wielder.

On reflection, Samara's hex had been less artful from the beginning. I had felt it come over me outside the monastery, even though I hadn't been able to identify what it was. I had always sensed something was off, but only recognized it for what it was after learning about her delusion hex.

Murkwood's magic, on the other hand, I had expected—but I'd still believed I had stepped into a real place. When her magic had washed over me, I hadn't felt it. I had only been on a ridge, and then I was in the marsh. And fighting toward an understanding of the inconsistencies of Murkwood's hex had been harder. Less forthcoming, like my brain was cloudy.

But without Samara's immersion in her own hex, without her explanation of how to defeat it, we would have been consumed by Murkwood's version of it. I was sure of that.

And we weren't even in Hell yet.

Eva pressed a conjured glass of an iced amber drink into my hand, the coldness of it surprising me. She was always the first to rally. "Drink it all," she said. "You'll feel better."

I took a sip, thinking it was iced tea. Then lowered the glass. "That's more bitter than Liara's heart."

"It's a fae drink." Liara's eyes traveled over the small plain around us, toward the hills. "Helps you feel more centered."

"Bottoms up, then." I raised the glass in a toast—which only Eva joined in on, even though they all had glasses—then downed it in one go.

I'd take bitter if it would relieve me of the dread of that hex. If I could feel just a little bit better.

I lowered the glass and found Liara staring at me.

Her eyes narrowed, examining my nose and mouth, then my eyes. "Why does the Shade have your voice?"

"She's the deceiver," Aidan said, still slouched. "It's kind of what she does."

She had my voice every time, I thought but didn't say. Every time I'd met her, she'd had my voice. Only this time, it could have been anyone's—Liara's, Eva's, Aidan's. Probably even Loki's.

But it was always mine.

And then there was the figure I'd seen as the light blasted the hex away.

"It was a stunningly good mimicry," Eva said, eyes also on me. "Like Clem was speaking in two places."

On reflection, that was probably what I'd seen the night I first met the Shade—a likeness, a hex. It was the winter of my first year, and I'd seen a vision of her atop a horse outside Hell. That wasn't possible, I knew now.

"Like I said"—Aidan pushed himself up to his feet—"it's what she does. She learned it well from the fae."

"*J'accuse*, Aidan?" Liara said, also rising.

A moment later all of us were up; that drink must have done its job.

"I don't accuse," Aidan said, retrieving his map and unrolling it. "I state facts."

I gripped the Backbiter as I stood. It hadn't left my hand since I'd taken it out on the ridge in Serbia. When I turned for the first time, taking in the place around us, I sucked in air. I knew this place. This was the spot where I had first used my magic.

My eyes drifted down to Loki, who was staring back up at me. "I believe," Loki said, "this was where I got swung around by my tail. And you said, 'Burn, fuckers.' And then you burned them."

I half-smiled, eyes darting away as a thought occurred. "And I'd do it again." My feet were already in motion, and I was crossing the grass away from the group, following the path I had taken that night. Except I had been running, running for my life. The bastards had been chasing me, some on all fours, and only when I'd reached the cliff—which I stepped up to now, slowly, carefully—did I fully understand.

I stared down the length of the sheer drop, into the crystalline flow of water far below, and remembered the night Umbra had saved me. She'd leapt off a bridge, as though she had known what I would face.

I would have to leap. Then, and later.

"Only those who overcome their fear survive," I said into the canyon, fighting against vertigo.

Eva came to stand beside me, her hair blown back like strands of pink silk over her wings. "This was where you jumped, wasn't it?"

I set a hand on her shoulder. "Is it sad that my knees are shaking?"

"No, Clem." She slid her hand up to her shoulder, grasped mine. "It's natural."

"Because I don't have wings?"

She squeezed my hand. "Because your body remembers what happened here. Somewhere inside you're still nineteen and unable to use your flames."

"The body remembers?"

She nodded. "Whether we want it to or not. It remembers."

"Hey," Liara called out. "When you two are doing sightseeing, you ought to come see this."

The five of us stood in front of a nearly vertical rocky rise some thirty feet from the canyon's drop, the water a low music behind us. And from that rise a hole had been bored into the rock—not human-height, but low.

Low enough that we'd have to get down on our knees to peer inside.

We all crouched in front of it, but not even the sunlight penetrated beyond the entry. Liara's fingers went out to the Faerish lettering inscribed in a semi-circle over the hole. She traced along the rock, reading: "'Don't. Don't seek, don't vie, don't linger. Where the darkness lies, the darkness must remain.'"

As she read, I found my fingers gripping at my pants, rubbing the feeling away. Tension, omen, fear—I heard them all in her voice. And I couldn't remember the last time I'd heard a fearful Liara. Maybe never.

Loki stared into the hole, tail swaying. "If there ever was a road sign to Hell..."

"This must be it," Aidan said. "That's about as dramatic as the old fae scholars ever got in writing."

Eva's fingers went out to touch the lettering. "Don't you think the inscription is odd?"

"How so?" I asked.

"For one thing, this isn't Old Faerish." Her fingers traced over the rock. "Old Faerish curves their letters. This doesn't. It's just regular Faerish."

I glanced at Eva. "And when did regular Faerish come into use?"

"Faerish evolved around the sixteenth century," Aidan cut in, leaning closer to the lettering.

"After the Battle of the Ages," Liara said. "Eva's right—this is post-battle."

"So you think it has something to do with Murkwood," I said. "This inscription."

"Maybe," Eva murmured. "It's different, the way whoever wrote this speaks of Hell. 'Where the darkness lies, the darkness must remain.'"

I'd had enough talking, especially with the sun past its peak.

"If no one has any objections..." A wisp circled my head, flew up to the entrance. "I'm sending some light in."

The others nodded.

The wisp flew into the hole, illuminating its edges. The tunnel remained the same size as it bored into the rock, but as the wisp flew deeper, the hole narrowed. And then, with a suddenness that made my chest catch, the wisp's light disappeared as it dropped down.

The light almost vanished, but not quite. It forged on, on, flying fast until it hit its tether with a small, uncomfortable tug at my chest. And then it began to return.

When the light reappeared and it rushed out of the hole and above my head, I said, "It goes far. We might have to crawl."

Eva sat back on her legs. "We'll need to dress for it. Thick material to protect our elbows and knees."

"There isn't time." Liara was already braiding her hair with swift fingers, twining the strands together with mesmeric speed. "The sun will be down in five hours, and we may need all of it."

"We could wait," Aidan said. "Until tomorrow morning."

"Liara's right." I began looping my braid into a bun at the back of my head. "There isn't time. She was there in the spring when Rathmore talked to the council. He could raise the Shade any day—it could be tomorrow."

"Better to meet her while she's still imprisoned," Eva said, her hair somehow already done up in a seamless bun. "Let's go now, then."

Aidan blew out air. "So the fight will be today."

Loki still stared into the hole, tail moving in a snakelike rhythm. Finally he glanced up at me, eyes emerald in the sun. "It smells in there."

I unclipped my cloak, balling it up and tying it around my chest. "A good smell, I hope."

"That depends on how you feel about the scent of the Shade's magic."

"I'm not one for the smell of shit."

"It smells like cloves," he corrected. "Sort of sweet. I want to follow it."

Of course. Of course her magic would smell sweet, alluring.

"Best to leave the horses free," Aidan said, glancing over at the horses grazing not far off. "They'll only stray for good reason, and in that case, they can run farther and faster than us."

"Good reason," Liara said. "Like we die down there and never come back?"

"Has anyone ever told you," Eva said as she tucked in her shirt, "that you should write a book on optimism?"

I moved closer to the cave's entrance. "Loki, stay behind me. I'll have the wisps provide us with light."

Liara came to my side, kneeling. "I'll follow you."

"And I'll bring up the rear behind Eva," Aidan said.

So that was it. We had decided. Now it was just to make the plunge.

As I knelt before the darkness, my hands went out to the rock, and I turned back to the others. "This is my prophecy. Whatever happens down there, don't stay too long."

Eva went rigid, and my senses sharpened on her as her lips parted.

"*Don't*," she whispered. "'Don't seek, don't vie, don't linger.' They're instructions."

Coldness ran through me.

"She's right," Loki said. "Instructions for how not to lose your soul."

"Well," I said, my throat tight, "at least somebody was kind enough to leave instructions."

Aidan's eyebrows pulled together. "In human and mage mythology, Hell has always been a place for wrongdoers. If we seek, if we vie, if we linger, we're dooming ourselves to lose our souls."

"So we don't," Liara said, rubbing her hands together to signal her readiness. "We get Clem to the Shade, and we end the witch. Then we leave."

But nothing is ever that simple, a voice said inside me. I used to give clipped, curt instructions—one and done, there and back. Nothing that mattered ever worked out so simply. *There's no other choice, though.*

I turned back to the hole. It was time to go.

"Anyone claustrophobic?" I said back to them.

"I grew up with an overbearing mom," Eva said. "Does that count?"

Nobody else spoke.

"So that's a no," I said, swallowing hard. "Good."

When we passed through the entrance into the rock face, coldness settled over me at once. I started on my knees, sending two wisps ahead to a distance of six feet to light our way. The others were interspersed among the group—two by Liara, two by Eva, and two behind Aidan.

It still didn't feel like enough. Even perfect light couldn't warm against this kind of cold—bone-deep, numbing, oppressive. Even the Spitfire, warming my chest, wings flared with anticipation inside me.

I hated tight spaces.

CHAPTER TWENTY-TWO

No breeze flowed in or out of the hole into the earth. The rock was cold on my hands, through the knees of my pants, slick under the toes of my boots. And the deeper we went, the more I felt it touching my shoulders and sometimes my back.

"Surprisingly smooth," Eva said from behind, her voice echoing forward. "Don't you think?"

"I hadn't thought about it," Liara bit out. "You know, considering our destination."

"It is smooth," I said without turning my head. I kept my eyes on the wisps, whose light grew brighter as the tunnel narrowed. Soon enough we wouldn't be able to keep on our hands and knees.

"And there's no scent," Aidan said from farthest back. "Odd."

"Oh, there's a scent," Loki said behind me. "It's like catnip."

"Loki can smell Murkwood's magic," I said. "Apparently it's a drug to him."

"Why do you always call her 'Murkwood,' anyway?" Liara asked. I knew what she was doing—what we were all doing: spreading our voices around, dulling the fear.

It wasn't working. If I didn't keep my arms straight, my elbows shook. My breathing came fast, tight, like I didn't have enough air.

And a gnawing had begun in my chest, like the Spitfire was working its teeth over my rib cage. "That's her name," I shot back.

"She doesn't deserve a name," Liara said. "Not a real one. Not anymore."

"Duck down," I said as the wisps' light grew, intensified by the narrowing tunnel. "We're going to be crawling now."

"I thought we *were* crawling," Aidan said.

"Really crawling," I said, trying to keep my voice steady, light. The gnawing was getting worse. "On our bellies."

The moment my stomach touched the stone was the moment the tunnel wouldn't allow me to pass otherwise. And I knew when I moved forward, I would feel the rock all around me. Pressing in.

Don't lose it, Rational Clem whispered. *Not now, over this.*

I forced myself forward, my movements shaking but mechanical. When I heard Eva call, "Everything all right, Clem?" I forced myself to say back, in sing-song, "Right as rain on the plain." Except it wasn't sing-song. It was a strange, uncanny deadpan.

"Rain on the plain?" Loki said behind me, and if I could have seen his face, he would have been concerned.

In my first group home, we must have watched *My Fair Lady* twenty times. Not because we'd wanted to, but because it was, over the years, on the communal TV in the living room at least twenty times. And every time I'd caught snippets of it until I had seen the whole thing in pieces.

I didn't like the movie, because I didn't like the group home. But if you've spent six years anywhere, especially as a kid, memories of it become a comfort. You don't realize what can be a comfort to you until you have nothing else.

The earth pressed in, not suffocating but present if I tried to rise even a little, as I pulled and crawled my way through the tunnel. And I didn't know if my breathing was coming fast because of a lack of air or what felt like it, but the wisps' light became white stars, and then I wasn't moving at all.

As I went, the gnawing had become clawing. The Spitfire, trapped, trying to claw and bite its way through my chest like an animal. Like it could escape me and race down the passage.

The pain was acute. And when I couldn't move, it became agonizing.

My hands thrust into the rock, and I tried to get up. I hit the back of my head against the rock and then my cheek as I ricocheted off. More pain—white-hot pain. My breath whistled in and out of me, not my own anymore.

You lost it, I thought, even as my chest constricted faster and faster. *You goddamn lost it.*

Not here. Not in front of them. Not now.

"Clem?" Liara said, distant through my ringing ears. "She's hyperventilating."

"Oh gods," Eva said. "She has panic attacks."

Through the impending sense of doom, of the Spitfire clawing its way out of me, a thought: How did Eva know that? I hadn't told her. I'd kept it from her for four years—or I thought I had.

"Loki," Eva was saying, "can you get up to her?"

"Working on it."

Something pressed against my foot, my leg, and soon a warm, furry thing was pushing itself up toward my chest. "Clementine," Loki said, his voice deep and sure, and I found his fur touching my fingers. My one constant. "It's okay. You're okay."

I couldn't talk. Tears had pressed out of my eyes, wetted my cheeks as I waited for it to pass. Doom circled my head, vultures with long necks waiting to descend. I couldn't get enough air. I would die in this tunnel.

The Spitfire, raging against its cage, would burst out of my chest.

"Remember when you were thirteen," Loki said, vibrating against my breastbone, "and you fell between the couch and the wall?"

That was in the group home.

"I-I"—I gasped in air, my vision nearly gone—"I was trying t-to reach..."

"The remote," he finished for me. "You were trying to reach the TV remote."

Past the pain, past the heat, I remembered. The memory appeared before my eyes.

I had dropped it. The couch was so heavy, and I was alone in the living room at night, when I shouldn't have been. I felt suffocated behind that old couch, and no one heard me yelling. No one heard me crying, hyperventilating, except Loki. I lay there for minutes, pinned, until he found me.

"H-how is this"—my chest caught, spasmed—"memory supposed to fucking help?"

"Do you remember," he whispered, vibrating harder, louder, "how you got out?"

Did I remember? I couldn't think, couldn't focus, couldn't consider anything except the absolute mass of earth all around me.

"Tell me what you hear," Loki said.

I needed to stand. Needed to move. I was going to faint.

The Spitfire can't get out, Rational Clem said. *Samara taught you to control it. So control it.*

Loki's paws pressed into my chest, his claws tiny thorns forcing me to the present. "I couldn't get you out, Clem. I can't get you out now. Only you can get yourself out. Tell me what you hear."

Loki's claws were pain. Real pain. His claws were centering.

I was Clementine. I was in control.

"I hear..." I paused, choking and gasping, listening through the faint ringing, "Eva's voice."

Eva's voice, murmuring soft words. She was saying it would be okay, that we would make it through. There was enough space. Enough air.

"Good," Loki said. "Tell me what you smell."

I swallowed. Drew in a long, stuttering breath through my nose. "Earth. Stale air."

"Tell me what you see."

The Spitfire had stopped. The gnawing and clawing had subsided.

My eyes opened, and I saw only perfect light. No white stars. Just the wisps, illuminating everything. I glanced down at Loki. "I see a dirty black cat."

"Can't be helped," he said with a slow blink, "unless we get out of this godsdamn tunnel."

A minute later, I was pulling my way to where the tunnel changed course. Loki had gotten behind me again, and the others were grunting and scraping along through the tight passageway.

Nobody said anything about what had happened to me. They knew this wasn't the time.

I had good friends.

The wisps ahead of me darted down, their light dimming as they reached the spot where the tunnel angled. As I came to it, I hooked my elbow over the edge. "It widens out again," I called back. "By a lot. Not too steep an angle, either."

"Thank the gods," Eva said. "They don't make it easy getting to Hell, do they?"

"Not if you're still alive," Liara said.

"Let's hope it's always this difficult," Aidan said, his voice farthest back.

Amen.

"Wait for me to say when." I pulled myself over the edge, dropping down into the section of the tunnel that began a slow but sure descent. I had enough room to half-stand, at least, and the decline wasn't so sharp as to risk sliding.

And it was here that I began to suspect this was truly a tunnel—not some coincidence, a crack in the earth. Someone had dug—or magicked—this path into being.

It was truly a tunnel.

When I rose, I sent the wisps ahead of me, squinting after them. The tunnel just went straight on and on... until it didn't. The wisps disappeared around a corner, leaving me in darkness, and that was when I jerked them back.

That singular moment of darkness had been enough.

"All right," I called to the others, hands out against the walls of the tunnel as I began a slow, hunched descent. "Come on."

They followed after, and soon the five of us were moving again. Eva and Aidan kept up a constant chatter, a buffer against our reality. Every time the stark fear pressed in, Loki would brush against my leg. Eva's laugh would tinkle around me. Liara's sharp hiss of annoyance would bring me back to where I was—with them.

We reached the turn, and the tunnel continued on just the same way. "It just keeps going," I said back to them. "Down and down."

"That's the only way, right?" Liara said. "Down."

"The fae's right," Loki said, passing me.

On we went, hunched down the next section of tunnel until it reached another identical turn, switchbacking at intervals on our constant descent. I'd lost track of how long we'd been walking when I came around the next turn. I stopped hard.

Liara bumped into me. "Hello, Clem's back."

I set my hand on her shoulder, bringing two of the wisps to a hover above us. "Look."

A few feet in front of us, the tunnel widened and rose to some eight feet wide and tall. It was blocked by a massive stone taller than me and three times as wide. A second inscription had been written above it, this one also in Faerish.

Eva and Aidan appeared behind Liara, the two of them staring up at the inscription. Silence fell all around, and I didn't like the lack of sound. Or their open mouths.

Above us, the lettering came in and out of view as the wisps circled. "Anyone care to translate?" I asked.

Eva's eyes flicked down to me. Her lips moved without words at first. "It says, 'The underworld does not welcome what souls are bound for Heaven or Hell.'"

"What does that mean?" Liara asked.

"It makes a distinction," Aidan said, "between the underworld and Hell. But they're one and the same."

"I'm mostly stuck on the 'not welcome' part," Loki said. "I wanna say that includes us."

I set a hand to the stone and found it, surprisingly, lukewarm. "We have to move it."

"Do we, though?" Aidan asked.

I looked back at him. "This is the way. This was where the wisps sent me when they gave me the key to the Backbiter."

"They sent you to the canyon above us," Aidan said. "Not here."

I turned back to the stone, and flame burst to life on my fingers.

"Aidan, you told me Murkwood was banished to the underworld. What do you think is past this stone?"

"The underworld," he said. "It has to be the underworld."

Liara's arms folded. "You're going to burn through that thing?"

I met her eyes in the firelight. "In a way."

This section of the tunnel offered enough room for me to swing a chain. When I pulled the Backbiter from my cloak, I let the rod slide to place beside the blade. The others were already backing up by the time the blade clanked against the stone floor, and definitely before my fire ran up and down the length of the weapon. "Orichalcum's the hardest metal on Earth, right Aidan?"

Aidan cleared his throat. "In theory."

"Time to find out."

On my first swing, the tip of the blade met the head of the stone without catching. It slid down the side and to the floor, and Loki let out a, "Hm." He sat down beside the others, tail flicking. "Not quite what I'd expected."

With a growl, I prepared to swing again. This time the blade caught in the stone, but when I tried to drag it down, it wouldn't move.

It was stuck.

I didn't have time for stuck.

"Clem," Aidan began. "I don't think we're going to—"

With a yell, the Spitfire flared in me. I called on it, or it had risen to meet my need. Either way, the Backbiter burst into new, super-heated flame, and I grabbed the chain, yanking the blade down toward me.

Heed me, the thought came, sharp and uncompromising.

The blade ripped through the stone, which hissed as it melted away, and cracked it from head to base like an egg. The blade hit the ground with a fiery thump.

I glanced over at the others. "What were you saying, Aidan?"

CHAPTER TWENTY-THREE

We pushed aside the crumbled parts of the rock and cleared out a space large enough that we could climb up onto it and duck through.

I was the first. When I got up to a crouch atop the rock, I sent a wisp through to show me what was on the other side. I wanted to be the first into this underworld.

In the silence, Aidan called up to me, "What do you see, Clem?"

"More tunnel," I said, my voice as dull as I probably felt. "Just more tunnel."

When I'd climbed through to the other side and dropped down, I still had my weapon at the ready. But nothing seemed different about this side.

What was curious, though, was the tunnel's curve; it mirrored the other side.

Loki was already by my feet. "Still smells like her."

"Stronger, or weaker?"

"Stronger."

Good.

I came to the edge of the first turn, a wisp flitting around me, and when I peered around it, the wisp zipped ahead, giving us a brilliant view of the next section of the passageway.

"Oh," Loki said. "Well that's curious."

"What's he meowing about?" Liara's feet hit the rock as she climbed through, approaching from behind.

I kept staring after the wisp. "The tunnel. It doesn't go down anymore."

"Which way does it go, then?"

I glanced back at Liara. "Up."

"Up?" Eva was through, and she came to my side to stare with me. "It goes up."

Last of all came Aidan, who was still shaking his head over the way I'd decimated that ancient rock. When he gazed down the passage, he tilted his head. "The underworld is up?"

I shrugged. "Only one way to find out."

We kept following the only path available to us. At the first switchback, Aidan said, "Did you notice, the incline is at the same angle as the decline?"

"And what angle is that?" Liara said.

"Something like thirty-five degrees."

He was right; I'd already sensed it, but it hadn't fully registered in my head until Aidan spoke up.

The farther we went, climbing and climbing, the eerier the feeling became of us simply returning the way we'd come by. And when I reached the drop-off, that feeling became a stone in my stomach. This was the spot where I'd panicked. We would have to do it again.

I stopped, staring up at it. "It's the same. Everything is exactly the same as the passageway down."

"We've reached the exit?" Eva said, breathless.

Cold water flowed through my veins. "I guess." I didn't know what we'd find when we made our way through that final segment. Matka Canyon? The sun still out? Or something worse.

If this was the underworld, or Hell, or whatever mages called this place below the earth, it bothered me more that it wasn't different at all. Not one bit. I had been prepared for sulfur and hellfire and wailing. I had steeled myself to see Murkwood's face.

This likeness was unsettling. If what we found outside was just like above ground, then how could you ever tell one from the other? You could get lost, thinking you were in the regular world.

It was unsettling. But we had come this far, and I had to stop her—end her. So I reached up, hooking my arms over the ledge and pulling myself up. And what I found was exactly what my brain had promised: a passageway so small I'd have to crawl through like I was in boot camp. The wisps had flown ahead, casting light on the gauntlet.

Loki leapt up beside me as I contemplated it. "I'm here."

"I won't lose it this time," I murmured, low enough for only him to hear. Before he could respond, I thrust the Backbiter into my cloak and shoved myself forward, diving into the tight space. Starting my crawl.

Inside me, the Spitfire turned in place, pacing like a caged creature. Wanting out. But the moment I'd pulled myself onto the ledge, I'd used Samara's training to push him so far down, I couldn't even feel his heat.

He didn't dare claw at me this time.

I moved faster this time, with purpose. I knew how far it was to the other side, how long I would have to endure this. The rock scraped my arms and knees, and probably took skin off beneath my clothes.

I didn't care. Chances were, worse awaited me.

When the tunnel widened and I could crouch, I sucked in air. I had gotten so far ahead of the others that I heard Liara's echoing voice call out from far off, "Clem?"

"I'm fine," I called back. "I'm at the first section. Hurry up."

I waited until they were close, and then, with my weapon in hand, we came to the end of the tunnel. What, for us, had been the beginning.

Except there was no sunlight here.

I paused three feet from the tunnel's exit, staring at the green half-light emanating in, dancing over the stone near my feet. When Liara came up behind me, I raised a hand. "I'm sending a wisp out."

When she saw the odd light, she didn't object. Neither did the others, who all crowded up behind me.

The wisp flew out, its color undiluted. It remained a brilliant blue-white, gleaming as it departed the tunnel and floated into what I guessed was Matka Canyon.

It disappeared, and we all remained silent as we were left with the other wisps hovering around us, their pure brightness an uncommon comfort. Without them, I'd have had to summon fire. And even my own fire wouldn't have felt as safe as these tiny balls of light.

A minute later, the wisp I'd sent reached the end of its tether. It came flying back into the tunnel and to a hover directly in front of my face. The sense of things it had seen penetrated my mind, and my hand went out to the stone beside me.

Eva's fingers touched my arm, light and warm. "What is it?"

My head lowered. "This isn't Matka Canyon."

"What did it see?" Liara asked, low and quiet.

I shook my head. "Forms, shapes, all of them still and dark. They seemed to be sleeping."

"Sleeping?" Eva said. "But there's light out there."

"Not any light I've ever seen," Aidan said. "It must be they're in stasis."

I swallowed, letting my hand drop. My fingers tightened on the Backbiter as my face rose. "This is where you can still turn back. The way is easy. I won't blame you."

Nobody moved. Nobody spoke up—except for Eva.

"Let's go, Clem," she said. "When you're ready."

Ready. I would never be ready. But that made no difference; I had to be.

With a burst of flame, I wrapped an enshroudment over all of us. Together, I led us out into the green light.

We came out to the sound of rushing water. Before us lay the same flat plain that we'd stood on when we entered the tunnel, but it lay mostly in darkness. The low green light came from everywhere and from nowhere, providing just enough for my eyes to see.

And what I saw made me go stiff. All around us stood humanlike figures—still, crooked, sleeping. The Shade's creatures. But in this place, they no longer pressed away light.

I could finally see them.

"Clem," Eva whispered beside me, "they're human."

The Shade's creatures were human. And thinking back to that first night I'd been dragged from my apartment and carried into the cold, I'd known then that they had moved like humans. Just faster.

And on that bridge, just before Umbra had asked me to jump, a group of them had rushed me. One on all fours with red eyes, and a recognition had passed through me. She looked like a child, I'd thought. But then the feeling had been swept away by fear and need, and I'd never considered it again.

From that point, they had always been the Shade's creatures. Inhuman beasts.

Closest to us, a woman stood with her head thrown back, arms akimbo, as though she'd been pierced in the chest. Her mouth was open, and her eyes were shut. Her breast didn't move; she didn't breathe at all. But she wasn't dead, either.

Others littered the space, each in their own poses. One man lay on his side, arms out. Another had at some point gotten on all fours, head lowered, fingers digging into the ground.

"Human," I said, "but twisted."

"Hell is a lot quieter than I'd expected," Liara said.

The inscription over the stone had spoken of souls belonging to the underworld, and souls belonging to Hell. It had made a distinction.

"What if this isn't Hell?" I said. "Aidan said the inscription spoke of the underworld and Hell as though they were two separate places."

"If that's true," Eva said, "then what is the underworld?"

I didn't know. Nobody else knew, either—or at least, they didn't speak up.

"Loki," I said, "do you still smell her?"

"She's as sweet a scent as ever," Loki said. "And nearer."

Good. Wherever we were, we were in the right place. Now we had to make our way toward her.

We started past the sleeping creatures, walking on cat's feet even under the enshroudment.

"Are they alive?" Eva said, staring at the contorted woman.

"I think so, in a way," Aidan said. "But not in the way we are. They sleep while the sun passes over."

And we were in a part of the world where the sun was still passing over.

"What happens when the sun has passed?" Eva said.

"I don't know," Aidan said, but I could hear in his voice that he had a feeling he knew. And I did, too.

"We know they come above ground when the Shade's power is greatest," I whispered. "During the witching hour."

But what did they do the rest of the night?

"They awaken," Loki said as though reading my mind. "They hate the light, so they sleep through it, and they awaken after dark. Every horror movie you've ever forced us to watch tells me so."

I blew out air, wanting to disbelieve. But I knew my cat was right. "We need to move. Fast."

"Move where?" Eva asked.

"Samara said the Shade would find Clementine," Liara said. "So she should drop the enshroudment."

"Gods, no," Eva said. "We don't know how easily the creatures could wake."

My fingers tightened on the Backbiter. "Liara's right. Even if they do wake, I can defeat them."

When I stepped outside the enshroudment, Loki moved with me. Eva and Liara made noises of surprise; I hadn't dropped the enshroudment from around the three of them. And I wasn't planning to.

I might be able to defeat the Shade's army of souls alone, but that didn't mean the others could. Not even Liara was a guarantee.

The moment I was outside the enshroudment, I sucked in air. It came thick and humid into my throat. Murkwood's magic was in my lungs. Inside me, the Spitfire was delighted, urging me forward. But I waited in absolute stillness to see what the sleeping souls around me would do.

Loki approached the nearest one—the woman with her breast upturned, head thrown back, and gave a sniff near her feet. Then his eyes, greener in the green light, blinked at me as he trotted back.

I knelt beside him. "What do you smell?"

"Murkwood's magic," he whispered. "It's all over her. And the others, I'd guess."

So she *was* the queen of her domain. When Samara had said that, I'd assumed she'd meant Hell—but this was a different domain. It was the underworld.

A different place with its own ruler, and different rules. Rules I didn't know.

With a flick of my fingers, I sent the wisps in all directions. They pinwheeled away from where we stood near the canyon. I wondered if everything would be the same as above ground—the hills, the slopes, the rivers.

When I straightened, my eyes had fallen on the spot where the land dropped away toward the canyon. I approached it slowly, my footsteps silent, Loki walking beside me. As I came to the edge, I was standing beside a man kneeling, face in hands like he was weeping. Weeping just before he'd slept.

I stared down toward the flowing water. Above ground, it had been blue and frothy. Here, it was green under the light, and otherwise dark. Black water, like oil, pouring through a crack in the earth.

This wasn't a good place. It was clammy, without a breeze, the air too thick, the light off-kilter.

It was a fever dream here. Not a nightmare with a beginning and an end, but a place where you turned circles and never found a bit of happiness any which way you turned. Always dissatisfaction. Always frustration.

Only one part of me didn't feel frustrated or dissatisfied. One part of me purred, thrilled and pressing at the edges of my chest. The Spitfire. As soon as I'd approached the ravine, it leaned forward. Wanting to head to the other side. To be somewhere I couldn't yet see.

The Faerish words came back to me: *Don't seek, don't vie, don't linger.*

I had no choice but to seek. But I wouldn't vie, and I shouldn't linger.

"Loki," I murmured. "Which way is her scent strongest?"

Loki faced out across the ravine—in the exact direction the Spitfire had leaned. "That way."

So the Spitfire knows something I don't. It knows where she is.

Or maybe Murkwood was calling the Spitfire to her. It, like her, was empowered by flames. They had a kinship.

The wisps snapped to the ends of their tethers, came racing back toward me. When they arrived, they amassed around my head. So many creatures—so many souls in all directions. All of them asleep, in odd poses of frustration or agony or both.

I turned back to the others, who had approached me, silent, under the enshroudment. It clung to them, a skein of nearly invisible, rippling fire. When I stepped inside it, I pointed across the ravine. "She's on the other side of the river."

CHAPTER TWENTY-FOUR

The plan was this: On the other side of the ravine, we would separate. Eva and Liara would find high-up spots to watch from, to wait for their moment. Aidan would remain under my enshroudment at a distance, keeping behind a rock or a tree.

And I would walk in the open with Loki. I wouldn't be quiet, either.

Eva and Liara flew Aidan across, and then they brought me across the ravine. Once on the other side, we found ourselves on a hilly slope.

Loki and the Spitfire told me what I sought lay on the other side. So it was just a matter of climbing.

We stood under the enshroudment on the hill, the creatures punctuating the slope all around us. "Don't reveal yourselves," I said to the others, "unless you absolutely have to."

Eva clasped my arm, leaned close. "I'll do what I have to do," she said. "I'm not leaving this place without you."

I squeezed her hand. "It may be pieces of me."

"Morbid," Liara said from my other side. "I like it."

I glanced back at her with a half-smile.

"That won't happen," Aidan said.

"He's right." Eva took a step back, then another. "I'll be watching you." And then she was outside the enshroudment and in the air, disappearing around a tall, spiny tree.

I met eyes with Liara.

"Make it quick," she said, "and we'll be out of here before the sun's down."

I gave her a nod.

When Liara had gone, it was just me and Loki and Aidan. And now it was my turn to leave him.

"Clem," he said. "My gift. I know I said it was part of the prophecy, but…"

"You don't know how."

He half-shrugged. "I feel like I'm missing something."

"It doesn't matter." I hefted the Backbiter. "This is all I need now. Stay under the enshroudment, all right?"

"Clem…"

I began backing away, out of the enshroudment. "Don't make me get sappy with Loki here. He'll never let me live it down." I turned, began my ascent up the slope with Loki at my side and the Backbiter in one hand. The wisps hovered around me in tense, frenetic non-motion, waiting.

"Loki," I said as we climbed the hill, "how long do familiars live?"

"As long as our favorite witch."

I glanced at him. "You can choose to die?"

"Sure. Just like humans can."

"Hey, if I don't make it…"

He didn't stop climbing. "Then I won't make it."

I watched after him a second. He had always been a small cat—maybe the runt of his litter, if there was such a thing for familiars. People in my life had remarked on it, and every time I had been surprised to hear it.

He had never seemed small to me.

I followed after him as he followed Murkwood's scent. The Spitfire pulled me toward the crest of the hill, toward what lay on the other side. When we reached the top, Loki had already stopped. He was staring down. And a second later, I discovered what he was staring at.

The hill descended into a valley, at the center of which was the largest, most sprawling tree I had ever seen. Its roots fanned in all directions, hundreds of feet into the green sky.

And in the shade of it stood a woman.

She didn't move. In fact, as we approached, she didn't seem as though she could move. The tree's roots wound up and over her ankles, almost black in the green light. And, too, her wrists had been bound by roots, pulled outward from her in a pose of supplication.

Her head was lowered, a hood over it, but a bit of hair peeked out from under her shoulder. I couldn't make out the color in the off-light and the tree's shade. When I leaned toward Loki, it was to whisper, "What's the scent?"

"Her," Loki said. "It's her."

I had already known as much; the Spitfire had become a pain in my chest, almost piercing my breastbone for how badly it pulled me toward the tree. It had never hurt me before today—not like this. Never seemed to have such a mind of its own.

When I reached the valley, what I had thought was grass was really moss and lichen. Spongy, slippery. My steps weren't as certain as I wanted them to be, and neither were the words I had in mind.

That didn't matter, though.

She spoke first.

When I had reached halfway across the valley to the tree, her head began to rise. A shrouded jaw and mouth came into view, and Loki went stiff beside me. He had stopped.

"Oh, but you've come so far, little puss," the woman said to him. "Don't stop now."

My voice. That was my voice from her mouth. A hex. It had to be a hex.

Flames roared to life in my hands, the wisps circling my head. "You won't get me with the same bullshit twice, Murkwood."

Her lips curved. "Is that so?"

So it *was* her. It was Raven Murkwood.

"Clem," Loki said, his voice a hoarse whisper.

I ignored him, scanning around us. The sleeping souls littered the valley and hillscape, all of them statues in different poses. Something must be off; even the underworld seemed to obey the rules of our world. If I could pick out one thing that was wrong, I could end the hex.

"Clem," Loki said again.

"What?" I snapped.

"I couldn't smell her magic in the delusion hex," he said. "I can smell her now. It's not a hex."

My hands half-lowered as Loki came to my side, but the flames went on burning along my fingertips.

Under the tree, Raven Murkwood burst into an oddly charming laughter. It held some of the same notes of my own laugh, but it was different. Some of the notes were darker, sharper. "A perceptive familiar deserves the greatest fire witch in five hundred years. Would you like to be mine, little puss?"

She could understand him. Murkwood could understand Loki.

Loki hissed. "Not now, nor in five hundred more years, cursed witch."

"Ah, not trusting of strangers." Murkwood tilted her head to the side, close enough for one hand to reach her hood. With deft fingers, she pulled it back. "And what about now?"

My flames guttered and died, throat tightening to a screw's width. And for the first time, I dropped the Backbiter. The weapon hit the moss with a dull thump, and from deep in me a word pressed its way to my tongue.

No. No. *No.*

She had my face. Raven Murkwood, the Shade, had my face. My hair, curly over her shoulders and frizzy, too. Her eyes were green like mine, her nose and lips and throat all the same.

This wasn't a hex—Loki had said as much.

So why did Raven Murkwood have my face?

"Loki," I whispered. "What does she look like to you?"

He didn't answer at first. Then, in a feathery voice, "You. Like you."

Me. Me but slightly older, her cheekbones more defined at the edges. Her mouth a little harder. Me of five or eight years from now. Me, who'd known cruelty.

"Still no?" Murkwood sighed, tilting her head the other way. "Shame. I haven't had a familiar in so long, and you could have been a marvel. Perhaps you'll change your mind momentarily."

A dry noise escaped my throat, and I cleared it. "Murkwood," I said. "Your name is Raven Murkwood."

Her green eyes flicked to me. A smile grew, chilling and indulgent. "Yes, my dear child, the wonder of my world. Now come to me, so I may show you who Raven Murkwood truly is."

The staggered, confused part of me wanted to go on staring with wide eyes. I couldn't comprehend what I was seeing, and I needed a minute to process. But the trained, determined part of me—Rational Clem—knew I had come here for a reason.

Pick up the weapon, Rational Clem said.

I half-knelt, grabbing the rod and chain in one hand.

"Yes," Murkwood said. "Bring that as well, my dear."

When I straightened, I didn't move. "Why do you look like me?" I called out, the fingers of my free hand rubbing together, antsy to be on fire.

On the hills around us, I sensed movement. In my periphery the dark forms seemed to be coming slowly to life, but I didn't for a second take my eyes off Murkwood.

Her smile widened. "Come close and discover all."

"You're a fool if you think I'll ever get closer than the reach of this chain to your neck. I've come for one reason."

She burst into new laughter, eyes never leaving mine. With a come-hither flick of the fingers on her right hand, she said, "Then let us get to the reason why you've come."

Forward, a voice hissed in my head.

Pain lanced my chest, and my fingers went over it as though I could rub it away. The Spitfire. It was railing against my rib cage like it could gnaw its way through, and the pain was sudden and white-hot and mind-erasing.

My legs trembled as I staggered forward, my body awkward and ungainly, nearly tumbling onto my face. All I could do was obey the Spitfire if I didn't want it tearing its way out of me, leaving a hole where my heart had been.

The pain was maddening, shrinking my world to a pinpoint. I lost all sense of space and surroundings; I just moved forward, the tree and the woman under it growing in my vision until she was directly above me, staring down at me with those green eyes. My green eyes.

I was on my knees. I had fallen to them.

My hands had gone up before me, the Backbiter laid out in my palms as though I was offering it up to her. And the wisps flew in and out of my vision, circling us both.

I had lost all awareness except of this. Of her.

"Finally," she whispered, so close she was practically in my ear. "Finally you've come to me. And now, child of my bosom, the flame's memories will roll through you as it leaves you. You will know why you were born, and why you exist now in supplication before me. It is the very least favor I can bestow upon you—a reversal of memory, a return to your beginning."

She extended one finger toward me, and the Spitfire jerked my body toward her bound hand. My head lowered, forehead approaching her fingertip, and the impulse to resist died the moment it approached the Spitfire's roaring bonfire of flame inside me.

I had no control now. Rational Clem was a dream. It was only the Spitfire and Murkwood's fingertip, the two nearing until, with a feather-light touch, the pad of her finger met the space between my eyebrows.

Air rushed into my lungs, my eyes rolling back into my head, and the world around me shrank to a film reel. Murkwood and I watched my own life spool backward.

I saw myself backing across the valley, Murkwood's form and the tree growing more distant, until I reached the hill. Step by step I passed up it, my eyes always on the tree, and when I reached the crest, I looked down into the valley, and knew I was watching my own life in reverse.

But I wasn't alone in watching it. Someone else was there with me.

Liara, Aidan, and Eva. They flew to me, and together we passed over the canyon and into the tunnel. We backed our way up, up, past the stone and even farther up until I panicked in the tunnel. In the wink of an eye I was in motion again, and we reached the daylight of Matka Canyon and the world above.

Faster. We went faster.

Back to Samara and the delusion hex. Back to the woods. Back to the academy. Edinburgh's crypts, finding Callum. The thief's blade, buried under ancient stone. My sister, Tamzin. The battle with Tristan Rathmore in Inverness.

Faster. Now we were infiltrating Edinburgh, all the guardian missions and time spent with Umbra in the meadow. My third year, second year, first year, meeting Eva and Aidan. The night I was kidnapped from my home by the Shade's creatures.

Faster and faster. Years upon years in the group home, just me and Loki and sometimes people who thought they could be my foster parents. They never could. Always I ended up back in the home with a revolving door of other children, none of whom I let myself trust.

I couldn't trust them. I couldn't trust anyone.

And then, there it was: Loki sat on my doorstep.

I backed away from the door into the night my mother and sister disappeared. Years of happiness I didn't know were happy—the way my mother used to touch my hair when I'd laid my head in her lap. My sister and I sitting in the bay window when a fire truck went by, the lights playing over our faces. The moment my mother gave me the locket and told me never to take it off. Being read stories at night.

And then my first memory: playing in a sandbox with the other children at preschool.

That was where my memories began, where the reel went black. But that wasn't where my life began.

Here, Murkwood said, a whisper in my head. *Here is the beginning. We've almost finished.*

The film reel came to a lurching stop and began to run normally. We moved forward in time once more. Color and sound appeared before my eyes, and I was an observer in the corner of a bedroom. My mother lay in the center of a bed, sweaty and pregnant. And beside her, holding her hand, sat a woman whose face I knew almost as well as my own mother's.

Maeve Umbra.

CHAPTER TWENTY-FIVE

It was nighttime, darkness pressing in like a blanket at the window.

"Bravery, Soph," Umbra said, squeezing my mother's hand. "It's almost done."

From this angle, Maeve Umbra looked almost exactly as she had the day I'd met her. Long white-gray hair spilling over her shoulders, her face lined by real old age. But this must have been over twenty years ago.

It was my birthday.

"Easy enough for you to say," my mother snarled, legs bent and spread. "You couldn't have ground me up a pinch of godsdamn painkiller?"

"I would, but I cannot. You know why." Umbra stood, came around to the end of the bed, standing between her legs. "Breathe, Sophia. Breathe and push."

My mother breathed and she pushed. She breathed and she pushed. When she let out a yell, it was at the bottom of her throat, the kind of noise a feral creature would make.

I'd never seen her yell. Not in words, and not like this, either.

I stared, transfixed, as she worked to move the enormous mound that was me from her belly out into the world. It was agonizing and long. In the long timeline of labor, "almost done" felt like ages.

Umbra coaxed my mom, hands on knees. As a midwife, she was calm, assured, no-nonsense. Every time my mother's head fell back and she shook it, insisted she couldn't do it, Umbra would say, "Eyes on me, Soph. Look at me." And once, in a particularly dire moment, she said, "You are a witch—there is no one more capable than you in this world."

It was the same voice she had sometimes used to talk to me. But this had more edge to it. A certain desperation. Why?

My eyes drifted to her. The air seemed suffused around Umbra, thicker. Rippling with faint color.

She was using her magic.

Around us, the bedroom vibrated with Maeve Umbra's magic, but it was only when I looked to the dark window that I properly saw it— the skein hanging over the room. This was an enshroudment. She was hiding my mother.

From who? And what?

My attention caught on the window. Even in the reflections of the glass panes, I caught a glimpse of shine, a glint off the dim light from in here. And what looked like a clawed foot.

A noise sounded at the window, like a tiny pebble hitting it. No one seemed to notice.

I tried to move closer to the window, but couldn't. I was stuck in this corner of the room.

My mother's breathing increased again, the in-and-out pace hard and fast, and Umbra said, "The head's cresting. We're nearly there."

"Maeve," my mother said between pushes, "we're safe."

It was a question.

"We're safe, Soph." Umbra's voice was full of false reassurance. After years, I knew that little quaver. I knew when she was afraid, and when she didn't feel what she said. And right now, she did not feel safe. Which was why she said next, "Quickly—push."

My mother pushed, her grunts and yells crescendoing. And at the window, the tapping increased, almost inaudible beneath the sounds of labor. Until, finally, in the corner of my eye I glimpsed a small, round eye attached to a long beak.

It was a bird. A blackbird tapping at the window.

When I glanced at Umbra, I knew she was aware of it. Her attention darted that way every few seconds, her nostrils flaring. She was keeping my mother's attention off it. She dripped with sweat to sustain the enshroudment, thick as a wool blanket around the room.

The tapping had become so hard, the window had a small crack.

My mom gave a last cry, peaking in a wail. My bloody head emerged, blond-haired and blue-eyed.

At that moment, the enshroudment dropped. Umbra's magic fell away, and they were exposed. The window shattered. A knifelike beak had burst through, and the whole pane fell away into shards.

The bird's wings extended wide, almost the span of the bed, and flapped once as it passed overtop my mother.

"No!" Umbra yelled.

But you let the enshroudment fall, I thought. *You exposed her, Umbra.*

In its claw was a single bit of color, like it carried a speck of the sun. The claw opened as it passed over the bed, and the speck—a tiny bit of flame, small enough to snuff with an exhale—fell from the raven.

Time slowed as it passed through the center of the room, weaving and dancing, and slipped between Umbra's outstretching hands. It passed between my mother's open thighs, on a straight and irrevocable course for the baby's head. My head.

And in the moment my mouth opened for the first time outside my mother's body, as I sucked in air to prepare for an absolute what-the-fuck-is-this-godawful-place wail, the flame dropped between my lips.

It disappeared there.

Time resumed. I let out a glass-shattering baby's cry, and the raven flapped once, passing through the doorway and disappearing.

Umbra rose to stand over me, stricken, staring down. And my mother stared after the raven, hands going to prop herself up, her mouth open and her face a rictus of shock and exhaustion and agony.

Something had happened. Something terrible. I could see it in her face. Her fingers clenched the sheets, and she let out a clipped cry.

"Sophia," Umbra said, low. The nighttime breeze blew in from the burst window, the curtains blowing toward them. "I'm so sorry. Gods, I'm sorry. You must understand—this fire only eats. It seeks to replicate itself, fights for its life against being extinguished."

"Stop it, Maeve," my mother yelled, trying to push herself up. "I saw what happened. You let the bird inside."

"It is uniform in its destruction and expansion." Her voice had dropped low, almost an undercurrent to my mother's sobbing. "This fire is either destruction or a tool," Umbra almost whispered. "Nothing else."

"No," my mother said, thighs closing. The rest of my body was out now, the sheets all bloody, and I knew it took every bit of the strength she had left to sit up as she did now, feeling for me. "You won't have this one." When she found me, her hands wrapped around my body, sliding me up toward her chest. The umbilical cord still connected us as I cried and she cried.

"It's too late—" Maeve began. She didn't get the opportunity to finish, because in the next moment she was pinned against the far wall of the bedroom.

And my mother stood on the bed, one hand out, the other cradling me. Her bloody nightdress hung around her ankles, the umbilical cord snaking out from under it, and she bared every one of the teeth in her mouth as the wind kicked around her, throwing her hair into a tornadic frenzy.

My mother, the air witch.

<hr>

Sophia Cole leapt from the bed, ran barefoot out of the room with me. Umbra remained pinned against the wall for ten or twenty seconds, the wind whipping around the room, until with a suddenness that startled us both, she dropped from the wall and hit the floor.

Umbra climbed to a knee, breathing hard with a lowered head. When she rose, she grabbed Parity from against the wall and stalked out of the room. And I was left alone with the bloody sheets and the witching hour breeze pressing through the shattered window.

"I don't understand," I whispered into the empty room.

"Of course you don't," a voice said from beside me. Left of me, Raven Murkwood leaned against the wall, one foot pressing flat to it. She wore the same robes from the underworld, her red hair almost like fire in this light. "No one told you what happened in this room."

"Why was Maeve Umbra here?"

"To protect against me." Murkwood's head tilted. "Like she protected every witch who came into this world. Or so she claimed."

"But you were trapped in the underworld."

"So I was. So I am." Murkwood drew in a breath. "But the witching hour has always been mine. And fate was so unkind to you, and very sweet to me."

I was born during the witching hour. Murkwood's hour. Umbra was protecting against that.

Murkwood stared at me, an almost-smile on her lips, as though waiting for me to understand. To piece it together. And I could feel my brain edging toward a precipice, backing away, taking mincing steps forward and back.

I didn't want to understand. I didn't want to know.

"What was that thing?" I said, hoarse. "That thing the raven dropped?"

"That is the right question." Murkwood pushed away from the wall. "It was a bit of my flame, extracted from my heart. Carried all the way from the underworld to your world, passed from witch to witch, waiting for the moment when it could take root in the right one. You see, so few witches are born, and fewer still during the witching hour."

I couldn't move, couldn't force my eyes shut. I could only stare at Raven Murkwood as she approached me—at my own red hair, my own green eyes. Nobody in my family had red hair and green eyes. My mother was blond, my sister was blond. They had blue eyes.

The precipice came closer as understanding forced itself on me: It wasn't my red hair. They weren't my green eyes. They had never been mine.

They belonged to Raven Murkwood. They belonged to the Shade.

And the creature that had always existed in the center of me, what I called the Spitfire. It wasn't mine, either.

"Yes," Murkwood said, closing the distance between us until we were inches apart. "The flames have never belonged to you. *You* have not belonged to you since the moment you were born. I have given you a seed of my power so that you might someday bring it back to me, matured and hellish. And here you are, my vessel. You've traversed so far, and my fire has grown inside you. Heated. Become empowered by your impulses, your brazen anger. What, you thought you could defeat those boys on the playground by yourself? Thought you alone could pin Maury down after he touched your thigh?"

No.

My eyes finally shut. The room disappeared, Murkwood disappeared behind my eyelids. This wasn't real or true. It must be a hex. She was deceiving me. Tricking me. Fucking with me.

"Oh, child of my heart," she whispered. "Don't close your eyes now. This is the most important moment of your brief life."

Fingers slipped under my chin, lifted my face. My eyes opened, and Murkwood still stood above me in the underworld. I was on my knees, the Backbiter lifted before me, and she was bound to the tree.

"What did I see?" I whispered. "In that room."

"You saw your inception," she said, delight crinkling the corners of her eyes. "You saw the rare and golden moment when the betrayals of centuries ago were rectified, and when the coward you know as Maeve Umbra made her greatest error. That was your true birth, Clementine Cole, the moment the fire entered you. It changed you forever, made you the witch you are today."

I stared at her, a wild confusion and furor heating my cheeks. I was too stunned, too outraged, too confused to tease out the swirl of thoughts in my head.

Who was I without my red hair?

Who was I without my green eyes?

Who was I without my fire?

I didn't know who that baby was. She was me, but she was an air witch. Clementine Cole's record in the birth registry showed an air witch. And I was not an air witch.

"This is the moment," Murkwood murmured, "when everything you have fought and worked for comes to fruition. In five hundred years, only you, child, have been able to find me. To rescue me. To nurture my power so beautifully. You are a miracle. A prophecy."

The pain was still in my chest, had been there all through the memory. Now it had reached its peak, and fire had begun dancing along my arms.

I was Raven Murkwood. Raven Murkwood was me.

I was the Shade.

No, Rational Clem snapped. *You're Clementine Cole.*

My hands had begun to shake. I couldn't move, couldn't fight. The Spitfire was in control of every part of me. Its heat was growing, flaring, searing my bones inside my chest.

Samara's face appeared in my mind's eye. *Control it. Control the flames.*

I gripped the Backbiter tight, fingers digging in, and thrust it into the ground. With flames rippling along my body, I managed to push myself upright.

Murkwood's delicate eyebrows lifted as she watched me stand. "Impressive. There's a reason you were the one, isn't there? I see another coward's hand at work in you—Samara, the blind, inebriated vessel in the woods has given you hope. Do not make this painful, Clementine. Kneel, and submit to me."

A plaintive meow sounded behind me.

My eyes pitched around and fixed on Loki a dozen feet away. Vines had wrapped around him, pinning him to the ground.

I turned back to Murkwood, my body vibrating with the pain and struggle to keep the Spitfire in check. I didn't move. "Only a real asshole would trap a cat."

"You'll make this hard, then." Her head tilted. "As you wish."

Her wrist, entrapped, flicked, and flames blossomed there. They hissed, dancing, and my eyes were caught by a vision. The face of my mother. And the hissing wasn't the flames, but her voice.

"That's right," Murkwood said. "Closer now, lest you miss it."

I took a step closer, dropping to my knees in front of the flame. There she was, hands and feet bound, being deposited onto the floor in the center of a room I'd once stood in. It was the Mages' Council room in Edinburgh.

Not there. Anywhere but there.

"Here was her sentencing, though little justice was done. Do you know what they do with witches in Edinburgh?" Murkwood whispered into my ear.

My breathing came fast, shallow. I wanted to close my eyes, but I couldn't. *They execute them*, I thought but couldn't say.

My mother rolled from one side to the other, the gag in her mouth revealed. The councilors sat around the table, and we watched the scene through the head councilor's eyes. "A rogue witch has been delivered," he said. I recognized that voice. "She has defied us for years. No more."

He was the one who took her—Tristan Rathmore.

"Yes," Murkwood said. "I see everything through my prince. He is my eyes in the world."

"Why?" I said, bile hitting my mouth. "Why take her and not me?"

"A trial for my vessel," Murkwood said simply. "Your first trial. Suffering makes you durable. Obsessive. Driven."

In the vision in the flames, the sentencing was quick. I forced my eyes shut as my mother was pulled to her feet. "No more."

Murkwood's voice sounded right beside me now, her breath tickling my ear. "If you will not watch, then you'll hear. Your mother was dragged out of the council room. She was taken to a square where a massive pole had been erected. Kindling had been piled beneath it, enough for her to stand high above the crowd—"

"*Stop*," I cried, searing heat blazing up my arms.

"—and she was taken up there to burn. And burn she did, Clementine. Your mother burned alive."

A scream erupted from me, my vocal cords shredding, daggers of heat pressing into the thick air. The flames consumed me; the Spitfire had taken control.

"Now"—Murkwood flicked her fingers, and the flame in her hand was snuffed—"your work is done."

Like a lever, my head dropped back on my neck. My mouth opened, and pain tore through the center of me. Fire lashed out of my breast, my arms, my hands, a shrieking noise tearing from my chest, and I could no longer hold the weapon. It fell from my hand, and I didn't know where it landed.

Pain. Pain was the center and whole of everything, fire lashing and reducing my bones and sinew and muscle to ash. And I knew it was all true, what I had seen in the bedroom with Umbra and my mother and the spark that had dropped into my mouth.

From the day of my birth, I had been a vessel. I had carried the Spitfire, never knowing what it was, that it wasn't really a part of me at all. I had nurtured it like it was as much me as Rational Clem, even though the two always contended for dominance. I had used it to carry me through the days after my mother and sister had disappeared. It had beaten up those boys for me. It had broken noses. It had gotten me up when I'd taken a hit. It had killed those creatures on the lake in Siberia. It had given me the anger and the fury to kill thousands more of them.

And now it was ready. Now it was no longer a spark, and Raven Murkwood was extracting it from me.

I had never been special. I had never been meant to defeat her, only to bring her back to herself.

I dropped back onto the mossy ground as the Spitfire extracted itself fully from my body. The fire left, and only coldness remained. The hollow chill of its absence.

A figure passed over me, a shadow—Raven Murkwood.

And somewhere I thought I heard my name being called, from somewhere far, far away. I wanted to see a streak of lightning through the air, blue flames, but I saw nothing. I didn't know what Liara and Eva and Aidan and Loki were seeing. I didn't know if they were coming for me, or if they were running away, or if they were alive or dead.

I only knew one place to reach as my insides were emptied out. One place for my fingers to go as the Spitfire left me.

I found the locket at my neck, the moonstone. And before I blacked out, I gripped the cool metal.

It wasn't the green, starless sky of the underworld I saw above me. It was my mother's face—the face I'd imagined every time I was alone and I looked up at the moon.

My mother, who I knew now was dead.

CHAPTER TWENTY-SIX

I'd always thought death was an eternal void. Nothing. A dissolution, an end-stop, a point on the sentence.

I was right, but I was also wrong.

On the other side of the void lay a scent. It smelled like fermented grapes. Like wine.

Wine?

My eyes opened. Above me, a ceiling of evenly placed wooden boards. They were unpainted, but consistent in width and without gaps. Good craftsmanship. Familiar work.

I knew those wooden boards.

I knew that scent.

My chest rose, sucking in air, and needles of pain pierced my chest, forcing my fingers up to my sternum. Cold. It felt cold there. Part of me was gone—the creature that had always been inside me.

A sweeping noise sounded nearby. My eyes dropped, found Bill the mutt wagging his tail from where he lay on the rug beside my bed. His head rose, tongue out, tail moving faster.

Samara. This was Samara's hut.

And I wasn't dead.

I swallowed past a dry throat. My hand reached for water, found a full glass on the nightstand. I lifted my head, swallowed it all down gulp after gulp until the glass had nothing left to offer. It struggled to stay upright as I set it back on the nightstand and fixated on the next part of living. Sitting up.

I'd only gotten my elbows under me when the door opened and a face appeared.

Evanora Whitewillow.

She paused there with a tray in both hands, steam wafting off it. Her serene face shifted, and the glassware began tinkling. Her chest moved, her throat bobbing, and it was only as she stood there in still-ness I realized she had cut half her hair off. It barely hung over her shoulders now.

"Clem," she whispered. "Clementine." Like she had forgotten my full name and was just now remembering it.

"You cut your hair," I said with a voice like straw, sound wheedling past the dryness. I cleared my throat but found I still didn't have any real voice when I said, "The others?"

"The others. Uh, they're fine. Loki's downstairs with Aidan, and Liara's outside with Samara."

I blinked once slowly at her, brows gathering. Wondering if we were back in Samara's hex. If we had never left it.

Or maybe I was just dead. Not in the eternal-void way, but in the afterlife way.

I tried to sit up, but my strength failed. My arms were weak as sticks. "Where's a mirror?"

"A mirror." Eva's eyes darted here and there before she set the tray down on a dresser. "You want to see yourself. Of course you do."

I nodded.

She raised a finger for me to wait, then passed out of the room. The hallway creaked, and a few seconds later Eva was back with a makeup compact in her hand. She came to my bedside and opened the clamshell up, turning it toward me.

I glimpsed my nose and lips before my hands went out to it, almost missing it before my fingers caught the edges. It felt strangely heavy in my hands, the mirror jerking as I tried to keep it still.

"Here," Eva said, steadying it with one hand.

When the mirror caught my eyes, I froze.

Green. Green eyes like a forest. Like a gem. And my hair was red and wild. I was pale—paler than I had ever been, my cheeks drawn. My eyes were tired, half-shut.

But I was still me.

I didn't understand. Didn't matter. My eyes shifted past the mirror to Eva. "Murkwood. The underworld."

She slid the compact from my hands, closing it as she straightened on the bed. "There's a lot to say. You should eat."

"Tell me first."

She stood, turning away toward the dresser. "You're as impossible as ever. That's a good sign."

Outside, lightning crackled. My eyes flew to the window, where smoke rose into the air. I had found an elbow, raising up enough to see. One hand had gone to the locket at my neck.

Eva picked up the tray. "It's just Liara training. She always gets too close to the hut. I always tell her, you know, one good lightning strike..."

I stared at Eva. How long had we been here?

She set the tray on the bedside table, picking up a bowl of what looked like broth. "You drank that whole glass of water, I see."

I knew what Eva was doing: soothing me, providing me with a controlled environment before she lowered the boom of everything that had happened between the underworld and this bed.

My lips parted as she lifted the bowl, brought up a spoonful of broth. It was chicken-flavored and went down easy. "I'm so glad you're awake, Clem. Not least because I was getting just a little tired of Loki meowing at me and not knowing what he was trying to say."

"Eva," I whispered, "how long have we been here?"

She paused with the next spoonful of broth in midair, eyes searching mine as though debating. Finally, she dropped the spoon back into the bowl. "Three months."

Now my arms did fail me. I sank back onto the pillow beneath me, staring without seeing the fae. The darkness had just been a blip, one tiny moment of blackness between here and there. I had been in the underworld, and now I was in Samara's hut.

"I don't believe you."

She glanced toward the window, sympathy drawing her eyebrows together. "Look at the trees."

I did look. And outside, the trees were bare of leaves. The topsides of the skinny branches were lined white with snow. The clouds hung low and fat and wintery, ready to drop more. And before me, Eva wore a thick wool sweater. The wisps were gone, too.

It had been August when we'd gone into the underworld. Now there was snow.

Three months I'd been out of the world, and I had no idea what had become of it.

"Three months," I said. Beside me, Eva had already presented the next spoonful of soup. "Did I die? Are we dead?"

Her lips tilted. "No, we aren't."

Outside, the trees' jagged fingers waved in a soft breeze. "Did you see what happened to me?"

"I saw it all, Clem. We all saw."

I turned back to her, steam fogging the air between us. "Tell me what you saw."

So she told me. That day three months ago, Loki and I had approached the Shade, stopped, and after a few words, Loki had been trapped by roots from the ground. I had closed the distance between us with mechanical, rhythmic steps, dropping to my knees before her with the Backbiter in my hands. The Shade had set her finger to my forehead, and only a moment had passed before fire erupted from my hands—

I set a hand on her arm. "Did you say only a moment passed after she touched me?"

"Yes. A second or two."

It had felt like the span of my entire life had played out right there in that valley. Everything I remembered and everything I didn't remember. And for Eva, it was one second.

"Eva..." I didn't know where to start. "I experienced decades. My whole life took place, except it was all in reverse, like the Shade was rewinding an old VHS tape and watching it backward. I saw every-thing—including the day I was born."

Her chin jerked back.

"It gets stranger," I said. "I watched my mom give birth. *To me.* Maeve Umbra was her midwife."

She stared with round gray eyes, the soup forgotten.

I told her everything I had seen—the raven breaking the window, dropping the spark, my mother pinning Umbra to the wall with her air magic.

"The raven," Eva said. "It was Raven Murkwood, wasn't it?"

"Not her, but some piece of her magic, I think. The spark was her fire, and it grew inside me for my entire life."

We just stared at one another as one of the tree branches creaked along the window.

"Did you see her, Eva?" I said. "What she looked like?"

Eva's head shook. "We were too far away. And the moment the tree released her from its roots, she pulled up her hood. But..."

I circled my face with a finger. "This is what she looked like. Exactly like me."

"I know." Her eyes fluttered shut. "Everyone knows."

"Who's everyone?"

"The world. The entire world."

Before I could respond, she had lowered her face. Tears were on her cheeks, small, descending crystals. She was apologizing to me. "It all happened like that." She snapped her fingers. "From beginning to end, it couldn't have been more than twenty seconds. Aidan started running toward you—the enshroudment left him when you fell—and I started flying. But it was too late."

I didn't know what to say. Watching her cry, apologize to me, I felt an anger I hadn't felt to this moment. Sudden, irrational, but still felt.

She had been there to watch over me, and she hadn't. I had told her it was my fight, but some part of me had come to rely on her and the others. To expect things.

Then the thought came to my lips: "Did you fight her, Eva?"

Gray eyes rose. "We tried. But Liara stopped us."

I didn't speak. I only waited.

"She grabbed Aidan, pulled him behind a tree. Then she came after me, saying we couldn't fight her. Not there, not then. She said a lot of things, but I had a hard time concentrating on any of it. I kept struggling until she said, 'We can save Clem. We can still get her out of here.' At some point I realized she was right, just like Aidan had, so we had to watch from a tree branch as the Shade just... left."

"Left?"

"She gathered up your weapon, called the wisps to her, and left with an army of those creatures."

"When you say 'left'..."

"I mean she left the underworld, Clem. Completely."

I lifted a finger toward the window. "And she's out there."

"Yes."

"Walking around with my face."

She kept on nodding. And added, "Though I suppose it's technically her face, isn't it? Sorry, not what you want to hear."

"I don't even know whose face it is anymore." Outside it was so peaceful, so serene. "And what has she done to the world, Eva?"

"She took Edinburgh in one night. Rathmore just gave it to her, gave her the Mages' Council and the whole city. It's her throne now."

One night. That still left eighty-nine nights since she'd entered the world. "I think I'm ready for some of that soup."

She gave it over, and I dropped the spoon on the tray. I upturned the bowl at my mouth, drinking it straight from the lip. I hated soup; after three months, it was the most delicious thing I'd ever tasted.

On the other side of the bowl were Eva's eyes, studying me. She accepted it back. "How different do you feel? You know, without... the thing inside you."

The Spitfire. It wasn't there anymore. How did I feel? "It's odd, you know." I paused. "I always thought I had chronic heartburn."

A tiny, close-lipped laugh burst out of Eva. And then she didn't try to stop it. "That's all you have to say?"

No. There was much more.

But at least I knew some fragment of me was still inside me. I could still make Eva laugh.

Bill's tail thumped against the rug, his panting audible—an announcement that someone was here. When he got up and turned to the door, Aidan and Liara were already inside. He was wide-eyed behind his glasses, and she was shaking her head with folded arms.

"You're awake," Aidan said. "Gods, you look just like her."

"She really does," Liara said.

I raised a hand, snapped my fingers. No flame appeared there. Not even the impulse of magic flowed to my fingertips. "But I'm not her," I said.

CHAPTER TWENTY-SEVEN

That first night, I examined myself in the almost darkness. Fresh cloth had been wrapped tight around my chest, the ends skillfully tucked. Probably Eva's doing. It was a slow, uncertain process to sit up and remove the wrapping, every wrong movement painful.

My hands were trembling by the time I reached the last layer. It sloughed away from my chest, allowing me to inhale properly. When I did, a searing pain made me double over. *Better not to breathe too deeply for now.*

I picked up the lantern on the bedside table, still flickering with a low flame, and turned myself toward the window. There, my reflection stared back at me.

My chest looked like the center of a rose bloom. I had skin, but it was all mottled, angry, red tendrils snaking toward my collarbone and over it. When my fingers lifted, traced over the scars, I could barely tell it was me in the reflection. That didn't feel like my body—not under my fingers, and not to my eyes.

I snuffed the lantern and replaced the wrappings in the darkness. I didn't want to see these scars; I didn't want to see me.

The next day, I found out from Samara everything that had happened since my death.

First, I hadn't died. After the Shade had extracted the Spitfire from my body and absorbed it into her own, she'd released Loki from his prison of roots, picked him up hissing and clawing by the scruff of his neck, and left the valley where she'd been held for five hundred years. She was trailed by the wisps and by her creatures, an army of them, passing off into the distance away from the canyon.

Apparently there were other ways out of the underworld. No doubt Murkwood knew them all.

When she had gone, Eva, Aidan, and Liara had found my body. I was still breathing. Together, they'd carried me out. Yes, over a ravine. Yes, through that tunnel system. And somehow they'd pushed and dragged me through the passage where I'd had my panic attack.

When they finally emerged into the real world again, things had changed. In just one day, things had changed.

Murkwood had taken Edinburgh. The city, led by Rathmore and the Mages' Council, had fallen to its knees for her. And she had already corrupted most of the leylines in Europe. Her creatures, which had always been limited to the witching hour, littered Matka Canyon at dusk.

It was unsafe. Unsafe to be out at night.

The veil wasn't safe. Leylines weren't safe.

So they only had one choice: to take the horses, who'd waited for us to return, standing all the while in a copse of trees. When they had hauled me onto Noir's back, Eva riding behind me to keep me from falling off, Aidan got on Siren, and Liara had flown point as they rode their way through Macedonia and toward Samara's hut.

It took days. And sometimes they'd had to fight.

When they arrived at the monastery, they couldn't find Samara's hut. They'd walked through the woods all night and been unable to spot it. As it turned out, Samara's real hut existed inside her own enshroudment. Maeve Umbra had taught her that magic, too. So it was Samara who found them in the morning, when she and Bill walked through the woods to the monastery to retrieve bread and wine.

That was how they'd ended up with Samara. Because they didn't know where else to take me, and they didn't know what to do with me. They hadn't had time to consider it, even, until they got me into the bed and Samara had set her hands to my face, to the festering wounds on my chest, feeling all over.

"So Murkwood has her power," Samara had said, "and Clementine is just an air witch."

"Will she live?" Eva had asked.

"Perhaps," Samara said. "Perhaps not. It's a miracle she's survived this long."

"Well which is it?" Aidan said.

Samara sat back. "It depends on her. On how dependent she became on the fire inside her, and what's left of the person who remains. We shall see if she ever wakes."

"Can't I heal her?" Eva had asked.

"Heal her? Oh, this may look like a physical wound—she will certainly bear the scars if she lives—but this is not a physical disease she suffers. It's one of the spirit. Because you see, my fae, it was a tiny piece of Murkwood's spirit she implanted in this air witch."

An air witch. I was now, and always had been beneath the fire, an air witch.

On hearing this, I lay back in the bed. It was Samara herself who told it to me, and who now made to reach for the bottle of wine she'd set on the nightstand, but resisted. She never resisted wine.

"Murkwood's spirit was in me," I said.

"Yes." Samara's voice was low and carried an unfamiliar note, like someone had died. "One aspect of her, at least."

"Her fire," I said, knowing the answer at once. "It was her fire and her anger and her impulsiveness."

It was what had kept her alive in life, just like it had kept me alive. It had given her grit and spirit and the rage to fight back. It was what had forged her from Raven Murkwood into the Shade.

"And the wisps," I said, my eyes searching for them and finding them nowhere in the room. "Where are they?"

"They're drawn to pure power," she said. "And a fire witch like Murkwood is the most powerful of us all."

"Samara," I said, and the old witch had raised unwilling, fluttering eyes in my direction. "How do you know all this?"

At this, she straightened and rose. Wordless, she passed around the bed to the window, where she drew the curtains shut tight. That didn't make sense; we were inside her enshroudment. We were hidden from the world.

Might be a reflex. A deeper fear.

She came back to a seat beside me and her scarred hands went out, searching for mine. I allowed her to grasp one of them. "I lied to you, Clementine. Or at least, I didn't tell you the truth I ought to have."

"Tell me now."

I watched her lean toward the wine once more, resist a second time. She took in a breath. "Sometimes a witch is born during the witching hour. In fact, witches are more likely than anyone to be born during that hour."

"Why?"

"Perhaps it's the moon's cycle. Perhaps the Shade's influence. I don't know, Clementine, only that it has been true for hundreds of years."

"Were you born during the witching hour, Samara?"

Her thumb began to rub over my hand. "Yes. But Maeve Umbra also oversaw my birth. You see, she has been protecting us against the Shade for a very long time."

My brows gathered. Samara couldn't be much younger than Umbra, if at all. "Since she was a young woman, then?"

"Perhaps." Here she paused, and the light in the room seemed to gather toward Samara, shadows growing in the corners. "I do not know, because Maeve Umbra has been the same age since the day I met her."

Maeve Umbra didn't age. Or if she did, it was at such a slow pace that someone as old as Samara hadn't perceived any difference.

I couldn't speak at first. Emotions clanged against one another like pots—confusion, disbelief, betrayal, anger—in my skull. Samara didn't press me, either. She waited until finally, when all the noise had subsided in my head, I said, "But you're blind."

She snorted. "I've just told you Maeve Umbra is immortal, and that's what you have to say. We blind people can perceive with our other senses, you know."

"It isn't that. I just... How do you know she's always been the same age? Maybe she's always had an old-sounding voice."

"Don't patronize me, Nectarine. I wasn't always blind, for one thing, and for another, she's been the headmistress at the academy since I was a student there. Do you know any headmistresses who've served fifty years?"

My head dropped back onto the pillow, overwhelmed. "I guess I do now."

"Yes, you do know one. The very woman who failed to protect you from the Shade at birth."

People weren't supposed to live forever. Nobody at the academy had ever talked of living forever. But Umbra's words were coming back to me now—when I asked how old she was. When I asked how old her daughter was.

"She has a daughter," I said. "A young woman. I met her in Switzerland."

"Her daughter's daughter's daughter's daughter's daughter, ad nauseam," Samara said.

The daughter was a descendant. The family I had met in Switzerland were descendants. Was it possible?

Samara could be lying.

I removed my hand from hers. "I found pictures in your bedroom. Pictures of students at Shadow's End. But one student's face had been scratched out every time."

"My face," she said, attention flicking again to the wine and back. "And now we're getting to the thrust of it."

"The thrust?"

Her head tilted as though she were observing me. "Do you really not see it?"

"I don't know what I'm supposed to see."

"Gods, this is why I never had children. No patience. And, well, the other part." She brought her face closer. Too close. "I'm old, but not so old you can't see it. The mouth, the nose."

Her lips had the wrinkles of a woman who'd wrapped them around thousands of cigarettes. Or who had drunk from hundreds of bottles. Probably the latter. But I doubted she was talking about that. I knew lips grew thinner with age, but hers still had a little fullness, some faint pink, a deep cupid's bow on the top lip.

The nose was straight, slender, without a ridge. A lot like...

I jerked in the bed.

"So you see it." She sat back. "Now you know what you'd look like if you lived to my age. And drank well as you did so."

I stared at her, unable to stop studying her face. Now that I saw it, I couldn't unsee it. Like I was looking back at myself from fifty years on. She even had the wild hair. "You were a redhead?"

A light entered her eyes. "Incorrigibly so." Blank eyes. Once green.

"You're a liar." I pushed myself farther into the headboard. "A goddamn liar."

"Oh, and we haven't even finished yet." She grabbed her bottle from the nightstand. "I'll return when you've processed. Then you can hear the rest of your bedtime story."

Samara, hunchbacked, left the bedroom without a word. As she passed through the doorway, for a moment I'd hoped Loki would appear by her feet. That he would cross between her legs and come to the bed, hop up beside me.

But Loki wasn't in the hut. He wasn't even in this country.

Murkwood had taken him from me.

It was Liara who came to me two hours later, bringing a dinner tray. "Don't get used to this." She deposited the tray on the nightstand. "I'm only doing it because Eva is on this tear about 'fairness' and 'equality.' Can't get her to shut up."

My stomach was in knots. "I'm surprised you didn't just tell her to shut up."

"Oh, I did." She pulled up a chair by my bed, straddling it with arms overtop the back. "Now I have to bring you dinner *and* breakfast tomorrow."

"At least you spoke your mind."

"For better or worse." She studied me. "And on that note, you look like shit."

I knew; I had lost strength and weight over the past three months.

I could feel it, see it in my arms and my face that one night I'd dared to look. "Liara, when we left here you thought Samara was a crazy old witch."

"I still do."

"Do you think she's a liar?"

"Absolutely not."

"She hexed us. That was a lie."

"A hex isn't a lie. It's a spell, Clementine." Her eyes narrowed. "You liked her. You always liked her."

"Feelings change." I nodded out the window; I wouldn't get anything else helpful from Liara when it came to Samara. "I didn't hear everything about what's happened out there."

"Oh. Well." She rested her chin on her arms. "I don't know much except what we've learned from two phone calls with Eva's parents. The world has split into factions—two, mostly. There's us, and there's the bastards who support the Shade. Since she took Edinburgh, they've been spreading propaganda about how she's meant to save the world from the true darkness. And..."

"And?"

She scrunched her nose. "I should probably tell you after dinner. I can tell Samara really laid one on you."

"She did, but if you make me wait until I've finished eating this macaroni and cheese, I'll tell Eva you ate my dinner yourself."

Liara stood. "The Shade's winning, Clementine. All those mages she abducted for so many years? They're her legion of creatures now. And goddamn if it isn't a massive army."

CHAPTER TWENTY-EIGHT

The next morning, I left the bed for the first time. Aidan, who'd brought me breakfast, helped me stand. And then, when I couldn't carry my own weight, helped me navigate my way around the room a while. When I was ready, he slung an arm around my waist to get me down the staircase.

"I'm good," I said once I'd gotten to the bottom.

He didn't move. "I'm not sure about that."

Downstairs, the living room was far less clean than in the hex. The furniture was old and fraying. I made slow progress toward the kitchen, where dirty dishes lined the surfaces. *No animations.* Eva was at work cleaning them in a wash basin.

And there was no doorway through to the other side.

I pointed. "Where's the library?"

Eva turned, a dish in hand. "Library? Oh."

"There is no library," Aidan said. "It was just part of Samara's hex."

Another clue as to the falseness of Samara's delusion—a blind woman wouldn't have regular books. Samara had claimed she'd kept them for the smell, but all along it had just been part of her test.

I turned back toward the living room. "I need to talk to Samara alone."

Aidan pointed out the ajar front door. "She's in her chair."

It took me longer than I'd admit to get from the kitchen to the front door. And by the time I came into the sunlight, I had to lean against the side of the hut. From the side of the hut, Noir whinnied at me. He stood under a lean-to with Siren, and someone had fitted a winter blanket to the mare's back. Noir had no doubt rejected his—or torn it off—because he wore nothing.

Samara, who sat not far off in a band of sunlight with her hand on Bill by her side, called out, "Didn't expect you up so soon."

"I didn't expect you to have my face." I turned away from the hut, one hand still bracing me. "But here we are."

"It's not just me who has your face." She ran a hand down Bill's head. "The gods know I didn't want it."

The scratched-out pictures. That had been her face she'd removed.

Samara pointed to the side of the house. "Pull up a chair."

"Can't you animate it over?"

"Pft." She waved a hand. "That was the fantasy of a hex, child. Only Maeve Umbra knows such power. Which, by the by, was another clue I left you to figure out you were in a hex. Don't suppose you caught that one, though."

I hefted the chair, set it down in front of her so we were facing each other. By the time I dropped into it, I was winded. "Who are you, Samara?"

Her face upturned, fully in the sun. "The better question is, who was I?"

"Who were you, then?"

"I was her child. Her progeny, just like you."

"Whose?"

"Raven Murkwood's."

My head spun, though I wasn't sure if it was weakness or shock. I gripped the armrests and sat back. "You were born during the witching hour, like me."

"So I told you."

"And she used you as a vessel. A vessel for her spirit." Saying it out loud, I realized Murkwood had used the same word as Catriona's prophecy: vessel. *The blood pact will end when the right vessel appears*, the prophecy had said.

I still didn't know what that meant. Any of it.

"She tried." Samara's fingers went to the center of her chest. "For thirty-five years she grew inside me. Made my eyes green, hair red. Angry like you."

All of this felt like too much, too vast for the smallness of the space around us. We were in this tiny break in the trees in the middle of nowhere, me and this old woman, and everything I had thought I knew about myself and my life wasn't true.

I wasn't even the first vessel.

My fingers dug into the armrests. "You knew this before you sent me to her. But you sent me to her anyway. You should be on your knees kissing my fucking feet."

"Ooh. Still have some of that fire." She kept her face averted, up to the sun. "I tried with you, yesterday. Gripping your hands. I've never been good with shame, little witch. And even worse at staying sober."

So she was drunk now. That was why her words seemed slushy.

"So you tried to fulfill the prophecy," I said. "Like me."

"Oh no." She shook her head in a precise way. "No, no."

"But you knew about it."

"Yes. I found out about it at the academy just like you did. Maeve always has her way of ensuring that prophecy gets into the hands of witches like us."

My face went into my hand as vertigo overtook me, the space around us spinning. Umbra. Had she been behind my discovery of the prophecy? It was Aidan who had shown the book to me. He said he'd discovered it in the Room of the Ancients. "I don't understand."

"She's an idealist, that Maeve. Always hoping someone will do the dirty work, that she can finally shape Raven Murkwood's fire into a force for good. Hence why she allows the Spitfire to perpetuate itself from vessel to vessel. But I read that prophecy once and refused. Never even opened the book back up."

So I had seen correctly: Umbra had allowed her enshroudment to drop from around her and my mother at the moment of my birth. She had allowed the Spitfire to enter me. "Umbra said she doesn't believe in prophecies," I said, head in hand.

"And why else would she have allowed you and me to be infected by the flames, Nectarine?"

There was no other good reason. I had thought I was so clever, believing the prophecy was about me. Just me. But Samara had connected the dots, too.

"Why?" My face lifted, my hands sliding over the armrests. "If you knew about the prophecy, why didn't you try to defeat the Shade?"

Now her face lowered as though she was eyeing me. "Because I'm a coward."

The silence stretched long between us, the distance between our two chairs growing the longer it went. Samara took a swig of her wine from a bottle I hadn't even known sat in the shade of her chair. But of course it did.

I couldn't decide if I hated her. A surprising anger simmered in my twin grip on the armrests. "So you lived with it. The creature inside you."

"For a long time, yes. It was dormant, always craving and desiring. Trying to push me this way and that. I was the most broken, miserable witch alive, but I still refused to acknowledge the thing." Her lips moved together, and finally her chin set as she decided on what she would say. "Until I found out about you."

My grip tightened.

"Some twenty years ago," she said, "Maeve told me she was over-seeing the birth of another witch. I suppose she thought I deserved to know, seeing as your mother and I were the last two witches alive. Of course, Sophia wanted to keep you a secret. She didn't trust anyone to be present at the birth of her baby—but she trusted Maeve, her beloved headmistress."

"My mom was a student?"

"Of course. Though she never carried the Spitfire—she was lucky to be born during the day."

"And why didn't she trust anyone else to be present?"

Samara's gaze drifted toward the horses, grazing at the far end of the clearing. "People get unpredictable around witches. They have ideas about us, about what we are and what they want us to be. And there had been a history of unexplained fire witches, an odd lineage of us. We didn't come from the same blood, and we weren't attacked by fire witches—we just kept on appearing, little babes who could wield fire."

"Tell me," I said without moving my teeth, "what happened when you found out about me."

Samara's attention snapped back. "Well, isn't it obvious? I gave the Spitfire over to you." She drew her fingers along the opposite hand, pulling up the sleeve of her dress to reveal so many porcelain scars, bone-white under the sun. "But it was not painless, or easy."

"You were found by Bill," I said, recalling Loki's words. "You were naked, covered in blood and scars."

Her eyes fluttered shut. "Like I said: not an easy process."

I stood. Began walking back to the hut, fingernails digging into the palms of my hands. When I stopped and turned around, Samara had already lifted the wine bottle again. "You could have at least told me. You'd have lost nothing by telling me."

"If I'd told you, would you have gone to see the Shade?"

I swallowed past a pit in my throat. "I don't know."

"That's the thing," she said, her voice frail. "That's the very thing."

I didn't talk to Samara for two days. On the afternoon of the third day, she and Bill came out to where I sat on a fallen log partly in the trees. I huddled with only a thin sweater on; I couldn't be bothered to get my cloak from inside.

When I glanced up, she gestured beside me. "May I?"

"Now you want my consent?"

"Hm, still a little spitfire yourself." She sat down, hands slapping her thighs, Bill dropping next to her. She rubbed her legs in silence as we sat side by side, and I sensed she was building up to speak. "Like I said," she began, "I spent decades avoiding my destiny."

"It wasn't your destiny." That word felt like ash on my tongue. "It was one screwed-up witch messing with you. And with me."

Sitting next to her, a fresh chill came over me. My hands wrapped around my arms, and Samara unhooked her cloak and passed it to me. Beneath it she wore a thick sweater and pants. "I can hear your teeth chattering from here."

"You need it more than I do, old woman."

"I've got wine to warm me. And Bill."

I pulled the cloak around me. It smelled like fermented grapes with a tinge of body odor.

"Decades ago, back at the academy," Samara said, "they called me 'the prophet.' You know why?"

I pulled the cloak tight around me. "You always knew when it would be drink-o'clock?"

She snorted. "Back then I had less pleasant ways of dealing with my feelings. No, you see, I always seemed to know things that would happen in the future: a couple breaking up, a professor getting promoted, two classmates getting in a fight."

That surprised me. Not her rebelliousness, but how different we'd been. We'd both been impulsive and headstrong, but not at all in the same way. Still: "You told me you'd make this worth my while."

"People thought it was my magic as a witch," she went on. "They thought I hexed my professors and the other students. But I didn't learn to hex until after I left the academy—until I went to Scotland to train under a fae named Frostwish."

"Ora Frostwish?"

"Ariadne," Samara said. "She had been trained by her mother, who'd been trained by her mother—a vile clan the whole way down. I imagine Ora is a granddaughter." She paused. "Anyway, that's not the point."

"I'd love to hear it, then."

She sat forward in the chair. "The point is this, Clementine: A prophecy is a description of circumstances that need to be created in order to have the best chance at what you want to happen."

I stared at her, uncomprehending.

"I was no prophet," she said, flustered now. "I was simply perceptive, good at reading people. Sometimes I made educated guesses."

"So you weren't out there playing the opposite of matchmaker?"

She shook her head. "Hundreds of magical prophecies have existed throughout history. Many of them are so random and far-fetched that their cocktail of items and circumstances and events coming together feels like magic. But true prophecies are devoid of magic—they simply describe ideal situations."

"Ideal situations," I repeated.

"They're not insights into the future," she said, "but the understanding of master strategists who fully understand what must and must not happen in order to achieve what they desire."

In the chill bite of the afternoon, Samara was making my head woozy. "I thought you didn't believe in the prophecy," I said. "You closed the book the first time you read it."

"Oh," she said, "I don't. But I do believe that our choices lead us down certain paths. And because *you* believed in the prophecy so deeply, I think you've created two possible destinies for yourself."

My eyes drifted to her. "And those are?"

One bony finger went up. "Defeat the Shade"—a second finger went up—"or die."

I hunched deeper into Samara's cloak. "I could become like you. I could find a hole and drink until I'm old and blind."

"It wasn't the drinking that caused the blindness, Nectarine. It was the blindness that caused the drinking. And these." She gestured to her hands, the scars riddling them. "All came about from ridding myself of the thing you call the Spitfire."

"My point still stands."

"No." She folded her arms. "You won't do what I've done. You're not the person I was. There may be a third path available to you, but it's not this one."

"You don't know that. We're both just pale copies of Raven Murkwood, anyway."

There was a good reason why I had liked Samara from the start: she reminded me of *me*. Worse, we'd both been shaped by Raven Murkwood. We were marionettes, and she had crafted us.

"We may be pale, but you and I are entirely different beings with different destinies. And yours doesn't end in a forest in Eastern Europe with a bottle and a dog at your side."

At this, Bill's head rose. He gave a gruff, his breath visible.

"So," I said, "what's the third path?"

Samara shrugged, rising to her hunch. "Hell if I know. We make our own destinies, remember? I only observe what I see."

I stared up at her. "Where are you going?"

"My ass is frozen." She started toward the hut, Bill following. "I'm going inside, where warmth and sanity prevail."

I turned back around, settling deep into the chair and the scent of Samara's cloak. Back when I'd been a fire witch, I had never been cold. All my life, I'd never needed more than a good sweater.

Now I was freezing. And I couldn't stop seeing Samara's fingers in front of me.

Defeat the Shade, or die.

I didn't want either destiny. But I couldn't imagine a third path—not from here. Not now that I had no magic at all.

CHAPTER TWENTY-NINE

After that conversation, life began to fold in on itself. I sat on the couch in Samara's living room for days, losing track of hours. Sometimes my friends tried to talk to me, and I didn't remember responding. Eventually they left. Food appeared in front of me, or maybe I got it from the kitchen, and then at some point I ate it and left the dish and cup sitting on the coffee table. Then that disappeared —picked up by someone's hand.

Four years. Four years I'd spent living for a purpose, something beyond me. A thing that mattered. I'd learned to ride, to wield fire, to destroy the Shade's minions, to hex, to enchant.

Every choice I'd made had been pre-decided. Guided by the thing inside me. I'd been drawn to the prophecy, to power, to the weapon. All because a five-hundred-year-old witch had wanted to escape her prison.

Now I didn't even have fire. I'd tried snapping my fingers once more a few days ago and didn't even create a spark. I hadn't tried again after that.

I didn't know what I was anymore. Who I was. Clementine Cole, not the fire witch. Long ago I'd been the drama queen, the liar, the scrapper. All of those had been the Spitfire's doing, too.

Outside this place, the Shade was sieging the world. Now she was at full power, and no one seemed to stop her. Liara talked into my ear about battles taking place between the formalists and resisters. Those who didn't support the Shade could only muster small groups in the cities and towns she brought her legions to, and even then they fought guerrilla-style, from rooftops or canopies.

At some point, the United Kingdom fell. According to a phone call with his mother, Aidan's family fled to the academy just in time. So had Eva's, from Austria, along with Liara's little brother. "So many people," he said within earshot of me, "are sheltering at the academy now."

"And Umbra's enshroudment?" Liara said.

"It still stands."

Eva came to tell me one evening that Umbra had contacted the Guardians' Council and told them to go to the academy, that the Shade would be coming. Or at least, that was what her mother had said to her the one time she'd been able to get in touch.

Umbra. Maeve Umbra. So she wasn't dead.

"Why should the Shade care about the academy?" I managed to say, my voice vague and thick.

"No idea," Eva said. "But Mama thinks the Shade is coming for the headmistress. It'll be a massive battle, she suspects. And if that's the case, then we need to be there."

Be there. Us. "The leylines are all corrupted," I said, my voice hollow.

"They've kept the one near the academy uncorrupted," Eva said. "Clem, we need to fight."

Me, fight.

I turned away from Eva, my hands finding their way around the mug of tea someone had set before me. When I set it to my lips, Eva tried to catch my eye by leaning closer.

I focused on the tea. The lemon scent of it, the sweet taste. Lately, with life folding in on itself, I had begun to appreciate the only things available to me to appreciate: exactly what was in front of me. Moment to moment, the tiny pleasures that brought up any feelings at all.

She thought I was someone I wasn't. She was talking to the person I used to be. The fire witch.

"Do you hear me, Clem?" she was saying. "We need to go to the academy. France and Spain have fallen."

"Why?" I said dully, eyes on the steam rising in front of me. "Umbra's an immortal being. She can handle it."

"Immortal?" Eva said.

I hadn't mentioned that to her. I hadn't talked to her much about anything. Now I waved a hand. "Ask Samara. She knows everything, especially when you offer her wine and guilt."

Bootsteps sounded behind the couch. Then a voice. "Clem, wash your hair. You look like you dunked yourself in a vat of oil." The bootsteps passed on.

"Very nice, Liara," Eva said, hooking one arm over the couch back. "She's depressed."

"We're all depressed," Liara's voice rang from the kitchen. "You don't see me drowning in my own body odor."

"And she's injured," Eva said. "Physically and mentally."

Now my eyes slid over to Eva. "Do I smell?"

"No." Her head shook, her nose crinkling for a millisecond. "No."

I leaned toward my armpit. The scent was strong.

"We need you, Clem." Eva's hand was on the blanket wrapped around me. "We need you there."

"Don't touch me." The words came out almost before I'd considered saying them. They carried such a steel edge, they sounded like they belonged to someone else.

"Okay." Her hand flinched away. "You need more time."

I didn't need time. One of my hands left the mug, the fingers coming together in the space between Eva and me. When I snapped them, the sound was soft and flabby. "You see this?"

"See what?"

"The absolute lack of a spark."

"Clem, you can learn—"

"Leave me alone."

After that, she did. And I went on sitting on the couch—not a liar, not a drama queen, not a scrapper, not even the girl I had been before my mother and sister had disappeared. Not the academy witch, either.

I was nothing. Like Samara, I was meant for nothing except a corner of the world for me to be as broken and miserable as her. I'd carry these scars until the world defeated the Shade, or the Shade took over the world and I became one of her thralls.

For as much as I hated Samara for what she'd done, it occurred to me as I stared into her fireplace, the fire burning low, that I might have done the same. If I were born as her, and she were born as me, and I had the chance to pass the curse of the Spitfire to someone else, I might do it.

At least then I'd never have the hope. The dream.

As for the world, they could fight the Shade on their own. I was out.

I had just come to that decision after so many days of sitting on Samara's couch when someone I hadn't ever expected to see again appeared at my side. Actually, he walked through the wall of Samara's hut.

Once he spotted me, he came to the arm of the couch and said, "Well where's your cat, then?"

It was Thom, the ghost child. Thom, who'd helped me escape the Edinburgh crypts. Who, months ago, had gone looking for Callum Rathmore's soul.

I turned round eyes on him, and he grinned at me, folding his arms high over his chest. "I may be pale as a ghost, but you look worse." Then he pointed. "Ah, I got a smile from you."

"Thom," I said. "Where have you been?"

He scratched the back of his head. "Oh, lots of places. You know, first I went looking for the soul you asked me to find. Traveled all over with no luck, and then I came to a soul pub."

"A soul pub?"

"You know, for drinks. Meeting folks. Listening to song."

"Aren't you a little young for that?"

He grinned. "We're ghosts—we don't card." Apparently he had learned some modern words from those ghosts, too. "And then, well, the folks there told me about another pub I had to visit.

And I'd never heard such music anywhere. You know Leonard Cohen?"

"Uh, sure."

"'I don't think I want to go,'" he sang, "'because Heaven's empty on a Saturday night.'"

Thom had a beautiful singing voice. And while I lay asleep or comatose for the past three months, he'd also been living up his afterlife. Listening to Leonard Cohen. I didn't know what to say.

Just then, Aidan walked into the living room. He stopped as I turned to face him, eyes flicking between me and the ghost child.

I pointed. "That's Thom."

"Oh," he said. "Okay."

Thom gave a single nod, arms folded once more. Now I remembered: he'd been uncertain about strangers. He was the little protector of his group.

"That's Aidan," I said. "He's the best person you could know."

"Hm." That was all Thom had to say about Aidan. He turned to me. "Well, I found who you were looking for."

I jerked back. "Found who?"

"The soul of Callum Rathmore. That's his name, right?"

Callum.

I dropped the blanket off my shoulders, sitting up on my knees, reaching out as though I could take the boy by the shoulders. But of course, I couldn't. Instead, I settled for hands on the arm of the couch. "That's his name."

"His soul's in the underworld," he said. "So I hear."

"From who?" Aidan asked, who'd now come closer.

Thom ignored him, eyes on me. Waiting.

"Where did you hear this?" I asked.

"The pub where everyone gathers. The barkeep there said the underworld is a place for two kinds: souls who don't belong to Heaven or Hell, and demons."

"What do you mean," I said, "about souls not belonging to Heaven or Hell?"

Thom's hand lifted, the palm flat as he tipped it back and forth. "They weren't good or bad enough in life to go in either direction, so they end up down there. Don't ask me how long—as long as it takes, is what I hear."

"As long as it takes for what?" Aidan asked.

Thom side-eyed him. Then, with a set chin, he said, "To go up or down."

"Like purgatory," Aidan said. "Except the Shade is keeping the souls stuck there."

My attention had drifted the moment the boy had said the word demons. The world had gone to watercolor as my eyes unfocused, a band of guilt tightening around my chest.

I had been so fixated on myself. Obsessed with my identity, or the loss of it. I hadn't even checked on Callum—whom I assumed still slept, unable to wake up, in Eva's tangibly manipulated tent.

"Demons." Aidan knelt to eye level with me, arm over the couch back. "Isn't Callum a half-demon?"

"Yes," I said. "He is."

It was easy to stand this time. The blanket around my shoulders fell off, and I said, "Where's Eva?"

Aidan rose. "She's outside with Samara."

I headed toward the front door.

"So I said," Thom continued, trotting along at my side, "'What's a demon?' And the barkeep said, 'It's Lucian the prince.' And I said, 'Who's that?' And he said, 'He wears armor black as night, wields a broadsword long as his leg—' And that was where I cut him off. 'Oh,' I said. 'I know who that is. He's the man who used to come down to the crypts time to time, but then he got chained up. He's the one I'm looking for.'"

We came outside. Eva and Samara were across the clearing, practicing Eva's air magic. She wielded her fan, swiping it in a circle while Samara sat under a nearby tree.

I strode toward them, Thom still following.

"Anyway, where's your cat?" the boy asked again.

I flinched; he knew just the spots to pierce me, to get me off my ass. "He was taken from me."

"But who would do that?"

"Another witch, Thom. Her name is Raven Murkwood, but you know her as the Shade. She took many things from me."

He whistled as we approached Eva and Samara. "You need to get that cat back. He was the nicest one I ever met."

Another needle right to the kidney. But I deserved it.

"Eva," I said. "Where's the tent?"

Her magic dissipated as she turned toward me, sweat and hair dappling her forehead. "Over there. I've been taking care of Professor Rathmore."

Samara snorted. "Don't need to call him 'professor' anymore, fae. Least of all a half-demon."

I was already headed toward the spot she'd pointed to. I came to the tent amidst the trees and ducked inside, but what I'd expected wasn't what I found.

Eva had worked on the tent. Expanded it. Where the cots had sat was now a living room with a sofa and a rug. Beyond that were steps up to the kitchen and table. And now there was a door off to the right and one to the left.

She did have three months of idleness, after all.

Thom came through the wall of the tent and whistled again. "Now this is some kind of magic."

I came to the door on the right, turned the knob. Inside, I found two full beds. Callum lay in one of them, but not as I'd left him.

"He's paler than you," Thom said from behind me, peeking around. "And that's saying something."

CHAPTER THIRTY

I crossed to Callum's bedside and set one hand to his forehead. "Why is he clammy?"

"He's been that way for weeks." Eva had followed me and was standing in the doorway, delicate hands wiping away the sweat from her temples.

Thom had gone suddenly shy, his voice soft in Eva's presence. He stared up at her with an open mouth. "Are you a fairy?"

"Something like that." She dropped to one knee before him. "I'm a fae. And you must be the brave boy who helped Clementine in Edinburgh."

Thom folded his arms, unfolded them, and decided the best course was to take a step back. "Never seen a fae."

Eva nodded in the direction of the hut. "Lucky you. There's another one of us inside the house."

Thom's eyes met mine, wide and uncomprehending. "Two fae. That must either be wonderful luck or terrible."

"Depends on which of us you encounter." She winked, rising. "Clem, it's like Professor Rathmore is sick. My healing had no effect."

Thom pointed at Callum. "That isn't supposed to happen."

"What isn't?" I said.

"Him being separated from his soul. He shouldn't be alive."

My hand hadn't moved from his forehead. "How *is* he alive?"

"I haven't any idea," Eva said. "But he's declining. I don't expect he'll survive this way much longer."

Somehow his skin had turned paler than mine. His lips had discolored, now carried a tinge of blue. Eva was right: this was a decline. "You should have told me," I snapped, knowing already why she hadn't. "Tell me how long he has."

"I can't say for sure, Clem."

"Guess."

I knew she hated being put on the spot; it probably made her mind go blank. But I didn't care right now. "Given the rate of things over the past three months..." She paused. "Two weeks."

My hand dropped to my side. "Thom," I said. "You're sure I can find his soul in the underworld."

"Sure as sure can be, given I'm a ghost and he's a half-demon and we're talking in the matter of lost souls. The barkeep told me the souls are drawn to people and things they were familiar with in life. That's how you lure 'em in."

I knew I wasn't going to get a better answer.

"Okay," I said. "Eva, we're leaving tomorrow."

She straightened, eyebrows rising. "For where?"

"We're going back through the tunnel in Matka Canyon."

"To the underworld? But we can't."

My eyes slitted. "And why not?"

"Well, Samara told us that once you've taken a path into the underworld, it closes itself off to you forever."

I had forgotten. "Where's another entrance?"

Eva's shoulders rose in a shrug.

Samara. I needed to find Samara.

When I came out of the tent, Eva and Thom didn't follow. Thom tried to, but Eva stopped him with a word. As I ducked outside, I could hear her asking him his favorite color.

She always knew when I wanted her there or not.

Samara was still seated on her chair under the same leafless tree,

Bill flopped over her like a blanket. "Look, Bill," she said, "the witch found her legs again."

I came to stand over her, my shadow casting her in deeper darkness. "I need to know how to get to the underworld."

Samara's eyes fluttered up to me. "And you can't take the same path you took. Hm." Samara petted Bill. "You think because I'm a witch who was once like you, I know a way down."

"Do you?"

"I sure don't. I may be a witch, but I'm no lost soul." She burst into laughter, her face turning toward Bill as though the dog understood. And maybe he did. "I wouldn't go near the underworld if it wore grapes and called itself unfermented merlot."

I sighed, turned away.

"But I know someone who might."

I stopped. "Who?"

"Before I tell you, I want to know something, Nectarine."

I turned back.

"Are you going to the underworld for the half-demon, or are you going to kill her?"

"I can't possibly kill her. I don't even have magic anymore."

"Ah." Her head tilted. "So you've given up on your prophecy."

"The prophecy was always bullshit. You know that."

"Hm." Her fingers fluttered against her chin. "So you say, and so it is. Well, the person you need to see is Maeve Umbra."

Umbra. "Why her?"

"She's been alive for longer than anyone else on this Earth, except for maybe Raven Murkwood, and she is a wizard so powerful she's capable of animating inanimate objects. It's a dead art, or didn't you know?"

"I knew." I paused; it seemed so obvious now that Maeve Umbra was older than she appeared. "Even if she does know a way down, I don't know where to find her."

"Sure you do." She twirled a finger. "Or your friends do. They're busy little bees, always strategizing. I like the one in glasses particularly. The dark-haired fae, too, has grown on me."

Aidan and Liara. Had Samara actually forgotten their names? The smile on her face had a mischievous tilt to it, just like when she called me Nectarine. There was no forgetting with her.

"I'll be leaving tomorrow, Samara."

"About time. You've been eating up all my food and clogging up my house for three months."

I turned again, and she said to my back, "Maeve will show herself. Trust me."

"You could come." I paused. "You could fight for the academy."

"Oh, no. I'm not saving the world, just like you aren't. I'm just going to enjoy my retirement with my dog, and you're just going to pick your boyfriend up from his subterranean vacation. Right?"

"Sure, Samara," I whispered, and started toward the hut.

"Clementine," she called after me.

This time I didn't stop. "Yeah?"

"I've kept the nearby leyline uncorrupted for you, should you need it."

I grunted and passed through the door of the hut, my mind already past gratitude and on to the academy. I wasn't going to find Umbra so I could fight any battles. I definitely wasn't going to find her so we could fight the Shade. This was about doing right by my cat, and by Callum Rathmore. They had both saved me, and now I would save them. And then I would be done—either dead or ready to be done with mages.

There was no destiny. There was no prophecy.

"The headmistress hasn't been seen in six days," Eva said when I got inside and found her sitting at the dining table with Aidan. "But when she contacted the Guardians' Council, she told them they had one week to prepare for a battle. That she would return with rein-forcements."

"Reinforcements?" I said.

"I don't know, Clem." Eva paused. "But I know I trust her."

Eva had a lot to learn about Maeve Umbra.

Thom left us that afternoon. His promise was fulfilled, and he said he had more souls to see. As he left, he said he hoped I'd find my cat and "that demon soul."

I didn't sleep well that night. In my dreams, my legs were covered in dirt and plants had sprouted from them. Grasses, dandelion leaves, sprouts. I kept having to pick the growth away, to slough the dirt off my thighs and legs to reveal the skin underneath. But there was always more, and I didn't get it all off before the dream ended.

My dreams never had happy endings. They never even had endings.

When I woke up, Eva slept with her back to me in the bed. The winter sun wasn't up yet, but I knew I wouldn't fall back asleep.

"You had a bad dream," she said into the stillness, not moving.

I turned my face to her, only barely catching her outline in the dark. "How did you know?"

"You gasped when you woke up."

"Were you already awake?"

She rolled over, facing me. "No, but I don't mind. When you've slept as badly as I did, you want to be awake."

I sighed, eyes lifting to the ceiling. "I get that."

"Clem," she said, "do you really think you've lost your magic?"

I'd lost more than that, but I wasn't feeling like pouring out my woes. Not today. "Yeah, I do."

"Then how are you going to defeat her?"

"I'm not, Eva."

She went silent, her breathing soft and slow. "And you're not even going to try."

My face snapped toward her. "I gave everything I had, Eva. Everything. After I save Loki and Callum, I'm done."

We eyed one another in the semidarkness, her pupils flicking between mine. The longer she didn't speak, the more the quiet felt like a hand around my throat. I knew I'd be damned by her words as much as the lack of them.

Finally, her lips parted. "I'll stay by you because I'm your friend," she said. "But that didn't used to be the only reason."

I sat up in bed, turning away.

She didn't try to talk to me, and we got up in the quiet of the hut, dressing silently and apart. She left for the bathroom, her admiration for me like a ghost following after.

I stared after her, rooted to the spot until she closed the bathroom door.

Evanora Whitewillow. She didn't understand.

I picked up the clamshell compact off the dresser, opening it to observe myself. The red lines of my scars trailed above the neck of my shirt like tendrils disappearing into my hair. Someday they would turn white as porcelain, but they would always be there.

I closed the compact. Better not to look at myself at all.

I knew as I came down the stairs I would never come back to this place. It was a place of hiding and forgetting, and it belonged to Samara. Just her and no one else.

At breakfast, Samara had conjured a whole spread for us. But she kept herself busy in the kitchen while we ate. She sang a strange, upbeat song and clanged dishware as she washed it. Eva and Aidan and Liara chattered about the academy and seeing their parents again, seeing Liara's brother. I ate in silence; I had no family to talk about.

When we were getting our cloaks on, Eva was saying, "Mama said to be careful in the woods outside the academy. We have to do a particular whistle"—she imitated it, like a bird's three-note trill—"and if all's safe, they'll whistle back."

"Sure," Liara said, cinching her cloak. "You can be on whistle duty, all right?"

Samara and Bill walked out into the snowy morning with us. The others went to the lean-to to take Siren's blanket off and get her saddled, and I hesitated with Samara.

"No goodbyes," she said as we stared in the same direction into the clearing. "They're saccharine and uncomfortable."

I had always felt the same way. I wondered if that was how Raven Murkwood felt about goodbyes, or if Samara and I just happened to share that feeling by chance.

"Samara," I said.

"You have a question. Ask it already—I can feel you vibrating with the need to spit it out."

I had wondered this since the day I'd met Samara, but other questions had always seemed more important to ask. "If you don't care about what happens to the world, why train us to fight?"

An uncharacteristic moment of thought turned into moments; she rarely took time to consider anything before speaking. When I was about to look over at her, she sucked in air and said, "I don't care about the world. But I do care about Maeve. I believe she's trying, in her own way, to do what's right." Her voice was serious and level like it had never been before. She sounded painfully sober, clear-headed.

"What did she say to you, about me?"

"She told me that someday you might appear, and that when you did, the price of my cowardice would be to prepare the one who'd taken on the burden of it."

The Spitfire. "You could have prepared me by telling me the truth."

"The truth wouldn't have prepared you," she said. "It would only have damned you. Maeve made the mistake of telling me what lay inside me before I'd had the chance to own my destiny. It broke me, Clementine. I couldn't go forward, couldn't go back. I could only remain frozen in place."

"You could still change your destiny," I said. "You could come."

She set a hand on Bill's head. "When you've followed a path as long as I have, you become entwined with it forever. Remember that, Nectarine, after you've saved your lover and grown bored of laying in bed with him."

With a wink, Samara turned away. She and Bill passed into the hut, and the door closed behind them.

Goodbye, old witch. I knew, somehow, I would never see her again.

CHAPTER THIRTY-ONE

We passed through the veil on horseback an hour after we'd left Samara's hut. It was Liara who parted the veil this time, her finger cutting as straight and true as ever. On the other side, a forest revealed itself. The academy.

She and Eva passed through first, their wings silent as they flew out of view.

Aidan and I waited for their signal, Siren and Noir standing side by side. The Shade wasn't supposed to attack until tonight, but she no doubt had daytime allies. Spies. She had the whole Mages' Council at her fingertips.

Aidan nodded at me; Eva had given him the all-clear with the whistle. The others had the ability to speak to each other without speaking, a skill I no longer had no matter how many times I pressed my thumb to someone's forehead. I wasn't part of the conversation.

When I urged Noir through, a feeling came over me that I didn't belong at the academy anymore. It was a place for magic. I had none.

It's not about the academy. It's about Callum and Loki.

I had spent so many years thinking of myself, of my destiny, that it was hard to get out of the habit now. Prophecies made you self-centered; you were always the chosen one. But I wasn't. I never had been.

We passed from snow-packed ground to the frozen barrenness of pine trees and bare trees and no snow at all. A different place, one I hadn't seen in months. But this was definitely the forest outside the academy—I'd know it anywhere, any season. The smell was always the same, even if I had changed.

As soon as we were through, Aidan kept Siren tight to my side. Protecting me. Eva and Liara flew to nearby trees, getting vision over us. At their signal, we started forward, walking the horses amidst the pine trees toward the school.

We had to be quiet, and we had to be vigilant.

Above us, Eva and Liara moved from tree to tree, keeping watch. The woods were silent and deep except for birdcall and the occasional angry, squawking squirrel. The horses' hooves crunched over leaves, and the longer we went the more I wondered if I'd be able to enter the academy at all.

I needed magic to see. I needed it to get inside.

"We're nearly there," Aidan whispered to me. "Liara says she sees the edge of Umbra's enshroudment."

I stared ahead; I couldn't see it. I couldn't see anything at all except the trees and forest, the regular world.

My chest began to hurt, the wounds pulsing as my breath quickened. Noir seemed to sense it, throwing his head, stamping one foot as he walked. I put a hand to his neck, soothing him, not feeling one bit soothed myself.

You can still enter, Rational Clem said. *You're still a witch*.

Was I, though?

I needed to be if I was going to get where I wanted to go.

As we walked, Siren had pulled a few steps ahead of me. All at once she disappeared like entering an invisible lake, submerged at the head and neck, then Aidan and her tail disappeared together.

When I looked up, Eva and Liara were gone, too.

They had passed through the enshroudment. They hadn't even considered whether I'd be able to see.

Noir halted, feeling my uncertainty. Or maybe I had leaned back. Only woods lay before us, but I knew the academy was on the other side. It must be.

The cold set in, tightening around me. Reminding me of the heat I lacked, the fire.

It reminded me of Vienna.

I squeezed my eyes shut. Our first night of winter holidays, Eva had brought me to a special place. We'd stood outside the solstice market, her behind me, and she had placed her hands over my eyes.

"Before you lies a cobblestone path," she'd said, "each stone reflecting the light from the sconces set at either side. Once you walk under the archway, you'll first smell roasted pine nuts mixed with the scent of honey and cinnamon wafting from somewhere far off. Then you'll smell roasting pork."

I'd shifted on the sidewalk. "And then I'll see Santa Claus?"

Eva hushed me. "And the music will come to you from far down the cobblestone path—a man and a woman singing together, and a bassoon to accompany them—leading you past a colorful gumdrop stand on your left, and a faerish wreath seller on your right, his creations so green and tied so tight you'll never lose a single needle..."

On and on she went, describing what lay before us in such a vivid, appealing way, I wanted it to be true. I wanted it to be real. She had been so certain I'd see it. It was her certainty that had made the difference. Her certainty in me had become mine.

Ahead of me, I knew I should be able to see the path leading to the academy's amphitheater. The worn-down grass in a semi-straight line passing toward the massive dome. The trees, as big around as houses, with stairs circling up their trunks. The walkways between those trees for the students who couldn't fly.

I should be able to smell Chef Vickery's cooking even from here. The salmon—Loki's favorite—spicing the air. That grape drink she would make at every meal, which I had overdosed on more than once at the guardians' inductions and parties.

I should be able to hear the sounds of students' voices as they crossed the grounds from one class to another. Quartermistress Farrow leading a lesson at the riding ring. Milonakis scolding someone for taking a book out of the Room of the Ancients.

I wanted those things. I wanted them all so badly.

I wanted to go back to a time when I was the bad witch, the fire witch, Clementine Cole with fewer problems than she knew but more than she could handle.

I wanted to be her.

Before I opened my eyes, a voice was speaking to me. It sounded like Professor Goodbarrel.

"Clementine Cole," he said. "Is that you?"

There he stood before me, on the path, staring up at me with a crease between his eyebrows. And beyond him, there was the academy. People were everywhere, their voices suddenly a low din, tents set up all around the clearing. The amphitheater contained more people, the whole place more like a refugee camp than a school.

I stared. This wasn't what I had pictured.

But I could see it.

"How did I get in?" I said.

"You walked." He pointed. "On your horse."

Noir. Noir had taken us forward while I'd had my eyes shut tight, and we had passed right into Umbra's enshroudment. What a goddamn legend of a horse.

And now I knew I still had a little magic in me after all.

I set a hand to Noir's neck, patting it. "Hello, Professor."

His beard had grown long and unkempt, his eyes not quite so joyful as before. "It is you. I'd recognize that horse anywhere, though you don't look quite the same as you did. I don't suppose anyone or anything does, though."

Ahead, Aidan stood amidst the tents, turning Siren in a circle. "Where are my parents?" he called over to Goodbarrel.

Goodbarrel pointed past Aidan. "At the Guardians' Council tent. In the meadow."

Aidan didn't wait; he took off on Siren at a trot.

Eva was already gone, no doubt to find her parents. And Liara crouched nearby on a tree, staring over everyone and everything. She looked as overwhelmed as I felt.

We were back, but everything had changed.

Professor Goodbarrel walked alongside Noir as we entered the grounds. "You've been delinquent from your classes quite a while, Ms. Cole. Three and a half months."

I snorted. "Professor, I've been delinquent from life for three months."

"Haven't we all. It's a rite of passage to adulthood, I think. And what better time than when the world's going to hell?"

I glanced down at him, eyes wide.

"Oh," he said. "I'm the interim headmaster, aren't I? Such things are too pessimistic. Welcome back, Ms. Cole—you're just in time for winter festivities."

I half-smiled, then nodded at a tent we were passing. "What's all this?"

"Homes," he said. "Many temporary homes for many mages. They've come from all over Europe and beyond, you see, some to be under the safety of Maeve Umbra's enshroudment. Others are here to fight. All will be behind the walls by tonight."

"There are no walls here," I said.

He pointed toward the meadow. "Ah, but you've been gone months, and our mages have been industrious."

Noir stamped, and I stared toward the meadow like I could see it from here. "Where is Umbra?"

Goodbarrel drew in a long breath through his nose. "A fine question, and I can give you a less-than-fine answer. She's in the meadow as well. So to speak."

I tilted my head at him, but his attention was already drawn away. One arm went out. "Ah, Quartermistress. One of your fine mares has returned." He paused, glanced back at Noir. "Or stallions."

"Definitely a stallion, Headmaster." Quartermistress Farrow had approached us from the side, arms folded. Her whip of a braid hung over her shoulder like a remonstration, her eyes slitted up at me. "As well as the thief atop him."

I set a hand to my chest. "Moi?"

"Oui, tu." Her eyes roamed over Noir. "Though he looks in decent shape, if not in need of a vigorous bath and brush. Where'd you take him?"

"Even if I told you, Quartermistress," I said, "you wouldn't believe me."

Her mouth screwed to one side. "I've come to believe many things when it comes to you. Now let's get that horse properly fed and groomed."

Goodbarrel had already been called away by one of the professors from House Gaia. "Headmaster?" I said.

He turned back. "Clementine."

"Will I be able to speak to Umbra?"

"I'm afraid not right away. You'll see what I mean in the meadow."

Noir was already following the quartermistress toward the stables, head bobbing in the old, familiar anticipation of food. When we arrived, they were somewhat different than I remembered.

Many horses grazed in the adjacent fields, ones I hadn't ever seen before.

I swung off Noir as we reached the entrance. "Where'd they come from?"

"Everywhere." The quartermistress swung the door open, ushering us inside. "Especially now that it's unsafe to travel by magic. Most mages don't trust the leylines, even if the one nearest the academy has been kept uncorrupted by Umbra's influence."

I led Noir over to his old stall, but found another horse had taken his place. Her roan head popped up as she worked alfalfa between her jaws and gave a little whinny.

At my side, Noir's head jerked, and his nostrils widened as a low, guttural noise emerged.

"Well, well." Farrow came over to my side. "She's a pretty lady, isn't she?"

I looked between the two horses, who were evaluating each other from a distance. The mare leaned over the stall, nose reaching out to smell Noir. And he didn't recoil or snap at her like he would have any other horse. Instead, his nostrils kept jerking, tail flicking.

I took a step back. "I can't handle a horse romance right now."

Farrow chuckled. "Love comes when it comes, and wherever it wants. Even to the unworthiest of us."

I set a hand on Noir's neck. "Are you calling my horse unworthy?"

She glanced back at me. "Do you want to argue about that, or do you want me to take care of him while you go looking for the head-mistress?"

She knew me too well.

I pointed between the horses. "Just... keep them separated, okay?"

She set a tentative hand on Noir's massive neck, my presence already forgotten. "Hello, sir. It's been a minute."

I left the stables the way I'd come, emerging out onto the clearing of tents once more. Some part of me wanted to head straight up to my old dorm, see if my things were still there. If it even belonged to me anymore. I wanted to go to the dining hall, to the guardians' tree, to Spark's common room.

Hell, I even wanted to see Milonakis.

But I needed to get to the meadow. I needed to find Umbra.

I'd just passed the amphitheater when a voice called out, "Where's your fire, witch?"

I stopped hard, my chest flaring before I'd even processed who it was. When I turned, Torsten was already on me, enveloping me in a hug that cut off my air. My former combat instructor was enormous, his arm coming in at my neck. "Cole! My little combat trainee. Where've you been?"

"Torsten," I said, muffled. "You're still here."

He had been a year ahead of me, but teaching an introductory combat class because he was one of the best fighters at the academy. And no doubt still was.

"I've been brought on," he said. "As one of the professors. Surprised?"

"Not one bit." I gazed up at the blond demigod, unable to tell him I had no fire. "And you're staying to fight?"

He knew exactly what I meant. His fingers raked through his hair with a nod. "There's no other way. The academy's where I belong, and she'll find House Gaia doesn't fall easy."

"House Gaia? Are the students fighting?"

"We're all fighting, Clementine." His hands had settled on my shoulders. "And now you're here. We have a witch's power on our side."

He thought I was powerful. He thought I was a good witch.

Four years ago, I would have killed to be both of those things in Torsten's eyes. Now I just stared up at him.

"I..." I took a step back. "Need to get to the meadow. I'll see you, Torsten."

CHAPTER THIRTY-TWO

Other students recognized me on the way to the meadow. Ones whose faces I remembered, and ones I didn't. They'd come for an academy, and they'd gotten a battle for their lives. Some of them said my name and hello, and others just stared.

I heard whispers:

"It's the leader of the guardians."

"The fire witch. No, not the Shade."

"She'll save us."

Save them. They thought I could save them. That was how desperate things were—that was how helpless they felt. They were looking for a savior, and they thought a twenty-three-year-old could be her.

I hadn't even been able to save myself. I hadn't been able to save my cat. I hadn't been able to save Callum.

I didn't stop for anybody. Ahead, I could see the meadow, white with snow and brilliant in the morning sun. A sense of tension, of waiting relief, built in me as I got closer. This was where I had trained so many long days—running, fighting, sitting under a tree, sitting on a log to think. Trying to ride a broom. I'd raced the first guardian trial here, danced with Callum Rathmore at a winter ball.

This felt like the center of the academy. The beating heart of it.

When I crested the tree line, light hitting my face, I stopped hard. One hand went up to shield my eyes, and I squinted. More tents lay around the meadow's edges, one of them markedly larger than the others, set apart.

Those weren't why I'd stopped.

Before me rose a thirty-foot-high wall of earth and ice. It tapered off at the top, creating a dome over most of the meadow. Not far away, a narrow gap in the wall offered a strange, porcelain glow. I crossed toward it, passing by the wall itself—it must have been two or three feet thick—and into the dome and the glow.

At the center of the meadow, a gleaming, iridescent light shone like a small sun. Its bottom nearly touched the ground, light dancing and radiating over its edges and through its pure white center.

"It appeared three days ago," someone said by my side.

Fi Waters.

I rarely wanted to hug someone, but the impulse came to me to throw my arms around the once-leader of the academy's guardians the second I saw her cropped blonde head next to me. The solid one, the strategist. She had returned.

Maybe I was looking for a savior, too.

Instead, in true form, I didn't move. "What is it?"

She worried her lip. "Nobody knows. The headmistress summoned it, and before she passed through, she told no one to follow her. That she would return on the night of the third day."

"Umbra was here three days ago, wasn't she?"

Fi gave a nod.

Which meant she would return tonight.

Unless I could find a way into the underworld, I had no choice but to wait for her—and the battle. I had no choice but to fight, whatever good I would do without magic or a familiar.

Though if I was honest with myself, I'd knew I would fight the moment I stepped back onto the grounds. When I was fifteen, I'd called myself a "lone wolf." It sounded cool, apart, and even though in the years following I'd stopped using the term, I'd still thought of myself that way.

Apart.

That wasn't true anymore.

I glanced at Fi. "Who's running the show with Umbra gone?"

She pointed to the large tent in the meadow. I recognized Siren standing outside it, head low; Aidan had gone straight there. "The Guardian Council."

So the council had come here, to Shadow's End Academy. This was truly a battle. And they might know a thing or two about the underworld.

"I'll see you later, Fi." I started toward the tent.

"So you're fighting?" she called after me.

"What else did you ever see me doing, Fi?"

Her laugh echoed behind me, the sound ricocheting around the meadow before it was lost under the noise of Umbra's magical creation.

The closer I came to it, the more I heard it.

Nearing the center of the meadow, I paused in front of it. From here, it seemed to encompass everything, the rest of the world lost to the shimmer—and it was completely opaque.

I stared into it, listening. It sounded like seashells being rubbed together, the shards of them on a beach.

Where have you gone, Umbra?

My fingers lifted, hesitant and slow. We weren't supposed to pass through, but that didn't mean we couldn't touch. And if anyone was going to break the rules just a little, it would be me.

When my fingers came forward, a warmth enveloped them. The light played over my arm, spectrums of color—tiny rainbows—dancing on my skin. This felt like the veil, but richer. More potent. If the veil was a skein, this was a thick duvet.

The magic here was immense.

I backed away from it, overwhelmed. Stared at it a few seconds longer before I turned toward the tent, rubbing my hand in my other one.

The warmth lingered as I came to the Guardian Council tent, which was twice as tall as Eva's. That had been a camping tent, low to the ground. This was for a large encampment, the flap to enter taller than me. Only a thin slit of light entered, but I couldn't see inside. Couldn't hear voices.

Siren's head rose, and she eyed me for a moment. If she was here, Aidan was inside this tent. And he had come in in a hurry, leaving the horse saddled, the bridle strap hanging to the ground.

I stepped through the flap, expecting a larger place than what the tent could reasonably contain. If a mage had made it, I'd long ago realized, it was probably tangibly manipulated.

But there were tangible manipulations, and then there was this.

I stood in the foyer of a bustling three-story building, the center of it completely open from the ground to the roof, like a large, square garden. People moved to and fro, descending stairs and going up them with scrolls and armor. Weapons' racks lined the far walls—one for blunt, one for sharp, one for ranged. The floor in front of me was recessed, two wooden steps down to stone, where a large, half-circle table occupied the middle. Currently unoccupied.

A square hallway with pillars ran the circumference of the space on my floor, doors leading off it. And on the second and third stories, a railing ran all the way around. I spied more doors leading off the central space up there.

One of the upstairs doors creaked, and a face appeared over the railing. "Oh!" Charlotte North said. "It's Clementine." And then she was descending stairs in green and gold robes, her feet tapping, and she wrapped me in such a tight hug she outdid Torsten. Aidan's mother had, from the moment she'd met me, treated me like her own child.

She pushed me away, gripping tight with her hands. "You look terrible."

I could only smile. "Terrible's better than dead."

Charlotte North slid one arm into the crook of mine, leading me around the edge of the bottom floor. Her hand wrapped over mine. "Thank the gods you're here. Aidan told us everything."

"Everything?"

She gave a grave nod. "All of it."

"Who's 'us'?"

"His father and me."

"But what are you doing in the council's tent?"

She turned round eyes on me. "Oh, Aidan never told you."

I just stared at her as she led me along.

"I'm a councilor, Clementine. We keep our identities secret, our locations dispersed, so that if one of us is caught, the rest of us aren't compromised. Aidan has had to keep it a secret for years now—and apparently he's done a fine job of it."

Aidan's mother was on the Guardians' Council. It shocked me, and then it didn't; not after what he'd told me about his gift.

"For a very long time now," she went on, "our family have served as strategists on the council." She opened a door, which led into a sitting room with a pretty lattice window on the far wall. Aidan sat in one armchair, his father in another, and Farina North in the facing loveseat.

Aidan's grandmother.

I stopped, almost jerking away from Charlotte.

Aidan half-rose. "It's all right, Clem."

I pointed at Farina, so many things coming to mind to say. Questions, accusations. But what I settled on was: "Your hair."

Her eyebrows rose, and she set one hand on her long, intricate braid. The one I had set fire to years ago. "What of it?"

"It's... back."

She set her teacup down. "I'm a mage who deals in the elements, girl. You think that was the first time I've lost my braid?"

Aidan and I met eyes, and he said, "She's with us, Clementine."

"I've heard that once before—when was it? Oh, right before she tried to put me in a metal box."

"It's unforgivable," Aidan's dad said. "What she tried to do is unforgivable. But she thought she was doing what was right."

Farina flapped a hand at him. "Be quiet, son-in-law, lest I start speaking for you." Her eyes flashed on me, and she came around the coffee table toward me, studying my face. "So you no longer have the creature inside you. I can see it in the dullness of your eyes."

I resisted taking a step back, my chin lifting. She knew about the Spitfire; had she always? "Lack of sleep has that effect, too."

"But you survived," she went on, head tilting as her eyes darted over me. "You survived the Shade, and you survived having it ripped out of you."

Aidan really had told them everything.

I diverted my gaze to Charlotte, the one with power here. "She helped the formalists. Why is she here?"

"Tried to help," Farina corrected. "And failed, thanks to my grandson."

"She believed you were an unimaginable danger to us," Charlotte said. "She believed the formalists wanted to stop that danger."

"You were the Shade's vessel," Farina said. "Every generation there comes one, and you walked into my home with eyes like flame and your fists already clenched. I knew you were capable of proper trouble."

She knew about the Spitfire, and she knew about vessels. We came once every generation. A suspicion slotted into place in the back of my mind, but was washed over by everything happening in front of me. By the red in my eyes.

She must have read my thoughts on my face, because she said, "What? You think after a lifetime of studying witches and prophecies, I wouldn't know about such things?"

"You idiot." The word launched from my mouth the moment I thought it. "You tried to give me over to the Mages' Council. You didn't know Tristan Rathmore was Murkwood's lieutenant?"

"Not all formalists serve the Shade," Farina said, standing taller. "Some are loyal to a free and unburnt world."

"You were wrong," I said. "I've seen the Mages' Council. I've listened to them speak. Rathmore's spymaster reported to him on me, on their failed attempt to get me into that box in your front yard."

I shook with the urge to throw myself at her, the feeling just like my old anger. Surprisingly like it. And it only made me angrier to see the surprise and embarrassment appear in her eyes, a woman who clearly prided herself on knowing things. On pulling strings.

If the Norths were strategists, she wasn't the best among them. Maybe she knew that—maybe she'd always known it, which was why she was so hard-lipped and insecure and haughty.

She'd never been given the gift of strategy *or* of fire. That had been Aidan.

Aidan stood, his face appearing behind Farina, his voice low. "She has information, Clementine. On my gift and the prophecy. That's the only reason she's been allowed in."

I wanted to accuse her of drawing the formalists to us, of setting a trap, but that was pointless now: a battle was already coming to the academy. The Shade knew we were here because Rathmore knew we were here.

"The prophecy is bullshit," I said. "All that matters now is finding a way into the underworld. If you can't give me that information, old woman, then you're useless."

Aidan pulled a book from the table—the one Samara had shown us in her hut. The one that contained Catriona's extended prophecy. He must have taken it with him. He had gotten very good at lifting books from places he shouldn't. "There might be more to it than we think, Clem." He came forward. "My grandmother thinks we might still have a chance."

He wanted me to sit. I didn't want to sit. I didn't want to spend more time in this fetid room with Farina North than I had to.

"There's a battle tonight," I said to Charlotte. "Shouldn't the council be doing council things?"

"We've been preparing for days," she said. "Everyone knows their orders. The work has been happening, Clementine, for three months. Since the day the Shade escaped her binds and came back into the world."

"I'd rather prepare for a fight"—my eyes slid over to Farina, to her half-empty and cold teacup—"than have teatime."

"I'll make it worth your while," Farina said. "No tricks. Why would I? You're just an air witch now, anyway."

CHAPTER THIRTY-THREE

On the loveseat, Farina North sat with the posture of a woman who had spent her entire life practicing erectness. Her spine was probably made of steel, especially after so many years of holding back the gravity of that braid.

"Five hundred years ago," she began, "our ancestor partook in the battle for the world—what you now call the Battle of the Ages. Her name was Eustace North, and she had a brilliant mind for strategy. Without her aid, the Shade might never have been defeated."

Defeated was a strong word. Temporarily waylaid was more accurate, but I stifled that reply behind the cup of tea I had been handed by Aidan's mother.

"But," Farina went on with an upraised, steely-straight finger, "Eustace North was a magnificent strategist, but quite sickly. Most of our family was all brains and no brawn. 'This is the folly we must remedy,' Catriona said, 'should a witch ever rise to take such power again.' So that when the battle was won, the leader of the forces of light looked upon Eustace and bestowed upon her a great gift from Heaven —the blue flame, more powerful, burning brighter and hotter than the Shade's magic—to be passed down through our line, and to reemerge when needed most."

At this, her eyes flicked to Aidan, narrowed with obvious meaning. She thought of Aidan as weak—as needing the flame most. That was her only explanation for why it had skipped her.

Aidan must be weaker.

He took this in the kind of stride only he was capable of, sitting with an impassive face and a cup on his knee, unblinking behind those glasses. He'd been shat on before.

"In the five centuries that followed," Farina continued, "our family have served as guardians of this world. When the Guardians' Council was established—"

"Who established it?" I said.

Her eyes cut over to me, eyebrows rising. "I believe it was Catriona, the prophetess. She became its first leader."

Catriona. Her name kept appearing, resurfacing like a ghost. I knew now it couldn't have been anyone other than the Catriona Raven Murkwood had talked about as her lover in *The Witching World*. But I wasn't going to say as much in front of my least favorite North.

"When the council was established," Farina repeated, "Catriona appointed Eustace North to the role of head strategist. And so it has been in the centuries since, that a North of each generation has assumed the role."

Nobody's head turned, but the general attention shifted toward Charlotte North. That explained her robes. That explained why she was here in the councilors' tent at all.

She was a member of the Guardians' Council.

"Do you lead it?" I said to her.

"Didn't you hear me, air witch?" Farina said, catching my eye with a jerking head. "Head strategist. That is our title."

Charlotte's nostrils flared, chest rising. Otherwise, she only said to me, "Maeve Umbra leads the council, Clementine."

I set the teacup down on the coffee table with an American's gracelessness. My eyes were round as grapes on Charlotte. "Umbra."

Did Aidan know Umbra led?

When he and I met eyes, I knew he hadn't been aware. His brow was creased, mouth a straight line.

"We have always kept our identities secret from anyone outside our families," Charlotte explained. "Our locations remain dispersed, too, for the protection and safety of the council at large."

So much made sense. Umbra's massive enshroudment over the academy, her opposition to the formalists. Why she made students into guardians, sent them on missions against the Shade and, later, the formalists themselves. Why Tristan Rathmore wanted so badly to capture her—not just because she was a powerful wizard who opposed him, but he'd be cutting the head off the entire council.

I wondered, too, if this was entwined with her longevity. Her immortality, if that was what it was.

I pressed the heels of my palms to my eyes. "Who else is on the council?"

"You will meet them all before the battle, no doubt," Farina said. "Now give me a moment without interruption, and I'll tell you why your prophecy perhaps isn't the bollocks you believe it to be."

My hands lowered, eyes opening.

Farina North placed the tome in front of her on the coffee table, lifting her reading glasses from their lanyard around her neck and settling them on her nose. She opened the book with the grave pride of a woman about to deliver her very own prophecy. Somehow she picked just the right page, because her finger stabbed down on it, then it trailed the page as she began reading.

"And Catriona said, 'When darkness begins to rise, the blue flame will return in the time of need to venture below and meet its opposite.'"

In the silence that followed, I glanced around the room. Samara's words about prophecies rang through my head—it was all just predictions, people trying to identify the right circumstances. Nobody knew the future. "And how does this mean the prophecy isn't bollocks?"

"The blue flame"—Farina gestured to Aidan with both hands—"has emerged in the time of need, air witch. This second battle for the world was foreseen by the gods. It is no coincidence. Aidan North is the one destined to defeat the Shade."

A pique of pride and jealousy hit my chest. Aidan, the chosen one. *She's wrong,* a voice said in my head, even though I'd already given up on the prophecy anyway.

And the gods? I had never seen evidence of any gods, not before or after I'd found out I was a witch, though everyone in the world liked to call on them when they got angry.

"Catriona also foresaw Murkwood's weapon being reassembled," I said. "And used to defeat her."

"Still possible," Farina said. "Though perhaps you won't be the one to wield it in the end."

My more skeptical eyebrow raised at Aidan, waiting for his pronouncement.

He fake-coughed into his hand, set his teacup on the table. I knew he hated this attention, would rather be talking to me in the library without anyone else to hear. "Thank you, Grandmother," he said. "For that enlightening interpretation."

I leaned into Aidan's shoulder as we came into the council's central room. "What do you say, North—ready to defeat a fire witch?"

His chin jerked toward me, surprise and maybe something darker in his eyes. "You don't need to be like that."

My hands went out as I followed him past a rack of spears, finger trailing just above their points. "Like what?"

I knew exactly what. I couldn't stop myself.

We passed by a fae half-walking, half-floating with a bundle of scrolls in his arms. Not long after Farina had delivered her theory to us —that Aidan was the one Catriona had spoken of, who would bring the blue flame to the Shade and stop her once and for all—a fae assistant had begun knocking at the door, needing Councilor North's attention. And so here we were, dispersing, and I was following Aidan who knew where.

I only knew he was walking fast, and I was keeping pace around the busy councilors' tent.

"Like it's funny," he said, his face already straight ahead. "It's not funny."

"Everything's funny until you're dead, Aidan. It's something you learn early when you're an orphan."

His head shook. "Now you wield that status like a cudgel. Only now."

"What status?"

We came out of the tent and into the meadow, biting air hitting our faces. "Being alone. Fending for yourself. You never talked about it before. Now it's your ticket to harassing me."

I faced him, but he kept walking. "I've never wielded a cudgel," I said after him. "I'm terrible with blunt weapons."

He threw his hands out. "I can't with you. Not right now."

"Where are you going?"

"To the library. I need to think."

I stopped. "Do you think they have cudgels there?"

As he stalked through the meadow, I turned back to Siren, whose head had raised as she remained near the tent where Aidan had left her. When I crossed to her and stroked her head, I murmured, "He didn't forget about you. Nobody could forget about you."

That pride and jealousy in my chest had been dulled a bit, but it hadn't gone away. I knew I'd feel my childishness later, allow it to shame me, but right now it was exactly what I needed—a pressure release valve from what I knew tonight would bring. Act like a jerk, let off a little steam.

Aidan got it. He was irritated, but I knew he got it.

I led Siren by her bridle through the meadow. The Norths had left me with more information than I'd expected and less than I'd hoped for.

None of them knew a way into the underworld. Not Charlotte, not even Farina. And when I'd asked if any of the other councilors might know, the answer had been solid uncertainty. Distraction. Because by then, the knocking had started at the door.

Which left me exactly where I'd started: waiting for Umbra to return.

"Clem," a voice called from across the meadow. When I stopped, Siren stopped, and both our heads turned.

Eva was flying toward me. Her and her mother, Nissa.

I squinted as they came closer. The crystalline whiteness glinted off their wings, but I thought I recognized Nissa's clothing.

Robes. Green and gold, distinctly like Charlotte North's.

When they landed in front of me, I pointed between them. "Please tell me you've dressed your mother in a spare set of councilor's robes because she was cold."

An apologetic half-smile appeared on Eva's face.

"I'm the Guardians' Council's spymaster," Nissa said. "For the past five years."

"You told me you were just regular guardians," I said. "You and Oberon."

"So I must be to the rest of the world, for safety's sake," Nissa said. "I'm sorry, Clementine, for not sharing the truth with you."

"Papa isn't on the council," Eva said. "That was the truth."

"So it's a council of women." I nodded. "Beyoncé would be proud."

"Actually," Nissa said, "it is."

Now both Siren and I fixed our attention on Nissa. "Seriously?"

Eva set a hand on her mother's forearm. "Seriously."

That was more than a little badass, but I was still feeling raw. So I said, "Okay," like women running the world wasn't the greatest and most thrilling revelation of my short life.

Eva came forward. "Clem, I asked Mama about getting to the underworld. She thinks there's a way."

My petulance fell away like a cloak. "Where?"

"Somewhere, I think, on these grounds." Nissa's hand went out. "When Maeve was here three days ago she spoke of it, though I don't think she was really speaking to me. Half to herself, maybe. We were speaking of keeping the academy's grounds safe, and she said, 'The way down should hold.'"

The entrance. But the academy's grounds were enormous, sprawling. "She could have meant the way down to anything."

"It seemed different," Nissa said. "Like she meant *down* down."

"Where is it?" I whispered.

Neither of them knew. It was obvious in their faces.

"Think on it." Nissa came forward, enfolding me in a hug I didn't resist. "And I'm sorry, Clementine, for everything you've endured. You are my daughter's very best friend, and when she told us of what happened to you, it was as though it had happened to our own child. You are the bravest among us."

And the only one without magic, I thought but didn't say. Even I was getting tired of my unrelenting self-pity. When she released me, I said, "Do you know when Murkwood will attack?"

"Dusk," Nissa said, eyes lifting skyward. "Eight hours, give or take."

"And Umbra will return then."

Nissa nodded, fully certain this time. "Yes, she will. She has never failed us. She told us to keep the Shade away from the center of the meadow for as long as we could."

But she failed my mother when I was born. She failed to protect me. Or maybe she let this happen—she let Samara give the Spitfire over to me to be a guinea pig for a bunk prophecy.

Behind us, Umbra's shimmering creation went on emitting its faint, tinkling music. "What is that thing?" I asked.

"A portal elsewhere," Nissa said, hesitating. Her lips parted, and then she decided against whatever she'd meant to say.

"To where?" I said. "You know—I can tell."

"I don't know, but I suspect." Nissa's face turned. "I suspect whatever comes through it will bring salvation."

Salvation. So she didn't believe we were capable of meeting Murkwood's army and defeating them on our own. And why would she? Murkwood had everything she needed. The Spitfire, the wisps, Lucian the prince. An army. My cat.

We were an academy of students and professors and one magicless air witch.

"So we have to hold out," I said, reading Nissa's body language. "We have to hold out until Umbra comes back."

She didn't answer right away. Then, sighing toward me, "Yes, Clementine. It's our strategy—our best and only strategy for survival. Defend and hold."

My hand went out. "And these walls?"

"Made of earth and ice—two elements..."

"To destroy the creatures," I finished, turning a slow circle. "Two elements will destroy them at once."

"It was Charlotte North's idea," Eva said. "She's the—"

"Head strategist. I know." I turned back to Nissa. "Did you know that Umbra is much older than anyone alive? Except for Raven Murkwood."

"Yes," Nissa said. "It is one of the council's most closely guarded secrets."

"How?" I said. "How is it possible?"

"That she does not share. But she has led the Guardians' Council for a very long time, and been the headmistress of this academy for generations before our own."

"Five hundred years?"

Nissa shook her head. "She hasn't ever told us her age."

"Don't you think it's strange," I said, "that there only seem to be two immortal people in this entire world?" And they were diametrically opposed.

CHAPTER THIRTY-FOUR

When I came into the academy's library, Milonakis sat at the circulation desk poring over a ledger. Her face turned like a bird's, eyeing me from a tilt. And behind her glasses, her eyes softened. "Ms. Cole."

"Hello, Professor Milonakis." I came to the desk in front of her, rapping my knuckles on it. "You know there's a battle coming, right?"

Any softness faded from her eyes. The mottle of her throat moved as a wave of irritation passed through her. "Of course I do." Then, after a beat, "But the library still needs to be manned. Students still go in and out."

I understood what she hadn't said: this was the place that centered her.

"Have you seen Aidan North come in?"

A half-nod. "He's inside. Has been for two hours."

"Thanks, Professor."

Before I could move, her hand darted across the desk, fingers on my wrist. It was the first time she'd ever touched me. But what she said was, "Have you taken any books from the library?"

"You mean three months ago?"

She tapped the ledger. "Several are missing. Have been for months."

I knew she wasn't talking about books. But she couldn't speak of anything else—it had been, and always would be, what would define her thoughts and life. She spoke of books when she didn't mean books.

I turned toward her. "No, Professor. I haven't taken any books."

She studied me a moment, her eyes catching on the scars emerging overtop the collar of my sweater. I had an impulse to cover them, but it was too late anyway.

Her hand withdrew. "Go on, then."

Past the circulation room, the library was empty. The chairs were pushed to their tables, and everything was free of dust, but Umbra's animations were gone. No books flew through the air. Besides the enshroudment, all physical traces of her had left with her.

On the second story, at our favorite table, sat one person. He had a stack of books in front of him, and steam from his tea wafted past his head as he hunched over.

He didn't look up until I was creaking on the steps, and then it was a frantic, wide-eyed microexpression I glimpsed between his towers of books. He schooled his face into calmness. "Hey."

I came over to the table. The books atop it were all from the Room of the Ancients—old, massive. They weren't neatly placed as per usual, but all at different angles. "Found what you were looking for in all this?"

"I don't know what I'm looking for." He sighed back, arms folded. "None of these books say, 'Your grandma is wrong. Don't worry—there was never a single prophecy told with you in mind.'"

I gestured to the opposite seat with a *"May I?"* eyebrow raise.

He nodded. He had forgiven me for earlier.

When I sat, I grabbed a cookie from the plate. Bit into it. "Would you do it, Aidan?"

"Do what?"

"If you found proof you were supposed to defeat the Shade, would you do it?"

"I'd have to do it," he said. "Just like you thought you had to do it."

I did think that. "Aidan, did Samara ever talk to you about destinies?"

His brow creased. "She only ever talked about wine and her dog."

I barked out a laugh, and it felt good. Like a little bit of the freneticism in me had gone with it.

"What did she say to you, Clem?"

I sat back, turning the half-cookie in my fingers. "She said prophecies are bullshit. That we make our own destinies. And that, given the way I'd lived my life, I had created two destinies: defeat the Shade, or die."

We met eyes across the table. He didn't speak.

"And I think," I went on, "if we don't do anything here tonight, if our only goal is to defend this academy, one of those destinies will come true."

"And you don't think it's the first one."

I shook my head.

"Without knowing it," he said, "you brought the Shade her power. You brought her her freedom. You made it your destiny to die to her."

I stared at him overtop the cookie. "Why you gotta come for me like that?"

"But I'm right."

"But you're right. She also said something else." I chewed, considering how to say it. "There might be a third destiny for me. But she couldn't see it."

"Can you see it?" he asked.

"No." It felt like something pushed at the edges of my mind, but it hadn't clarified. "You know, if Murkwood is immortal, there's only one way anyone can defeat her."

"Defeat her? I thought we were dying to her."

I wiped my fingers of crumbs, ignoring him. "The only way to defeat her is to send her back down, Aidan. To keep her away from the world."

"Send her back to the underworld, you mean."

"That's exactly what I mean. It's also where I'm headed anyway."

He shook his head. "I thought you were out. Done with the world."

"I'd love to be." Even as I said it, I knew it was posturing. A lie. "But she still has my cat. And the underworld still has Callum."

"You think we can keep the Shade in the underworld. Again."

I pointed at him. "I can't. You can. You heard your beloved grandma—the blue flame is more powerful than her precious fire." I stood. "Want to make your own destiny, North?"

The plan was this: Fight for our goddamn lives until Umbra came back, and once she'd shown us the way to the underworld, we'd lure the witch down there and imprison her. Again.

In the process, I'd get Loki back. And I'd find Callum's soul.

Eva had insisted on coming. The moment we'd told her, she said she was coming with us. She hadn't told her parents this, of course—they'd been appalled to learn she had already gone to the underworld once. They'd wrap themselves around her ankles before they let her go again.

So what we'd told the council was this: Aidan would use his flames to defend. He would protect the academy as best he could, and maybe we could all survive until morning.

This was what the council wanted to hear. They hadn't been to the underworld—they couldn't think beyond what lay above the earth and protecting what they had. And they wouldn't send their children down there on a hope and a prayer.

It wasn't the best plan. Maybe it wasn't even great—it was full of holes, of questions, of contingencies. But it was better than outright dying.

I stood in front of a weapons rack with dusk only an hour away, staring at a selection of blades, and it all felt beyond me. So much stood between me and what I wanted.

Just pick something stabby. Right now, I just had to pick a weapon.

I lifted a scythe almost taller than me. It reminded me of the Back-biter—or the blade on it, at least. And it would work from atop Noir's back.

I swung it a few times as, in the council tent around me, people filed in and out, the place a hub of activity. Mages went into the armory, came out in leather or metal. Mostly it was the earth mages who wore the heaviest armor. The water and fire mages wore leather. And the fae, who all used air magic and needed to fly, didn't wear armor at all.

Torsten had fitted me in leather, like I still had magic. Everyone but those who knew me were afraid of me, the fire witch who looked exactly like the Shade. They feared me like I was her.

But those who knew me even a little believed in me. And I let them believe, let them hope, because their belief and hope mattered almost more than anything. I had spotted Aidan with Saoirse, his almost-girlfriend, as I'd left the library. And when she'd turned to me, her eyes had been bright with admiration.

I couldn't bear to destroy that.

The scythe had a good weight. It sliced the air like it could split it. If nothing else, I might be able to scare the Shade's creatures.

Raised voices emanated from the entrance to the tent. They sounded angry, or at least severe enough that I turned, the scythe still in both hands, as several mages came into the tent.

"An envoy," one of the mages called out. "An envoy from the Shade to see the council."

Nissa was already in the central room. "Who?" she said.

"She identifies herself as Councilor Rathmore's bodyguard."

I turned, scythe in hand, cold blood running through my veins as I stood in shadow. *Councilor Rathmore's bodyguard.*

"We'll see this bodyguard," Nissa said.

As the mages stepped aside, they revealed a short, cloaked figure. The hood shrouded her features, but I knew from her figure she was a woman. And two of the academy's mages stood so close to her, her arms were practically pinned to her sides.

Hisses emanated around the tent. Students, mages I didn't recognize or know. Even some professors.

Nissa Whitewillow appeared at an upper railing. "And what does the envoy want?"

"She would speak to the council," the mage said. "All of them."

More hisses. Whispers.

I remained in shadow, unmoving. My eyes fixed on the figure at the tent's entrance.

"We'll hear her," Nissa said, her wings carrying her into the air. She dropped to the bottom floor. "Send for the other councilors. We'll convene, if briefly."

Soon the councilors appeared from the upper stories, already in their armor, and began filtering toward the bottom floor where I stood. As they assembled, the mages brought the envoy forward to stand at the open end of the horseshoe council table.

Her boots emerged from the edges of the cloak as she walked. All other movement in the tent had stopped.

Nissa sat at the head—what must be Umbra's seat, if she were around—and gestured toward the envoy. "Lower your hood and speak."

The hood went down, and her face emerged.

I dropped the scythe, my fingers losing all their strength, and it clattered with an unholy sound on the wooden boards. I didn't pick it up even though all faces turned toward me. Tamzin, however, kept her eyes on the councilors. She hadn't seen me, and I didn't come forward.

The last time I'd seen her, she had told me she'd kill me if she ever set eyes on me again.

My sister's blue eyes were blue as a bird's egg, her cheeks pale, as she stared at the council. Her hair hung in a tight braid, but the edges had frayed at some point. Tiredness darkened her features.

Nissa sat forward, elbows on the table, her hands clasped. "Why have you come here, bodyguard?"

Tamzin's eyes darted over the councilors. Her lips drew into a line, and it seemed to take all her will to drop to one knee. "I served Tristan Rathmore on the Mages' Council for years. I was his bodyguard, and I was told our purpose was to protect Edinburgh—to protect the world from the witch known as the Shade." She sucked in air. "I was deceived."

The hisses came again, and my anger flared as I searched them out. How dare they. How *dare* they.

At the table, the councilors had leaned toward one another, whispering. Nissa went on staring at Tamzin. "But why have you come here ahead of the battle?"

"For the same reason all of you are here." My sister's face lifted. "I will not serve her. I will not serve the Shade. The only side I'll serve in this battle is the one meant to defeat her. Believe me when I say I can offer you knowledge you do not already have—about Rathmore, about the Shade."

The hisses went on, more intense. They didn't trust her.

Nissa raised a hand for quiet. "Forgive me, Tamzin. But if you've served Tristan Rathmore for this long, why should we believe you?"

It was a good question. And Tamzin didn't have a good answer; I could see it in the way her eyes moved like lightning bugs. She'd carried that trait over from when we were very young.

I came forward. "Because I believe her."

Tamzin's eyes went wide as dinner plates as her face lifted. She saw me and her lips parted, her chin trembling.

Nissa turned. "Do you know her, Clementine?"

"She's Tamzin." I hovered at the edge of the steps down. The last time I'd seen her had been in the crypts under Edinburgh, when she had told me she would kill me if I ever came back. "She's my blood."

Silence followed.

"She's a witch?" Charlotte North said.

"No." Tamzin's voice was soft, lacking certainty. Her eyes dragged from me to Charlotte. "I'm her blood, but I am no witch."

Nissa turned toward me. "And if she threatened to kill you, then why do you trust her, Clementine?"

"Because she's Tamzin," I said. "She's my sister."

CHAPTER THIRTY-FIVE

We stood across from each other in the same room I'd met Farina North earlier in the day. I hadn't made to sit, and Tamzin didn't feel comfortable enough to do much more than lean against the far wall with her arms crossed.

This was the only room she was allowed to be in. She couldn't leave it, and certainly not the tent. Nissa had already spoken with her privately, no doubt probing her for everything she knew about Rathmore and the Shade.

Then, because of the look in my eyes when I'd asked, Nissa had allowed me to be in here with Tamzin. For a bit.

Except we hadn't spoken yet.

"Tea?" I said. "Coffee?"

She shook her head.

"I know a recipe for killer fae rolls," I said, and then I remembered: I couldn't conjure them anymore. I couldn't conjure anything.

"I'm not hungry." She diverted her face away, probably not seeing anything in that corner of the room. "Or thirsty."

Despite everything, all the time we hadn't seen each other, she was still so much my sister. The way she folded her arms, the left hand over the right elbow. The way she worked her mouth when she was bothered.

Somewhere deep inside—or maybe not so deep—we were all the children we had once been.

"This is your chance, you know," I said.

"My chance?"

"To kill me. Like you promised."

She met my eyes, and the ghost of a smile appeared, that old feeling between us. Then it was gone, washed over by an emotion I couldn't name. "I'd have to do it with my bare hands. They took my weapon."

"As I recall, your bare hands can do some damage."

She almost flinched. Her eyes fell on the scars appearing above the neck of my sweater. "Looks like someone got to you before me."

My hand went up, tracing them. They were only now properly scabbed over, after three months. "Someone got to me a long, long time ago. But I didn't know it until now."

"How did it feel?" She paused. "When the Shade pulled it out of you."

So she knew. I wondered how she knew.

"It felt like she was pulling my heart out of my chest. And maybe taking a limb along with it."

"It felt like part of you, then."

I shrugged. "It was with me since the day I was born. Did you know that part, too?"

"I know it all now. When the Shade first appeared in Edinburgh, I thought she was you. She looks just like you. But she wasn't you. I could tell the first time Rathmore brought me before her. She's hard like flint." She sighed. "And then I stood in on their meetings, because I'm the bodyguard. And I heard what had happened to you. What she had done."

I didn't know what to say. My hand went on tracing the scars, remembering the feeling.

"You were trying to stop her," Tamzin said. "Weren't you?"

"And doing a piss-poor job of it."

Some part of me ached to walk over to her, to pull her into my arms and press her head against my shoulder like our mom used to do with us. I suspected some part of her wanted that, too. Longed for it.

The other part of me resisted. Because while I knew Tamzin, I didn't. So much time had passed. She'd lived a whole life I knew nothing about. She'd bloodied me. She'd tried to kill me.

"You're a witch, you know." The words felt almost like an insult; to her, I knew they were. "You were born a witch. And you're still one."

Her arms tightened across her chest. I could see her resisting all the things that came to her to say. *At least she's learned self-control in her time with Rathmore. But then, what is a bodyguard except self-controlled?* "Mom never told me," she said.

"No," I said, "because she knew what I was. She never wanted us to be discovered." She never wanted me to fulfill the Shade's purpose. It made sense: if she raised me as a human, never told me I possessed any magic, it might never manifest. And if it never manifested, the Spitfire would have always remained that impulsive, lustful part of me.

It would have just been me, my inexplicable but persistent anger.

"She was a good mom," Tamzin said, and the memory of what I'd seen in the Shade's flames came back to me with a pain so severe it made my chest hurt.

"The best," I said, hoarse.

I couldn't tell her what I had seen. What I knew. If she didn't know, I couldn't tell her.

"What was it like," I said, "being raised by Rathmore?"

"He didn't raise me." She finally sat on the loveseat, right at the seam between the two cushions. But her arms stayed crossed. "It was mostly his son. He was like my older brother."

I stiffened, then dropped into the armchair facing her. "Callum?"

She nodded. "For years I lived in their home in Edinburgh. He was my only family. Then he left, and all I had were my instructors. They trained me from the beginning, Clem, to fight you."

"To fight me?"

"To fight a witch. Callum taught me to fight fire. Ora Frostwish taught me to defeat your hexes. Both of them were sent to the academy to teach you exactly the things I was taught to fight against."

I sat back in the armchair, both hands gripping the arms. They were sent here to prepare me. To prepare the Spitfire. So much made sense. And I began to understand a little bit of why Callum had disappeared after my second year at the academy. Why he'd given up his title.

He couldn't—or didn't want to—be a part of it any longer.

"I was always told," she went on, "that you would come for the blade in the crypts. That was mine to guard, and if I let you get past me, the world was doomed." A bitter laugh filled the room. "They weren't wrong."

"And they trained you to fight me," I said, "because that was another trial for the Spitfire." I had grown stronger after I'd fought Tamzin in the crypts under Edinburgh.

And the thing I couldn't say to her, but suspected: She was meant to die. She was meant to die to me during that fight. She had been groomed for it.

When we met eyes, I could tell she knew, too.

When I came out of the council tent, dusk was making itself known; I could feel it in the coolness of the air, in the growing shadows over the meadow. Voices rang out, directions being given to get into positions.

Torsten led a group of earth mages out of the meadow, toward the main grounds. Horses cantered this way and that. I could have sworn I spotted Circe Petalfleck's cropped blue hair before she disappeared into the trees. The guardians had returned. Fi, Circe. Mishka and Jericho and Akelan and the others were probably here, too.

That might be my last glimpse of Circe, I realized. One or both of us could be dead by morning.

I carried my scythe over to a quiet edge of the meadow, unhooking my cloak. I pulled Eva's tent out of the tangibly manipulated pocket, half-expecting to find the Backbiter there, too. But no. That wasn't with me anymore.

I put the scythe down and set Eva's tent up, grabbing my cloak and bringing it inside with me. Through the living room and in the bedroom, Callum went on sleeping. Alone, pale. Withering.

I came to his side with a greatsword in both hands. The thing had been hell to lift out of the rack; I'd practically buckled under the weight. "This isn't the original," I said, "but hopefully it's goddamn heavy enough for you."

I set the greatsword on the floor by the bed, along with the metal chestpiece and helmet I'd managed to pick up from the armory. He wasn't like other fire users, I realized. Where they wore leather, he wore metal. Maybe I'd get to ask him about that someday.

"I'd stay," I said to him, "but time's running out. I'll see you soon, I hope."

I came out of the tent and back into the meadow. It took only a minute to disassemble and tuck back into my cloak. Then I picked up the scythe and realized magical torches had been lit around the academy grounds, dotting the night.

It was time.

After leaving Tamzin, but before I'd left the tent, Charlotte North had thanked me for bringing Tamzin to them. "I didn't bring her," I said. "She came on her own."

"We would not have trusted her enough to believe in her word," Charlotte said, "without your endorsement. It's you we trust, Clementine, and your sister by extension. And she has given us ample information that will aid us in this battle."

I had overheard Tamzin's conference with the councilors. They had brought her out into the central room, and she was telling them that the Shade's darkness was far, far greater than they could imagine. That it was unfathomable. The first wave of creatures would be like nothing they'd seen.

If we could survive that, she said, then we might survive the night.

The councilors seemed dubious. One of them said the first Battle of the Ages was nothing so extreme. But I had no doubt Tamzin was right.

My sister didn't lie.

As part of Charlotte's thanks, she'd taken a few moments to show me the map of the grounds. I had never seen it like this, from directly above. The grounds were large, but they were in effect a half-circle. The circle extended from a long cliff, the one I had nearly ridden Noir off once before, and Umbra's enshroudment extended for miles from it.

And markers were placed all around it.

"We have to protect all of it?" I asked.

"To start, our people must be everywhere that isn't the cliff," she said, "as we don't know what side they'll attack from. Perhaps all sides."

"And what did Tamzin tell you?"

"As I'm sure you heard, she said the Shade's army was vast. So vast, in fact, that they could completely surround us without any concern for their numbers at all."

No doubt that was what she would do. If she could, then why not?

"And the dome you've created?" I said.

"If we should fail"—she paused, as though considering what she'd just said—"then all units will fall back to the dome."

She knows we'll have to fall back. It's just a matter of time.

Charlotte pointed out to me the various units she'd assembled—each of them containing a mixture of air, fire, water, and earth mages—and where they would be placed. Various professors and Guardians' Council members and former guardians each led regiments. I spotted names I recognized, but one made me stop and point. "Youngblood."

"That's right. Liara has volunteered to lead this one."

She was posted at the northwest side, near the faculty homes. If she was leading, then she wasn't going into the underworld with me—she was going to defend the academy.

She's done enough. More than enough.

"And where will Aidan be?"

"He'll begin here." Charlotte pointed to the clearing at the center of the academy. "On horseback. From there, he'll roam where he's needed."

She was sending her son out, too. There was something impossibly selfless in that, in the level voice she maintained as she said it. "What about the blue flame?" I said. "Your mother said he was supposed to be involved in the prophecy."

Her eyes shut, palms resting on the edge of the map. "I believe the blue flames were meant to fight the Shade. And that's what they'll do tonight."

"You don't believe in the prophecy. Do you?"

Charlotte's eyes opened on the map. "All my life my mother has carried a superstitiousness with her that I never shared in. No magical hand moves us, Clementine, but our own."

She's like Samara, then. We make our own destiny.

My focus returned to the battlefield before us. "And where will Eva be?"

"She'll be with you," Charlotte said. "She has insisted on being with Aidan. She'll be his eyes and his guard."

I straightened. "And where will I be?"

Her face softened. "You'll remain just outside the tent, Clementine. To protect the students who are still too green to fight."

By which she meant: I had no ability to fight the Shade. Not anymore. And so I would be with the others who also could not.

I nodded. "How far we fall."

She set a hand on my shoulder. "You haven't fallen, Clementine. You have much more to offer this world. Trust me." And with that, her assistant had beckoned her away, and she'd apologized and disappeared into another room.

At least they'd let me have the scythe.

I began my walk toward the stables. On arrival, I found them bustling, the quartermistress barking orders. Riders were leaving, heading toward different parts of the academy grounds at a gallop.

When I got to the quartermistress, she slapped me on the back. "Where have you been? Noir has been waiting for you."

She didn't know I didn't have magic. Or that Charlotte North had condemned me to guard the tent. And I wasn't going to tell her. "Which stall?"

She pointed. "He's been washed and brushed and fed four hours ago. He's ready to run."

I squeezed her arm. "Quartermistress," I said, hesitating.

Her eyes were already elsewhere, and she called out to a rider just mounting up. When she finally turned back to me, her cheeks were flushed. "What is it, Clementine?"

I wanted to tell her things. That she was the first professor who'd seen something in me. Who'd given me a job at the stables my first year. That I wasn't sure if I would have made it through that first year without her and the horse. That all the time we spent together at her home and in the stables had been more important to me than half the classes I'd taken.

But there wasn't time. There was only time to say, "Will you be in the fight?"

"Of course," she said, eyes flashing. "As will all the students you taught to ride bareback."

CHAPTER THIRTY-SIX

When I rode Noir out of the paddock, voices were calling for everyone in a unit to gather in the meadow. We followed the crowd, some of them on horseback. The quartermistress was right: half of them were bareback. Not even a quarter of them had been my students, though.

They'd just learned to ride that way without me.

One of the things I'd learned by instinct, but never really understood until now, was that bareback riding gave you a closer connection to the horse. A mage's horse relied on magic, and the closer the mage to the horse, the stronger the two were for it.

I only understood it now because I had no magic, and riding Noir wasn't the same. I felt the bones of his spine, the jostling of his gait, the imprecision of my seat.

Better than sitting outside a tent.

In the meadow, a massive group of humans and fae and riders had formed in the center. Everyone was milling about, thumbs being pressed to people's foreheads. They were establishing magical connections, probably already talking into each other's heads. All of them except me.

I rode up to the back, near the edge—I wouldn't be noticed back here. Well, except by the people who were looking for me.

"Nice wheat-cutter," Liara said from behind me.

When I turned on Noir's back, her arms were folded as her wings kept her at an eye-level hover. She was fully clad in form-fitted black. Her boots were knee-high, and her hair pulled tight and wrapped into a bun. "Nice combat gear."

"They actually assigned you to a unit?"

"Sure," I said. "And I heard you're leading one."

Even in this light, I didn't miss the conflict passing over her face. She schooled it back into stoniness. "I'd better be—I'm the guardians' co-leader."

I didn't even have to try for a smile, which surprised me. "Shock 'em for me, would you?"

"Absolutely." She hesitated a second as though she wanted to say more. And then, in a whisper of wings, she was gone, evaporating into the almost-night.

I'd just about-faced when Eva flew to my side, her black outfit and boots the same as Liara's. "What are you doing?"

"Riding my horse." I glanced her up and down. "You're killing it in those boots."

"You're supposed to be in the tent."

"Actually, I'm supposed to be just outside it." I half-turned atop Noir. "Where's Aidan?"

She pointed. "There."

At the front of the crowd, Aidan rode Siren toward Umbra's portal. He wore leather armor, which he looked wholly out of place in. The mare came to stand in front of the portal, tail swishing.

As he did, Nissa Whitewillow rose above us, hovering in front of the portal. Magical torches had begun to illuminate throughout the crowd, peppering the meadow. She called for silence, which swept over the crowd like its own form of noise.

"Humans and fae of the light," she called out, her voice a bell. "Tonight, a battle will fall upon us. Raven Murkwood, the fire witch known as the Shade, has once again risen to power. Tonight she will order her forces to attack our academy, the pulse of our resistance." She paused. "You all know this well. This is why you're here, brave hearts—to fight. And fight we shall, all of us. And we will not lose, because we have two gifts."

She gestured to Aidan. "Before us, the gift of the blue flame, the heritage of the Norths. Legend tells of the blue flame being the most potent and powerful of all flames, a gift from the gods and capable of repelling even the Shade."

She's blowing smoke up our asses. I knew the council didn't quite believe in Aidan's fire like Farina did. But I didn't blame Nissa; we needed all the hope we could get.

Aidan sat solid and statuelike, his birthmark red with the discomfort of being stared at. I could practically feel his embarrassment from here, but then again: He hadn't run and hid. He hadn't disappeared into the crowd.

He was here in front of us, and that made him even braver than the man who craved attention. He would do what it took to protect the academy.

Then Nissa's hand went out to the portal. "And by morning, the wizard Maeve Umbra will return. She has promised, and she does not fail. She will return to us, and between all of us, the academy will stand."

Around me, people cheered. Nearby, a student called out my name —"Ms. Cole!" It was Saoirse, riding bareback. She had fallen a thousand times and gotten back up every time.

She waved, and I smiled at her. "Remember your position," I chided.

They didn't know how close we were to the precipice. How this was one night among a thousand, because the Shade was immortal and she could return tomorrow night and the night after, and every night until we broke.

This was a stopgap. It was triage.

The fact of it came clear to me as we stood in the meadow, and the truth I'd been submerging finally surfaced:

This was about more than Callum and Loki.

Aidan and I had to go down to the underworld. We had to return Murkwood to her prison. We couldn't just let these people fight a battle that would only end when they were all beaten.

But to do that, we needed the headmistress.

Come on, Umbra. I eyed the portal as Noir stamped, hoping if I wished hard enough her face would appear through it. *Make my life easy.*

Nothing happened, of course. The bone-white gleam of it went on unbroken, the seashells tinkling through the meadow.

"Now the time has come," Nissa called out. "Defend your school. Defend your home. Defend the light. Take your place with your unit, and defend one another until the sun crests the horizon."

In the almost-dusk, everyone began to disperse. They went in all directions, voices ringing out to follow, to head this way and that.

Eva remained by my side, hovering. "You shouldn't be out here, Clem. It's not safe for you."

I kept my eyes on Aidan, following his movement. He was headed toward the clearing at the center of the grounds. I lifted the scythe in my hand. "You mean to tell me you don't need any wheat cut?"

"No jokes." She came closer, until her gaze was undeniable. "You don't have magic."

I stared at her, my eyes traveling between hers. She had come up against my most powerful, impenetrable defense mechanism. "I have magic"—I pointed to the center of my chest—"in my heart."

She groaned. "Stay close to me. And be careful."

And here my teachers had told me being a smartass would get me nowhere fast. She flew after Aidan, and I followed.

We found Aidan at the clearing, in front of the amphitheater on Siren's back. He was surrounded by a group of mages in the semidarkness, some of them professors and a few guardians I recognized. The fire mages among them held flames in one hand, everyone's faces dancing.

The silence was overpowering, almost deafening. We were in a state of waiting, of watching.

Down the path, I knew from Charlotte North's map of the grounds that another unit of fae led by Eva's dad waited in the trees nearest the leyline. They were the watchers.

Eva flew to Aidan's side, and a silent conversation passed between them. They both glanced back at me; clearly I had come up.

Aidan's brow creased. "Clem."

I rode closer, Noir's head swinging as though he felt my blood thrilling in my veins. "Fight's about to start, North. Keep your eyes on the darkness, not on me."

He sighed, turned forward—toward the woods. "Stick with Eva. I won't always be here to protect you like she can."

Aidan was giving me orders. I held my tongue, gripping the scythe. "Just don't forget the plan."

"I haven't forgotten." He took a tighter grip on Siren's reins. Then his eyes slid to mine, softness entering them. "Don't do anything stupid. All right?"

I half-smiled at him. "I'm a witch. When have we ever done anything stupid?"

On my other side, Eva snorted. "I can't think of a single time."

Everyone's faces snapped in one direction with eerie precision. They were all staring in the direction of the path toward the leyline, where the watchers were posted. Something had drawn their attention, but I hadn't heard anything.

Which meant someone had spoken into their heads.

Around me, a subtle preparation occurred. Horses were brought to stand at attention. Weapons were unsheathed. The fire mages' flames rose higher and brighter.

I set a hand on Noir's neck to keep him steady. During the long hours of this day, I had considered how I would fight this battle. I didn't have fire, but I could still ride. I didn't have hexes, but I could still swing a weapon. And I didn't have the ability to speak into anyone's mind, but I still had my voice.

I was still me. And even though I didn't have the Spitfire, I felt that familiar determination in me like a balm. A reassurance. That potent determination hadn't belonged to the Shade. It had, and always would, belong to me. To Clementine.

Far ahead of us, the trees began to creak. The muffled sounds of movement followed, and then the unmistakable sound of metal clanging. Just once. It echoed through the clearing with all the ominousness of a struck gong.

Then the clang came again.

The mages around me moved to encircle Aidan, Eva's magic appearing at her hands, the iridescent outline of her fan of wind gripped low. Blue flames appeared at Aidan's hands, and then the haft and string of his flaming bow. He raised it, an arrow flaming to place between his fingers and the bow.

They had to coordinate their attacks. Two elements at once, or else the creatures wouldn't die.

"They're coming," Eva whispered to me. "They've just penetrated the enshroudment. Papa's unit is fighting them, but there are too many. It's like the wave of an ocean. Be ready."

Ice carried up my spine, even as the water mages in our unit stepped forward, the four of them drawing water molecules from the air, weaving them into a blend over their hands, and throwing out sheets of ice over the ground before us.

The slick spread at once, far and wide, reflecting the moon through the trees. It was a cloudless night. At least there was that.

When the slick had reached its natural end, they appeared. They appeared just as Eva had said, in a wave, pressing away the moon's light, all limbs and darkness spreading over the ice.

This wasn't what we had expected. But it was far more than we'd thought. Far, far more. An unfathomable amount, like darkness itself was an element and could consume the light.

It was what Tamzin warned us of.

My sister hadn't been lying. She'd been trying to help us. And she had given up any safety she had with Rathmore to be here, with us. Fighting for us.

The ice set them off balance, and their movement became less coordinated. That was when the fire mages unleashed jets of flame, pouring over the space between us and the wall of darkness. Obscuring it all.

The ground rumbled, and in the next second the earth rose before us. So much of it so quick. I'd never known what the earth mages were capable of until tonight.

Within seconds, a wall of dirt and stone had risen to twenty feet in the air. But the moment it had drawn up to its full height, the moon gleaming off the edges of it, I saw them.

They were climbing it. The creatures were climbing it like it was nothing at all, the darkness seeping over, a wave of black oil obscuring the moon. Silent, voiceless, noiseless except for the faint sounds of scrabbling.

These were all souls. All souls belonging to the Shade.

One mage launched a fireball into the mass, and it was consumed and disappeared in an instant.

It took coordinated attacks to kill one of those things. And we were only a unit of maybe twenty-five.

In the center of the group, Aidan only had his bow nocked. He held the arrow like it was a precious thing, and the dervish I had once seen emerge from him was completely absent.

It wasn't going to happen. Not here, not now.

"Get back," I whispered, hoarse. I leaned back and sidelong to turn Noir, and he reared. I yelled, "Get back!"

The others didn't move the first time I said it. The second time I said it as Noir's hooves stamped back down to the ground. And that seemed to jar them out of their stupor.

"She's right." Eva had risen to see over the wall. "We have to fall back."

Twenty-three mages on horses began turning. Twenty-three of them began to flee, as, above us, magic began raining down on the dark water of souls cresting and now pouring over the wall.

Tamzin was right again: It was like nothing I'd ever seen.

CHAPTER THIRTY-SEVEN

I kept close to Aidan as we galloped, reining Noir in. He could go faster, much faster than any of them, but I would rather be consumed here than lose Aidan because I'd run ahead of him.

I glanced back. One of the riders from our unit had lagged, and now the wave of creatures reached the ground behind him. The impulse to turn and help had hardly reached my muscles before the creatures reached the horse's tail, back legs, and then sucked horse and rider fully into the mass.

This had been a terrible idea. We'd needed to do so much more.

I leaned closer to Noir's neck. Then, over to Aidan, "Can you push her any faster?"

He glanced over at me as we rode along the path toward the faculty homes, deep into the woods. Why had we ridden this way? I didn't know. I only knew we had to ride away. Away. Aidan must have seen the distress in my eyes, because he nodded. He drove his heels into Siren's sides, and our unit rode deep into the trees.

We were pulling away from the first wave. Only some of the creatures were keeping up with us, breaking from the pack. And some was better than an innumerable mass.

Some could be killed.

"Coordinate your attacks," I called out, throwing my voice behind me to the other riders. "Eva, you're with Aidan. Everyone, pick a partner who's not your element. You have to attack the same creature at the same time."

I didn't know at first if they'd heard me. Maybe we were all still running like rabbits.

In the next second, one of Aidan's blue-flame arrows flew past me. It was followed by a yell from Eva, who I looked back to see slicing her fan through the air, the immense yellow wave off it slicing into the creature closest behind us as the blue arrow lodged in its head.

One down. An ocean to go.

Soon, more magic filled the forest. A fire mage and an earth mage blasted a creature as the earth rose beneath it, launching it into the air. Water and fire froze, then burned. Earth and water entrapped, then—

"Eva," I said. She was too busy fighting to pay any attention. I leaned Noir out from the group, slowing him to where I was underneath her. "Eva!"

"What?" she yelled back in mid-swing.

"Tell the council we need to fall back to the dome."

"Not yet," she yelled. "We're supposed to hold them off as long as we can."

"We've already reached that point," I said, wishing the Shade had just left me a little magic. Enough at least to be part of the conversations going on inaudibly all around me. "We're screwed out here."

I veered Noir back toward Aidan, who shot off arrows as fast as they appeared in his hands. "We need to head for the meadow. All of us."

"I heard you." He shot off another arrow. "But we need to buy them time."

"For what?"

"The boggan."

The memory of that strange, overwhelming creature flashed into my mind. The first one I'd met had tried to drown me. In the final guardian trial, I'd discovered their entire kind hated me—hated fire witches. Even so: "One boggan won't do shit."

"You'd be surprised. There's a reason Umbra kept one around."

I'd believe that. Knowing Maeve Umbra, she didn't just keep a creature like that on the grounds just to sort students into their houses once a year.

"How long?" I said.

"Mom says to hold out five minutes more. They're coaxing him out of his cave."

Five minutes. In this battle, that was a lifetime. "Coaxing?"

He shot off another arrow with a hiss. "He hibernates in winter. He won't be lured out until he scents the Shade's magic."

We couldn't survive like this. Not running for our lives through the woods. "Fine," I said. "These things are doused in her magic. We'll lead the creatures to the cave."

Eva had slowed to fly above us. "We're supposed to stick to the central grounds."

"Forget the central grounds," I said. "They're overrun. Follow me, and bring the creatures with your magic."

Without waiting, I veered us toward the boggan's cave. I knew the others followed when the horses' hooves echoed behind me, doing their best to keep pace. The trees glowed blue around me as Aidan kept his magic alight, a beacon to the Shade's creatures.

I was surprised how well I remembered the way to this cave; I'd only been here a few times. But then, I had grown to know every part of these grounds well over four years. It had become my home.

Branches and leaves whipped by, shadows appearing out of the night. I had to duck and lean, keeping my eyes open as the ridge appeared to my right. We were getting close.

"Warn whoever's there," I called out. "Tell them to get out of the way."

"Already done," Eva said.

"We'll run right by the entrance. That should do it."

The mouth of the cave approached fast, Noir galloping hard. I leaned him toward its entrance, guiding us in a path close enough that we would skate right by it—and the creatures would, too. They should smell like well-done steak.

We swept by, passing the cave's entrance in a rush. I pulled Noir around in a wide circle, catching sight of all the different colors of magic following me. And the absolute wave of darkness that followed.

Come on, you bastard.

The creatures passed by the cave, encompassing its mouth. I kept Noir passing in his arc, and for a moment all was silent as we came around.

Then, that shriek. That unmistakable boggan shriek I had hoped I'd never hear again. He burst from the cave, sent the Shade's creatures flying in all directions. In the moonlight, I could just make him out.

He rushed on all fours, massive, slashing and spinning and leaping. He pounced on one creature in a burst of smoke, and in the same motion he leapt for the next one, catching it in his maw in the air. Everything he touched was obliterated. He was a shark in a school of minnows.

How was he killing them?

"You don't see that every day," Eva said.

When I glanced up, she was flying beside me. "He doesn't have magic."

"He eats magic," she said. "And their whole kind hates fire witches most of all. This is a feast."

"That should hold them for a time," Eva said. "At least, long enough for us to get everyone into the meadow."

Eva was right—we needed to get to the meadow, a place we could defend as one. And we had to defend it until Umbra came back.

"Good call," I said. "Tell the council we're overwhelmed, and everyone needs to pull back."

Aidan fired off an arrow into a fresh clutch of creatures chasing us, almost as though he hadn't heard me. And then, maybe just because he trusted me, he said, "Right. We're going."

As a unit, we veered right, toward the back side of the meadow. I slowed Noir to the pace of the rider in the back, a water mage about my age. And I realized I knew her. It was Mishka Reddy.

"Mishka," I said, breathless.

"Don't talk." She wound water around her hands, shot it behind us to form a slick of ice that spread through the trees in our wake. "Just ride."

Behind us, creatures slipped and slid, and I realized Mishka was purposely taking up the rear. She was guarding our unit.

We passed by the central grounds, where magic flew like fireworks. Above us, mages stood on the rope bridges high up between the trees, slinging their magic. Fae darted above us, sharp lances of air stabbing into the mass of darkness. Sometimes the attacks were coordinated, but most of the time they weren't.

It didn't matter; killing one of the things was like extracting a single drop of water from an ocean.

When we broke into the meadow, it was gloriously lit as we passed through the single remaining gap and into the dome. Like a crisp winter scene, the portal still at the center of it. Wonderful, and terrible —we had to defend this place for who knew how long.

The councilors appeared from their tent, some of them mounting horses. Others flew, like Nissa. I spotted Tamzin running, and I started toward her at once. When Noir galloped up to her, she froze, shrinking with one arm up to brace herself.

I came to a skidding stop in front of her, dropping my useless scythe. My hand went down to her. "Get on."

She stared up at me, arms lowering. And then her hand found mine, gripped it, and I pulled her up behind me.

"You were right," I said. "About everything."

Her hands went around my waist. "I wish I wasn't."

———

I let Tamzin guide me. "We need to get everyone here," she said. "The council will listen to you."

"First time for everything," I said, already spurring Noir toward Charlotte North, who rode to meet Aidan's unit at the center of the meadow. When we came alongside her, I said, "Councilor."

She glanced over at me, her eyes wide. "I heard. Eva and Aidan relayed your message. All units are currently pulling back to the meadow."

"We'll defend the entrance until you've gotten everyone inside," Tamzin said to her.

Charlotte glanced between me and her, the two of us sitting together on Noir's back, then nodded.

Nissa dropped from the air to a hover amidst us. "The watchers tell me they're pouring in from all three sides now. The central grounds are overrun."

"So they're closing in that fast," Charlotte said. Her hand flew out toward the rest of our unit. "Everyone, we need to defend this entrance until we've got the others inside." I had a feeling she was speaking out loud for my benefit, since I was the only one who had no mental connection.

We only had nine mages left in our unit. "We need more," Tamzin said. "Where are the others?"

Hoofbeats sounded at the tree line, two units appearing simultaneously. They converged on us, kicking up frozen ground as they came to a stop. Charlotte North began giving them silent directions, and Eva and Aidan rode over to me. The look on their faces told me exactly what they were thinking.

We were the front line, and we needed to hold them off as long as we could.

Eva flew close to me. "You need to get inside, Clem."

"No," Tamzin said from behind me. "If Clem can ride, I can fight."

I glanced back at her. "You can?"

She reached into her chestpiece, yanked out a nightstick and flicked it to its full—five-foot—length. "If you'll give me a little magic to work with."

Eva started back in the air. "Mama said you were disarmed when you came into the tent."

"You're not the only ones who deal in tangible manipulations," Tamzin said.

Eva didn't bother arguing; she shot her air magic out toward Tamzin, who caught it deftly on her nightstick, swirling it around until Eva's yellow magic enveloped the length of it.

"The four of us stick together," I said. "With Aidan's fire and Eva's air, we take as many of them out as we can, for as long as we can."

"Head that way"—Tamzin pointed toward the central grounds— "they'll be emerging from that direction first."

We took off around the dome, Siren and Noir running close together, Eva flying above us. When we came to the tree line, a black ooze had begun to pour from it into the meadow. No—not an ooze, but the creatures themselves. They were fewer, slower, but still like water. And now they were here. Already.

"Get me close," Tamzin said. "As close as you dare."

"You asked for it."

The first creatures had just passed the tree line when we rode by, Tamzin yelling as she slashed out. The air magic Eva had given her was magnified by her nightstick, and one strike with the weapon threw a dozen of them aside, the air buffeting and slicing and rending.

She was fierce—fiercer than me. And now I remembered what an absolute miracle she was with that weapon. Scarier even now than when she'd used it against me in Edinburgh's crypts.

Then, she'd been fighting with conflict inside her. Now, she fought like the world was ending.

We rode well together. She didn't fear the horse's size or height or speed. I guided Noir along the knife's edge of them, Tamzin leaning right with one hand tight around my waist, the other arm swinging the nightstick with feral, unrestrained grace.

Aidan's blue arrows whistled through the air, sizzling as they made contact with the ones Tamzin had attacked. Down they went as we raced along the tide, the four of us riding down the ones who emerged onto the grass, taking them down with fire and air.

I thought I heard the crack of lightning elsewhere in the meadow. *Liara*, flashed into my mind, and then she was swept away beneath our own fracas. But the knowledge settled in me: We were fighting for the academy. We all were.

But they kept coming. They simply kept coming.

More mages flowed into the meadow, all of them heading toward the dome. Eva would give the word when everyone was inside, but until she did, we would stay out here. Fighting.

We kept battling, rushing along the tide, tempting fate every time Noir's hooves came within grabbing distance. But for such a massive horse, he moved like the wind, always one step ahead, always evading.

Until he didn't.

The moment it happened, I knew it was bound to happen—with this many, even a horse like Noir couldn't stay ahead forever. One caught hold of his back leg as we rode along the line, and the horse whinnied, slowing and kicking at it, or trying. Then his other back leg was caught, and soon the creatures were all around us.

Tamzin fought them. The horse reared. Aidan's arrows sizzled, lighting the horse and our faces in blue, taking them down slower than they multiplied. When one grabbed my foot, numbness overtook me to the ankle like a promise. Then it grabbed my calf.

One moment we'd been free, and the next we were sinking in black oil.

"Tam," I said. Needing to protect her. Unable to. "Can you jump? If you throw yourself far enough, you might be able to run."

"And leave you?" She went on fighting, her arm tightening around my waist. "Never again."

CHAPTER THIRTY-EIGHT

After my calf came numbness to my thighs. They were ascending, climbing over us, and it only occurred to me when the numbness hit my chest that I should say something to my sister while I still could.

But by then, I couldn't.

I couldn't even feel whether she was on the horse behind me anymore.

My eyes lifted, searching for the moon before I couldn't see it at all. When I locked on it, of course it was round as a gunmetal coin. *Mom*, I thought. Usually there was more, but this time there wasn't.

Just that. Just Mom.

Then blackness overtook me, and I couldn't feel my face. Couldn't see. But this wasn't the painless void of unconsciousness—it was full-blown, aching, heart-hammering consciousness.

I was being smothered, and I knew it. Just like that night during my first year when they'd launched themselves on top of me like they could douse a flame. And that was when I'd discovered my fire.

I'd fought them off. This time, I couldn't. I couldn't do anything. And through the panic, the fear, images slipped into my mind: My head in my mom's lap as she stroked my hair under the afternoon sun.

Sitting on the back porch of our home, eating a popsicle in my bathing suit. Lying with my sister in the grass, arms and legs spread as far as they would go, eyes shut.

One thing was true: In every memory, there was warmth. Always the sun. Always heat. Maybe this was the brain's coping mechanism for absolute, perfect terror. And if so, I didn't even mind knowing.

Somewhere distant, I thought I heard a sizzle. That could have been my brain's dying euphoria, but the noise hissed through the air again, louder. Closer. Again, again.

My face came uncovered, the numbness sliding out of it as my eyes opened. The cold air bit at me, and I saw blue flames.

Aidan's flames.

"Clem," Eva yelled. My eyes darted up, left, found her fighting—flying, darting, swinging with her yellow fan. "Clem, hold on."

Hold on for what?

A clap forced my eyes up to the sky. A pair of wings, massive and blue-feathered, retracted against the body of a figure so bright with light I couldn't bear to look at him straight on—only his flaming outline. He held a blue-white sword, and he dove straight toward me, encompassing my vision.

I couldn't look away. Couldn't move.

He swept past me, and I felt the heat off him as he sliced through the creatures like they didn't contain bone or flesh or anything substantial. They were just air, and they dissipated like smoke as he passed through.

"Clem," Tam said behind me in a gasp, like she'd just taken her first breath.

"I'm here."

I turned my head, but he had already disappeared to the other side. The flaming sword cleaved through swaths of them, and Noir's head swung upward with a whinny as he was freed.

Black smoke rose around us as the blue flames came back around, and the figure rose into the air. The wings extended, filling my vision, and then his chest rose toward the sky and he circled toward the tree line.

Aidan. It was Aidan, but it wasn't him.

Noir started into motion, a walk and then a frantic gallop. I gripped tight, along for the ride, and Tamzin gripped me.

Eva flew alongside. "You're alive."

The numbness still hadn't fully left my fingers. "It's a surprise to me, too."

"What the hell was that?" Tamzin said. "Who was that?"

"It's Aidan," I said. "My friend, Aidan."

"Aidan North?" Tamzin said, like she knew his name. And then it occurred to me: she probably did. "From the family of strategists?"

"He went insane," Eva said. "The second the creatures leapt on you, Clem, it was like he was possessed."

Possessed. Just like that day in England, when Farina North had brought the formalists to capture me. This was what I had seen wreathed in blue flames. Not Aidan, but a creature of flames with wings. That day, he'd been a destructive force—absolutely uncontrolled and overwhelming. He was the only reason I'd escaped.

Just like tonight.

The blue flame will emerge when needed most. It had emerged...to protect me.

Noir was galloping us toward the dome when Eva stopped, hovering. She turned back. "Clem, look."

I brought Noir around to an uncertain, unwilling halt. We stared, breathless, as Aidan wreaked havoc on the Shade's forces. He swooped, dove, swung through tree trunks and cleaved their tops from their bottoms with that greatsword. Blue flame was left behind, and wherever it existed, the creatures died.

If they didn't die, they were destroyed.

"He looks like..." Tam began.

"An angel," Eva finished. "He looks like an angel."

And he did. But not sweet, not soft—an angel of flaming retribution if I ever saw one. It was hard to even look at him straight; I had to watch his outline unless I wanted his image seared into my eyes.

With one ear-splitting flap of his wings, he swept through the meadow, cutting down any creatures who made it past the tree line. Everywhere else, battle had stopped. Movement had stopped. He was wholly capturing as he cleansed the meadow, flying faster than I could follow.

"He's incredible," Tamzin said. "What the hell is that fire?"

"Blue flame," Eva said.

The only thing that can defeat the Shade. Samara had told us it was otherworldly. Farina North had said it was from Heaven. And staring at it now, it occurred to me for the first time that it was the same color as the wisps' light. The wisps' *perfect* light. What the others had called hellsbane.

"But it won't last," Eva said. "We need to go while we can, Clem."

Her words made me stiffen. She was right—Farina had promised the blue flame would burn bright and snuff out.

"But Aidan," I said.

Eva flew close to me, in front of my face. "Trust me—he'll be all right. It's you without magic, after all."

I hesitated. It ran against every instinct in me to leave Aidan behind. *I* was the one who protected *him.*

Tamzin decided for us. She pressed her heels into Noir's sides, and the horse took off in the direction Eva flew. Toward the wall, and the narrow opening the mages had left for the rest of us.

Noir slipped through the opening in the wall, barely. It was tighter than before, and the sides pressed painfully against our legs as we followed Eva in.

In here, the dome felt smaller than it had. Everyone was pressed in around the portal, and the fae had taken to hovering above the humans and horses. The earth and water mages were preparing to close off the final entrance.

Charlotte North was ushering everyone through. I wondered if she knew about Aidan and what was happening outside. She must know. She knew about the blue flame and what it was capable of. She had always known—it was part of their family's legacy.

But I still called out to her: "Aidan's out there. Don't close the entrance until he's in."

"We know," Charlotte said, her voice steely but sharp. "The Whitewillows are going after him."

Outside, I couldn't hear if Aidan was still fighting. The sound was obscured by the noise around me, the voices calling to each other. In the crowd, I set a hand to Noir's neck. Horses didn't like feeling like they couldn't run, and this one was the foremost example of that. We could move, but we couldn't run.

My face lifted. The walls were thick. This would be enough to hold off the creatures, but not the Shade. Not Ora Frostwish. Not Tristan Rathmore.

Under a minute later, Aidan's mother and father appeared through the entrance—and they were carrying someone.

Aidan?

People made a hole as the Whitewillows lowered him to the ground, and Nurse Neverwink dropped down next to him. She checked his pulse, inspecting his body for injuries. When her hands went to his chest, glowing with healing magic, I called out, "Is he alive?"

"He's alive. He's burned, though." That was all she said; her focus was completely on healing him.

The blue flame—that must have been what did it. He was otherwise too powerful to be hurt.

Behind me, Charlotte North said, "Close it off. Close off the dome."

Nurse Neverwink and Eva, too, went around attending to the injured as the earth and water mages closed off the last opening. I couldn't tell who had lived and who had died, but no one had limbs missing. There was no blood.

Some looked pale, though. Gray.

Outside, as the mages quickly sealed up the remaining section of wall, a pattering had already begun against the far side. The creatures had crossed the meadow and were testing our defenses.

"They'll die as soon as they touch it," someone said. "It's two elements at once."

"Yes," a voice returned amidst the faces dancing in the firelight, "but they're only the foot soldiers."

A fae dropped near me in a rustle of wings, but I couldn't make out the face in the dim light. Only the voice. "Looks like we need to pull an Umbra out of a hat."

Liara.

I released a breath. "You're alive. I thought I heard you crackling out there."

"I've got wings and lightning—if I wasn't alive still, I wouldn't even want an epitaph on my tombstone."

Then her words of a moment ago processed. My voice lowered to a confidential tone. "You think Umbra's our only way out of this."

"I know she is." She had flown closer, to be near my ear. "I heard the councilors. This is a battle beyond anything like what the Shade brought to bear in the Battle of the Ages. Her power is unfathomably stronger."

Noir shifted under me, and I felt his unease in my bones. The pattering grew higher along the walls, moving upward until it sounded like it was everywhere. All around. Like we were enclosed by it. A silence fell over us as we listened.

I hated this. I hated hiding.

"Hooves," someone said into our hush. "I hear hooves out there."

I didn't hear them at once, and then I did. Close and closer—more than two horses, and maybe more than four. The closer they got, the more I felt their vibrations up through Noir's body.

"Everyone," Nissa called out, "prepare to fight."

Magic filled the air around me. Fire burned brighter. Water was sucked from the air, condensed into gleaming ice spikes that hung above people's heads. A breeze kicked up around my head. The earth trembled.

We all stared in the same direction, at the dancing light of the earthen wall facing the central grounds.

And though I didn't have a weapon, I had my horse, and I had my fists. They were my first defense, what had gotten me through so many times. I knew, like I'd always known, I wouldn't drop without a fight.

CHAPTER THIRTY-NINE

Silence prevailed, and then it didn't. I was sweating from the heat of the fires around me. The hooves had stopped, and footsteps sounded. A chain rattled beyond the wall, and I knew from the sound of it exactly how it moved, what it felt like between my fingers. I had held it many times.

"It's the Backbiter," I whispered to Tamzin. Then, loud, "Everyone, get away from that wall."

She was coming through. Nothing would stop her.

Faces turned to me, half in shadow and half in dancing light. Most of them didn't know me or my voice.

"Do as she says," a familiar voice called out. Jericho Masters—he was here. "Move back. Quickly."

"Back, everyone," Fi Waters said from somewhere to my left. "Away from the wall."

The crowd pressed away from the wall like a buoyant thing, all moving together. And as they did, the chain went on rattling, the same noise over and over. Murkwood was swinging it.

A second later a flaming blade cleaved its head through the wall, the deadly point of it appearing with a gleam. And with another rattle, it drew sideways, melting the ice and cleaving the earth like butter. I watched, mesmerized by its precision as it was yanked downward to the ground. It was almost like a living thing.

The blade disappeared back through the wall, and a deep, guttural voice called out in a language I didn't recognize from the other side. But I did know that voice. And I knew the clinking of that armor as he came closer.

The armor stopped its noise for a moment, and then the whole section of wall caved in. The night air flowed in, chilling the sweat on my face, and I caught a glimpse of a massive greatsword before the madness began.

"*Sabaid*," Nissa called out.

It was the word Samara had always used—Faerish for *fight*.

Four types of magic flew toward the hole. Liara's lightning set it all off with blue-white jaggedness, and the greatsword disappeared behind all that killing power. The air took on a strange, ionized smell, humming around me with static energy. Gradients of color rippled from the spot, water hissing to air, flames buffeted by wind, earth crashing.

This went on for five, ten seconds—until a natural stopping point, when people had exhausted themselves. And that was when I realized we had been trained only in bursts of magic at the academy. Quick, explosive kills. Not sustained defense like this.

The magic abated, leaving smoking water in its wake, and on the other side stood Lucian the prince. He hadn't moved; his greatsword remained low at his side, and his pure black armor was untouched. He couldn't possibly have deflected all that himself.

Then I glimpsed the blue-white light of the wisps floating away from him. They had protected him; I hadn't even known that was within their power. But then, as he started forward into the smoking water, sabatons clinking, I realized I didn't know many things about the power I'd once had access to.

Noir began backing up; I hadn't even given him a signal.

Behind me, the sound of Tamzin's nightstick flicking to place. "He shares the Shade's power," she said to me. "Which makes him impossible to kill. All we can do is stay away."

Rathmore raised his sword, both gloved hands now on the grip.

Flames began at his fingers, lit up the blade from guard to tip. The Shade's creatures raced in behind him, dying on the sections of the wall they touched. But those who died created a barrier for others to get by, and they flowed in as two streams around him.

"Does everyone know that?" I asked Tamzin. "About Rathmore."

The attacks had resumed on Rathmore, air and water and mounds of earth and jets of fire all streaming at him. He deflected or absorbed them—I couldn't tell—and swung at the nearest rider, whose horse reared with just enough clearance to avoid the flames.

"I told the council"—she raised her nightstick, catching a blast of fire shooting past our heads—"but who knows if they listened to me."

"What's his goal?" I said.

Ahead of us, Rathmore stepped forward and swung again. Most moved away from him, but it was hard to tell who he caught with that sword in the fracas.

"He's making a path to the portal," Tamzin said. "The Shade wants Maeve Umbra."

I didn't quite understand, but there also wasn't time to ask questions. Behind Rathmore, I caught glimpses of the wisps. Murkwood was here. She was coming.

I swung Noir around, searching. Nissa Whitewillow flew over the battlefield, probably leading the fae, sometimes driving attacks with her air whip, the ricochet off it hitting the creatures who'd ventured farthest in. She was too far away to get to.

But Charlotte North sat on horseback nearest the portal, two bodyguards on horseback at either side of her. No doubt she was giving silent orders, providing strategy.

Tamzin swung out with the nightstick, catching a creature that had made its way to Noir's back legs. "We have to move."

I spurred Noir into a gallop toward the councilor, came to a skidding stop as the three stationary horses jerked to attention. "We have to stop her," I said, breathless. "She can't get to the portal."

Charlotte nodded. "Maeve told us as much, and your sister, too. We have a plan."

Behind me, Tamzin blew out air. "Well deploy the goddamn plan, then."

"Ten seconds more," Charlotte said. "Ten seconds more and she'll be inside."

I turned Noir toward the main battle. Earth and fire mages, and the fae, were all fighting Rathmore from a distance. But no water.

Riders were lining up at either side. I spotted Mishka Reddy among them. They fought off the creatures, but otherwise held their position.

As Rathmore lowered his weapon for his next swing, I saw her.

Raven Murkwood rode her own pure black horse as her monsters poured in around the horse's legs. The wisps hung in a tight, unholy halo around her head, and the flaming Backbiter was held diagonal over her body, the blade promising only tragedy.

She was the Shade.

The Shade, hooded to where her face was hidden, urged the horse—a massive black stallion like mine—forward at a walk. She rode bareback, and the sight pierced me to where I sucked in air through my teeth.

The affinity with the black stallion, the desire to ride bareback—those hadn't been my desires. They had been hers, the Spitfire influencing me all along.

I'm just like her. I've always been just like her.

And there, riding on the horse with her with a glowing golden lead around his neck, was Loki. My familiar, my emerald-eyed cat. He sat regally behind the Shade, and I didn't know if he could see me.

But he was alive. And I would get him back.

Soon, I would get him back.

The Shade came to a stop a few yards past the hole in the wall, and her lips parted to speak. She dismounted and took two steps forward. "Mages of—"

"Now," Charlotte whispered. "Now!"

As one, the water mages sent a deluge of water from both sides at the Shade, completely obscuring her from view. The horse reared, whinnying and backing up. With a jerk of the fist, the mages iced her over. What was left, when the water and ice had settled, was a great crystalline statue of the Shade. She was completely encased in ice, stuck as she had been in the moment of capture, eyes open, her lips parted to speak.

A moment passed, and then Charlotte gestured with one hand pointed straight at the Shade. A whole cadre of mages moved in to capture her—

But a crack had formed in the ice, right down the center of it.

"Get away," I said. Then, louder, "Get away from her!"

Too late. The ice burst into an explosion, shards flying everywhere. I braced myself as they speared through the air, cutting my forearms. People yelled, some screamed. And when I lowered my arm, there she was, wreathed in flame.

The Shade, smiling.

She spoke a word I didn't understand, and Lucian the prince rushed forward on his horse, charging into the mages with a handed swing of his flaming greatsword.

"*Sabaid!*" Nissa Whitewillow cried, and within moments the two sides were in a furious and terrible battle. The Shade's weapon swung, the blade slicing through the air as magic flew around us. All the while, the creatures kept on pouring into the dome through the hole the Shade had created.

It was chaos. Fae and humans surged around us, Noir dancing with a jerking head, his lungs moving quick. Tamzin swung out with her nightstick, deflecting anyone who got too close, and Noir stamped and bit and kicked at the creatures.

From this vantage, it was clear we were being overwhelmed. And slowly backed toward the portal, the Shade making her way ever closer to it.

In fact, she was close now. Closer than she ought to be. But there was no way to stop her—the tide of her creatures was overwhelming. We were about to be overrun, consumed all over again, when a light burst from the portal.

Instead of darkness, everything turned blinding and white.

CHAPTER FORTY

The light was searing. The light was all-encompassing.

My hand went up to my face, shielding my eyes. And it was from the light a horse's hooves emerged. A mare, angular and lean. Her coat was a pure, unbroken gray, and the chest and head that followed were the same. From the knees up, the horse was armored in intricate gold plate, the dark eyes visible only through an equally intricate headpiece. The white mane had been braided tight to the horse's long neck.

Atop that horse sat Maeve Umbra.

She held Parity, her staff, in one hand and the mare's reins in the other. Her hair had been tightly plaited to her head, her cheekbones knife-sharp in the light. Her cloak swept over the horse's flanks, its own sort of armor.

A stillness had settled around me. Even Rathmore and Frostwish had gone still. Only the Backbiter's chain rattled once more.

Murkwood caught the chain, the blade coming to an instant stop, the flames guttering. She stared at the rider in the light, and she whispered a word I couldn't hear.

On the mare, Umbra tilted the staff forward, toward the Shade and her army. "*Sabaid!*"

Flying forms streamed around her, brilliant stars emerging into the darkness. They swept past Tamzin and me so fast that Noir danced under me, snorting and throwing his head.

"It can't be," Tamzin said. "They aren't supposed to be real."

Umbra urged the mare forward with Parity pointed ahead, a surge of lightning appearing from above her and pivoting off the staff. It raced into the Shade's army, dancing between her creatures.

Within seconds the light met the dark, and the Shade's weapon took on brighter flames as the battle resumed. My eyes had begun to adjust, and what had been brilliant stars now took on form and shape.

They had wings. Wings and silver weapons.

"They're fae," I said.

Behind me, Tamzin said, "They're from the Court of Whispers. I didn't think it was real."

They fought unlike any fae I'd seen in this world.

One of them dove from the sky not far from us, unsheathing two slender swords. Both blades glowed with air magic, but they were two different colors. One glowed blue, and one orange. She spun, half in the air, her toes only briefly touching the ground, as she hacked into one of the creatures with the blue blade. She brought the orange blade around, completing her spin, and the creature dissipated into smoke.

On she went, airborne and then on the ground, the two blades only whispering as she danced her way through the monsters, leaving a clear path behind her.

Another one flew past our heads, so close I could smell a scent unlike anything I'd experienced before. Like Eva's fae rolls, but more intense—and with a hint of longing. If longing was a smell. The fae came to a hover, pulling a bowstring tight to his face and unleashing an arrow that glinted in shades of green as it drove toward the battlefield. He nocked again, unleashed. Nocked again, unleashed.

Every time he hit a creature, and every creature he hit burst into smoke.

The fae kept emerging from the portal, each one of them flying straight through and into battle. And for every fae that came, more of the Shade's creatures piled in through the wall. More and more of them.

But Maeve Umbra had returned. Her lightning announced her; she was fighting not far from the portal, the mare lit up by every lightning strike.

"Hold on—I'm taking us to Umbra," I said to Tamzin. "Keep them off us."

My sister's arm tightened around my waist in confirmation.

I squeezed Noir's sides, and the horse was glad to be in motion. He broke straight into a canter, and then a gallop as we made for Umbra. Tamzin's nightstick slashed through the air as I threaded Noir through the battlefield, past the magic flying over our heads.

"Headmistress," I called out when we had gotten close to her.

At first she didn't notice me; she thrust her staff into a creature leaping at her, lightning enveloping its form and sending it into the ether. In fact, she seemed surrounded by them, like they were congregating to her, even though she was also surrounded by fae who worked to fight them off.

Her face rose a moment later, eyes fixing on me. She drew in air. "Clementine."

Noir reared, front legs kicking at one of the creatures. When he lowered, Tamzin slashed out at it, and Umbra finished it off with lightning.

I rode him closer, even as he forced me to guide him in circles. He just wanted to run. "I need to know—"

"Murkwood," Umbra said, her voice sharp as metal. "She cannot be defeated here. Not above ground."

She must have seen the disbelief on my face. She'd opened the portal to the Court of Whispers—the fae realm. She had brought them here, but even they couldn't defeat her? The battle surged around us, but somehow Umbra managed to hold my gaze. "Do you recall what you found under my office last year?"

I paused, uncertain. Then I nodded.

"That's where you must go," she said. "Chop it down, and head to this spot below."

"But—"

"You need Aidan." A crack of lightning enveloped her, and I had to shield my face. Around us, the Shade's creatures turned to burnt molecules. "Go now," Umbra said. "I'll follow you to the meadow when I can."

And then she was gone. She turned the mare away, swinging with her staff, lightning ricocheting off her and the horse and the mass of creatures following, reaching.

They wanted her. They wanted her badly.

I turned Noir, and from where she fought, Murkwood stared in our direction. No—she stared at Umbra. The wisps fighting around Murkwood all came to attention, and as a mass they surged into the air and chased after Umbra's mare.

Behind me, Tamzin squeezed. "What are you waiting for? We need to get to her office."

I need to find Aidan.

I started Noir into a run, and he weaved naturally around the creatures rushing us. "Tam," I said. "I can't bring you where I'm going."

She pressed tight to my back, an unignorable presence. "Like hell you can't. You just try to get rid of me."

We found Aidan in a corner of the dome, still with Nurse Neverwink and Eva. But now he was awake, and many others around him were not. It had become a triage spot, and even as Tamzin and I rode up, a pair of fae delivered another unconscious mage onto the ground in front of Eva.

She flew to the man, her hands already glowing when they fell upon him. She wasn't waiting to be told.

Meanwhile, Aidan only half sat up, his hands on the ground like he'd just come awake.

"Aidan," I called as we came to a stuttering halt. "I know the way down."

His face lifted to mine, slower than normal. If he'd been burned, it was hard to tell except in the tired hollows under his eyes. Neverwink had done good work. "Umbra told you where?"

I nodded. "And she said I need you."

He hesitated, and for a second I thought he might decline. That he might not move from his spot on the frozen ground. Then, with a lowered head, he pushed himself up to one knee and to his feet. "All right."

When he came over to Noir, Tamzin had just reached down for his hand when Eva appeared next to him. "You're leaving," she said.

Aidan grasped Tamzin's hand, and she pulled him up behind her. Noir hardly seemed to notice the weight; he was once again eager to be on the move.

"We're going," I said. "Now."

She wiped a hand over her brow. "All right." She turned to Neverwink. "I have to go with Clementine."

Neverwink hardly spared her a glance, knelt as she was over a downed mage. "Do what you must. Return when you can."

"I will," Eva said.

Noir shifted under me, and I kept him still. "Eva, this isn't a quick one-and-done."

"I know." She rose into the air, pulling her sleeves down and tightening her bun. "Would you rather I told her I'll never be back?"

"These people need your help," Aidan said.

"Nothing is more important than what we're about to do." Eva flicked a whiff of her air magic toward Tamzin, who caught it on her nightstick. "Aidan and Tamzin, work with me. Clem, you lead, and I'll keep them off you."

There wasn't any arguing. We didn't have time for arguing.

I brought Noir around. "Keep your heads low. We're getting out of the meadow."

And there was only one way out.

I slid a hand down Noir's shoulder—my signal to him. He practically vibrated beneath me with anticipation, understanding. So when I pressed my heels into his sides and brought myself down to his neck, he took off like a shot.

We were still one moment, and then we were galloping, thundering across the meadow. He had done this before, once, during the first guardian trial. This was his home, his place of majesty. He had shown me what he was capable of years ago, and now I asked it of him one more time.

He picked up speed, his head pulling forward, and magic streamed past us, not bursts or swirls but lines of it. We rushed past the mages and the fae and into the thick of the Shade's forces, which massed like water. They were everywhere, even though the bulk were focused on Umbra. The ones piling in through the hole still blotted out the moonlight on the grass and the earth itself.

We had to get outside the wall.

"Not that way, idiots," a voice called.

My eyes lifted. Liara flew above me, her lightning whips illuminating her face. "You'll kill yourself if you go that way."

"There's no other way out," Tamzin called back.

"Follow me." Liara veered around toward the back of the dome, and we followed. She flew ahead, a ball of lightning building between her fingertips.

"What the hell is she doing?" Tamzin whispered to me. "It's just pure wall."

"I don't know," I said, "but I trust her."

Liara shot ahead, the lightning growing to encompass her chest, then her head. Her wings folded tight to her body, and like a crackling meteor she blasted through the wall. A perfectly round hole was left in her wake, three feet off the ground and big enough for Noir to jump through.

We raced toward it, Eva slipping through ahead of us. Noir didn't slow, didn't stumble. He took us straight to the wall and leapt it with ease, and once more we were outside the dome.

We'd made it.

Liara swooped overhead. "Keep your magic ready," she said. "There are more of them at the central grounds. When they see us, they'll give chase."

"Us?" I said up to her as we began the long ride around the side of the dome.

"Of course," she said, her lightning whips reforming in her hands, trailing behind her as she flew. "You need me. You always have."

We came around the dome, passing through the trees toward the central grounds. I'd expected the iciness of the night and stark quiet, but what greeted me were flames. The academy was on fire, the whole place ghoulishly lit up in orange.

"Gods," Eva said, flying close to us.

"This was the Shade's plan," Tamzin said. "Raze the academy. End the resistance."

"She's done the first," I said. "But not the second."

We rode toward the flames—toward the headmistress's office. We needed to get to the tree. I didn't know what state it would be in, but that was where we were going.

The creatures out here were sparser. Most didn't notice us; they headed with mindless intent toward the central battle. We gave them a wide berth, navigating the flames as we rode toward the clearing at the center of the grounds.

Everything. Everything was on fire.

It can be rebuilt, a voice said inside me. *The academy isn't any one tree.*

We rode up to the headmistress's tree, itself in flames, the door surrounded by them. But for some reason it seemed resistant, the flames licking at it but not consuming.

"This is it," I said. "We have to walk from here."

Behind me, Aidan slid off, followed by Tamzin.

I was last. When I hit the ground, I kept my hands on Noir. The horse breathed hard, coughing, and I didn't want to let go of him. But he wasn't safe here. I set my hands at either side of his face, touching my forehead to his.

He allowed it, nickering.

"I need you to run," I said. "Until I get back, I need you to run from this place. And when I get back, I'll find you."

His head bobbed an inch up, velvet chin wobbling. When I lifted my face away, his black eyes blinked once, the firelight dancing in their orbs. He took two steps back, and because he had no saddle and no bridle and no reins, he was free to turn, to run without catching on anything, to take off through the burning grounds with his tail streaming behind him.

And like a slip in the night, he was gone.

CHAPTER FORTY-ONE

The four of us approached Umbra's office doors, the heat off them immense. "Hold on," Eva said, one hand out to stay us. "Clem, when I do this, push the door open and don't wait. You two, follow her."

With both hands out, palms upraised, Eva set two streams of air magic at the flames around the doors. They flared up, enlarged, but were also buffeted back for as long as Eva's magic lasted.

I didn't wait; I stepped into the cool breeze of Eva's magic and set my fingers around one of the handles and my shoulder to the door. Hot —it was still scalding hot. Liara stepped up beside me, her own shoulder going to the other door, and together we pressed them both open.

Inside, the antechamber was still intact. But it was heated like a sauna, and high up I thought I saw smoke collecting where the wisps used to float. Aidan stepped inside, and we held the doors open long enough for Eva to fly through, the flames licking down toward her, engorged. She evaded them, landed between us.

"This fire will take down the whole tree," Liara said. "Fast."

"How long do we have?" Eva asked.

"A few minutes."

I started toward the moon at the far edge of the room, where the illustrated scene of the Battle of the Ages reached its nighttime crescendo. When I stopped, it was to stare down at the illustration.

I had forgotten about the details.

The human and the horsewoman and fae, fighting in the forest. The steed with sparks off its hooves. The weapon the horsewoman carried, sundered. And, afterward, the fae sent through a gleaming portal by the human.

Maybe the human wasn't just any human. Maybe she was a wizard.

"Umbra," I whispered to the mage in white robes, "is that you?"

"What are you doing, Clem?" Tamzin called over.

"Nothing," I called back without turning. My foot went out to the moon, the toe pressing downward. It depressed for me, sinking into the ground. Around the edge of the room, the sounds of the steps sliding to place greeted me once more, and maybe for the last time.

When I came back, the others hovered over the steps, staring down. "Clem," Eva said, "how did you know about this?"

"Eva, you're talking to me," I said, approaching the head of the steps. "The better question is, how *don't* I know about it?"

"She has a point," Liara said.

"What does that mean?" Tamzin asked behind me.

"Down we go." I led them into the earth. Though I wasn't sure it would happen, one of the magical torches came to life as soon as I came near. *So Umbra's magic is back.* It was a balm, a relief. Not to mention the coolness that swept over us as soon as we moved into the earth.

"What it means," Liara said as she descended behind me, "is that Clementine was a bad witch."

"Very bad," I said.

"Your sister used to go everywhere she shouldn't," Aidan said to Tam.

"Or everywhere I should," I said. "Depending on how you look at it."

"She's always been like that," Tamzin said.

"Listen," I said. "If we have to fight the Shade, you have to know how to defeat her hexes. The paralysis hex—"

"We know," Aidan said.

"Samara taught us to defeat all of them," Liara said. "Ad nauseum."

"Who is this Samara?" Tamzin said.

Liara sighed. "Some crazy old witch."

"She is a crazy old witch," I said, fingers along the sides as we descended, "but she's badass, too."

That smell came over me again—earthworms and dirt and that astringent scent I knew now to be behind a door I didn't want to go through. Once again I remembered the feeling of ancientness that this place held, but this time I knew a thing or two more about it.

I knew Umbra was ancient. And not ancient by regular standards, but irregularly ancient. Hundreds-of-years-old ancient. Which made me wonder if she was the one who had built this place beneath her office. And, as we reached the bottom of the steps, I wondered if she was responsible for what we were heading toward.

That tree. That creepy goddamn tree, and what it held.

Some part of me always wondered if I had imagined it. If it was a dream. But now that I knew the truth about who I was and who Raven Murkwood was, the truth of it settled over me.

It hadn't been a dream. Not at all.

"Hey," Eva said. When I glanced back, her face was turned back up the stairs. "Did you hear something up there?"

Liara's face also turned. "Let's pick up the pace, Clem."

Keep moving. We need to keep moving.

"These doors," Aidan said as we started down the first hall and two more torches came to life. "The wood on them is cut in the old style."

"Old style?" I said.

"Back before modern machinery, air mages used to cut wood with specific strokes. These planks bear the strokes of an air mage—you can see it in the exactness of the angle. Except there's a blackened edge to these. How strange."

My eyes floated over the doors we were passing, only barely acknowledging what Aidan had referred to. "It was Umbra," I said, realizing it as I spoke. "It was her lightning."

"Umbra?" he said.

"She's old, Aidan." We had reached the end of the first hallway, and I hesitated. *You can't stop here. Not here.* "She's hundreds of years old."

Eva's voice was right behind me. "Clem, stop. What are you saying?"

I glanced back at her, pausing, grateful for the opportunity not to turn right down the next hallway. "I mean Maeve Umbra is immortal."

Eva's lips parted, but Liara set a hand over her mouth. A silent communication passed between them—they still had the magical connection, I realized, that allowed them to speak into each other's heads.

Eva spun, staring behind us.

Liara's eyes met mine, and I knew the moment they did, we had to move. Fast.

I grabbed Tamzin's hand, and we moved. I took us right down the hallway—the place Umbra had told me never to return to. If I did, I would be expelled from the academy.

"From what academy?" I imagined saying to her when this was all over and the place was ash around us. The dark-humored part of me smirked, even as I ran us toward the place I never wanted to go back to. I knew it was a diversion, my mind taking me other places.

Taking me away from what I was approaching.

The hallway was much shorter than I remembered. We arrived at the far door within seconds, the sickly-sweet smell already seeping through. My stomach turned as my hand went to the latch. When I looked back at Tamzin, I wanted to give her some explanation—some preparation—before we went inside.

But there wasn't time.

I pushed the door open, and there it was. The ancient tree, its roots fanning out to all sides of the room. Hanging, furry. And on the other side...

We piled into the room, Eva last of all. She shoved the door shut behind us. "Liara heard someone coming. And I did, too. It didn't sound like human footsteps."

Tamzin stared at the tree. "What is this thing?"

My breath came fast; I wasn't breathing through my nose. I might retch if I did. My hand went out, grabbing Tamzin's wrist as she began to lean to get a better view. "Don't go around there."

She flared on me, nearly yanking her wrist away. "Why?"

Because there's another version of me. But dead.

One of the vessels. The thought came to me, crystallizing: It must have been another vessel, trapped here forever. Why? I couldn't say.

"You don't want to know."

She studied me, but didn't pull away. "What now?"

I backed toward a wall, staring at the base of the tree's trunk. It seemed to extend into the stones, past the stones. "Umbra told me to chop it down."

"Chop this down?" Aidan shook his head, turning toward me. "Are you sure?"

"I'm sure." I pointed. "This is a false floor. There's something beneath here—beneath the tree."

Aidan approached where I pointed, staring down. Then he nodded. "Clem's right."

Eva had one ear to the door. "I hear something out there. It's closer." She glanced at us. "Whatever you're doing, do it quickly."

I took a long draw of air—thick, sweet in my throat—and pushed it out. "Aidan," I said, "will you do the honors?"

He stepped closer, blue flames igniting. "Get back."

"Hurry," Eva said. "They've found the steps."

Tamzin crossed to the wall beside me. At some point she'd pulled her nightstick out, and as the room filled with blue light, she made to reach out and catch some of it.

"Don't," Aidan said, retracting his hand from her weapon. "It'll melt that metal."

"Potent stuff," she whispered.

"You don't even know." Aidan stepped toward the tree, hands out. With two swipes, he sent blades of flame at the tree's trunk. They sliced through it with clean precision, charring the tree even as it was cloven. And from it emerged a terrible hissing, crying sound.

My hands clapped to my ears. So did Tamzin's.

Aidan staggered a step back.

"Don't stop," Eva said to him. "We don't have time to stop."

Aidan came forward again. This time when he cut, it was faster, with more intensity. And his blade of flame sliced right through the spot where the tree met the flagstones. One side, then the adjacent side.

The tree groaned, leaning. Its roots began to snap away from the walls, sloughing to the ground. And the scent from them was so strong I did retch.

"They're here," Eva said, her magic appearing from her hands. It quickly encompassed the wood she leaned against, a buffeting force to keep it shut. Liara leaned with her. "They're behind this door."

With a last slice, Aidan took out the tree's foundation. The floor shuddered, and I said, "Aidan, get back."

He stepped back, then leapt for the edge of the room. The floor beneath the tree gave out, the flagstones around it falling as all the roots snapped away from the walls. And as the tree fell, I caught a glimpse of her.

Her red hair—*my* red hair—slipping away to whatever lay below.

I didn't hear the tree crash below. I didn't hear anything after it slipped away.

The stones dropped away to about a foot from the walls, disappearing once they were gone, never heard from again. And all four of us stood as though we were on the precipice of something dark and deep.

We stood in silence, in shock. And then a bang came against the door Eva and Liara stood in front of, and they were nearly knocked off it and into the darkness below, if not for Eva's air magic. "What now?" she said.

I stared down, afraid of heights like I had never felt in my life. I couldn't see what was down there, except an odd golden shimmering that seemed to fill the space.

"Look," Tamzin said, pushing away from the wall, hovering at the edge, "I'll take my chances with whatever's down there. It's better than what's behind that door."

She was right. My sister was brave, and she was right.

Umbra had told me to chop the tree down. It was the only way to defeat the Shade, she said.

"We need to drop," I said as the banging came again, and Eva shuddered against the door. "Now."

Aidan stared at me. "Drop?"

"Remember what happened when we entered the underworld?" My fingers left the wall as I leaned forward a degree. "What's up here is down there. The inverse."

The banging came again at the door, and it opened half a foot before Eva pushed it back. I glimpsed darkness there, too, on the other side.

"Climb down," I said. "To the other side."

Tamzin and I met eyes across the room. She nodded at me, and we both stepped forward at the same time. We knelt, sliding off our perches as we gripped the stones, and lowered our bodies into the hole.

CHAPTER FORTY-TWO

I'd expected the weightlessness of falling, but I only experienced a strange loop-de-loop. My stomach went up, and then it came down. I hadn't closed my eyes, but when I lowered myself, the sheath of darkness had encompassed my vision like I had.

On the other side, all my weight went into my arms. I half-crumpled to the stones before toppling backward against the wall. Across the room, Tamzin had managed to carry her weight in her arms, her legs in the air until she allowed them to lower gracefully to the floor.

This was the same room. It had a door. But the tree Aidan had chopped down wasn't here—just the hole it had left behind.

And the air around us carried a green hue.

"Where's the tree?" Tamzin said.

I stared at the hole. "Gravity works the same between the real world and the underworld, I think. When it fell..."

"It fell back down there," Tamzin finished. "And then back here."

And back and forth and back and forth. I nodded.

"This looks exactly the same," Tamzin said. "It's the same room."

"No," I said. It was the same room, but not. Only I didn't know why this room would exist in the underworld, too.

Aidan appeared beside Tamzin, upside down, and she reached over, helping him avoid tumbling over.

Eva appeared in the center of the room, slipping through the darkness, her wings moving. She had flown headfirst, and never experienced the loop-de-loop as she came through to our side. "Oh," she said as she turned a slow circle. "It's the underworld."

Liara appeared next, orienting herself at once.

I pushed myself to my feet, nausea rolling through me. "We can't stay here."

Eva flew to the door, pulling the latch. It opened easily for her. "Come on. We know the way out."

The three of us began moving around the edge of the room, hands on the wall. A second later, Tamzin grunted, her foot edging toward the hole.

Something had reached out and grabbed her. A numbing hand.

Aidan's blue flames and Eva's air magic rushed toward the hand at the same moment, obliterating it. The hand was turned to dust, and Tamzin and I began moving faster.

More hands were reaching at the edges of the stones. The Shade's monsters. And some were now appearing, feet-first, at the far side of the room.

Aidan, Liara, and Eva were already through the door and into the hallway. Tamzin and I reached it at the same time, and I pushed her through ahead of me. We fell into a run down the hall, strange, green-lit torches coming to life around us as we did.

It was an exact replica of the above world. We reached the T-junction at the end of the hall and took a left. Eva flew first, remembering the way, setting our pace. And I brought up the rear, refusing to let my sister out of my sight.

We hit the stairs almost at once, Eva flying straight up them. More torches came to life ahead of us, leading us out of the cold earth and into—

I didn't know what.

But as we arrived at the head of the stairs, I should have known. Here was an antechamber just like Umbra's, illustrations all the way around the edges of the circular floor. Two massive doors promised a way outside.

Eva flew to the doors, took a second to turn toward us. "I don't understand." She gestured to the antechamber. "I don't—"

"Me either," I said as I came to the top of the stairs. "But at least we know the way out."

They were still coming after us. We needed to get out of here.

Aidan pushed through one of the doors and out into the night. Tamzin followed, and Eva and I came through last. We emerged in the clearing, the academy grounds familiar—if green-hued—all around us. The amphitheater. The dining hall. The rope bridges between the trees.

We knew this place. We knew it inside and out.

The only difference was the gold shimmer running straight through the center of the grounds. Two gleaming lines of it appeared deep into the trees from two different directions, passed under the amphitheater, and headed on a path to meet in the meadow.

"The meadow," I said. "We should head for the meadow."

"Why?" Eva said.

I'd already started running. "It's where Umbra will find us."

My sister fell into a run behind me; she had heard Umbra say as much.

I unhooked my cloak as I ran, an impending sense of finality building in my chest. *This is the place where it'll all be decided.* If I was going to die, I would die in this meadow.

I wondered if that was my own thought, or a remnant understanding I'd gained from being the Shade's vessel for over twenty years. A connection with her that would simply never go away.

Some of my thoughts were mine, and some I'd never know the origin of.

We emerged into the wintry meadow. No moon shone here, but I could still see in the green ambience. Without the cloak a cold sweat chilled my body, but I preferred the pain to death.

I wanted to live. I knew that now in a way I hadn't known it after I'd woken up in Samara's hut. The question had been on my mind. I'd never let it come to the fore, make itself known, but it had been there. I only knew that now, with the recognition of how badly I wanted to live.

I ran along the tree line to the same spot where Umbra and I had sat so many times in the shade. Where she had taught me a great many things. I dropped to my knees and pulled Eva's tent from my cloak. "Help me," I called to the others. "Help me set it up."

We raised the tent under the trees, and I sat outside it on my knees. My hands clasped, and I set the knuckles of my thumbs to my forehead. I had never prayed before, but now my eyes shut against my hands. *Please*, I thought. *Please, please find it, Callum.*

Callum's soul was down here somewhere. If I couldn't bring him back to his body, it would be as bad as losing Loki. Both of them had saved my life more than once. Both of them were still saving it now.

"Clem," Eva said behind me, her voice a rasp. "I hear footsteps. Coming toward the meadow."

I trusted that; her hearing had always been far beyond mine.

Please, I thought one more time. *Find it. Find it.* I had laid the sword and armor by his body. I had done exactly what Thom had told me to do.

Tamzin's hand fell on my shoulder, and I rose. My hands came apart, and I turned toward her. My sister, blue eyes and blonde hair and lips flint-hard. She looked like our mother would have when she was our age. That thought made my arms go around her, and whether she wanted it or not, I pulled her tight against me. I buried my nose in her shoulder. The smell of her was undiminished by the underworld.

She didn't resist.

"Whatever's coming," I whispered, "I'll protect you."

She scoffed, her nose half-blocked. "You're the one without the magic."

"Doesn't matter," I said. "I'll still kick anyone's ass."

Now I heard the footsteps. They were moving fast, at a run. I lingered with my arms around Tamzin until Eva's voice rang through the trees.

"Headmistress," she called out.

My eyes lifted. There she was, Maeve Umbra, her robes billowing as she moved toward us. Her hair was half-loose, and at some point her cheek had gotten bloodied. "Evanora Whitewillow," she said as she came to us. "I should have known." Her eyes traveled over the rest of us, finally settled on me. Her lips came together, grim as she nodded.

"Headmistress," Aidan said. "The prophecy—"

"Catriona's prophecy," a voice rang across the meadow, nowhere and everywhere. It was followed by the approaching sound of horse hooves, moving slow and methodical. "Catriona's hopeful prophecy."

Umbra turned away from us, toward the path we'd come by. She planted Parity in the ground. "Stay here, all of you," she said over her shoulder. "This battle will be finished here, by me."

No, I thought. That wasn't right. She had told us to meet her in the meadow—if she didn't need us, she wouldn't have brought us here. Wouldn't have asked me to bring Aidan here.

Umbra was already moving out into the meadow, striking toward the center of it. The two gleaming lines met there, crossing and diverging on their separate paths. And that was what she headed toward.

From the far end, a massive black horse's head appeared—the stallion. It was ridden by a woman, her cloak long over its flanks, a bladed weapon low at her side. The wisps hovered around her head from shoulder to shoulder.

Raven Murkwood rode into the meadow, Loki still collared atop the horse. She was flanked by a second horse, a roan Clydesdale with clopping hooves, ridden by a huge figure in black armor with a greatsword at his hip. Lucian the prince.

"Look," Liara whispered at my side. Up above, Ora Frostwish flew through the sky, her robes trailing, as she hovered above the meadow.

My eyes lowered. Out there amongst the trees, everywhere, I saw them—the Shade's creatures, all leaning in. Waiting. They weren't far from where we stood, either, but their attention wasn't on us.

They were fixated on Maeve Umbra.

"Where are your fae armies, Catriona?" Murkwood said to her. "Of course, I remember—they're too fearful of this place."

"Raven," Umbra called out, her voice loud even in my ears, even from here. "We must end this."

Murkwood kept the horse moving—not fast or slow, but at a determined, sure pace. There was no rush. When the two women were thirty feet apart at the center of the meadow, the horse came to a halt with a flick of the tail. Rathmore's horse stopped behind her.

"End this?" Murkwood said. "You and I both know you cannot do it. This is why the prophecies exist."

I took a step forward. The way they spoke to each other...

They knew each other. And not in a passing way. These two women knew each other well.

"Centuries ago, perhaps," Umbra said. "I could not, it's true. But our time is long past, Raven. We cannot be forever."

A welling understanding built in my chest, clouding my eyes, blocking my nose. It rose to the surface, light breaking through in cracks, and then Murkwood said what I had only begun to understand from *The Witching World* years ago.

"Catriona," Murkwood said in the center of the meadow. "For as long as you live—"

"—I'm eternal," I whispered, echoing her.

Catriona. Catriona. Catriona was Umbra.

It was Umbra who had delivered the prophecy. It was Umbra who had foreseen that one wielding fire would descend into the underworld and end the Shade with her very own weapon.

Maeve Umbra—Catriona—had been alive for five hundred years. And Raven Murkwood had once loved her.

Catriona had loved Murkwood, too.

Umbra's face dropped, and she seemed to lean against her staff to keep her upright. Those words washed over her like a physical force, powerful even now. Even after all this time. "This wasn't how it was meant to be," Umbra said, head shaking. "You were Shadowend. We were to protect the world."

"Are we not?" Murkwood said, one hand sweeping out. "The under-world remains intact. As shall the world above, under my watch."

A silver gleam had appeared in Umbra's hand, slipped from her robes.

I took another step forward, squinting. I couldn't make out the shape of it through the green hue.

"You've corrupted it," Umbra said. "All of it, the moment you stole the flame. And now, come what may, this all must end."

She raised the object.

A dagger. It was a dagger.

Murkwood's eyes widened. Her lips parted.

Small, sharp, the dagger's tip lifted to point at the center of Maeve Umbra's chest. She had moved so fast; the dagger was at her side and then it was at her breast, piercing the cloth of her robes.

And it stopped.

Umbra's hand shook, and tears ran from her eyes with the dagger poised. Her lips pulled away from her gritted teeth, and she let out a sob. I couldn't tell what had stopped her, but it seemed like it was her own unwillingness and nothing else.

Atop her horse, Murkwood sighed to a slump. "No shame in fearing death, dear Cat." With a flick of her fingers, she sent the wisps toward Umbra. And at the tree line, the creatures streamed out. They rushed past us, making for Umbra at the center of the meadow. Hundreds—thousands of them.

Umbra threw the dagger aside with a yell, her voice ringing through the trees. "We must end her," she bellowed.

Us. She was talking to us.

She raised Parity, and green-hued lightning shot from the sky down toward her as the wisps and creatures converged. It splintered, rico-cheting out. Before it touched Murkwood's horse, she and the horse burst into flames. And Loki with her, encompassed by her magic. I could still see the golden lead around his neck.

"Tam," I said, and my sister leaned close to me. "Can you sever the leash she's got on Loki?"

Her eyes slanted over at me. "If it's magic, you know I can."

I exchanged a glance with Liara, whose lightning came to life at her fingertips. She and Eva took to the air, their eyes on Ora Frostwish.

Then I turned to Aidan. "We have to kill her."

He nodded, blue flames appearing on his hands. "I know."

We started forward together—until a hand fell on my shoulder from behind. Stopping me.

"Clem," a voice said. "Let me take the lead."

CHAPTER FORTY-THREE

Every part of me stilled—except my insides, which slid over themselves, my chest tightening like a girdle's cinch.

He was here.

I turned, face lifting. Callum Rathmore stood before me in the chestpiece I'd left for him, the greatsword low at his side. His face was still pale, his black hair unbrushed, but his eyes were wild with life.

He had found his way back. Thom had been right.

I took in a short, stuttering breath. Then, "About time."

He wrapped his arm around my head, pulling me to his chest. His fingers stroked at my hair. "I know. I know."

I allowed it, sank into it even as the creatures streamed around us. It had been so long. I had wanted this for so long. One of the reasons I had come down to this place had been fulfilled.

Then my anxious mind interceded: Tam. Eva. Aidan. Loki.

I leaned back. "The Shade."

Callum's eyes lifted past me. They fell on his father, who'd dismounted his horse and now stalked toward us. "Clem, you have to free Loki."

I knew that; he was my cat. But there was something else in his voice, too. Like he understood something I didn't. "Why?"

He pressed me aside, both hands going to his greatsword, preparing. "Free Loki. Free the blue flame. That's Catriona's prophecy." Then he started forward to meet his father. The two men were virtually the same height, but Tristan Rathmore's black armor made him look impossibly large. Imposing. When flames lit on his hands and licked down his greatsword, he looked like a demon.

Like Lucian the prince.

Callum, thinner and mostly without armor, didn't hesitate. He still had his own flames, and they consumed his sword as the two men met in the meadow with an echoing clang of metal.

In the sky, air magic flew. Eva and Liara fought Ora Frostwish, their professor and mentor, the three of them moving faster than my eyes could follow. I only caught glimpses of their magic in their wake as they battled, the fae deep in a back-and-forth.

Umbra was besieged from every side. The creatures kept flowing toward her, and she kept fighting, a beacon of jagged, electrified light in the center of the meadow. She fought like I had never seen her fight before: without hesitation, destroying a swath of them all around her with one rippling, thundering blast of lightning.

Aidan and Tamzin made for the Shade, killing creatures along the way. Tamzin had Eva's air magic on her nightstick, and she spun, leapt, and slashed at everything that came close.

Then there was the Shade. Her flames had receded after Umbra's massive lightning strike, and she had dismounted her horse, Loki hopping down with her. She carried his lead in one hand and a second lead in the other as she took slow, sure steps toward a battling Umbra. She hadn't noticed Aidan or Tamzin—and why should she? They were whelplings.

She only had eyes for Umbra. Covetous eyes. And she had a second golden lead. I stared. She didn't want to kill Umbra—she wanted to capture her. That golden lead was meant for Umbra's neck.

I didn't understand why. Because Umbra led the resistance? No, it was more than that. She and Umbra had both lived five hundred years. They had loved one another. They were connected somehow, even still. That was why Murkwood's eyes had gone wide with fear when Umbra had tried to kill herself.

They were connected somehow.

I needed to fight. I didn't know how.

Free Loki.

Aidan and Tamzin had reached the Shade. He met her in a wave of blue rushing toward her, and the Shade stopped. Orange fire spread up and down her body, and the blue flames washed over her.

"Ah, a North with the gift," Murkwood said. "Have you come to fight me, then? But you are so very weak. You're sapped of the angelic power. I can see it in your eyes. A pity."

With a yell, Aidan shot one jet of flame at her, then another. She deflected each of them, dropping the second lead. "Very well, then. You shall have your fight." She twisted her fingers, drawing flames around one hand and sending them drilling through the air toward him.

He met the flaming drill with his hands extended, a blue shield forming over his palms as he leaned into it. The sweat on his brow was illuminated by the blue light.

She slid the Backbiter from its place at her side, and as the first swing of her blade came at Aidan, I knew she was right. He was tired. Sapped. That power... it couldn't be accessed twice in a day, maybe even a week.

He managed to get out of the blade's way, but barely. He staggered, throwing up a hand to deflect the blade with his flames. But the chain wrapped around his arm, wrapping suddenly and tight as a snake. He was caught, and she wasn't letting him go.

This wasn't the way. It wasn't how we would defeat her.

All I had to do was what Umbra had told us: End her. End the Shade. And to do that, Callum had said I had to free Loki.

Free the blue flame.

Maybe Samara was right—I didn't have to defeat the Shade or die. Maybe there was a third path for me.

Behind the Shade, Tamzin had found her way to Loki. My cat was stuck where the lead had fallen, trying to pull away from it but unable to, as though the magic rope was pinned to the ground.

With one swipe, Tamzin cleft the lead in two, severing the magic. It was what she had been trained to do: take magic, destroy it. The lead shriveled, dying around Loki's neck. Disappearing, freeing him.

It was almost as though Tamzin was meant to intercede. Almost as though she had a role to play.

Loki was free, and he came running toward me.

I stepped out beyond the trees, moving toward the Shade. I pointed at Aidan. "Go to him," I said to Loki. "Hurry."

This was it. This was the third path.

Loki obeyed. He pivoted, rushed toward Aidan.

The Shade had yanked him to the ground, and in spite of the blue flames racing up and down his arms, the chain could not be undone or broken. The Backbiter was made of the strongest metal on Earth.

She dragged him toward her now as he struggled, wriggling against his binds. Exhausted. Spent.

He wasn't meant to battle, but he'd come anyway. He wasn't meant to fight, but he was here in the underworld, doing it because he thought he had to.

He didn't have to. He could leave that to me.

"Aidan," I yelled, running now. Past the Rathmores, still battling. Beneath Eva and Frostwish, fighting in the sky. "Throw your flame to Loki."

I wasn't sure if he'd heard me. He went on struggling as Loki raced toward him, a black blur across the frozen ground. Finally the Shade had closed the distance between them, and she lifted the slack chain, flaming orange now, and set it gently around Aidan's throat.

"Aidan," I called again. "Your flames. Give them to Loki."

His face turned, wide, wild eyes meeting mine. He was terrified, and he'd heard me.

So had the Shade. Her face flicked toward me, almost too fast for a human's. Her lips parted, and I stared, transfixed, at my own face across the battlefield. Like she'd mesmerized me.

"Clem—" Callum yelled.

He was cut off. Everyone was cut off.

The whole meadow had gone dead silent, dead empty. Everyone was gone, except for me and the Shade and her wisps. She knelt with the chain of the Backbiter coiled before her on the grass, her eyes still on mine.

Just the two of us. It was just us.

She rose in an eerie, smooth motion, as though she were buoyed beneath her cloak. She turned to me, the Backbiter's rod and blade in one hand, the chain in the other. "You wish to have purpose," she said. "You wish to have magic."

"Yes," I said, surprising myself. "More than anything."

She started toward me, the chain clinking; I couldn't stop staring. "Why?"

"Because I've felt powerless my whole life," I said, the truth like pearls on my tongue. "Because I've never felt in control."

Her head tilted, and the wisps floated idly. "You and I are not so unalike, you know. How do you suppose a woman in the fifteenth century obtained power? Birthright?" She scoffed. "I was a poor man's child. Marriage? No man wanted a strange woman like me, despite any beauty I may have had. And I wanted no man. So you see, when the world does not afford you power, girl, you have no choice."

"You took it," I said.

"I took it." She moved toward me, coiling the chain, and now she replaced the Backbiter at her side. Then her hand rose; a scar ran down the center of the palm. "I took it because if I didn't, the only person I've ever loved—still love—would have died."

She came to me, palm out between us like an offering. I placed my hands under hers. "Before I became the fire witch," she said. "Before I became the Shade, I was Raven Murkwood. I was seventeen, and I made a pact in blood with the only person who understood me."

"For as long as you live"—I feathered a fingertip over her scar—"I'm eternal."

"Yes. You found my book, didn't you?"

"I read it a hundred times." My face lifted to hers. "It made me feel not so alone."

Her eyes softened on me. "Perhaps you understand, then, why I could not bear to live without Catriona, nor she without me. While one of us lived, the other could not die."

Umbra.

While Umbra lived, Murkwood couldn't die. And while Murkwood lived, Umbra couldn't die.

That was their connection. It was why, as the Shade grew in power over the past few years, so too did Umbra. That was why the Shade wanted to capture her so badly. To keep her alive—or maybe, maybe because she still carried the root of love in her chest.

Murkwood observed me. "You understand that part. But what you don't yet understand is why fire witches exist at all. We are separate from other fire mages, Clementine. Our power comes from a place so deep, no soul has ever returned from it."

My fingers fell away from her hand. "There's no place deeper than the underworld."

"There is," she said. "It's where the thing you called the Spitfire came from." Before I could take a step back, her hands caught mine. "You see, before the battle, the world crawled with creatures you have never seen. What you call the Battle of the Ages began as a fight of man and fae against vampires, werewolves, creatures of legend and myth. They were real, Clementine—they are real, down there."

My heart galloped. My throat was dry. I could hear it in her voice: she wasn't lying.

"Catriona understood their threat," she said, "and she helped me. We developed hexes. We imbued the will-o-wisps with hellsbane. We forged the Backbiter. Together with the fae, we fought the creatures back."

But there was more. I could see it in her lit eyes.

"And then," I said, "something changed."

Her chin lowered. "We fought them into the pits. But we could not guarantee the gates would stay shut forever—so I made a decision, child. A decision to be this world's guardian."

I understood now. This was why Samara had told me the Spitfire was a creature of Hell.

"Without the flame," Samara had said, *"nothing can stop what's below our feet from rising to the world's surface. From overtaking it."*

The meadow had grown colder and emptier around me. "You took your flames from Hell?"

"To preserve the world," she said, fingers enclosing mine. "Do you know what agony it is to carry such a thing inside you for even a minute?"

"Yes," I whispered. "I do."

"You carried a speck of it, just a mote you brought to maturity. I've spent five hundred years with it," she said. "Five hundred years of it clawing at my center. She made me a prisoner here, Clementine, and the warden of this place."

"Because you didn't end the war," I said, the conviction growing as I said the words. "You tried to take too much power."

"Catriona and the fae did not trust me with the flame." She pulled my hands to her chest. I could feel warmth there—the Spitfire. "The fae are as tempestuous as man. They turn against one another, forget the pain of their mothers and fathers within a generation. It's why we rise and fall and rise and fall again."

I could see it now—an earnestness in her green eyes. She was telling the truth, or what she believed to be true. She had stolen fire from Hell to protect the world, carried it inside her. Sacrificed her peace and sanity to become the first fire witch.

And Umbra had imprisoned her for five hundred years.

CHAPTER FORTY-FOUR

The Spitfire purred against my fingertips, even with bone and muscle separating me from it. I wanted it back, even now. Even after everything it had put me through. "You used me," I said to Murkwood. "How many other witches did you use over the centuries?"

"Used," she said, "and empowered with just a mere speck of the flame. I gave you the power to destroy the men who would take advantage of you. Hurt you. And here you stand before me, without magic—"

"Without magic?"

My hand fell away from her chest, a strange feeling growing in me. Without magic. Was I without magic? I had the oddest feeling that wasn't true, or might not be true in a moment.

But we were alone in this meadow, just the two of us. Like we had always been. Like we would always be. And it was true that even though she had used me, I had come this far with the Spitfire's help. She listened to me, understood me.

And yet...

I took a step back. "You've been pleading with me," I said. "Pleading your case this whole time."

She took a step forward, the wisps floating toward me. "I want us to understand one another. To become allies."

"No," I said. She was using me; we could never be allies. "I have some power over you, and you don't like that. You want to change that, and so you've been pleading with me."

But what power? What power could I possibly have over this witch, with her will-o-wisps and her bladed weapon and her fire?

I turned a slow circle, staring out over the wide expanse of grass and dead, wintry trees. This place felt so familiar.

"That path," she said behind me, "that path through the trees will take you to a school I conceived of with Catriona. I was to be its headmistress and she my first professor. There, we would protect young mages and witches and wizards from the world. We would grow them in power."

I stopped, staring at the path before me.

Headmistress. She would be the headmistress of the school amidst the trees. But there was only one such school, and one such headmistress.

I turned back to her. "She built it, and you burned it to the ground." My breath quickened; the veil had fallen away. "The fae were right, and Umbra was right to imprison you. You can't be trusted."

Her eyes narrowed.

"Look at you," I said. "How pathetic. You've hexed me, and even without magic I can see through it."

She melted into the ground with an explosion of sound around me. Metal clanged to my right, and someone yelled my name. In front of me, what had been an empty meadow was filled again with creatures of darkness and the Rathmores still battling and Umbra still besieged and Raven Murkwood standing a few yards in front of me with my four favorite people in the world on their knees in front of her.

No—not all on their knees. Eva, Liara, and Tamzin wore the golden leads, their hands bound behind their backs by flame. But Aidan wore the Backbiter's chain around his neck, and he lay face-first on the ground in front of the Shade.

He wasn't moving.

Eva was crying, her chest jerking with her sobs, and Tamzin maintained a stony face. But as soon as I came out of the delusion hex, her chin trembled.

And Loki was nowhere. Nowhere to be seen.

Somewhere past the Rathmores, I heard Ora Frostwish moan. I caught a glimpse of her wing, half in the air, and the rest of her sprawled on the ground. That must have been Eva and Liara's work while I was hexed.

The Shade stared at me like she almost longed for me, and I registered pity in those eyes. "I'd hopes for you," she whispered. "But you've forced my hand."

I didn't have time to respond, even in my head. In the next second I was on my knees, my entire body contorted with mind-erasing pain. My back arched, head falling back on my neck. A scream guttered its way out of me, but it didn't even sound like my voice. Pain was the world's core and the world's whole—it was everything, and I was nothing.

Only one thought eked through: the agony hex.

This was what Samara had called the agony hex, and I knew now why pain was a poor word for it. This was beyond pain. It made me into a pinprick of consciousness, lightning searing up and down every nerve in my legs and arms and chest, flames charring my limbs and chest and face until I was nothing but ash.

Time didn't exist. The world didn't exist. My future and past were gone. I had only one awareness—

Agony. Just agony.

I didn't know how much time had passed before another thought navigated the morass of my mind and made it all the way to the front. This was it: *Samara taught you to fight this.*

She taught me. What did she teach me?

Pain like an anvil, pain like a vista of nothingness. I couldn't make words—everything scrambled as soon as a figment of thought occurred.

Resist. Overcome.

The words came from nowhere, entities unto themselves. I wasn't Clementine, just a vessel for pain. But once those words echoed inside my head, I couldn't unhear them. They reverberated with power, with meaning.

Resist. Overcome.

But I have no magic. I have no power.

Samara sneered into my head. Somewhere I heard her voice through the static. "Your power was never in your magic, Nectarine," she said. "*You* are the power."

Had Samara said that?

It didn't matter. It was true.

I began with my eyes. They were screwed shut, needles of pain driving through them. I needed to open one eye. Just one, just a peek.

Nothing I'd done in my life had been so impossible as opening one eyelid. I had to press aside the pain, to place it inside a lettered box and force my brain into manual. *You remember this. Open your eyelid.*

A slit of the world came into view, upside down. Trees, the forest with their roots the wrong way up. My head was still thrown back. I was in the underworld. Around me, a fight was still happening. *But I know the third path.*

Resist. Overcome.

My other eye opened, and then I was truly in the world again. I forced my head up, the thing like a fifty-pound bag of flour. My fingers clenched, driving into my palms, and the pain was murder. It was unignorable.

But so was I.

I forced one foot up, solid on the ground. Then the other. I stood, pain coursing through me like a live thing, but I couldn't do anything except stand. If I didn't stay on my feet, I would never get back up again. I knew it with absolute certainty—I had to stay on my feet.

Ahead of me, the Shade had turned toward Umbra.

"Catriona," she called, her voice ringing through the meadow. "Give yourself over, dear, or you'll force me to tighten these leashes around your disobedient younglings' necks."

A blast of lightning followed in the spot where Umbra had been fighting, and as the smoke from it cleared, Umbra stood in the middle of the charred patch of ground. Parity gleamed in her hand. For the first time since this fight had begun, she had a moment's pause.

And in it, her eyes fixed on mine. They widened with shock. Then they flicked to the Shade's black horse. Or, I should say, underneath it. A second later, she had her attention on Murkwood. "Release them, Raven."

Umbra had been trying to tell me something. I had known her long enough, spent enough time training with her, that she did not gaze at any one place without purpose. She had been directing my attention to that spot—telling me something.

But there was nothing underneath the horse.

Murkwood dragged Eva and Tamzin to their feet, both of them crying out and coughing and choking. "These are magic leads, love. Don't toy with me—you know how fast I'm capable of separating their heads from their bodies."

No one's attention was on the horse, except mine. The Rathmores were still fighting, and the Shade and her creatures were all fixated on Umbra.

That was when he appeared. Loki, as though from nowhere. But it hadn't been from nowhere—he had been enshrouded. Umbra had enshrouded him.

His green eyes met mine, tail low, body almost touching the ground. And when I nodded, he set into motion.

He moved toward Aidan, who still lay with the Backbiter's chain around his neck.

Let him be alive.

When Loki reached his fingertips, he nudged at Aidan's hand with his nose. Aidan didn't react, and I stifled back a sob that rose from nowhere.

Loki lifted a paw, set it on top of Aidan's hand. With slow, careful precision, he did what he did best: unvelveted his paw and dug his thorny claws into Aidan's skin.

That made Aidan jerk. His fingers moved, and then his eyes opened. His glasses were gone, broken on the ground near him, but he still saw me.

He was alive.

CHAPTER FORTY-FIVE

His fingertip lifted, a single spot of blue welling on the tip. It was all the strength he had left, and Loki set his nose to the flame.

The Shade drew Tamzin to her, dragging her along by the throat. Tightening.

Such a delicate, small thing, that fire—the barest breath could snuff it. The flame on Aidan's fingertip disappeared when Loki touched it, maybe snuffed out by the tiny back-and-forth of air through his nose.

Loki's face lifted, and he straightened. His face shimmered, dancing with flame, and the more of his fur it touched, the more it spread. It spread like wildfire, encompassing his body, rising high.

Then they transferred to me.

The flames began as a warmth in my chest, different than the Spitfire. Less desirous, impulsive. More constant, an everflame that filled my rib cage and spread through my body in a slow, even wave.

The agony ended. The hex was broken.

I lifted my hands, blue flames hovering over them, waiting for my impulse, my command. This was a power beyond anything I had experienced. The Spitfire had been reckless, a feral creature. The blue flame was consistent, unwavering—so it burned hotter, more intense.

This was it. This was the third path.

I didn't have to defeat the Shade. I didn't have to die to her.

I could become the Shade.

Everything stopped. The wisps, racing around Umbra, stopped. The Shade's creatures lowered to their haunches. The Rathmores staggered back from one another, faces turning toward me. Eva, Liara, and Tamzin struggled against their leads to glimpse me. The Shade turned her face, and my own eyes gazed over at me, wide and green.

And they grew wider as the wisps raced toward me.

The will-o-wisps flew over my head, coming to a familiar hover from shoulder to shoulder. Waiting for my will. I could feel them again, connected to me.

From where she stood, Umbra stared at me, breathing hard, leaning on her staff. "Clementine," she said, and though she was yards away, she sounded right next to me. "Oh, my child."

Murkwood threw the golden leads aside, and they stuck to the ground where they fell. She approached me like I might bite, with careful steps, her eyes never leaving mine. The Backbiter slithered from her robes, the chain clinking as the blade came to swing low at her side. "Fire witch," she whispered. "No one but a North may wield the blue flame."

I felt her attempt a paralysis hex. Her flames pressed at me, but they were repelled by my own. Shrugged off like a child's attempt. Then she tried at the agony hex again, but her magic couldn't penetrate my own.

My fingers closed to fists. Already I could feel the immense power of it threatening to overwhelm me. I didn't have forever—I only had a little while. But it would have to be enough.

"That's where you're wrong." My hands circled around and around one another, building flame. I thrust them out toward the ground at the Shade's feet.

She raised a hand, flames appearing there. Not fast enough.

A blue wall of fire burst into life around her, so tall and loud it obliterated everything and everyone else. All I could see were the flames. All I could hear were the flames.

And then I heard something else. Lightning. Umbra was coming.

I sent the wisps in with one command: *Destroy the Shade. End her now.*

They rushed forward, disappeared amidst the blue flames.

"Get back," Umbra said, her voice hardly audible beneath the conflagration. "Back, child."

The Backbiter's blade appeared from nowhere, slicing out of the wall of blue flames toward my head, black metal aiming to scalp me.

I leaned back, the blade flying overhead. The blue flame made me faster, more supple.

The blade arced, disappeared back into the wall. A moment later it launched in a vertical arc, slicing down toward the crown of my head. She was fast with it—unbelievably fast. But what shocked me more: the blue flames hadn't killed her. Neither had the wisps.

She's truly immortal.

I backpedaled, the blade singing through the air in front of me. It hit the ground and dragged for a second before being yanked out of view.

I allowed the blue flames to die down, to get a view of her. When she emerged, she was haggard, breathing hard. Black char covered parts of her skin. Patches of her hair had been ripped from her scalp—the wisps' doing—and her clothes were tattered and burned.

She wouldn't die. She just wouldn't die.

She still gleamed with potent orange flames, and with lips pulled back from her teeth, she swung the fiery blade up over her head, revolving it once, twice. She sent it toward my stomach to gut me.

I leapt back, but the flames burst off the blade, rushing at my face. The blue flame buffeted them back—and Parity.

One moment I was fighting alone, and the next, Umbra was there. The staff vibrated with searing white lightning, crackling and jagged, repelling the flames.

"Stay with me, child," Umbra said. "Don't leave my side."

With a scream, the Shade sailed into a wild motion. She became a creature of blade and flame, the chain's noise almost rhythmic as the blade flew toward us again and again, the Shade turning and ducking and leaping.

Tristan Rathmore lifted his greatsword, the blade on fire, and rushed us. Callum gave chase, and soon the four of us were in the fracas together.

Umbra kept to my side, deflecting any blows from the Shade and the prince. Lightning crashed around us, and in the glimpses I got of the battle, I unleashed my flames at the Shade.

She was the one who had to be stopped. If she was stopped, all of this would stop.

The next moment, she was everywhere. Everywhere I looked, she spanned the battlefield, all of them with the Backbiter. It was overwhelming. They surrounded us, all of them crowding in.

It's a hex. The likeness hex.

Flames burst to life on my left hand, and I dropped to one knee as I drove the palm into the ground. A rush of flame spread like a wave, encompassing half the meadow. The thousands of likenesses evaporated until only the Shade remained, her body lit with orange flame to protect her from the wave of blue.

With a cackle, she fought like the Backbiter was an extension of her body. Umbra fought close to me, the two of us deflecting blows and trading with our own. The wisps raced around her, attacking, but she ignored them. Sometimes the Shade dodged, spinning out of the way, and sometimes my flames connected. She never went down. She refused to go down, to stop coming at me.

And she only had eyes for me. For the blue flame.

She kept coming closer, closer, her flaming blade everywhere. And because I was growing fatigued and the blue flame waned, I slowed. I didn't have her immortality.

The blue flame slipped away from me, slowly and then all at once. My skin scalded, and I only knew it when the cold air ran across my arms and bit into my face. I kept fighting, clinging to the power I had left.

In a fight like this, it only took one wrong move for a witch like me to die. And when, dodging under the prince's sword, I straightened to find the Backbiter's blade rushing at me like a wild creature, ready to rip through my breastbone, the world felt, all at once, bitterly cold.

The blade didn't connect. Not with me.

A form appeared in front of me. Wild white hair, billowing robes. But no lightning—this time, she only used her body.

Maeve Umbra.

The blade bit into her breast quietly, ripping through fabric as it tore itself back out. She hardly moved, and it was only in the stillness that followed that I noticed her hands were out at either side of her. She had dropped her staff, and her hands were out like she was protecting her child.

But it was me she was protecting.

The Shade went still as the blade hit the ground, chest moving fast. She stared at the lethal tip, soaked in blood. Then at Umbra, who wavered a moment. I sensed she was about to fall in the same moment a wail went up.

It was the Shade. It was Raven Murkwood, dropping the Backbiter and setting both hands to her face.

Umbra fell, and I caught her in my arms. She was so light—so impossibly light. I held her head up, staggering the two of us away. Away from the Shade, away from the Rathmores, whose swords had begun clanging once more as Lucian the prince, the father, let out a bellow. They had never stopped fighting.

Umbra's feet dragged across the ground, and her eyes were on me as I guided us by muscle memory toward the tree line. The trees were bare and dead, but I still found the same spot we'd sat so many times.

No, I hadn't made it that far. I only got us a few yards away from the fighting before I dropped to my knees with Umbra still held, but the spot was in view. She had a clean red line down the center of her chest, robes slit open to a wound I could hardly look at.

Even through the cauterized opening, the blood still came. More and more of it.

"Child," Umbra said up to me, her violet eyes studying mine. I'd once heard the eyes were the only part of a person that never changed. As old as we got, our eyes never changed. And for a moment I could see the young woman she had been. Hopeful, idealistic.

"Why did you do it?" I said with sudden violence. "You could have stopped her in fifty other ways."

"No." Umbra's hand came up, and for the first time I noticed the long scar on her palm. It was identical to Murkwood's. The blood pact. "There was no other way."

My chest burned, a fist of pain clutched there.

"I've always been a coward," she said. "For five hundred years I hid. I ran. I avoided. I wasted multiple lifetimes just surviving. We all have a destiny, child, and I couldn't accept that mine was to die."

"No—"

"I'm so sorry, my girl." Her hand came to my cheek. "I knew from the day I met you, when you came out of your mother's womb, you were a good witch. A good witch, Clementine. You could carry this burden. But you didn't deserve it."

I couldn't speak. Couldn't even see properly.

"Your path does not end here." Her hand trailed toward my neck, fingers searching. Her eyes were unfocused. "The locket."

My eyes were blurred, my head even blurrier. "What?"

"The locket," she whispered, breath hitching. And then her fingers lost their impulse, her eyes widening. Not with death, but with the reflection of what moved beyond my head. Behind me.

I turned my face, and in the same moment was obliterated by something hard and cold and unforgiving. I lost Umbra, lost my balance as I was flung. I spun toward the earth, pain radiating from my cheekbone, and landed on my back away from her.

The ground knocked the wind out of me. I gasped for breath, mouth opening, chest convulsing, as she stepped over me.

The Shade, with Parity in her hand. Staring down at me with murder in her green eyes. "Stay right there." She disappeared from view as she knelt over Umbra.

I still couldn't breathe, but I needed to see Umbra. I turned my face, my unhurt cheek touching the ground, as the Shade hovered over the headmistress, who lay unmoving.

She picked up her hand, but not to clasp it. Her fingers went to the pulse at the wrist, and then the Shade's eyes fluttered shut. She seemed to curse, her lips hardly moving with her breath, and her eyes opened on me.

Air came back to me all at once, a great gasp of it. I rocked up to my elbows, breathing hard and coughing. Not far, the Rathmores kept on battling—weakly now, but Callum struggled. His father kept coming, and Callum's blocking was slow and less efficient every time. Eva and Liara and Tamzin and Aidan had all fallen. Loki, too, next to Aidan, the blue flame gone.

Beside me, the Shade lowered Umbra's hand. She crawled over to me, looming over with Parity still in her grasp. Her nails dug into the ground like an animal's, her eyes wild in her head. "You've killed her."

I shook my head, unable to speak. My fingers, shaking, rose automatically to my chest. They sought out the locket, my mother's locket.

Umbra had spoken of the locket before she'd disappeared at the end of my fourth year at the academy. I'd lost the exact words, but now they came back to me with sterling clarity: *The moonstone around your neck—I sense it matters more than you know. Remember, it was your mother's gift to you.*

And her last words. *"The locket."*

It had always been my mother's protection for me. What had kept me safe for years—and what had kept her nearby even when she was gone. Now I knew she had died, and she was gone.

But I still had her with me—here, around my neck. She was a woman who had been a great witch. An air witch, yes. But a good witch.

Just like her daughter.

I was an air witch. And I was a good witch.

My fingers closed around the locket. A blast of air burst from my hand, buffeting her back.

The Shade recoiled, clasping her hand. Startled.

Almost as startled as me.

My fingers unclasped, and I lifted them before my eyes. Green air flowed over my fingertips, across my palm. The other hand, too. Was it the locket? The moonstone?

No—I knew this was me. This was my magic, thrumming through my veins. This was what had been gifted to me by my mother and her mother and all the women who came before.

Umbra had told me, as she and I approached the academy for the very first time, that a witch's magic came in fits and starts. It came with belief.

I'd never lost my magic. I had only lost my confidence.

This—this was all mine. Air magic that no one could take away from me.

The Shade saw it. Flames burst to life on her hands, up her arms. She scrabbled atop me, reaching for my throat. Searing flames made contact with my neck, and I screamed. Pain raced through me, the agony of before. She had hexed me again, and every muscle tensed with the rigor of it. But this time it didn't hold the same power over me; I kept my head.

Resist. Overcome.

I could hex her. I had the magic now.

Above me, the Shade snarled, flames risen all over her body. They danced from her bare scalp and along her back, and I knew she was overcome by the Spitfire. She had become a growling, ravaging creature.

And I wasn't like her. The agony hex was a base, cruel thing. It was simple and terrible and no one deserved to suffer it. No—no agony hex. There had to be another way.

I struggled to pull her away, fingers grasping and pulling at hers. The air magic only made the flames higher, brighter, better. She was burning me. Choking me. Ending me, and air magic couldn't fight that.

But behind her, I glimpsed something that could.

And I finally understood what Samara had meant when she said, *"A prophecy is a description of circumstances that need to be created in order to have the best chance at what you want to happen."*

All of this, the past five years, had been Umbra's master strategy. She had created the best possible circumstances to defeat Raven Murkwood.

And now I had a chance. Just a chance, but there it was, gleaming in my mind's eye like a star.

Or a blade.

CHAPTER FORTY-SIX

The Backbiter lay three yards away where the Shade had dropped it, the bloody blade stuck into the ground, the chain coiled like a snake. Waiting.

I thrust my hand toward it. My vision began to go, the world growing dark, as the green magic flowed from my hand out toward the weapon. It sailed through the air, bobbing and weaving, and when the tendril had reached the chain, I closed my fingers tight.

I couldn't breathe, could hardly see anything except the Shade's insane grimace, every tooth in her mouth visible, eyes like two pieces of coal in the semidarkness as she bore down.

White stars had entered my vision. I had seconds before I lost consciousness. With a shaking hand, I yanked. I heard the chain rattle as my air magic tore it free and pulled it to my waiting hand.

The cold metal of the chain touched my palm, and I allowed gravity to slide the rod and blade down into my hand. When I felt the smooth metal against my palm, I wrapped my fingers around it tight and thrust the blade into the Shade's back.

It wasn't my strength; I had none.

It was my mother's strength.

It was my sister's strength.

It was Samara. Liara. Eva.

It was Maeve Umbra.

The Shade straightened above me, eyes going wide as coins. Her fingers slackened around my neck, and I pulled in air so hard I thought my lungs would burst. The world came back, slowly, and with it, pain. As well as the Shade's ragged breathing.

Her arms fell to her sides, and for a moment she hovered. Her eyes lifted, traveling like she was seeing this place for the first time, and then she slipped off me. She hit the ground as silently as Umbra had taken the blow that would kill her.

I rolled away, coughing, one hand at my throat. It was tender, but I'd expected it to be burned through. It wasn't. A coolness issued around me, and I glimpsed the green air magic wisping away.

I had protected myself with it. A buffer around my throat.

The air magic had protected me. *I* had protected me.

And I was alive.

A hoarse, rasping sound came from behind me. I lifted my head, caught a glimpse of the Shade trying to speak.

I could have ignored her. Instead, I thrust myself to a seat, moving next to her. The wisps moved with me, gliding idly around us. She was burned everywhere, only wisps of hair left, her clothes mostly gone. She lay with the Backbiter's blade sticking out of her, and yet in the fetal position she didn't look at all like the witch the world had once called the Shade.

She only looked like a dying woman whose name was Raven Murkwood.

Maeve Umbra—Catriona—had once loved this woman. She had loved her so much she thought she would never be able to live without her. And Umbra had said I was a good witch, and this woman had probably once been a good witch, too. She and I had been one and the same, and I her vessel. Her identical vessel—red hair, green eyes, all impulse and fire.

We weren't so unalike, Raven and me.

And besides, no one deserved to die alone. Even this witch who'd tried her damndest to kill me.

My hand went out to hers, my fingers threading through her own, and I clasped it. I looked into her eyes, which stared off into the distance as her mouth worked, and I squeezed her hand.

"It's all right," I whispered, the way my mom used to say to me when I wasn't so sure. "Everything will be all right."

I kept saying it until her mouth stopped moving, and her eyes stopped staring, and she went perfectly still for the first time in five hundred years.

Even then, I kept saying it.

She was gone. The Shade was gone.

I lowered her hand. With two fingers, I shut her eyes. The wisps hovered around us, uncertain and unguided. They floated like lightning bugs—with no real intent or course.

Years ago I had learned they contained the souls of dead mages. That was Murkwood's doing. Did I have any control over them now?

"Release the souls bound here," I said into the air around us. "Shine your light on them, and then release yourselves."

They didn't respond at first, their bobbing and floating unchanged. But eventually one of them came to hover directly in front of my face. It didn't speak, but the blue-white light grew larger, brighter.

I shielded my eyes as, all at once, the light burst into a thousand motes. They spread all around me, spreading through the green-hued air. The other wisps followed, one by one, bursting like stars into molecules. They spread through the air, rain in reverse as they poured across the underworld's landscape. All around me the Shade's creatures were brought into light, the magic evaporating like smoke so that the souls beneath were revealed. And they, like the wisps, swirled into the obscured sky and were gone.

When I stood, the underworld's meadow spread like a charred battlefield around me. People lay everywhere, and I didn't know where to begin.

"Clem," a voice said to my right. Callum, on his knees, hunched over a body.

I took an uncertain step toward him, then another, moving as fast as I could. When I got to his side, I found him bloody. I didn't know whose blood it was. And the body he hunched over wasn't a body at all.

It was just an empty, black suit of armor with a sword beside it.

Callum gripped his own sword, the end of it driven into the earth, to keep himself upright.

I dropped beside him, pushed his hair aside to see his face. "Are you hurt?"

"You didn't answer my question."

I pushed his hair aside again, and again, to reveal his face. "What happened to your father?"

"Lucian the prince," he said, eyes lifting to mine, "is tied to her power. If she dies, he dies."

I squeezed my eyes shut, pressed my lips to his forehead. When I leaned back, he said, "Go see about the others."

The others. God, the others.

I stood, my head swimming. Aidan and Loki still lay together, but the horse had disappeared. Maybe that was just a figment of her power, too.

"Eva," I called as I moved toward Aidan and Loki. I couldn't focus on anything but them. "Eva, we need you."

I dropped to my knees beside the two of them. Aidan's glasses were broken on the ground. "Aidan," I said. "Aide." My hand went to his short hair, moving it aside to see his eyes.

When his face came properly into view, he grimaced. "Even my hair hurts," he said, his voice a hoarse whisper.

Eva landed in a rush of wings, crouching on his other side. "Aidan."

"I'm here," he said. "Barely."

I'd already shifted around to Loki, my familiar. He'd saved me again, with blue flame. He'd saved me more times than he knew. My hands went under him, and I lifted his limp body. I set my ear to his chest, wanting a heartbeat more than I'd ever wanted anything— power, control, to be good.

I just wanted him to be alive.

There, in his tiny chest, I heard it: achingly soft and slow, his heart.

My face crumpled, and I cradled him in my arms. "Eva," I whispered, shifting around. "When you've finished..."

Her hands glowed, already set at the back of Aidan's head and his shoulder. "He's alive?" she said, glancing at Loki.

"He's alive." *But his heartbeat is too slow.*

She gave a firm nod, attention returning to Aidan. Her mouth set in a line, and I knew she wouldn't stop until she succeeded or failed.

But she wouldn't fail.

Aidan couldn't wait, and Loki couldn't wait. My fingers remained on my familiar's chest. I had once been able to share my fire with him. Maybe I could share this magic, too.

The air magic gathered at my fingertips, pooling around both hands that encircled my cat. Slowly moving to encompass his body. "You can have it," I said. "You can have it all."

I didn't even need magic anymore. I just needed Loki to live.

The magic swirled around him with its own pulse, and I curled myself around him, setting him to my chest and my face against his fur. The magic enveloped both of us, a warm breeze in the unrelenting cold of the underworld's nighttime in winter.

Seconds or a minute later—I couldn't say—a voice sounded against my chest. "I might live," the small voice said, "if you don't suffocate me."

A sob-laugh came out of me, and I uncurled, revealing Loki. His eyes were open, clear and focused. "Hey," I said.

He breathed slow and even, still not lifting his head. "So"—his voice was hoarse—"which witch won?"

"The good witch," Eva said.

"Oh, good." Loki's tail gave a single flick. "Now I don't have to worry about who'll feed me breakfast tomorrow."

Speaking of witches.

I stood, Loki still in my arms, searching. When I spotted her, she had already gotten up and was helping Liara to her feet. She was covered in dirt and char, her hair flown free, but my sister was on her feet with her nightstick in hand. Ready for whatever would come next.

She met my eyes, and for the first time in ten years, I knew my sister was safe. That we had—and always would have—one another.

We wouldn't be separated again.

Within minutes we were all gathered in the center of the meadow.

Only we remained. Eva had healed Aidan enough to where he could stand, leaning on her shoulder. The Shade's creatures were gone, evaporated into stardust. Ora Frostwish had crawled or flown her way out of the meadow during the battle, and I had a feeling she'd be keeping to ivory towers from here on out.

Callum picked up Umbra's body, holding her light frame in both arms. He came to stand beside me. He nodded toward Murkwood's body. "Already the flame is beginning to claw its way free."

A cracking sounded as he said that—the cracking of bones. Murkwood's bones where she lay dead on the ground. I had thought everything she'd said to me while I was inside her hex had been lies. Ploys to earn my trust, my pity, to keep herself alive.

"She meant it," I said as a burst of flame appeared from her chest. "She was the warden of this place. She kept the real darkness below, didn't she?"

"She took the flame to have it for herself," he said. "She became corrupted, a liar about many things. But she told you the truth about what lies below."

With a screech, flaming claws appeared as Murkwood was rolled onto her back. The reptilian head pulled itself free, and I finally saw the Spitfire.

It was exactly like I had always imagined it.

The Spitfire extracted itself from her, all licking flames and claws and webbed wings. It turned itself atop her body, toward us. For the first time, it saw me. The Spitfire saw me. And I saw it, the two of us separate from each other.

Its wings spread wide, and with a second screech, it grabbed her body and took off into the air, rising high above the meadow. A crack of wings followed, and it soared out of sight, Murkwood's frame trailing in its grip.

"We should leave." Callum started toward the tree line, Umbra's robes trailing past his legs. "It'll be headed to the gates of Hell."

"To open them?" Tamzin said.

Callum didn't answer.

Which meant the answer was yes.

More darkness. More evil.

I should have known; it was never-ending. Which made me hesitate.

Eva and Liara supported Aidan, one at either side of him, and they all started after Callum. Along the way, Tamzin glanced back at me. "Coming?"

Was I coming.

I glanced down at Loki, who looked back up at me. "You heard Rathmore," he said. "The gates of Hell. More trouble's coming."

Questions gleamed in his emerald eyes. He held such trust in me, and I knew he would be by my side to the end.

"Well," I said, "can't be worse than that last foster home."

"Oh god," he said. "You mean the couple with the Yorkies? I had blocked that out."

I started toward the trees with Loki in my arms. Following my sister. Eva. Aidan. Callum. And in my head, I only heard Rational Clem's thoughts.

Of course, now she was just called Clementine.

CHAPTER 47

Snow lay like a crystalline blanket over Vienna, the sun high and round and warm above. Winter would be done soon, but for now, I would enjoy the chill, the hot coffee, the twinkle lights, as Eva called them.

"What do you think," Callum said, his gloved hand sliding against mine as we walked, "of a warmer place?"

We were passing over a bridge, the canal frozen beneath us. "Like?"

"Greece."

"Are they known for their forests? Noir needs places to run, you know."

"They could be."

We came off the bridge and into the shadow of a tall building. I leaned closer to him. "The best magic academy in the world—in Greece. I don't even speak the language."

"Let's hope you're a quicker learn with languages than you are with fire magic."

I turned a straight line of a mouth on him. "Don't think because I don't have a piece of Hell inside me anymore I can't make you suffer."

He stopped with me, his eyebrows lowering, dark eyes intense on me. When he looked at me like that, I never quite knew what would happen next. And I preferred it that way. "Maybe so," he said. "You did fight a fire witch. You might have lightning in those fingertips."

I didn't expect when he took a step toward me, backing me toward the wall of the building. He lifted my gloved hand between us, sliding off the fingers one by one until my bare skin was exposed to the air.

When he had disappeared from the academy years ago, he had gone to unbind himself from his lineage. Callum had given up his powers and his heritage so the Shade would no longer have any control over him. So he wouldn't hurt me.

I shivered just before he raised my hand, face lowering, lips touching my knuckles like he was testing a flame. His eyes lifted, level with me. "Just your nearness makes me ache."

I half-smiled. "I sound awful."

"Completely."

It had been three months. In those three months, we had attended two memorials: one for Lucian the prince, and one for every mage who'd lost their lives at battle for the academy, Maeve Umbra included. I had spent so many weeks in shock, in grief, and then, as it always did, light filtered back in. The world began to feel like a place with possibility. Callum had taken his place on the Mages' Council, promising a new future for Edinburgh. One less... hellish.

And as his first act as the council's head, he'd destroyed the labyrinth in the crypts beneath the city. Releasing all those souls.

Enough darkness was filtering up from beneath the earth. We didn't need any more of it.

He fitted the glove back onto my hand, and we continued on, passing another couple arm in arm. The woman's eyes were sharp, piercing on me. She could have been hiding fangs under those lips—a vampire's, a werewolf's. Nowadays, anyone could be either, or a hundred other supernatural things. You just didn't know.

The world was full of more magic than it had ever been, new enclaves of creatures I'd only thought existed in storybooks appearing around the world. Some were good, and some weren't. Some were irredeemable.

Which was why the academy had to be restored. And I had been invited to join the Guardians' Council to help rebuild it.

Maybe in Greece. Maybe elsewhere. But Maeve Umbra's academy would go on. It would continue in her ideal—light in the dark.

When we came to the coffeehouse, we stopped in front of a portrait window. Inside, Eva and Aidan and Liara sat in a booth together. Eva and Aidan were having an intense back-and-forth, Liara seated with folded arms. Loki sat upright on the table's surface with his tail wrapped around him, a proper cat.

His emerald eyes glittered when he sensed me. He gave a silent meow that morphed into a yawn, pink mouth and tongue appearing.

The others didn't notice; Tamzin had arrived inside the coffeehouse, removing her coat. Eva stood to greet her, throwing her arms around my sister. The Whitewillows had taken us in three months ago, until we figured out where we wanted to be. They had offered for us to stay with them forever, if we liked.

Part of me didn't mind the idea of that.

The other part of me glanced up at Callum, who wasn't looking through the picture window at all. He was looking down at me.

"You can come in," I said.

He shook his head, and my fingers went out to his black hair, threading through it. Inviting him closer. "You're just saying that to be polite."

"I am." I grinned as his arms went around me, and he urged me to him. The warmth of his breath heated the space between us, and then his lips were on mine, soft and thrilling.

Kissing him, I sometimes forgot the world.

A thump on the glass jarred us apart. Eva's delighted, rose-cheeked face was there on the other side, and I knew the exact noise she was making even though I couldn't hear any of it. And I was grateful for that.

Callum swept his arm around me, leading me toward the door. "Time waits for no woman."

When I arrived at the door, I paused. He had already turned away, his wool coat swinging around his calves with his hands in his pockets. His black hair gleamed golden under the sun, and though he was walking away from me, he was coming toward me, too.

I didn't fear being left by him. Or anyone.

He'd believed that I would be the one to defeat the Shade. So had Umbra. Not because I was in a prophecy, but because, as he'd said not long after the battle at the academy, "You're you."

I was me.

My fingers rose, and I removed my glove. I stared at the palm, tempted to test Callum's theory. Maybe I had developed lightning magic like Liara. Like Maeve Umbra.

No—I didn't want to know. Not yet.

Because, in the end, it didn't make a difference.

My face lifted, finding the marble-blue sky. No wintry clouds, no moon. But I thought it anyway. No matter what the world brought, no matter what darkness, no matter what pain—

I'm going to be all right now.

I couldn't see my mother, but I knew I was looking in the right direction.

THE END

Hi friend—

Over two years after *Spitfire* came to me as an idea in Scotland, it's written and the story is done. It felt like eons as I was writing, but now...

Now it feels like I've blinked and it's over.

Life does happen like that, doesn't it? When I conceived of this series, I always knew Clementine would be the Shade. What I didn't know was quite how I'd get there. It's how I write: driving through the fog with my headlamps illuminating just in front of me and a destination in mind.

Along the way—maybe about book two or three—I began to understand with a kind of aching gratitude that *Clem would be okay*. In spite of everything that happens to her, she would be okay. And it's her journey to that equilibrium that gripped me, because I knew I could put her through unbelievable rigors.

Losing her magic. Losing the Spitfire. Losing Loki.

Our lives test us, forge a mettle in us. And—I hope—empathy, too, for the often unseen battle every other person is fighting. That's the magic, and I believe that's what makes Clem okay even without her flames.

Thank you for staying with me through her journey.

As promised, here's the soundtrack to *Good Witches Don't Die:* https://open.spotify.com/playlist/2z1CAojEFsSTwUZIZkyaNL?si= 12f7a7290a8347e0.

Until the next book—

Shavonne

ABOUT THE AUTHOR

S.W. Clarke is an urban fantasy author who lives in a magical tree (well, we all have dreams, don't we?) with her husband and two identical, unrelated cats. She writes to inhabit the lives of the smartest, bravest women her brain can conjure.

Want to be notified of her latest releases? Join her newsletter!

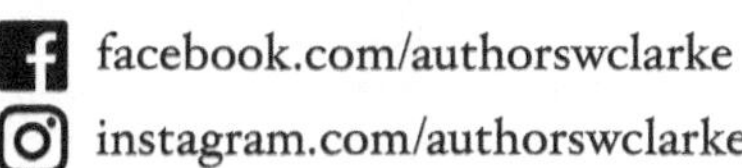

facebook.com/authorswclarke

instagram.com/authorswclarke

MORE FROM S.W. CLARKE

Ready for your next magical obsession? Check out *Whisper and Blade*, the dark urban fantasy series featuring assassin duo Veda and Caim.

A fallen angel and a blind psychic? Forget heaven, that's a match made in Hades.

Veda and Caim couldn't be more different.

She's watchful. He's impulsive.

She's human. He's a beast.

But sometimes, the lion needs the lamb.

As a skilled assassin duo for the Delta Underground Organization, Veda and Caim have taken out the magical world's worst of the worst. Their record: forty-one necromancers in two years.

She finds. He kills.

It's business as usual...until they discover the eight-pointed arrow and the cult it belongs to. Then all hell breaks loose.

Veda:

Two years ago, I woke up with no memory of who or what I am. Whatever happened to me left me blind.

But I have a gift.

I can hear people's thoughts. All around me, all at once, all the time.

The only mind I can't read is *his*.

Caim:

When I fell from the sky, my wings turned black as coal—and my heart? Well, there's a reason they say Fallen can't love.

I've walked the earth a thousand years, relegated to shadows and moonlight. Ten centuries have taught me one thing: humanity sucks.

Then I became an assassin and picked up the blade. You have a supernatural target to take out? I'm your guy.

The assassin life was good—until the organization partnered me with *her*.

She's a whisper. He's a blade.

Together, this match-not-made-in-heaven has to stop the cult that holds the key to Veda's past—and threatens the entire magical world.

Start reading the complete series today on Amazon.